I0831741

All Is Well

A Novel

Lisa Jensen

Wild Ground Publishing

For my big sister,
who taught me to write
my own story.

Chapter One

Emma's steps are swift and soaring, as if she is running down a mountain, rather than traversing the flat sidewalk that extends to the glass entrance of Brigham Young University's Student Center. Three separate students yield their right of way. Never mind that they are in college, and Emma is a mere high schooler. One of them holds the door for her. She doesn't notice.

Nor does she notice the smells and sounds of the Cougareat, all of them familiar and therefore immaterial: the buzz of voices, the whirr of blenders, the waft of burgers and fries and those curry bowls that she orders when she's dragged here for her annual lunch date with Dad.

Emma is not here with her dad (thank goodness), and she's not here for the curry. Something new is tingling on her tongue, ringing in her ears, and growing in her belly. Emma is running away—or trying to, anyhow.

She rushes past the tired, old paintings of Jesus, immune to his mournful stare, hurries down the steps to the basement, and there it is: the ride board. It's a large map of the continental United States, mounted on wood and framed by small pockets, each labeled with a destination. Western states to the left of the map, eastern states to the right, destinations within

Utah listed below. Emma's eyes scour the bottom—Salt Lake, Sandy, Orem, Payson. Near the end of the row, she finds it: Moab.

Her face opens in a smile. She feels that burning in the bosom, as Mormons call it. It's supposed to mean that something is true. Supposed to be a fact detector of sorts that can confirm, for example, that Jesus and Heavenly Father *did* actually appear to fourteen-year-old Joseph Smith in the woods of upstate New York. Except that Emma's never felt this while thinking of the prophet Joseph. For Emma, this sudden warmth is usually an on-the-mountain feeling or a listening-to-music feeling. A staring-at-stars, talking-with-a-friend feeling.

She hopes the heat in her chest means she is on the right path. But when Emma reaches out a hand, she finds the pocket empty—no one soliciting rides to Moab, no one offering space to passengers. Her shoulders slump. She can't write her own name and number on a card and risk one of her parents answering. "May I ask who's calling?" Mom would chirp sweetly into the corded phone, benignly ruining everything.

I'll try again tomorrow, Emma tells herself. She'll race back to campus as soon as the bell rings, releasing her from school. And until then? She'll just have to keep pretending—keep squeezing herself into the familiar a little longer.

***

Across campus, Graham Madsen is pretending, too. He's been doing it for so long now that it escapes his awareness—the shoving down of nerves, the squelching of that flustered self-consciousness that arises when his students whisper to each other across the aisles. He grips the side of the lectern and, as he does at the start of every class, clears his throat. It's a loud noise—rattling, but vaguely melodic. A bugle call of sorts.

Half of the troops come to attention. The remainder continue their chit chat. Graham clears his throat again. This time it's a single, sharp note—a musket shot. The stragglers turn to face him.

Graham—"Brother Madsen" to most of his students, "Professor" to a fawning few—releases the lectern and paces into the silence. The tap, tap, tap of his Oxfords is rhythmic and soothing in its precision. He would prefer to just keep tapping, but it's his job to speak, and regrettably, he must ask a question.

Last week's dealing with the department chair is still fresh—nay, *pungent*—in Graham's mind. "I'm getting the same complaint on nearly every student evaluation," the chair had carped. "The point of these classes is to *engage* students with Philosophy, not strafe them with arcane details. They don't all have your brilliant mind, but it's your job to get them thinking. Make them wonder whether they're brains in vats! Get them grappling with the problem of evil! You need to *ask them questions.* Non-rhetorical ones."

The thing about questions, in Graham's opinion, is that they tend to inspire more movement of the mouth than movement of the mind. These undergrads come here so crammed with certainty that a single question is enough to open a floodgate of prepackaged answers. Still, he swallows this objection and parts his lips.

"What is the highest good?" His voice is a crisp staccato, timed to the tapping of his shoes. Several hands sail immediately into the air, but Graham doesn't notice. He presses on: "Or, to come at the same question from a different angle: what is the meaning of life?" He wants to say more—wants to offer his own in-depth and soon-to-be-published analysis of the differences between Aristotle's and Kant's answers to this question. He wants—well, it's no use. *Non-rhetorical*, he reminds himself and turns toward the class.

Half a dozen hands wait in the air. Graham grimaces at the sight and can't help adding an addendum: "Please recall, as is stated multiple times in the syllabus, that when you make a comment in my class, I expect you both to demonstrate your engagement with the reading and to advance an argument in support of your views."

At the mention of the word "syllabus," two students in the back row exchange knowing grins. One of them, a young woman, lifts her pen and makes a tally mark on the top corner of her notebook page.

Only one hand remains in the air now. Graham eyes its owner with a touch of suspicion. The young man, with his blond hair neatly parted on the left side and his collared shirt freshly pressed, is practically bouncing out of his seat in his eagerness to be called on, and it is not unreasonable to wonder if, given permission to speak, he will shake your hand and offer you a Book of Mormon. They are easy to pick out: the students newly returned from their missions.

"Yes?" Graham sighs.

"I just wanted to say how moved I was by the ways in which Kant's philosophy aligns with what we know to be true. Because he says that the highest good is, like, when morality and happiness are in proportion to each other, right? And that's exactly what the Plan of Happiness is. It's a promise from Heavenly Father that if we do what's right, we'll be rewarded with eternal happiness. So, the highest good is eternal life. Kant didn't have the gospel, but reason alone took him really close to the truth."

Graham is about to retort. To indicate the errors in this student's thinking. But another hand is in the air, this one in the very back of the room, and Graham remembers the rest of that oral treatise from the department chair. "You don't have to point out every mistake. If you let them respond to one another, you'll be surprised how often your students will do that work for you."

Graham hesitates. He has an inherent dislike of students who opt to sit in the back row, and this one looks like a vagrant, what with his tousled tresses and ratty band t-shirt. Graham stares for a full beat, which is one beat longer than he usually looks at his students. The vagrant interprets this squinty-eyed pause as permission to speak.

"Personally, I find the claim that happiness is the purpose of our existence sort of offensive. I mean, what about victims of genocide? Or slaves? Or little kids who are abused? Their unhappiness has nothing to do with their own morality. Kant isn't saying that the purpose of life is some cocktail of happiness and morality in the *afterlife*. I think he's saying it's in *this* life, and that strikes me as seriously unfair. I mean, someone endures horrific abuse as a kid, and then we're going to tell them that since they aren't happy, they've failed in some way and as a result, their life is meaningless?"

Something about this student is too much for Graham. And who turned the thermostat up in here? He feels sweat prickling his hairline. He tugs at his necktie, paces, then abruptly stops, swivels, faces the assailant.

"What's your name?" Graham croaks.

"Ben Rogers."

Graham marches toward the lectern. Another student is chiming in. It seems bottomless—their ability to speak without saying anything of substance. Or maybe Graham simply can't absorb substance right now. He feels strangely choked. He wonders briefly whether he might be having a medical emergency. This thought does nothing to calm him. He needs to take control of the situation.

He cross-checks his attendance sheet, prints *Benjamin Rogers, honor code violation*. The shakiness of his handwriting makes his jaw clench. Lips pressed, he clears his throat. The bugle sounds strangled but suffices to silence whichever student is prattling away.

Graham turns to the vagrant. "Benjamin, as a student at BYU, I assume you have read and signed the honor code. You have also read and signed my syllabus, which states in no uncertain terms that the honor code will be upheld in this class. As we all know, young men at BYU are required to keep their hair neatly trimmed. Yours nearly covers your ears. Take care of that before you come to class again, or I will be compelled to take action, as is detailed on page seven of the syllabus."

It is a relief to say these words. Graham's breathing eases. Meanwhile, the bit of lobe peeking out from Ben's hair turns scarlet, but he rallies and turns to smile at the young woman across from him, who is making a second tally mark. "Syllabus"—Brother Madsen said it again. She had bet that he'd drop the word four times in today's class; Ben bet on six.

For a moment, silence—gratifying to Graham and awkward to his students—prevails.

Chapter Two

For the third day in a row, Emma walks to the Student Center. For the third day in a row, this walk is the closest thing she knows to silence—no ringing bells, no teacher droning on, no clicking shut of binder rings. No nagging parents, no squabbling siblings, no Spice Girls blasting from her best friend's stereo. There is only the occasional whirr of passing cars—and the incessant whirr of her own mind.

Emma needs to find a ride *today*. She cannot face another weekend.

A sunny voice chirps lyrics in her head. *Saturday is a special day, it's the day we get ready for Sunday*. The words feel menacing. Emma sees it: Mom sweeping, mopping, dusting, and ironing so that everything and everyone will be immaculate for the Lord's Day. Dad seated in the study with a yellow legal pad and his quadruple combination—Bible, Book of Mormon, Doctrine and Covenants, and Pearl of Great Price, bound in a single volume—planning the Sunday School lesson. Her six younger siblings scurrying about, desperately snatching up all the bits of fun before they get swept away or ironed flat. No playing outside on Sundays. No TV. No comic books. No music, except hymns. It's all journaling, naps, scripture study, and church meetings on the Sabbath.

It's not the lack of fun that troubles Emma, though. It's the dissonance between how she feels and how she has to act. She can't stomach another Sunday of sitting elbow to elbow with her family, locked in a lie, sharing hymnals, taking the sacrament, pretending that it is the holiest and best three hours of her week. To make matters worse, this Sunday is a fast and testimony meeting.

Emma can sneak her way around the twenty-four hours of fasting easily enough, but the testimony meeting is a different matter. The bishop is expecting her to stand up and bear her testimony for the whole congregation. *She can't.*

It's possible that he'll forget, of course. Or that he'll catch a stomach bug and have to stay home. Emma has spent a fair bit of time imagining this latter scenario. And even then, her whole body rises up in rebellion at the notion of another Sunday in church.

She knows how it would play: the knot in the pit of her stomach, cynicism and snark rattling the inside of her skull until it feels like her bones might crack. All the while, she would be expected to sing, to bow her head, to smile. Odds are, her youngest sister Sariah would ask her for help bearing a testimony. It's a ritual that Emma used to enjoy: holding Sariah's hand, walking up to the podium with her, whispering one line at a time into her tiny ear. "I bear my testimony," Emma would say, and then Sariah would squeak the same words into the microphone for the whole, smiling ward to hear. The script never changed much. Whisper, squeak: "I know the Church is true." Whisper, squeak: "I know Joseph Smith was a prophet." Whisper, squeak: "I know the Book of Mormon is true." They usually whispered and squeaked their way through a declaration of God's love and then on to expressions of gratitude before finishing it all off (as everyone does) "in the name of Jesus Christ. Amen."

Emma couldn't do it again. A few months ago, she had still halfway believed the words that she whispered into Sariah's waiting ear. She had at least *wanted* them to be true. Now she doesn't know what to believe, but she knows she doesn't believe *that*; she doesn't even want to anymore. What she wants is—well, she hasn't quite figured that part out yet. But this much is clear: seven-year-old Sariah can't actually *know* that the Church is true. It's brainwashing! Buzzing all of that into her sister's ear!

Of course, Emma has also been that seven-year-old. She remembers standing at the podium, Mom whispering sweetly in her ear. She asked her mother one time, around that age, how she could *know* the Church was true or that Heavenly Father and Jesus were real, and Mom had told her in that honeyed voice of hers, "The Holy Ghost will tell you by giving you a warm feeling in your heart."

Moms and teachers and bishops were always saying things like that. The good old "burning in the bosom," that infallible guide! This answer was almost satisfactory at age seven. At seventeen, not so much. Emma picked the question up again in recent years, turning it over, willing the whole thing to make sense. Faith is one thing, but how could she *know*? Mormons, the good ones, don't just believe; they *know*. If you say "I *believe* that Joseph Smith was a prophet" or "I believe that the Church is true" instead of "I *know*," then you might as well just say "I doubt," which of course no one says.

Emma has never loved the idea of claiming to know things that she only believes—a compunction made more distressing by the fact that no one else seems to share it. "Do you really know the Church is true, or do you just believe?" Emma had asked her best friend Cami a few years back, as they sat shoulder to shoulder, eating bowls of sugary cereal.

Cami looked up, startled. "I *know*," she insisted, wiping milk from her lips.

"How? How do you *know*?" Emma pressed, more out of yearning than skepticism.

"I just do. I feel it. Don't you?"

"I dunno," Emma shrugged. She spooned the last marshmallow from her bowl and stared down at the mass of oat cereal left behind.

Maybe she was the only one who ever doubted, who ever felt uncertain. Her teachers insisted that "a testimony is found in the bearing of it." It must have been a quote from some old, dead prophet because Emma heard it over and over. A testimony is found in the bearing of it. *Fake it until you make it.* Emma never managed to find a better interpretation of those words. And so, she did fake it for years, taking her fragile, embryonic belief and declaring it fully formed knowledge. But when she paused, when she dared to look within? There it sat, a flashing neon sign: *DOUBT*, it proclaimed. To unsee a light like that, you have to either squeeze your eyes shut or get really good at explaining your own reality away. Emma tried both. Occasionally, she ignored or pretended so well that she felt brief flutters of certainty. It never lasted, though. It was a mothlike faith, inevitably scorched by the neon light of doubt.

When you have been told so many times that shouting "I know the Church is true" from the rooftops will help you to *actually* know, and instead you feel the words carving away at your insides, feel yourself growing hollower with each repetition—well, then the DOUBT sign just flashes brighter, bigger, until your barren insides glow like the Vegas strip.

Maybe this doubt was just one of Satan's many temptations, Emma told herself. Maybe it was her thorn in the flesh, her cross to bear, her own unique and awful inadequacy that she must strive to overcome. *Maybe.* But regardless of its source, on and on the light flashed.

Now, Emma doesn't want to squeeze her eyes shut anymore. She doesn't want to believe that the problem is something internal, something about her, something about which she should feel ashamed. She recently began allowing herself furtive glances at DOUBT. When she did, the letters shifted. *We're Open, Come In,* they seemed to spell.

Maybe it was just curiosity getting the better of her. Maybe it was weakness. Maybe it was Satan. Then again, maybe it was some deep inner wisdom or daring. In any case, something clicked. Or cracked. Or opened. Or shattered. Something illuminated or went dark. And now, here she is. In this moment, one truth burns in Emma's bosom: she has to get away from here, from Provo, from her parents, from the Church, from this life in which she doesn't belong. And to do that, she needs a ride.

Emma's feet hurry down the steps of the Student Center. Her eyes search out the familiar, always-empty pocket: Moab. But it's not empty today. A yellow slip of paper peeks from the top. Emma pulls it out and reads her golden ticket. *Dan Christensen - up to 8 passengers – Moab – Saturday, 11/4.* That's tomorrow. Emma exhales so forcefully she wonders where all the air came from. There's no phone number listed, just *TA in 1119 TMCB Fri 3:00-7:00.*

It's 4:30 now. TMCB? Emma only knows the JKHB, home to her father's tiny office with its towering stacks of books written by dead guys. She hopes the TMCB is nowhere near there. She'll have to ask. That's fine. She's not shy, and at 5'8" and seventeen years, she's not likely to be called out for being a high school student on a college campus. She makes her way out of the Student Center and onto the quad, a sprawling lawn crisscrossed by paths connecting the most prominent buildings. Chattering students spill in and out of the library, and Emma picks one, an impeccably groomed young woman with shining, auburn hair. "Hey, do you know where the TMCB is?" Emma asks her.

The woman tilts her head, puzzling. "Oh, isn't that the Talmage? It's right over there, next to the JKHB."

Emma's eyes drift across the quad, squinting to make out the small sign: *James E Talmage Math Sciences and Computer Building*. It's a nondescript building—pale brick and concrete, dissected by narrow windows. The only remarkable thing about it is its tight proximity to her father's office; the JKHB practically spoons the Talmage. Emma will have to walk directly under her dad's window to make it to the front entrance. She could circle around and look for a backdoor, but she's sick of tiptoeing. Instead, she lifts her chin and strides forward. If this works—*when* it works—everything will be different.

The odds are in Emma's favor on a campus bustling with thirty thousand Mormons. Or perhaps Heavenly Father intervenes on her behalf. Emma's father does not see her. He is searching his filing cabinet for the folder marked *Honor Code Reporting Forms*. Ben Rogers still has not trimmed his hair.

Dan Christensen, Emma's ride to freedom, is just where he promised to be. He sits at the entrance to room 1119, headphones on and discman perched on the desk in front of him. Whitney Houston wails faintly from his direction. Emma takes in the room—the smell of stale Doritos, fluorescent lights flickering down on a couple dozen computers, most of them occupied, all of them by men.

Dan looks up, and his face brightens. He slides his headphones down from his ears. "Hey, can I help you with something?"

"Um, are you Dan?"

Dan nods, looking both confused and exhilarated—as if he has won the lottery without even buying a ticket.

"I found your paper on the ride board. I was hoping to catch a ride with you to Moab?" Emma plays it cool, as if she doesn't care much either way, but her stomach clenches as she speaks.

Dan does not play it cool. "Oh, dude! That's rad! I thought it was gonna be a really lonely drive. All my roommates have dates this weekend—well, *every* weekend—so I figured I might as well go home and hang out with my family. My mom just got called as the ward organist, so I wanna be there for her first week, you know? But going down there alone seems sort of lame, right? It's a long drive. I didn't think a *girl* would want to go with me, but yeah, you should totally come! Don't even worry about helping with gas, okay? I'm just super stoked that you're coming."

"Wow, thanks." Total creeper or just an awkward geek? Emma feels too relieved to be troubled by the question. *This is actually going to work*, she tells herself. The knot in her stomach loosens.

"Sweet, I'll pick you up at 7:00 tomorrow morning! What's your address?"

"Oh, um, I live in the foreign language housing," she lies.

After a few exclamations from Dan over how "rad" that is and repeated lamentations about how desperately he wants to live in the Portuguese house and how much he misses speaking the language because his mission to Brazil was, as he tells her, the best two years of his life, the arrangements are finally settled. Emma will meet him in the parking lot the next morning.

It's hard to say who feels more anticipation when they part ways. Emma, who finds an escape hatch, suddenly opened. Or Dan, who will be spending over three hours alone with a girl, which is three times his previous record, not counting his mother and sisters.

Chapter Three

As far as Dan can tell, he is the only guy at BYU who doesn't have a date this weekend. Well, him and that kid in his ward—the one who isn't going on a mission. That dude is probably the only nineteen-and-a-half-year-old male on campus. He might as well have a red letter on his chest. A "U," perhaps, for "unworthy" (and "unmarriageable"). Dan feels sorry for him. Admittedly, Dan feels sorry for himself, too. His roommates, all RM's (returned missionaries), go on dates almost every weekend. Three of them have steady girlfriends of a month or more and so, will likely be married by summer at the very latest, and the other two ask different women out just about every weekend, searching for the one. "You learn a lot about a girl on a first date," his roommate Travis tells him.

Dan wouldn't know because he's only been on one date, and it didn't go well. His date insisted that he take her home within the first hour. Dan was befuddled. "I bought her flowers, and I paid to get her into the skating rink! And she didn't even give me a chance," he groused to his roommates, who exchanged knowing glances behind his back.

Dan tried asking a few other women out, and they turned him down. "It's not like I was asking them to marry me or something!" Dan sputtered, but this was just bluster. There is nothing that Dan wants more than to find a wife. And so *of course* he had imagined the possibility of proposing if the first date went well. In his heart of hearts, though, Dan knows that *he* is the problem. He is the misfit.

So imagine Dan's excitement over the fact that an eligible female has responded to his ride board ad. He had only been hoping for someone to split the cost of gas with him. A few dollars one way or the other are nothing to the prospect of finding his eternal companion, though, and this is his first real opportunity to show a girl all that he has to offer. His first opportunity and, if the present trend holds, maybe his *only* opportunity. Dan is determined not to squander it.

This won't be easy. When he's nervous, he gets clumsy and awkward, even by his own standards. The one date he went on, the one where he took a girl ice skating and she insisted on going home early? Well, that might have been precipitated by Dan's tripping over his own feet, flailing wildly, and grabbing his date's breasts to right himself. A simple apology would likely have eased her shock and embarrassment, but instead, Dan blushed scarlet and stammered something about falling on pillows.

His mortified date was saving her downy breasts for after the altar—a place she certainly wouldn't be approaching with an impudent clown like Dan Christensen.

After meeting Emma, Dan prays with particular earnestness. "Heavenly Father, thank you so much for sending your beautiful daughter my way. I know you must get tired of hearing me pray for a wife, and if you'll just help me make a good impression, then I won't have to keep bugging you about that all the time. Please help me not to mess this up!"

Heavenly Father helps those who help themselves, and so, Dan is careful to do his share of the work. He cleans his car, throwing away weeks' worth of soda cans and crumpled homework assignments. He buys an evergreen air freshener at Walmart and then, inspired by what can only be the Holy Ghost, he tapes a small picture of his favorite temple to the front of the dangling pine. Dan holds it in the air, beams at the swaying edifice. Now any time he looks at his rearview mirror, he'll be reminded of his most important goal—an eternal marriage, sealed in God's own house. And each time Emma looks there, she will glimpse the purity of his intentions.

Dan thinks long and hard about what he really wants to show Emma. With his other first date (Dan is thinking of this drive as a date by now), he had tried to act cool. The reason he had flailed and grabbed the girl's breasts was that he was attempting to show off with a crossover. This time, Dan won't show off. Instead, he'll show his future helpmeet who he really is—a righteous guy, a good guy, a geek perhaps, but also a guy who will treat her like a princess for all eternity. And so, on the evening of the day on which he first met his would-be eternal companion, Dan shaves and showers with extra care and stays up a bit later than he ought, burning a CD for the road, then spends most of the night tossing, turning, sleeplessly praying.

Chapter Four

Emma can't risk goodbyes. No one can know she's leaving until she's already gone. But she cuts three pieces of white paper down the middle, folds each one in on itself, and labels each with a name: *Eliza*, *Joseph*, *Hyrum*, *Brigham*, *Nephi*, *Sariah*. Inside each folded paper, Emma writes a short note apiece for her two younger sisters and four younger brothers. She'll tuck the stack under Eliza's scriptures before leaving in the morning.

Emma needs to write Cami a letter, too—but how to begin?

She won't write *him* a letter. There's nothing to say. She doesn't know anything for sure yet, and even if she did—well, why ruin his life? It's one thing to find yourself knocked out of a life you never wanted in the first place. But to be expelled from a life that you chose? She won't put him through that. Disappearing is a kindness, and it's one that costs her nothing—or almost nothing.

She'll miss talking with him. She'll miss the evaporation of hours—the way time disappeared when they were discussing things that no one else seemed to understand. He understood. She loved that about him, but she wasn't *in* love with him.

It was curiosity that propelled her forward. Curiosity about being kissed, and then . . . well, the thing about curiosity is that, in Emma's experience, it's bottomless. Every seemingly buttoned-up answer spills new questions from its pockets. Or more to the point: when you unbutton one question, revealing its answer, the next thing you notice is more buttons—tiny, shining invitations.

How many times had Emma heard the words "necking" and "petting" on the list of absolutely-do-not-do-this prohibitions? To hear a word so many times but not try the thing even once? When she parted her lips and his tongue slid into her mouth, she almost giggled. *Necking*, she noted silently. When his hands cupped her breasts, the inner voice chimed again. *Petting*. And *this must be heavy petting*, as he unfastened her jeans, sliding his fingers into her underpants.

Then, the voice went quiet, and Emma just felt it all unfold, neither reaching nor resistant. For a stretch of moments, she was a *body*. And she was *alive.*

Afterwards, her inner commentator returned to summarize the evening's events. *Fornication. Second only to murder.* The thought made her smile. He saw the sudden twitch of her lips and asked what she was thinking. When she repeated the words aloud, his face went white.

"I'm sorry," he stammered. "I thought you were right there with me, I—"

She laughed and grabbed his hand. "I was. I *am.* I'm not saying I regret it. I just thought of the words, and they struck me as funny."

The color returned to his face, and he smiled, too, rippling relief.

When she was alone again, driving home in her family's Ford Club Wagon, Emma found herself laughing aloud, found herself charmed by the secret she carried, delighted by the realization that she had done something so forbidden and not been struck by lightning. She didn't even feel the white, hot heat of shame. Instead, she felt almost like—could it be—almost like her own person. A person who made her own choices.

This light-souled secret popped just days later in a CVS bathroom. Emma knew what the blue + sign on the plastic stick meant. It meant she was her own person making *terrible* choices. She returned to the shelves and grabbed two more tests.

"Are these things ever wrong?" she asked the woman at the counter, whose double-pierced ears suggested to Emma that she might know about such things.

"You'll get a false negative if you test too early," the woman replied, scanning the boxes without expression.

Apparently, this was normal to her—girls buying pregnancy tests, disappearing to the bathroom, then returning to the counter to purchase more. It was not normal to Emma.

"How about a false positive?" Emma asked, her voice unnaturally high.

"I've never heard of that. You're supposed to take it first thing in the morning, though. It's more accurate that way."

Emma's hands trembled as she buried the pregnancy tests at the bottom of her canvas messenger bag. Morning was an eternity away.

She didn't sleep that night. It didn't help, of course, that she was up every hour, racing to the bathroom to pee. But even in the lull between, she tossed, restless. The backs of her lids lit up like screens, projecting possible futures. Some held scraps of hope, others were impossibly bleak, but they all shared one common necessity: escape. Escape from this life—whether that came in the form of exile or flight. There was no use pretending that she belonged here any longer. As her belly expanded, what was already obvious on the inside would become obvious on the outside: she didn't fit in this life, in this story, on this straight and narrow path. One way or another, she would have to leave.

Should she try to explain all of this in the letter to Cami? Should she tell her best friend about the second pregnancy test, the single line without the telltale cross? Emma chews on her lower lip, her pencil hovering aimlessly over the still blank page. No, that would just be more confusing. It is certainly confusing to Emma. *I think I might be pregnant*, she writes.

What next? *I'm sorry I didn't tell you. I was afraid you would think less of me.* Emma pauses, writes *I think less of me, too,* then erases it. It's only half true. She feels like an idiot for possibly getting pregnant. But the other half of the truth—the part where she doesn't see why sex is such a big deal—isn't something that she can share with Cami, or with anyone for that matter.

***

The first time that an old man asked Emma about her sex life, she was twelve years old. She walked into Bishop Peterson's office, and he shut the door.

"Happy belated birthday," he offered with a smile, seating himself behind a large wooden desk. "Your twelfth birthday marks a special milestone—your transition from being a child to being a young woman. These next few years will be some of the most important years of your life."

Emma knew this and had been feeling very grown-up all week.

"This is the time to begin preparing to be a mother and a wife. You and I will meet once a year now to check on your progress and make sure you're staying worthy of the goal of a temple marriage. I'm here to counsel you if challenges arise. I have a lot of questions for you today, but first I want to see if you have any questions for me?"

Emma shook her head no, trying to match her gravity to the bishop's.

He began the standard list of worthiness questions. Most of them she had expected: did she "have a testimony," as he put it, that The Church of Jesus Christ of Latter-day Saints was the one true church on earth? Did she have a testimony that Joseph Smith had been a true prophet and that Gordon B. Hinckley was the true prophet today?

She was glad he didn't ask if she *knew* these things. Emma hoped *belief* was enough to count as a testimony. She answered "yes" all around with only a twinge of worry that she might be lying.

Then Bishop Peterson left the familiar ground of faith. He asked her about the Word of Wisdom; did she abstain from coffee, tea, alcohol, cigarettes, and illicit drugs? The question seemed comical. Where on earth would she get drugs or coffee from? And why would she want to? The next question, about something called "masturbation," left her even more confused.

"Do I what?" she asked, unsure.

"Engage in masturbation or self-gratification?" Bishop Peterson's gaze broke with hers for a moment. Did she imagine that he was blushing?

Obviously, masturbation must be something bad, so Emma feigned certainty. "No," she answered and then spent the rest of the afternoon fidgety with agitation. Had she lied to a servant of the Lord?

At home that evening, she stole a private moment with Merriam Webster, fingering pages until she found it. "Masturbate, masturbation, masturbatory - erotic stimulation of one's own genital organs commonly resulting in orgasm." Emma's face felt hot; Bishop Peterson had asked her about *that*? Gross. She wasn't sure what orgasm was—something dreadful, to be sure—but she had heard from Cami that teenage boys mess around with their private parts and that if you saw that one of them wasn't taking the sacrament on Sunday, you knew for certain that he had confessed it to the bishop. But she wasn't in danger of that kind of sin. She was a *girl*, and girls are pure. That's what everyone said, anyway.

Girded with a fuller understanding of pertinent terminology, Emma breezed through the annual worthiness interviews at thirteen, fourteen, fifteen, and sixteen. She got used to the questions, and of course she was already used to the idea that old men were entitled to judge her—old bishop, old Dad, good old Heavenly Father. Sure, the whole thing was a bit uncomfortable, but it wasn't much worse than playing in the Christmas piano recital or standing up in Social Studies to present a report. Her ears and cheeks turned a bit red, and she avoided looking at her audience, but she was still able to do what she needed to do: to play the keys in the appropriate rhythm and sequence, to distinguish between the branches of government, to reply that yes, she obeyed the Law of Chastity, and to mumble a blushing "no" when asked about masturbation.

Around the time of her seventeenth birthday, though, Bishop Peterson was called to be Stake President (a promotion of sorts, albeit unpaid) and was replaced by Bishop Harrell. Bishop Harrell asked all the usual questions, and then threw a curveball: "Do you ever think about breaking the Law of Chastity?"

Emma wondered if she had misheard him. "Do I ever *think* about it?"

He nodded, leaning back in his chair, elbows on armrests, fingers steepled together.

"Well, I mean, it's obviously *crossed my mind*. But I haven't thought about it in the sense of actually intending to do it."

Bishop Harrell pressed his lips together, drummed his fingers, then released them, leaning forward. "Your tone of voice suggests that maybe *thoughts* don't seem like a big deal to you."

Her tone? Emma swallowed the first retort that came to mind. If she had a dollar for every time her father had issued an indictment on the same subject, she would owe a hefty tithe. "I guess I don't really get the point of the question," she finally answered, her voice pulled into an even line.

"The point, Sister Madsen, is this: you're turning seventeen. You're almost a grown woman. Soon, you'll head out into the world and leave the protective shelter of your parents' home. Without them physically present to guide you, whatever temptations you're feeling now are going to get stronger."

He had misunderstood her, she realized. He thought she was saying she felt *tempted*. That was what he had meant to ask. She just needed to set the record straight. "Oh, it's not a *temptation*," she interjected. "It's just a passing thought. I mean, my Young Women's leaders are always talking about how we shouldn't, like, neck or pet, and of course when someone says something, you get an image in your head, right? Like if I told you not to think about an elephant, you would automatically think about an elephant, just for a second, anyway."

The bishop pursed his lips. "I see the apple doesn't fall far from the tree. I'm afraid waxing philosophical isn't going to protect you from temptation."

Emma's face burned. He had asked a question, and she was explaining her answer, and now he was accusing her of being like her father? She swallowed hard, forced her fists to unclench. "All I was trying to say is that they're passing thoughts, not actual temptations. I'm not going to act on them."

Bishop Harrell was silent for a moment. When he spoke, his voice was slow and pondering. "Tell me more about these thoughts."

Emma gaped at him. Tell him about the pictures that came to mind when she heard words like "necking" or "petting," or worse still, "fornication"? Tell him that when she heard the phrase "sex outside of marriage is next to murder," she imagined some dark, deviant, nearly murderous version of herself having sex? There was no way on earth she was going to tell the bishop about any of that. She didn't even want to *think* about it with him in the room. Images arose unbidden—tousled hair, wild eyes, bare shoulders, and a wickedly handsome boy. Emma tried to think of something else, anything else—elephants, breakfast, Book of Mormon prophets!

"You look troubled." The bishop's voice interrupted the flood of unwanted thoughts. "I understand this is hard to talk about, but it's important."

His voice was softer now, but there was no way Emma was taking him on an excursion into her imagination. She wished she could go back in time and assure him that she had never once had a single thought about breaking the Law of Chastity. Voices hummed from beyond the closed door. Oh, to be there instead of here!

The bishop stared at her, barely blinking. He would wait her out. She had to say something. "Look, it's really not a big deal," she began. "Like I said, when I hear a word—*any* word—I get a picture in my head. But it doesn't stay. It's gone *really fast.*"

If there was doubt in Emma's voice, it was only because she could still see that image, playing like a movie in her mind—herself and some boy and a sin second only to murder. She felt herself blushing.

"How are you fighting that temptation?"

Her annoyance flared, and the image went up in smoke. Why did he keep calling it a temptation? It was just a flipping picture in her head. There was no use in defending herself, though. He would only accuse her of arguing. If she wanted this to end, she had to play by his rules. "I sing hymns," she lied.

"Wonderful! That's a great strategy. And are you reading your scriptures daily?"

"Most days," she answered, and this was technically true if you averaged the answer over the past few years rather than, say, the past few months. Emma's lack of an ironclad testimony wasn't for lack of trying.

"Good. It sounds like we're catching these temptations early and like you're taking important steps to combat them. This can get tricky, though. If you believe you're doing so well that you don't need to worry about these temptations, that creates a door through which Satan can enter. Humility is a better defense than confidence—humility and a strong testimony."

Emma nodded, and the bishop paused, drumming his fingers together again. "Hmm, I don't recall ever hearing you bear your testimony in fast and testimony meeting. I know this might feel a little awkward, but let's have you do that right now."

"Bear my testimony? Right now?"

"Yeah," he nodded, smiling. "Go ahead, whenever you're ready."

Emma shifted side to side in her seat. She wondered if she was supposed to stand up. She wondered what to do with her hands. Mostly, she wondered what to say. She had already lied about the whole hymn thing. In theory, she could lie now, too—*in theory*, but not in practice. She had been eroded by the same question for so long—*how can I know that the Church is true?* She could no more feign a solid testimony than a valley could pretend to be a mountain.

"Well, I believe that Heavenly Father loves me," she mumbled. "And I believe that Jesus died for our sins . . . and that the Church is true . . . and that Joseph Smith was a prophet." She could hear her volume fade with each successive claim, as if her belief were wired to a dimmer switch. She really did believe that she was loved by something bigger than what she could understand. Maybe the rest was true, too? She would give it 60/40 odds. Or maybe 50/50?

Emma hadn't noticed just how faint her own belief had become. It used to give off a *little* more light, didn't it? What had happened? The question captivated her: what was the genesis of her unbelief? And what should she do with it?

All these years, she had been a child in the back of a car, asking the same question over and over: the spiritual equivalent of "are we there yet?" Now suddenly, she could sense the possibility of far more interesting questions. *What does this sign mean? Where does that road lead? Why are we going where we are going? Where else could I go instead?* Emma forgot the bishop's presence in the room.

"Is that all you want to say?" his voice broke in.

"Umm, yes," Emma answered, and she was telling the truth.

"It sounds like your testimony needs some work. You used the word 'belief' a lot. Heavenly Father wants you to *know* that His church is true. Have you prayed to know for sure?"

"Yup." There was no apology in her voice.

"Sometimes we have to ask more than once. When our faith is tested like that, the rewards of the testimony that come are even sweeter. If you keep asking in faith, you *will* receive a sure testimony of the truthfulness of the gospel."

Emma gave him a smile that she hoped would hurry things along. She wanted to leave here. She wanted to go for a long walk or write in her journal. She wanted to be alone with her thoughts. There were doors ajar in her mind.

Bishop Harrell kept talking, though. He quoted the warrior prophet Moroni's promise from the end of the Book of Mormon—the assurance that if you ask God for a witness of the truthfulness of the Book of Mormon (or any teaching of the Church), "with a sincere heart, with real intent, having faith in Christ," then you will receive an answer. He bore his own testimony and encouraged Emma to fast and pray. Then, he paused and stared at her expectantly. Had he asked her a question? She nodded her head, smiled at him again. It seemed to do the trick. He stood up, reached out his hand, and took hers in a hardy shake.

"I look forward to fast and testimony meeting," he said. "You'll find that your testimony is much stronger by then if you do the things we talked about, and there's no better defense against temptation than that."

Emma nodded again, told him goodbye, and was out the door before she grasped that she must have unknowingly smiled and nodded her agreement to stand up in front of the whole congregation and bear her testimony in one month's time. A boulder tumbled into the river of her thoughts. She couldn't possibly bear her testimony next month! She didn't have one. And what's more, for the first time, she was ready to consider the possibility that she didn't need one—didn't *want* one.

"Emma!" a voice interrupted the swirling.

She turned to find Brother Pingree, who doubled as her family's orthodontist and home teacher. "Happy birthday! This week, right?"

"Yeah, thanks."

"Hmm, you don't look all that pleased about it. Let me guess, your dad still isn't buying you a car?" Brother Pingree sighed in mock dismay, shaking his head. "Fathers are a sorry lot these days."

"Definitely no car," Emma laughed, and the boulder loosened.

"I'll have a talk with him. I'm sure he'll listen to me," Brother Pingree's eyes twinkled. "I'll tell him you need a . . . hmm, how does a red Mustang sound?"

"Do you think you could talk him into a silver Dodge Viper convertible instead?"

Brother Pingree's laughter bounced from the walls. "I'll be glad to try. Now get along with you. You're supposed to be in Young Women's, aren't you?"

Emma turned to walk toward class, but when she reached the door, her feet kept moving—down the hall, around the corner, to a bigger door, labeled *EXIT*. There were still doors ajar in her mind.

When she pushed her way out, a thrill rushed her body like wind. Maybe doubt is one of those things that looks its worst just before you take the plunge. Like inching up to the edge of a cliff, gaping down at deep water and summoning the will to fall. You feel such dread. And then you leap, and the fear is gone, and you are a gull, swooping weightlessly, joyfully toward the catch.

***

Not that Emma feels weightless or joyful today. There is too much to do, too much that is uncertain. Is she plunging toward water or a jagged boulder? Maybe it doesn't matter. Maybe all that matters is she can't stay, coiled and compressed in this place. It can only be her springboard to something—*anything*—else.

And so, she begins packing. Just the essentials, just what she can fit into her schoolbag. She pulls out her binder and books and tucks them under her bed. The final unopened pregnancy test still sits at the bottom of the bag, the box smashed and bent. She leaves it where it is and begins adding items: toiletries, a few changes of clothing, pajamas, socks, underwear, and her wallet, containing $243 in babysitting earnings. She hesitates at her nightstand, looking down at the black, leather-bound scriptures with their gilded pages that her parents gave her when she was baptized at age eight. For so many years, she read from them every night, imagining that if she worked just a little harder—if she did all the right things—a testimony would follow. Her world would make sense. She lifts them now, but only to reach the envelope of photos that is tucked underneath. She rifles through the pictures, finds one of her and Cami smiling side by side and another of Eliza, Brigham, and Sariah seated hip to hip to hip at the piano. She slides both photos into her journal, then folds the messenger bag shut.

Bag packed, she heads downstairs to say goodbye without saying goodbye. Emma's mother and six younger siblings are in the family room, watching *The Princess Bride* for the umpteenth time. "Anybody want a peanut?" André the Giant asks, and the Madsen children erupt into their umpteenth round of giggles.

"I'm heading up to bed, just wanted to say good night," Emma tells the room.

"Already? Everything alright?" Her mother turns toward her, eyebrows tilting up and together in that look of concern that Emma usually finds so annoying.

"Yeah, I'm fine. Cami and I are going for an early run, and then we have to spend the rest of the day working on our German presentation over at her place. So I just want to get a good night's rest." There—she's justified her early departure and prolonged absence. She's bought herself time.

"Why don't you two work on your project over here? I could help you."

"Oh, uh, I told Cami I'd go over to her place. Her parents have something going on, so she needs to be around to keep an eye on Mikey," Emma improvises.

"Well, let me know if you want me to look it over for you later." Mom smiles, but the inner edges of her eyebrows remain creased. German and homemaking, these are Heidi Madsen's offerings, and her daughter isn't interested.

Emma casts a last look toward the two couches, the two lines of blond heads turned to face the screen. "Good night," she whispers and heads up to bed. Amazingly, she sleeps like a child.

***

Graham Madsen sits where he always sits on Friday evenings: at the large mahogany desk in the study. The door is closed against the sounds of clanging swords and quests for vengeance. Heidi and the children always watch a movie together on Fridays, and Graham cloisters himself here, preparing his Sunday School lesson. He teaches Gospel Doctrine, the adult Sunday School class, and has done so since first receiving the calling three years ago. Though it was just plain, vanilla Bishop Peterson who beckoned Graham into his office and extended the invitation to serve as Sunday School teacher, Graham performs this role with such zeal that you might suppose it had been Jesus Christ himself sitting across from him in the swivel chair. All callings are said to be inspired—that is, the bishop seeks revelation as to who should serve in what capacity, but the "revelation" that Graham Madsen ought to serve as Sunday School teacher must have come easily. Graham knows the scriptures better than anyone else in the entire ward.

He has a scripture for everything. For whole wheat bread, lovingly baked by his wife. ("Grain is ordained for the use of man.") For Jello salad, prepared with equal tenderness. ("Man saw that it was good for food.") For the teasing and squabbling that often overtake his children. ("Is there one among you that doth make a mock of his brother?") For muddy boot tracks in the foyer. ("Put off thy shoes from off thy feet!") For rain, sun, wind. (Ecclesiastes 11:3, D&C 88:45, and Ether 6:5, respectively.) When his eldest daughter runs away, scriptures will stream from his lips like expletives. Graham doesn't swear, of course. If he has a linguistic vice, it is his propensity for punning.

Apart from puns, he is rarely intentionally funny. His quirks are so abundant, though, that much like his college students, members of his Gospel Doctrine class tend to overlook this. "Brother Madsen is hilarious!" they say, rattling off some amusing habit or anecdote.

There is the way he unconsciously chest bumps the chalkboard when he gets enthusiastic about what he's writing, so that his tie and jacket and sometimes even his chin end up powdered with white dust. There is his daily run through the surrounding neighborhood, exactly four miles, begun at precisely 7:00 AM and concluded between 7:32 and 7:34 AM. Purple spandex running tights when the temperature drops to forty-nine degrees or below (as measured by the thermometer that hangs on his kitchen window), purple jogging shorts for fifty and above. There's also the tenacity with which he returns to his carefully plotted Sunday School lessons, interruptions notwithstanding.

Just last week, he was interrupted mid-sentence when a fly sailed straight into his open mouth. Brother Madsen coughed, spat it into his bare hand, wiped the phlegmy carcass onto a paper torn from the yellow legal pad that never leaves his side, then spluttered, "Matthew 25:35. He was a stranger, and I took him in."

And then? He returned to the lesson, as if nothing had happened! As if he couldn't hear the buzz of laughter.

Tonight, Graham's quadruple combination is open to Jacob 5, the longest and densest chapter of the Book of Mormon, as well as the subject for this week's Gospel Doctrine lesson. The chapter consists of a wordy allegory, detailing the painstaking efforts of a man—"the lord of the vineyard"—to care for and protect his olive trees. Jacob 5 catalogues every move that this master and his servant make in their efforts to ensure that tame rather than wild olives flourish in the vineyard. Privately, Graham chafes at the use of the word "vineyard" in this context. Shouldn't it be an "orchard" or "grove?" Graham is not the only faithful Latter-day Saint to object to some aspect of this chapter. The more common complaint, though, is that the master and servant prune, nourish, dung, and graft for *seventy-seven* verses, so that by the end, the average reader finds herself vicariously exhausted from their labors. Graham is not the average reader, though. Semantic imprecision notwithstanding, he feels a deep sense of kinship with the lord of the vineyard.

It is no easy matter to be lord over anything. As a parent and professor—lord over young minds—Graham can sympathize with this. This is why he scaffolds his classes and his household with syllabi and rules—to prevent the unpalatable outcomes that might otherwise emerge.

Midway through the allegory, the lord discovers that wild olives have overtaken his trees. "What could I have done more for my vineyard!?" he grieves, then makes one final effort to save them. He tastes the fruit of every branch, prunes the very worst branches from the trees, then burns the offending limbs. And it works! The tame fruit again outcompetes the wild. The lord celebrates but also issues a warning: If wild fruit ever invades his vineyard again, he will burn all of the wild trees without mercy.

"It would serve them right," Graham shrugs, shaking his head in condemnation.

He will focus his lesson, he decides, on seven carefully chosen passages from Jacob 5, introduce six relevant verses from elsewhere in the scriptures, and share one pun. (If the lord hadn't sacrificed the wildest branches to the flames, then *olive* his vineyard would have become corrupted.)

***

When her alarm rings at 6:00 the next morning, Emma dresses in running clothes—Adidas track pants, *not* purple spandex—then tiptoes down the creaking stairs. She pours a bowl of Cheerios and eats hurriedly. Too hurriedly, perhaps. The cereal clumps in her throat, demanding more time than she's willing to grant it. She washes the sludgy remnants down with a glass of orange juice and carries her dishes to the sink. The water is icy cold, but Emma doesn't notice. Her mind is running south and east toward Moab. And from there? The possibilities have been playing over and over in her mind for days, some of them thrillers, some survival stories, some romcoms. All of them saturated with color and sound and destiny. They share a common beginning: Emma's urgent departure.

It's no wonder, then, that she doesn't register her surroundings. Doesn't see the worn oak table, with its scratches and dents and nine empty chairs. That her eyes can't absorb the forest green wallpaper with its white, leafy vines and the red crayon marks that Hyrum scribbled as a toddler. Perhaps, if she inhaled deeply she would smell the pumpkin pie that Mom baked late last night. But she doesn't inhale, not really. Her mind is alert and racing, but its path is far from this room. Emma hurries along with it, out of the kitchen, through the family room, and past the upright piano with its yellowing keys around which her family has gathered, singing and re-singing the same unchanging hymns in voices that change and crack.

Emma unbolts the front door. It sighs in relief as the weather seal breaks. She steps into the twilight, schoolbag slung over her shoulder. Cami's place is on the way, just a few houses down the street. Emma tucks a red envelope into the mailbox. *CAMI*, it proclaims, big and bold with little hearts at the corners of each letter. And then she continues her trek. She's walked this route so many times before—south and just a bit west, past the temple, toward 900 East. Today, though, each footstep is a seal breaking, a rush of air, a rebellion.

Chapter Five

Emma makes it to the FLSR parking lot fifteen minutes ahead of schedule. Dan arrives just two minutes after her. He pulls up to the sidewalk and painstakingly rolls down the window of his burgundy and faux-wood station wagon. "Hop in!" he calls out.

Emma yanks at the metal handle on the passenger side and slides into the plush seat—also burgundy.

"I'm super stoked you're riding with me," Dan says, as she pulls her door shut.

"Thanks. It's nice of you to drive me. And I'm gonna pitch in for gas. That's the whole point of the ride board."

Dan steers the station wagon onto Temple Hill Drive, approaching the traffic light at 900 East. "It's also a way to meet people." He turns to look at Emma, hoping to mark the significance of his words.

His gaze is unyielding, and Emma inches her body closer to the passenger side door. *Why isn't he looking at the road?* She meets his eyes briefly, hoping this will satisfy him. It seems to. Dan turns his eyes back to the street just in time to safely execute a right turn. Emma's own eyes take in the evergreen-scented temple hanging from the rearview mirror.

"What temple is that?" she asks him.

Perfect. She noticed it. "It's the Monticello temple. It's the closest one to where I grew up in Moab. It's brand new, it just opened while I was on my mission, but I'm getting married there." Mission and marriage, all in the same breath. Dan impresses himself with his own twofer.

"You're engaged?"

Dan blushes, "Well, no, I still have to find the right girl." He should look at her again, should mark the significance of his words with his eyes, but he sits rigid, tense, his neck refusing to move. *Heavenly Father, help me not to blow this,* his mind pleads.

With new courage, he begins again. "What's your favorite temple?"

"Mine? I dunno. I grew up here, so I guess the Provo Temple is sort of my favorite, even though it's kinda weird looking." She hadn't meant to tell him anything about herself, and she's annoyed to have let this much slide.

Dan could ask about where her family lives now. He could ask any number of personal questions. Emma hopes he'll merely weigh in on the particulars of the Provo Temple with its strange, cakelike physique. Instead, he turns to look at her. "Whoever gets to take you to the Provo Temple will be a very lucky guy."

Emma's forehead crinkles and her eyebrows slant toward one another as if whispering together about the sheer awkwardness of this moment. What on earth is she supposed to say to that? Is this guy going to spend the whole drive hitting on her?

Dan is unsettled by his words, too. Would he really give up marrying in the Monticello temple just to make this beautiful daughter of God happy? He would, he realizes. He would do that and so much more just to have a sweet little wife like her by his side.

"I have no intention of getting married." The sharpness of Emma's voice cuts right through his warm epiphany.

Dan is dumbstruck. She might as well have said, "Oh, I'm not really interested in happiness," or, "I prefer that my existence remain meaningless," or perhaps even, "All I really want is to become a drug-addicted prostitute and die a miserable death." *All* Mormon girls want to get married. They want it even more than the boys do, which is a lot! Just like all Mormon girls want to have babies. That's what it means to be a girl!

"What do you mean? Why not?"

"Well, why should I? So some guy can boss me around?"

Dan's own father is a much milder sort than Graham Madsen, and so her words bounce when they hit him, meaningless, impossible to take in. "That's not what marriage is," he frowns, rubbing the back of his neck.

"Well, maybe I'm just not the marrying type."

Dan's missionary spirit kicks in. "But marriage is central to Heavenly Father's plan for us. To return to live with Him in the Celestial Kingdom, you *have* to be married. That's why he gives us these beautiful temples, so that we can have eternal marriages and return to live with Him. Besides, don't you want to bring His spirit children into this world and give them bodies? There are babies just waiting up there in the preexistence, hoping to be born into a home that—"

"You don't have to be married to have a baby," Emma snaps.

Dan's mouth hangs open. He has no answer. A full minute passes in silence. It's too much. His fingers fumble with the stereo, twice hitting the wrong button, before he finally manages to press play.

His freshly burned CD begins. The Mormon Tabernacle Choir fills the space. Dan selected the songs so carefully—artfully weaving together hymns about the temple and eternal families with romantic pop songs. He realizes now that this may not have been the best choice. "*I have a family here on earth*," the choir sings. "*They are so good to me. I want to share my life with them through all eternity.*"

Emma turns her face away from Dan and presses her forehead against the window. She feels caged. She left one zoo, only to find herself locked in another. None of the futures she imagined included this. Maybe it's Heavenly Father's sick idea of a joke. The familiar song continues its auditory assault.

It dawns on Dan that there is something more tragic than his own unrequited righteous desires. What if you just didn't desire the right things in the first place? *This poor girl.* How did she get so mixed up about what matters? Girls are born pure and good. Something must have happened to her. *Someone must have treated her badly*, he decides. Well, he won't be guilty of that. Whatever it may cost him, he will make sure that for the next three hours, she is treated like a daughter of God. And so, for the first time in his adult life, Dan Christensen initiates a conversation with an eligible female without hoping it will lead to marriage.

He turns the volume down. "So, what do you do for fun?"

"For fun?" The side of Emma's head is still pressed against the glass. "Umm, I run," she answers without inflection.

"Me too!"

"Neat." Emma's voice invites no further commentary. Her gaze stays trained out the window, where south Provo whizzes past.

"They have a rad half marathon in Moab every March. I'm doing it for the second time this year."

"Mmm." Emma still refuses to look his way.

"The course is along the Colorado River, so it's flat or slightly downhill most of the way. You just follow the water. And it's beautiful! You run through these red buttes and bluffs. One of them looks like Yoda."

Against her will, Emma finds herself picturing it—blue water reflecting a cloudless sky, red rocks rising into Jedi formations. Something in her softens. She peels her face from the glass. "I've never been in any races," she says.

"Really? Dude, I would have given up running ages ago if it weren't for races. I get pretty lazy unless I have something to train for. Plus, there's something so rad about the energy of a race."

Emma is quiet again. She and Dan run for different reasons, that much seems clear. He runs toward something, whereas she is always running away. Motivation isn't really a problem when you have something sufficiently awful chasing you.

Emma imagines the half marathon, hundreds of runners lined up beside a wide, snaking river. The shot fires, and the runners break loose down the road. Half of them have their gazes trained ahead, a thought bubble hovering in front of them, just beyond their reach. They run toward their bubbles, strain for them, excitement and anticipation on their faces. A lean, muscular man at the front of the pack sprints toward a gold medal. At the rear, a fellow in sweatpants plods toward a fitter vision of himself. A pretty, blond woman in the middle runs toward the crowd of friends who will cheer and congratulate her as she crosses the finish. Others are running away, chased by their own thought bubbles. She sees a harried looking middle-aged woman, running from a bubble-encased gaggle of whining children. An old man, his muscles atrophied but still visible on his thin frame, is chased by the Grim Reaper.

Where is she on the course? Emma looks for herself, looks to see what's chasing her. Is it Dad? The bishop? A baby? An oversized pregnancy test with legs? Maybe it's just a voice, booming over and over that she doesn't fit, doesn't belong in the rigid storyline that is supposed to direct her life. Or maybe it's the burning awareness that she doesn't *want* to.

Emma remembers her first run up Rock Canyon. The run that sent her sprinting up—or down—her present path. It was just after that worthiness interview with Bishop Harrell. Emma pushed through the exit and raced home in her Steve Madden heels, but the house was just another cage—another too-small space for the ocean of thoughts and feelings crashing inside her.

She stripped off her Sunday dress, yanked on shorts and a t-shirt, laced up her shoes, and tore out the front door. Running on the Sabbath obviously wasn't allowed, but what did that matter? If the Church wasn't true, if she was giving up the quest to find a testimony, then what importance could the list of dos and don'ts that had chased her for her entire life possibly have?

Emma turned uphill and ran full speed. Running was nothing new. Her feet had pounded out hundreds of miles on the sidewalks and streets of the foothills. But today, her legs pumped up, up, up, off the asphalt and into the mouth of

Rock Canyon. The fire in her lungs, the screaming of her heart, the uneven ground beneath her feet—they felt like the truest things.

And truth felt *good*. Emma's body cut the air, shedding gravity as she moved. She could feel mass slipping from her head, her shoulders, her belly. It shattered behind her as it hit the ground. The boulders that had pressed on her broke into gravel and were suddenly insignificant bumps on the trail. Something for her to run across and beyond.

Everything Bishop Harrell had said? Unimportant. What Captain Moroni or anyone else thought of her? Irrelevant. What her parents expected of her? That was *their* problem.

A whitecap of forbidden images rode the wave of her thoughts. Emma saw herself bare shouldered again, a modern Jezebel. She still looked wild. She looked *free*. She didn't chase the image from her thoughts.

Instead, Emma stopped running. She dropped to her knees, and let a hymn shake from her lips—all music, no words. It was *laughter*, wild, full-bellied, joined by an echoing chorus from the canyon walls.

Maybe this song is still echoing, even as she sits, strapped to a seat in Dan Christensen's car. Maybe the laughter never dissipated once it left Emma's lips. Maybe it hung in the air and wrapped itself around her. Remnants of laughter, puffs of air between her and all those weighty, serious things that wanted to press themselves into her, wanted to shape her to fit their story. A *haha* cradled in her palm, filling the space between her skin and the hymnal, the scriptures, the sacrament cup. A breathy chortle, between her and Dad, between her and the bishop, between her and Captain Moroni with his unkept promises.

Air whistles past the windows now. Dan is still talking about running. "It's a road race, but most people come to Moab for the trails."

It takes Emma a moment to process what he said. "Really? Are there a lot of trails around there?"

"Yeah, there's loads of trails. Have you never been to Moab?"

"No, my grandma just moved there. This is my first time visiting."

Emma's heard somewhere that the most successful lies combine truth and falsehood. It's true that Oma lives near Moab and true that it's Emma's first visit. Oma's been there, though, for as long as Emma can remember. Explaining why she's never visited her own grandmother—and why she's going now—isn't an option.

"Well, if you're into hiking or mountain biking, you'll love it. You'll never run out of trails," Dan tells her.

"I like hiking, but I *love* to run on trails. It's basically my favorite thing." True, she's only been running trails for about a month now, but it *is* her favorite thing. A month can be a lifetime.

"Really? That's rad! I haven't done any trail running, just hiking and road running. You must be pretty adventurous."

"Maybe." She leans back into the headrest. *Adventure.* Is that what she's after? Is this leap into the abyss proof that she is adventurous? Or just that she is desperate? Maybe the answer will be clear when the freefall is done.

Chapter Six

The lunch dates were Heidi's idea. "It would be good for you to spend some one-on-one time with the kids," she urged her husband. "So you can get to know them better."

She tucked the bedsheet neatly at the corner as she spoke, her voice casual, but she glanced furtively in his direction. Heidi rarely offered suggestions to her husband. When she did, he rarely accepted them.

Graham knotted his tie, his lips pursed. "You think I don't know the kids?"

"No, of course you do. It's just, I get to spend a lot of time with them, and well—" her voice bobbled as she searched for words. "They're growing up so quickly, and it would be a way for you to connect with them. To counsel them."

Counsel them. Now she was speaking his language. It wasn't what she wanted, really, nor was it what her children needed—more lectures from their father. But sometimes, Graham was softer when you caught him alone. And she wanted *that* for her kids. She wanted them to know his gentler side. The part of him, however deeply buried, that she had fallen in love with so many years ago.

Graham furrowed his brow. "I'll consider it."

And thus, the tradition began: an annual lunch date with each of the kids, beginning after their twelfth birthday. Emma was already fourteen when the tradition commenced. Dad arrived at BYU's food court armed with two copies of the Church's *For the Strength of Youth* booklet. He handed one to her. "Go ahead and read aloud," he instructed.

"Which part?" Emma asked.

"All of it. From the beginning."

She groaned heavily—a sound she knew her father hated—and opened the booklet from the back. Nineteen pages. "Can I *please* eat first?" she asked.

"One bite," Graham replied, the sharpness of his tone muffled by a half-chewed mouthful of ham sandwich.

Emma heaped curried chicken and carrots onto her fork and delivered them to her waiting mouth. Her taste buds zinged with discovery—with flavors she couldn't name. Her mother made curry exactly once a month, mixing a single teaspoon of spice with a full cup of mayonnaise and two cans of cream of chicken soup, before pouring it into a casserole dish of broccoli and chicken. This was something different. Emma chewed slowly, savoring.

Graham cleared his throat—a sound his daughter hated—and looked at Emma. Not full in the face. He rarely did that with anyone, but it wasn't necessary; he could bore a hole through your chin.

Reluctantly, Emma swallowed and began to read. Her throat dried, and her curry grew cold. Graham chewed his sandwich, listening for the passages that required exposition.

"Begin to prepare now for a temple marriage," Emma rasped, and her father's head nodded in time with his chomping. He looked to her chin and raised a hand, like a traffic control officer might—his cue for her to yield to the impending rush of his words.

Emma gulped her water and shoveled bites of chicken into her mouth, looking up just often enough to give a faint impression of attentiveness. Nothing he said and nothing she read was new to her. She knew what was expected: sabbath observance, modest clothing (as if her mother would ever buy her a tank top!), and a ten percent tithe on her babysitting earnings. Emma knew to avoid music with intense beats or vulgar lyrics, to shun rated R movies (and most of the PG-13 ones), and to limit her circle of friends to those who shared the Church's standards. She knew of course that masturbation, petting, homosexuality, and pornography were sins, but that didn't make it any easier to read those words aloud in front of her father. If she had looked up while reading them, she would have noticed that his face burned the same shade of red as her own. He was in his element now, though.

"Your mother was nineteen when we got married. That's just six years older than you."

"Five," Emma corrected, wiping her mouth.

Graham's face tightened with confusion or consternation or maybe merely calculation. "Five," he finally conceded. "The point is that it's time to start focusing on becoming a worthy wife and mother. You can't be an unruly little girl forever."

Subsequent "lunch lectures"—as Emma came to think of them—were, if not better, then at least briefer. Her father always brought two copies of *For the Strength of Youth*, but they only read the sections he considered most pertinent to her personal inadequacies. The selected reading passages were bookended by dense monologues of fatherly admonition. "Your mother tells me that your bedroom has been messy of late," he chastised the following year. "Cleanliness is next to godliness, and in just a few years' time, you will have a home of your own to care for."

Report cards, household chores, dress and grooming—it was all fair game, but Emma's future as a wife and mother was indisputably his favorite topic. "Motherhood is your highest calling," Graham orated in his fourth annual lunch lecture, just a week prior to Emma's escape in Dan's station wagon. "President David O. McKay referred to motherhood as 'the greatest potential influence either for good or ill in human life.' Fathers hold the priesthood—the power of God on earth—and your husband will be the head of your home, but *you* are divinely tasked with the sacred role of bearing and raising children. As you know, it's Heavenly Father's will that mothers remain home with their children, but it's still important for you to receive an education. You could end up widowed, after all, and need to support—"

Emma's ears perked up. An education. Finally, he was saying something interesting. "I'm working on college applications," she interrupted.

Graham's eyebrows drew together. "Your mother mentioned that. That's what I wanted to talk with you about."

"I'm applying to the U." Emma's face shone as she said the words. The University of Utah was forty minutes to the north, in Salt Lake City. Cami was applying there, too. They would get a dorm room or maybe an apartment together. The thought of such freedom, just a year away, made her skin prickle with excitement.

"You should've come to me before making any plans, Emma. I thought your mother and I were on the same page—well, we are now—you'll be attending BYU."

Emma's mouth fell open with surprise. "What?"

"If accepted, which I'm certain you will be, you'll have free tuition and can live at home. It makes good sense financially, and there's no better place for you to find an eternal companion."

"An eternal companion? Dad, I'm seventeen. I don't want to get married yet, and . . . live at home?" Her voice was aghast.

"Your mother said you might react poorly, but I prayed about it, and it's the right decision."

"*You* prayed about it," Emma's voice rose in pitch and volume. A few heads turned curiously in their direction. "It's *my* life!"

"And *I* am the priesthood holder in our home. I'm entitled to receive revelation for you. You know that perfectly well."

"Well, what if I've received revelation, too!"

"*Wanting* to do something does not constitute revelation." He spoke without looking at her, then leaned in for another bite of his sandwich. His meal was apparently more interesting than her future, more pressing than her autonomy, and certainly more palatable than her feelings.

Emma shot to her feet, nearly tipping her chair to the ground. "Oh, but *you* wanting me to do something? That comes straight from God, I suppose?"

At home, Graham wouldn't have stood for such behavior. But in a crowded food court? His face burned and his spine stiffened, but his eyes flickered only briefly to his daughter's retreating form before returning to his sandwich. It clumped in his throat, nearly impossible to swallow. A less principled man would have given up; Graham did not. He saw the hoagie through to its soggy end, then picked up his napkin and carefully wiped his hands and mouth, before bussing first his own tray and then his daughter's. Cleanliness is next to godliness.

Chapter Seven

Twelve years earlier

Oma didn't sit like the other women Emma knew—spine erect, body tucked neatly in its designated spot. Instead, she sprawled as if space were an infinite commodity. When Emma scrambled down from her twin bed and pitter-pattered to the living room that morning, she found her maternal grandmother draped across the couch, her thick brown waves swirling and tangling like vines against the backdrop of cabbage rose upholstery. Baby Hyrum sat on the soft cushion of Oma's belly, bouncing and giggling, each bounce eliciting a loud exhalation from Oma—something between a laugh and a grunt.

Emma was delighted to wake to something different. Saturdays often felt empty—no kindergarten or church (which meant no Cami), just a day filled with the sameness of her family's restrained rhythm. Three meals, one snack, too many chores, and a few hours to "play"—unless your notion of play involved noise or messes, because those were right out. With Oma in town, though, everything was fresh and new and just a bit chaotic, as if spring had come early.

Oma's eyes smiled to Emma in welcome. "*Guten Morgen, Schatz*!" she chirped. *Schatz,* treasure, jewel. Emma saw herself shimmering, clad from head to toe in rubies and emeralds—that's what it was like being with Oma.

"Toss me a pillow?" Oma asked, and Emma brought her a pale blue throw pillow embroidered with a picture of the Salt Lake temple.

"Mom says we can't play with them," she warned Oma.

"Well, your Mom's at the grocery store." Oma's eyes sparkled with mischief. She turned her head and plopped the pillow down across her face. It looked so silly, Oma with a temple for a face—two darkened windows for her eyes, spires forming sharply arched brows, her hair still billowing out in every direction. Baby Hyrum looked puzzled, unsure of what to make of this change. Without warning, Oma curled her torso upward, sending the pillow flying from her face to the floor. "*Kuckuck*!" she cried exuberantly, and Hyrum burst into a fit of giggles, waving his fat fists in delight. Oma laughed too. Her belly shook, jiggling Hyrum's cheeks. Again, she hid her face behind the opaque veil of the Mormon temple, and again she burst free with a triumphant "kuckuck," the couch shaking with shared laughter.

"It's like a cuckoo bird," Oma explained to Emma, "popping out of a clock. You need one too." She motioned toward the other throw pillow, the one with *Families Are Forever* stitched in dainty cursive. Oma donned the temple, Emma shrouded herself in familial harmony, and together they erupted with shrieks of "kuckuck," flinging both pillows to the floor.

They tried on other cuckoo clocks as well—several more pillows, a baby blanket, Emma's favorite princess costume, copies of the *Ensign* and *Friend* magazines that the Church mailed out each month. The pile of discarded clocks mounded higher and higher on the floor until Oma, Hyrum, and Emma all spilled giggling onto the pile.

The door from the garage creaked open. Emma's mother walked into the living room, arms filled with paper grocery bags, her legs trailed by little Joseph and Eliza, Irish twins. She stopped in her tracks, and the toddlers bumped against the backs of her legs. "Mutti!" She was surprised. "What a mess! Emma, hurry and clean this up. Your father will be home any minute."

Your father will be home any minute. Emma knew the heft of those words, though she was still too young to spell them. She scurried to tidy the room. Magazines on the table to the left of the couch. Blankets folded in the basket. "No, Oma," Emma corrected her grandmother's cleaning efforts. "The temple pillow has to go on the other side of the couch, and that one goes on the armchair."

Oma raised an eyebrow but complied, the sparkle in her eyes replaced with something that Emma could not yet read.

The next morning before Church, Oma wove Emma's hair into its first ever French braid. Emma sat as still as a five-year-old can possibly sit and loved every second of it. Oma's cheerful chatter and thoughtful questions. The tickle of the comb as she traced lines across Emma's scalp, dividing the hair into sections. The way each section perched on one of Oma's deft fingers, which then wiggled and danced until—voila! It was a masterpiece. Of course, Emma could only see it with the help of two mirrors, one held behind her head at an angle, the second one in front of her. At first it was exciting, with Oma's help, to train the back mirror just right and discover that she could see the rear of her head. But at church, where four different people complimented her hair, Emma found herself increasingly upset. It wasn't fair. Here she had this beautiful braid, and she was the only one who couldn't see it. She could *never* really see the back of herself. And that was a whole half of who she was!

She tried telling Mom all of this after Church, but it was no use. "Honey, it doesn't matter what the back of you looks like," Mom soothed, unsoothingly.

With Oma, it was different. "You know, I think you're wiser than a lot of grown-ups," Oma mused. "You're right, none of us see ourselves all the way. Some people barely see themselves at all."

"They should make better mirrors." Emma's face was earnest.

Oma smiled. "Yes, they should. But you know, people who really love each other and look at each other closely can be like mirrors, too."

"How?" Emma asked.

"Well, why don't you tell me what the back of me looks like?" Oma said, turning.

Emma paused, considering. "Your hair is big and brown, and in one spot, it looks like a ribbon after you curl it with scissors. And you look very tall and strong and not very ladylike because you aren't wearing any pantyhose."

Oma spun around, laughing, and scooped Emma into a hug. "*You* are my favorite mirror ever."

"You be my mirror now!" Emma demanded.

Emma twirled, and Oma paused to consider. "Well, your hair is beautifully braided, like a golden rope. But little strands of it are popping out, like wild animals refusing to be tamed."

Emma giggled. "Like lions?" she asked.

"Yes, like naughty little lion cubs!"

With this, Emma roared, and Oma pounced, and the two fell giggling, yet again, to the floor.

Mirrors, Emma would decide. Oma had mirrors in her eyes, and that's what made them sparkle. And let her see things that other grown-ups couldn't.

***

Graham Madsen does not have mirrors for eyes, never did. He cannot see behind himself. He rarely even looks to the left or the right. Why bother, when the tunneled line in front of your retinas reveals everything you need to know?

That is, in part, what made it so easy for Emma to lie to him. She was always the wild one, the impulsive one, the too-curious-for-her-own-good one. They each had a role, Emma and her siblings. Joseph was the know-it-all, the rigid one, clearly his father's son. Eliza was the good girl, polite, proper, unfailingly sweet. Hyrum was the joker and prankster, as different from his father as a circus performance is from a sacrament meeting. Brigham was the sensitive one, an old soul, intelligent and introspective. Nephi was the rough and tumble one, the one who lived for trucks and balls and needed stitches three times before starting kindergarten. Sariah was the baby, the princess, the one who could do no wrong.

Sariah could do no wrong, and Emma could do no right—not in Dad's constricted eyes, anyway. As the oldest child, she ought to have demonstrated obedience, tidiness, faith, and humility for her younger siblings. In this, she was chronically disappointing. Emma learned that it was a waste of her energy to strive for the impossible—that is, to try to please her father. Besides, she knew things that he didn't. She knew for a fact that he was wrong about plenty of stuff.

Nothing made Dad's limitations clearer to her than his attempts at discipline. He wasn't malicious—not really. He was committed to perfect justice. The trouble was that he was equally committed to an *image* of himself as perfectly just. Emma, whose eyes bounced in every direction, saw this, even as a young child.

She saw it when Joseph wrote *Joe is a butthead* across his own drawing in order to get Hyrum in trouble. Once Hyrum had been spanked—justice served—Dad could not contemplate the possibility of error on his own part, evidentiary handwriting samples notwithstanding. In fact, he spanked Hyrum a second time for attempting to plead his own case. Emma tried to intervene on her brother's behalf and was asked whether she would like to have a warm bottom as well. There were consequences for questioning Dad—well, for questioning *out loud*, anyway.

Emma wasn't arbitrarily bad. When she disobeyed, it was often for a good cause. She was a righter of injustice, a defender of the defenseless, quick to step in and protect her younger siblings. Like Emma, Hyrum was a scapegoat. Something about him was bewildering and therefore offensive to his father. Joseph's pretension, Brigham's quiet intelligence—these, Graham could understand—but Hyrum's way of being in the world (much like Emma's) registered as an affront.

Emma knew almost right away that Hyrum was the culprit when Dad barked them out of their beds late one Tuesday night. *The lineup*. It happened now and again. Emma glanced at her clock: 11:23. She had been asleep for less than two hours.

Emma and Eliza exchanged glances as they left their bedroom together. Eliza's glance was worried, Emma's indignant. She was fourteen years old—old enough to know that this was not normal. *Dad* was not normal. "You know when your parents get you out of bed in the middle of the night, like as a punishment," she had once begun a complaint to Cami.

"What are you talking about?" Cami had laughed, as if it were a joke.

Emma stood now in the hallway with her younger siblings. The boys yawned and rubbed their eyes. Sariah was still in bed. She was only three and cute as a button, therefore exempt from this particular family ritual, at least for the time being.

Dad's voice filled the hallway. "Honesty. I had hoped I could count on my children to be honest." He always began with a sermon.

Graham Madsen clasped his hands behind his back and paced the narrow corridor as if it were his classroom. His children pressed against the wall, shrinking to make space for him. Emma donned her mask, the one she always used in a Robin Hood moment: the look of respectful concern. Underneath it, her brain bounced about, straining to imagine who had done what this time and what the plotted consequence would be. Last time they had been dragged from bed, it was because Hyrum had used Dad's flathead screwdriver (for a task his father had assigned) and neglected to return it to its designated spot. All of the Madsen children had been compelled to follow Hyrum from room to room until he located and returned it.

Then Hyrum had stayed up to clean Dad's already gleaming tools, while the other kids returned to bed.

The time before that, Dad had stumbled over a stray shoe in the foyer. All of the shoes had somehow spilled from the shoe bench and been strewn across the floor. It was almost certainly Sariah's handiwork, but the older children were pulled from bed to clean the mess and then assigned extra chores for the next day. The message was clear and constant in the Madsen home: mistakes, messes, forgetfulness, disorder will not be tolerated. Cleanliness is next to godliness. God loves those who obey Him.

Dad's requirements for love seemed no less exacting. "You are better than this," he would say to Emma sometimes by way of rebuke, but she knew he didn't mean it.

He was still pacing, still sermonizing. "Among all the forms of dishonesty, one stands out as uniquely deplorable," he orated. The Madsen children, by necessity, had advanced vocabularies for their respective ages. "Theft," Dad's voice boomed.

The word filled the corridor, a complete sentence. Dad slowed his march and looked at each of his children in turn. If he could have had one superpower of his choosing, he would have chosen the power to read people the way he read logical proofs. The power to deduct meaning from facial expressions, body language, and vocal tone. For every X, if X is a child and X glances to the left when accused of a crime, then X is guilty of the crime in question. For all B's and C's, if B attempts to correct C, and C's lip trembles and C looks down, then B's rebuke of C has succeeded and B ought to cease scolding because if B persists in scolding, B will experience diminishing returns in the improvement of C's behavior.

Some people seemed to have this superpower. Graham did not, and it made moments like this quite taxing. He had to take decisive action, had to establish order, but he had to do this with only partial access to the facts. He would, as always, simply have to wield the tools at his disposal: religious doctrine, rational argument, and a healthy dose of fear. The culprit would be frightened into confessing.

Emma watched him scanning their faces. She knew he had no clue who had done it—whatever it was. She had no clue *what* had been done, but she knew precisely *who* had done it. There was a soft glow of triumph on Hyrum's face. His jaw was set, but the corner of his lips twitched ever so subtly, evidence of a battle between fear and mirth. If Dad got desperate enough, he would pick someone to blame—probably her or Hyrum, depending on the infraction. If he picked Hyrum, the punishment would be doubly severe. Never mind that Hyrum was in fact the guilty party; a warm wave of protectiveness washed over Emma.

She stepped forward. "It was me!"

The words tumbled out of her without deliberation, one line in the part she had been playing for years. The hero's part.

"*What* was you?" Dad seemed surprised.

"The . . . the theft. I took it." She had forgotten to hold out until she knew what she was supposed to confess to.

"You ate a bite of an uncut pie directly from the center of the pan?" He said the words slowly, lingering over the gaps between them, as if willing them to fit together.

Of course, she had done no such thing. "Yeah, I did," she answered, her voice deliberate.

"That seems like strange behavior for a fourteen-year-old."

He didn't believe her because it didn't make sense. But then, why would she lie? None of it made sense to a mind like Graham's, and so, as he often did when at odds with his wayward eldest, he played the part of the confident monarch while inwardly aching for superpowers he didn't possess.

"Well, I was mad." Emma's chin lifted defiantly, and she held her father's gaze. She felt a thrill of power. She could know things that he didn't know, and she could use that knowledge to protect, to derail. "Mom's always baking things for people at church but we don't get to have any. I figured if it was messed up, we would get to eat it for once."

Graham didn't need superpowers to see that Emma felt no remorse. Her eyes were *sparkling*. Occasional disobedience was one thing, but this total lack of contrition! This dearth of respect!

His face turned red, and his voice hardened. "So, you were hoping to eat more of it, then?"

"Yeah, maybe it was dumb, but I'll bake a new pie for Mom after school tomorrow." She sounded almost flippant. The nerve!

"*After school*? You'll bake a new pie for your mother *right now*. 'Let him that stole steal no more: but rather let him labor, working with his hands.'"

"Dad, it's like midnight. I have school in the morning."

He snorted derisively, "That's something you ought to have considered before embarking on a rampage of theft and vandalism."

It was Emma's turn to snort. *A rampage of theft and vandalism?* She rolled her eyes, then pushed past him to descend the stairs.

The hair on his neck bristled. Some day she would be a parent and see what hell she put him through. But she needed a taste of it, just a little taste, right now. Emma might be too old for the rod, but Graham Madsen would not see his child spoiled. "There's one thing you need to do first," he announced.

Emma twirled midway down the stairs. "Oh yeah, what?"

"Finish the pie." His voice was matter-of-fact.

"Finish the pie?"

"Yes, finish the pie. You wanted to eat it so badly that you destroyed it, so now go ahead and finish it before you bake a new one."

"Whatever, Dad, I'm not hungry."

Such lip. "I didn't ask if you were hungry. We'll all come down and join you. Kids!" he barked, and the rest of the Madsen children followed Emma warily to the kitchen.

Heidi trailed behind them. "Graham—" her soft voice floated across the room.

Emma hadn't even seen her mother there. Mom had a knack for disappearing—for standing back from her husband's disciplinary actions, invisible, uncomfortable, but rarely, it seemed, uncomfortable enough to intervene. "She'll be sick," Heidi said. "She doesn't need to eat it. She can just bake a new one."

Heidi was right, of course. Graham knew she was right. He already felt that uncomfortable prickle of regret, of having reacted too quickly. But that prickle had to be squelched. Because if Heidi was right, if the prickle was right, then Graham Madsen was acting wrongly—an insupportable conclusion! Even if one allowed such a possibility, strictly for the sake of argument, it would lead to an impossible place. Because if he was acting wrongly—so wrongly that he needed to veer from his course—then how could he ensure order in his own home? After an admission of fallibility? No, it was better to be too severe on occasion than to make the greater mistake of ceding authority, inviting questioning, practically begging his children to stray from the straight and narrow path. This was all for their own good in the end.

Graham didn't look at his wife when he spoke. "I'm handling this. Go put Nephi back to bed."

Heidi pursed her lips but lifted five-year-old Nephi from the kitchen floor, where he had already collapsed in a sleepy ball. Holding him tightly, she left the room.

Emma's stomach dropped when she caught sight of the vandalized pie. Pumpkin, her favorite. But there were only three or four bites dug from its center. She would basically have to eat a whole pie. She hated Mom for abandoning her, hated Dad with his perverse sense of justice.

"Sadist," she mumbled beneath her breath. Only she pronounced it "saddist." Advanced vocabulary notwithstanding, it was a word she had only read, never heard spoken aloud.

Dad's punishment, though "saddistic," wasn't especially creative. He had swiped it from Agatha Trunchbull in *Matilda*, Emma was sure of it. Mom had just finished reading the book aloud to Hyrum, Brigham, and Nephi the week before. Dad must have overheard that part.

There was more to the punishment, of course. He was still lecturing. The importance of honesty, *blah, blah, blah*. Emma watched his face fatten into the sneering, double-chinned countenance of Mrs. Trunchbull, the savage headmistress in Roald Dahl's tale. Dad's hair—always short, always tidy, always neatly parted on the right side—pulled back from his expanding forehead into a tight bun. His long, lean frame broadened into the looming mass of a giantess, his flannel pajamas becoming a military style dress, tightly belted around his widening waist.

And Emma knew what her part must be. She was Bruce Bogtrotter, the guilty schoolboy who would be forced to eat an impossibly massive chocolate cake in front of the entire school. She felt herself broadening, too—her flesh doubling and tripling to meet the challenge. Bruce was not afraid. She would not be afraid—not of an oversized confection and certainly not of her dad.

"Who knows a hymn or a Primary song about honesty?" The question mark heralded the end of her father's castigating line of periods.

Joseph was the one to answer. "There's 'I Believe in Being Honest.'"

"Do you know all the words?"

Joseph nodded, his spine lengthening.

"Go ahead and give the starting pitch, then lead your brothers and sisters in song while Emma enjoys her pie."

Tentative voices filled the kitchen. "*I believe in being honest . . . I'll form good habits in my youth . . . to speak up in defending right and keep my name and honor bright.*"

The irony of the words made Emma feel strangely *hungry*. She would show him. *She* would speak up in defending right. It was *his* name and honor that were dull and filthy. He had dragged himself through the muck in the moment he chose to yank a bunch of kids out of bed just for the vindictive pleasure of scaring them. Dad was far from honest—a harsh dictator at home, and a bland, buttoned-up Sunday School teacher at church.

"*I believe in being honest*," they sang again, and Emma stuck the fork into the center of the pie. She might as well eat it that way once in her life. The chorus of voices fell into the background as Emma ate her fourth, fifth, sixth, seventh bites. As her stomach filled, the voices morphed. To Emma's ears, they were no longer singing. They were chanting. It was a low chant at first, but it rose like a wave: "Bruce! Bruce! Bruce!"

Emma was suddenly aware again of how her body had ballooned. Her arms, her chest, her belly—they were massive. Her long blond hair was short now, hanging dankly above her fleshy forehead.

"Bruce! Bruce! Bruce!" She looked at her siblings' faces. Eliza was crying. Hyrum gave Emma a look that she knew was meant to be grateful and encouraging.

She, Bruce, had spoken up in defending right. She was equal to her fate—equal to any punishments her father might dole out. Bruce ate faster, not even tasting the food, elated by her strength, her mass, her rebellion. She would show him.

"Bruce! Bruce! Bruce!"

The orange center of the pie receded. Her stomach squeezed. She felt ill; it was the feeling of speaking up and defending right.

"Bruce! Bruce! Bruce!"

Only the crust remained. She grabbed chunks of it with her hand, devouring large bites. The sooner it was done, the better. She would not give him the satisfaction of seeing her slacken or get sick. *Defending right*, she reminded herself, looking down to be certain she was still Bruce—still sufficient to the challenge. By now her actual belly had swollen and was pressing against her pajama shirt. It was hardly any work at all to see herself as Bruce—large, powerful, defiantly taking up space.

"Bruce! Bruce! Bruce!"

The last bite. The chorus died. Dad delivered a final lecture on the importance of honesty and on the punishments that await those who steal or bear false witness, and then Emma's siblings shuffled back up the stairs to bed. The clock read 12:17.

"You *do* like pie." His voice cut through the heaviness. Did she only imagine that he sounded unsettled? "Get up and bake a new one. You know where to find the recipe?"

"Yes." She was weak at the thought of getting up and moving about in her present state—suddenly too tired and sick to be Bruce. Besides, the Trunchbull hadn't put Bruce to work right after eating. He had been allowed to vomit in peace.

Mercifully, her father walked out. Emma stood up, trudged toward the pantry, stopped, turned, wretched in the trash can. She let herself hang there, trembling for a few moments. Maybe Mom would come? Would pull her hair back from her face and tuck it behind her ears, like she used to when Emma was little? But Mom didn't come, not until later, when the crust was nearly finished. She was upstairs, busying herself with putting the younger kids back to bed, busying herself by soothing the wounds that she knew how to soothe. "Don't worry, your sister will be fine. Go back to sleep," she told the littler ones.

Hyrum allowed his mother to tuck him in and turn out the bedroom light, but as soon as the door closed, he snuck into his closet with a flashlight, a sheet of paper, and a box of crayons.

Emma righted herself and resumed her hunt for the Libby's. The recipe would be on the back of the can. She finished the baking and cleanup just before 2:00 AM, climbed the stairs, and collapsed into her bed. Where the softness of her pillowcase should have been, her cheek landed instead against the crispness of paper. Emma flipped on her bedside lamp. *SORRY* the paper read in bold, blue letters. Beneath the one-word apology, an orange pie as large as a house crushed a yellow-haired man, who—apart from the ruby red slippers on his feet—bore a striking resemblance to her father. Sick and tired as she was, Emma couldn't help giggling. At least it hadn't happened to Hyrum.

Chapter Eight

The drive passes more comfortably than either Dan or Emma would have predicted. They talk about running. Dan tells stories from his mission, most of them self-deprecating and humorous rather than proselytizing or self-aggrandizing, and he teaches Emma a few phrases in Portuguese (*Voce linda*! *Voce lindo*! *O Livro de Mormon*). Emma, in turn, attempts to teach him a few words of German.

"*Ich heisse* Dan," she models.

"Eesh. Heisse. Dan."

"Not 'eesh' like 'quiche'. 'Ich,' like, well, I guess there's no English equivalent. But it's a harder 'ch' sound."

"Eesh," Dan repeats, more emphatically.

"No, try this. 'Chhh.' It's kind of guttural but maybe a little higher in the throat. Like you're trying to hawk a loogie but don't want anyone to notice."

"CHHHH," Dan's throat rattles, and Emma bursts into laughter.

"Okay, now just add the 'ee' in front of it."

"Eesh," he says again. "Did I get it that time?"

"Close enough," Emma smiles.

"So where does your grandma live, anyway?"

For just a second, Emma had forgotten what lies ahead. "She's in Castle Valley. But she's gonna get me in Moab."

"Castle Valley!? No way, that's rad. I'll drive you there! It's up the road I was telling you about—the race course, you know? I can introduce you to Yoda."

"Oh, well, my grandma wants to get brunch together in town. I told her I'd meet her there," Emma lies.

Dan's smile briefly falters. "Well, you could come to my house and have her pick you up from there?"

"Thanks, but I'll just wait in town."

"Okay," his voice deflates. "Where do you want me to drop you off?"

Buildings are popping up alongside the road now—a gas station, hotels, followed by denser clusters of shops, restaurants, and galleries. They've arrived more quickly than Emma expected.

"How about there?" she points. *Information Center* is printed in large, red letters across the face of a boxy stucco building. Dan pulls up to the curb across the street.

"Thank you so much, Dan. Let me chip in for gas." She reaches into her bag.

"No, don't. Seriously. This has been awesome. You don't owe me a thing. And hey"—he pauses to scrawl something on a piece of paper—"that's my parents' number here in Moab on the top and my number in Provo on the bottom. Call if you want a ride back. I'm heading to Provo on Monday. Or if you want to come see your grandma some other time, maybe we can ride together again."

"Thank you," she smiles, swinging her legs out of the car to meet the pavement.

And that's it. Emma walks, bag slung across her chest, to the corner, waits for the light, and crosses the street toward the information center. There will be phones there. As she approaches the building, she hears her name and turns to see Dan, his window down.

"Eesh. Heisse. Dan," he calls, grinning.

"Voce lindo," she calls back, with a wave, and the station wagon rumbles off.

Emma walks into the information center and turns to stare at the phone. Is she seven buttons away from everything—or from nothing? It's been eleven years since she's seen Oma. All Emma has are memories—memories and a hint, dropped unwittingly by her mother, that Oma still thinks of her.

***

Heidi Madsen is not as spineless, it turns out, as Emma had believed her to be—a fact that brings Emma's blood to a simmer. No one would call Heidi assertive, to be sure. She allows her husband to shape almost every detail of their family life, while she tiptoes in the rigid contours of his shadow and encourages her children to do the same. "Your father will be home any minute! Hurry up and clean this mess!" "Lower your voices. Dad's trying to read." "If the two of you can't stop bickering, I'll tell your father."

But she rarely does tell him anything. Because for all her lack of assertion, Heidi loves her kids more than she loves her husband. It wouldn't be quite right to say that she doesn't love Graham at all, but the affection she feels is tangled with thick strands of resentment and fear. She started out loving him deeply. And so, noticing that Graham was a choosier eater than she was, she encouraged him to build the family menu. Observing that he cared more about where they lived—it *must* be brick, even in the back; it must be walking distance from campus and from the temple; it must have an office with a door that can be closed; the neighbors must keep their grass and trees neatly trimmed—she had allowed him to choose their house himself. Seeing how much rules and routines mattered to Graham, she let him dictate them. Heidi can be content with just about anything, after all. Letting Graham make the choices seemed like the loving thing to do.

It was the loving thing to do, until it became the safe thing to do. Heidi knows how to hold her sadness inside. She knows how to put on a good face and pour the scraps of herself that remain into building a better life for her children. This means, of course, that she has to protect them from the unpalatable realities of home life. They *must* reach adulthood intact. They cannot break—Heidi couldn't bear it. And so, she shows her children how to tiptoe, how to disappear into the shadows, how to avoid the worst of their father's eruptions.

Some of her children are more willing to learn this lesson than others. Emma has always refused to walk on her toes. And it's Emma who discovers Heidi's small, safe, barely visible rebellion.

Every year or so, Heidi buys a new calling card at the grocery store. And every Wednesday, when Graham is at work and the children are in school, she digs the calling card from her purse and uses it to call her mother. After a quick hello, they hang up the phone, and then Mutti calls her right back so that Heidi doesn't use up the calling card too quickly. Graham doesn't inspect the phone bill, but weekly long-distance charges would surely catch his notice.

They don't talk about Graham—not anymore. What is there to say? When Mutti first began dating an attorney, there were long, tearful talks and a couple pro bono consultations, but Heidi always got stuck on two points: first, she had never finished college. How would she support her kids? And second, she knew the pain of growing up without a father. Surely, this father that her children had was better than no father at all? He loved them. She knew he did. He wasn't a bad man, he was just . . . *interesting*. That's the word. Well, it's the word Heidi uses, anyway.

Heidi and her mother mostly chat about the children now. Mutti is always eager to hear about Emma, the grandchild she had known best. She had been there for Emma's birth, for her first birthday party, and for a host of other short visits until Graham forbade her from coming again.

Mutti talks a bit about what she is up to—hikes she has taken, the extremes of desert weather—but Heidi never asks many questions. Mostly what she wants to hear from her mother is her own name. Not "Heidi," as Graham (and consequently everyone else) calls her, but "Heide," its consonants rich and warm and the last "e" pronounced as a soft "eh" rather than a harsh and final "ee." When Mutti says her name—"Heide"—Heidi Madsen feels that she once was and might someday be more than she is at present.

And so, it happened on a Wednesday not so long ago, that Emma—her mind still coursing with energy from that first run up Rock Canyon—left a paper for her English class sitting forgotten on her father's printer. It was one of those occasional days on which Mom had let her drive the van to school, and so she rushed home during lunch hour to retrieve it.

When Emma burst in the front door, she was greeted by the sound of her mother's voice, speaking in German. "Mutti," she heard her say, followed by a flood of meaningless syllables. Emma froze, straining her ears to hear. Her years of high school German were not enough to make sense of all of the sounds, but she pulled words from the flood. "*Schule*," she knew: school. "*Kinder*": children. Then "Emma," her own name. Mom was talking to *Oma*—about *her*.

It can be unsettling to discover that one's mother has an identity that transcends her relationship to you—that the one planet that might plausibly orbit around you pays clandestine visits to some other solar system. Even if you find this planet annoying and smothering and claim to wish it would circle someone else for a change, its unfaithfulness throws out shockwaves.

Emma's hands clenched, and her pulse raced. So, her mother was capable of some sliver of independence, after all—some sliver of strength and resolve, a small but deliberate bite from the center of the pie. She was *capable*, but as far as her eldest daughter could tell, she used that strength—that appetite for rebellion—for herself, rather than for her children.

Emma staged her own rebellion. Heart pounding, she retraced her own steps, carefully avoiding the floorboard that creaked. She opened the door softly, stepped out, then closed it with a deafening slam, satisfied at the thought of her mother's alarm. Mom would panic, Emma knew. Had Dad come home and overheard her? Was there an intruder? Emma sprinted to the van, driving it away too quickly to allay her mother's fears.

Revenge can be sweet, even when it's chased by the bitterness of docked points, of a "B" that should have been an "A."

Emma was too angry and too satisfied with herself to drive back to school. Instead, she just drove. She wasn't going anywhere in particular, just burning gas. Moving to not be still.

And then she found that she *had* gone somewhere. She was just a few blocks from Juice and Java. Cami's mom had taken the girls there several times. For juice, of course, not java. For orange, carrot, and ginger squeezed into a delicious concoction. Emma turned into the parking lot, her hands finally relaxing on the steering wheel. She deserved a treat.

It could have been an innocent treat like orange and ginger or carob and banana. It *should* have been innocent. There was no premeditation of sin. But maybe the Holy Ghost had abandoned Emma after she slammed the front door and left her mother in a state of nervous agitation. Or maybe the Spirit of God left her a few days earlier, when she pushed through the exit and traded church for mountains. Maybe Emma had been too good for too long. Maybe she was in the mood for a taste of uncut pie.

"What can I get you?" the barista asked.

"I'll try a latte." The words poured out of Emma's mouth. Where had they even come from? A *latte*? She knew it was some sort of coffee drink and therefore expressly forbidden by the Word of Wisdom, but beyond that, she was clueless.

"What size?"

"Umm, medium?"

"Any flavoring?"

"I don't know. What do you recommend?"

The barista, a tall boy with green eyes and a mop of wavy brown hair, smiled knowingly. "Your first latte?" he asked.

"Yeah." Emma felt a blush and a smile on the face that used to belong to her, felt a giddy flutter in the chest that used to be hers. What on earth was she doing? And why didn't she stop herself? "I've never tried any kind of coffee before," her former face confessed.

"Well, this is a big day, then! We need to get a bell for occasions like this." Emma laughed, and he continued. "I'm not actually a coffee drinker either—"

"Juice boy!" his pink-haired coworker sang out, and it was the mop-haired barista's turn to blush.

"They all make fun of me because I don't drink coffee," he explained. "I go to BYU, so I'm the odd one out here. But anyway, most people like to put some sort of syrup in their latte to sweeten it. How about vanilla?"

"Sure, I like vanilla." The face that used to be Emma's chatted with Juice Boy for a bit longer and was clearly in cahoots with the hand that rummaged around in Emma's purse, pulled out her wallet, paid, and even added a tip. Was Emma the face and the hand after all? Or was she the whiny voice of admonition that followed her to the table, buzzing like a cartoon mosquito: "Heavenly Father is watching you. He sees everything."

"First latte *ever*!" The barista's voice broke through the mist.

Legs carried her back to the counter. A hand reached for the latte.

"Let me know how you like it. If you're not a fan, I'll make you something else."

Everything paused: the admonishing voice, Emma's face, the war between them. Even Juice Boy. The whole world stood still to witness Emma's first taste of steaming, foamy transgression.

The hand lifted the cup, the face took a sip, and warmth—sweet, bitter, all-consuming warmth—poured down Emma's trachea, burned in her bosom. The admonishing voice fell silent. The face, the hand, they were Emma's own.

"How do you like it?"

"I *love* it."

***

It was a slippery slope, an exuberant slide, from that first transgressive taste to the present moment: to Emma knocked up and running away.

Emma eyes the wall-mounted payphone. Knowing that Mom and Oma were in contact made it easy to find Oma's number. Sometime between midnight bathroom trips, between the lightning of a positive pregnancy test and the thunder of a negative one, between horror show projections on the backs of her lids, between turning to the left and tossing to the right, Emma rolled into the realization that it was time for drastic action. She crept down the stairs and pulled her mother's address book from the kitchen drawer, checked under *D* for *Dietrich*, and there it was, *Claudia Dietrich*, plain as day. Emma jotted the number and address down on a yellow Post-it note, and a plan tornadoed inside her.

She reaches into her pocket now, pulls out the folded yellow square. Will Oma be glad to hear from her? Will she even answer the phone? There's only one way to find out. The clink of a quarter in the Moab payphone, the buzz of the dial tone, seven beeps, and then the ringing begins.

Chapter Nine

Eleven years earlier

Emma had just finished telling Oma what she liked best about Primary—singing time—when Dad came home. "I even know a song about when dads come home!" she exclaimed happily, forgetting restraint in a way that seemed to happen when Oma was around.

"Sing it for me!" Oma smiled, and Emma bounced up from the couch, half marching, half dancing as she trumpeted:

I'm so glad when Daddy comes home
Glad as I can be!
Clap my hands and SHOUT for joy—

"Emma! There's no call for such a racket," her father scolded, passing through the living room on his way to the kitchen.

Emma's voice faltered. If Dad had been her intended audience, then she would have stopped immediately, but it was Oma she was singing for.

"Keep going," Oma mouthed, holding a finger to her lips, as she stood to join Emma in the now muted dance.

Emma whisper-sang, matching her motions to the lyrics. Oma followed along, making a big show of bending low, letting Emma wrap her little arms around her neck, then feigning mime-like astonishment as Emma patted her cheeks and planted a kiss square on her nose, all in time to the words of the song.

"That was wonderful! Is there a song for when moms come home?" Oma asked.

"Moms are always home, except when they go to the grocery store."

Oma chuckled. "*Your* mom is usually home, but not all moms are. When your mom was a little girl, I went to work every day, just like your dad does."

Emma puzzled over this for a moment. She realized, of course, that some mothers do go to work. Her first-grade teacher, Mrs. Money, had a two-year-old at home, who stayed with his grandmother during the day. But this knowledge had sat unconsidered on the periphery of her little world—a world in which mothers stayed home to care for their children and fathers went off to work. Cami's mom stayed home. All the moms at church stayed home. And the dads went to work all day. That's why the Primary song about dads coming home was exciting and boisterous; a father's involvement in your life was intermittent, unpredictable, and therefore worthy of spirited attention. Emma privately liked the idea of a scary song about dads coming home, too, something akin to the theme song that accompanies the Wicked Witch of the West.

"There is a song about moms," Emma told Oma.

"Yeah, how does it go?"

Emma sat up straight, folding her arms, just like she had learned in Primary, and sang in her clearest, most reverent voice:

Mother I love you
Mother I do
Father in Heaven has sent me to you.

Oma waited patiently through the ballad-like song. "Well, it's very pretty but not nearly as much fun as the song about dads," she mused, once Emma was finished singing.

"Dad didn't think my song was fun."

Oma whispered again. "Maybe your dad has forgotten how to have fun. That happens to some grown-ups."

"But not to you."

"No, not to me. And it won't happen to you either."

"How do you know?" Emma hoped Oma was right. How awful, to forget how to have fun!

"God didn't make a giggle like yours with the intention of letting it go silent," Oma declared, tickling Emma under the armpit and eliciting a shriek of laughter.

"Emma"—Mom's head peeked into the living room—"please come set the table for dinner!"

Emma hopped up from the couch, but her grandmother grabbed her by the hand.

"I'll do it, Heide," she interjected. "Let Emma play."

"No, no, you stay put, Mutti. It's Emma's job," Heidi answered.

Emma traipsed cheerily toward her mother. "When I grow up, I want to be just like Oma!" she chirped. Mom turned, her pregnant belly swinging into view, but she looked past her daughter. Emma's eyes followed her mother's gaze.

Dad stood at the sink, drinking a glass of water. "There are better examples of womanhood than your grandmother," he rebuked, barely looking up from the book held open in his left hand.

Emma wasn't quite sure what he meant by "examples of womanhood," but she knew that Dad didn't like Oma. She saw how he looked at her grandmother—almost as if she were one of those noisy children in sacrament meeting who weren't his to punish and scold. He *did* scold her sometimes, but Oma always laughed and said things like, "Loosen up, Graham," which made the vein on his forehead bulge.

Oma was right, she decided. Dad must have forgotten how to have fun.

"Well, I'm going to be just like Oma. I'm going to be a grown-up who still has fun!" Emma proclaimed.

Dad lifted his head. "*Fun*?"

"Oma doesn't just stay home all day doing boring things. Oma goes to work!"

"And that's your idea of fun?" He turned to glower at his wife.

Emma heard them, later that night, talking in their bedroom. Dad's voice was rigid, even the soundwaves refusing to bend. "She sets a bad example for the children."

Emma could hear him pacing back and forth, holding his unwavering line—a sentinel, guarding against fun.

Mom's voice was harder to hear—soft, meek, as it always was around Dad. It sounded as if she had protested, though; as if for some fleeting moment, she had held an opinion of her own.

"Heidi, you heard Emma. She idolizes her, which is exactly what your mother wants. She wants to turn our girls into mini versions of herself. And I'm not going to let that happen!"

"I don't think she's trying to make anyone be like her."

"You don't *think*?" His voice was ice. "Well, thankfully, thinking is *my* job, not yours. And I'm done—done with these visits, done with allowing her to influence this family. She leaves tomorrow, and that's the end of it. She's to have no further contact with the children."

If Heidi held an opinion, it was fragile, translucent. A dandelion puff, dispersed in the wind of her husband's righteous anger. Emma pulled her ear away from the door. Oma was going home the next morning, and after that, Emma wouldn't see her again.

Emma tossed and turned that night, angry, sad, confused. She had a dream that Dad dressed up as a police officer and took Oma to jail, then a dream that Dad brought his toolbox into the living room and began wrenching the keys one by one from the piano, and finally a dream that she folded herself into Oma's suitcase and went with her to Castle Valley.

In the morning, Emma stayed in bed, the covers pulled tightly over her head. She heard Mom preparing breakfast in the kitchen, Oma lugging her suitcase down the stairs, and the sounds of her siblings' feet pattering up and down the halls. And still she stayed in bed. Finally, Oma came to find her, knocking softly on the door. Emma didn't answer. The door cracked open. "Schatz?" Oma approached the bed. "Are you okay?"

Emma buried her face in her pillow, shaking her head no.

Oma sat down next to the small, prone figure. The mattress shifted with her weight, Emma's little body rolling involuntarily toward Oma's larger one, revealing a small, splotchy face.

"What's wrong?" Oma's fingers caressed Emma's hair.

Emma screwed her eyes tightly shut. Maybe if she refused to say goodbye, Oma wouldn't leave. Maybe Oma would fold her into the big, brown suitcase and take her along.

"It's alright if you don't want to tell me. I'm sad, too—sad to be leaving. Can I stay here with you for a bit before I go?"

Emma nodded a grim-faced assent. Oma laid down beside her, pulling her granddaughter in, baby spoon nestled in soup spoon. Emma never knew how long they laid like that or whether Dad had told Oma that she wouldn't be allowed to come back because the little girl fell asleep in the woman's arms, and Oma tiptoed out, leaving a kiss on the unruly golden crown of her granddaughter's head.

That evening, Emma sat down with her parents and younger siblings for their nightly scripture study. Most of Emma's friends read with their parents from the simplified and illustrated Book of Mormon created especially for children. Not the Madsens, though. Graham's children received the word of God directly from the source, even at the tender ages of six, four, three, and one.

Every evening, it was the same ritual. At Graham's behest, Heidi gathered the children to the living room, seating them in a row on the couch, with Hyrum on her ever-shrinking lap. Graham pulled up a chair and sat opposite his family. And then he read. Always in his most somber voice and always from the Book of Mormon. Emma was beginning to understand bits and pieces by now, and Dad sometimes stopped to explain or summarize the text. Tonight, he read from 1 Nephi 8, the story of Lehi's vision of the Tree of Life. For the first time, Emma didn't need him to translate the verses into ordinary speech. She had heard the story so many times at home and in her Primary class that it had become real to her. As he read, she imagined herself into the scene.

Her thoughts floated upwards, away from the heavy solemnity of Dad's voice, beyond the archaic words and into a beautiful, grassy meadow. At its center, stood the Tree of Life. It was prettier even than the aspens in her backyard, its trunk thick and golden. Its branches fanned out in every direction, culminating in dazzling clusters of brilliant white fruit. Two figures stood by the tree, eating the fruit—the prophet Lehi and his wife Sariah. They *glowed* with righteous joy, and Emma knew it was because of this magical fruit. Emma's taste buds prickled. She wanted to taste it, too, this miracle fruit that would grant her eternal life in the Celestial Kingdom. She watched as the glowing prophet and his glowing wife waved their arms, beckoning to the rest of their family to join them by the tree.

Their four sons stood some distance off. Two of them, Sam and Nephi, hurried toward their parents. Emma scampered to keep pace with them, but a dark mist blew in. It swirled around her, growing thicker with every second. This, Emma knew, represented the temptations of the devil. It was frightening, this cold mist that hid everything from her view. She couldn't see Lehi and Sariah, couldn't see the tree, could barely make out her own hand as it groped in the darkness, searching for something to hold onto. It must be here somewhere, she thought, and then her right hand found it—the certainty and solidity of the iron rod, which stretched through the mists of darkness to the meadow where the Tree of Life stood. The words of a hymn danced in her mind: *The iron rod is the word of God. 'Twill safely guide us through.*

Emma clung to the rod, walking hand over hand alongside it. She could hear someone moving ahead of her in the darkness and knew it must be Nephi or Sam, the righteous sons. Their disobedient brothers, Laman and Lemuel, were undoubtedly lost in the darkness by now. Should she call to them? Beg them to grab hold of the rod? She knew where Laman and Lemuel wanted to go, and it wasn't to the Tree of Life. Only righteous people strive toward the Tree of Life; the rest are lured by the Great and Spacious Building.

As soon as Emma thought of the building, there it was, hovering over the mist like a castle on a cloud. Music and laughter poured from its turrets. People danced on its balconies. It looked like fun. Emma blinked her eyes hard. It *wasn't* fun, couldn't be fun. It was *sin*. Those laughing, dancing people had chosen the temptations of the world over eternal life with Heavenly Father. Emma would not make that mistake. Hand over hand, she inched her way toward the tree.

Another sound broke through the mist. Not the rustle of Nephi and Sam's robes as they moved ahead of her, clinging to the rod. Not the merrymaking of the men and women in the Great and Spacious Building. It was the sound of her father's leaden voice, pressing down. *Oma?* Had he said "Oma"? Emma shook her ears loose.

"Your Oma has chosen the Great and Spacious Building rather than the Tree of Life. She loves sin more than she loves Heavenly Father—more even than she loves her own daughter or grandchildren. She won't be coming to visit anymore."

Oma in the Great and Spacious Building? Oma *not love her*? Emma was back in the vision again, turning toward the hovering edifice in search of answers. As if her eyes had willed it, the building grew steadily closer and more distinct. There were Laman and Lemuel now, standing on a balcony. They pointed, jeering, at their parents by the Tree of Life. On all the balconies, men and women stood mocking in this way. One woman—beautiful, with wild, brown curls and kind, laughing eyes—leaned out from the uppermost railing. She didn't point or mock like the others. She just jutted her head forward, chirping "Kuckuck! Kuckuck!" The grip of Emma's tiny fists loosened from the iron rod.

Maybe it was this softening of white knuckles that set Emma apart—that put her on a slightly different trajectory than that of her siblings and friends. Maybe this is the reason that she would never *know* the Church was true. The reason that when she ran to the mountains like Jesus or the prophets, the clearest prayer to cross her lips was laughter.

Good Mormon children cling with ever increasing fervor to the iron rod. They absorb the faith of their parents, the Primary lessons, the scripture stories, the exhaustive list of dos and don'ts. *Straight is the gate, and narrow is the way, which leadeth unto life.* Good children plant their feet firmly on the narrow path, their eyes trained ahead, tunneling through the mists of darkness toward the only acceptable goal: eternal life in the Celestial Kingdom, the highest kingdom of heaven.

Emma *wanted* to be one of these good children. But at six, she knew that Dad was wrong about Oma. By seven, it was clear that he was wrong about other things, too: that he couldn't reliably determine which child had made a mess of his papers or swiped a finger full of frosting off the cake. Coming up on her eighth birthday, she found herself *wanting* to believe him, wanting him to be like other dads—cheerful and funny like Brother Pingree or steady and kind like Cami's father. She wanted her father to be reliable and wanted the straight and narrow to be, well, straight. But where Dad proclaimed straight lines, she saw squiggles and curves. And when Dad and her Primary teachers declared the narrowness of the way, Emma found herself inconveniently plump and protruding, like an unwieldy piece of furniture that has to be turned every which way and its legs removed before it can be coerced into the intended room.

Eight is a hard age for imperfect Mormons. It is the "age of accountability"—the age at which children officially know right from wrong and are baptized as members of the Church, thus becoming accountable (responsible, blamable, punishable) for their sins.

Emma was lucky, at least, to have an older and wiser friend who could guide her through this rite of passage. By the time Emma's eighth birthday rolled around, Cami had already been eight for over a month. "I've sinned a bunch since getting baptized," Cami whispered to her after Primary class. "It's gotta be at least twenty times by now. I have to repent almost every night before I go to sleep."

This was bad news. Cami was, in Emma's estimation, far sweeter and more obedient than Emma was ever likely to be. And still it was comforting to think that maybe Cami wasn't quite perfect either.

"I wish I could just wait and get baptized when I'm older," Emma lamented.

"Why?!" Cami looked scandalized.

"So that more sins will get washed away."

"But what if you wait to get baptized and then you die first? That would be really bad."

"I know," Emma nodded solemnly. "That's why I don't ask my parents about it. Plus, I'm pretty sure it's a sin just to think it. It's like wishing I'm allowed to sin."

"Well, you're getting baptized on Saturday, so it doesn't really matter. That sin will just get washed away with all the other ones."

"Yeah. I feel like I should hurry up and sin while I still can. Like if I want to hit Joseph on his stupid head, I'd better hurry and do it." The two girls giggled before Emma fell into somberness again. "But it's also my last chance to practice being good."

"You'd better practice. It's really hard to be good all the time."

Emma sighed deeply. "It will be harder for me than it is for you. I have to do way more chores. And my parents don't let us play in the mud or get dirty or watch cartoons or do any of the fun stuff you get to do."

"Getting muddy isn't a *sin*," Cami countered.

"In my family it is. And my dad loves the commandment about how you'll die if you don't obey your parents."

"What?!"

"You know, 'honor your mother and father, that your days may be long upon the land.' Dad says that one all the time. He says 'honor' means 'obey' and the other part means it will make you live longer. So, if you disobey, you're more likely to die. Which basically means I'm doomed."

"I don't think that's what it means. I've heard 'honor your mother and father,' but I've never heard anything about dying."

"Well, either way, obeying *your* parents is a lot easier than obeying mine," Emma said, kicking at the ground. The list of potential sins and shortcomings felt impossibly long. It was awful, this tug of war between righteousness and fun. A constant battle, and she was the field.

The night before her baptism, Emma couldn't hold it in any longer. She asked the question she knew she wasn't supposed to ask.

"What happens if I don't get baptized?" she croaked from deep beneath her blankets, just as Mom switched off the light and began her exit from the room. Heidi stopped mid-stride. Emma held her breath, peering out at the frozen silhouette.

Finally, her mother turned, her hands clutching the sides of her own neck. "Then you wouldn't get to live with Heavenly Father. We wouldn't get to be an eternal family."

"Who would be my family instead?"

"You wouldn't have a family, Emma. You have to go to the Celestial Kingdom to have an eternal family. That's why baptism is so important—so special. And since you're the oldest, it's *extra* special and important. You're setting the example for your sister and brothers."

Emma picked at a stray thread on her quilt.

"I know you'll make the right choice," her mother said, her voice sunny again. She crossed the room to Emma's bed, kissed the tiny forehead peeking out, then left, closing the door behind her.

Emma lay awake, pulling at threads. When she awoke the next morning, she saw that the seam of her quilt had opened in one spot. Its inner edge spilled out jaggedly as if some small creature had chewed on it in the night.

The morning should have been perfect—perfect like Emma would be when she rose from the water. Mom made waffles for breakfast, Emma's favorite, but she could barely eat. Something inside her felt gnawed, too.

When the time of the baptism neared, Mom took her into the master bathroom and wove her hair into a tidy French braid—the second French braid of Emma's life. "We don't want your hair floating up to the surface of the water," Mom said. "This will keep it in place."

Would it, though? Emma thought of Oma, of lions, of mirrors.

"Do you want to see the back?" Mom asked, offering a small hand mirror. Emma faced away from the counter and held the glass at an angle. Behind her, she found a perfect line—straight, shining, thoroughly domesticated.

"You need one more thing!" her mother beamed, placing a small, white box in Emma's hand.

Emma lifted the lid. Inside was a silver ring with a navy-blue shield, etched with the letters *CTR*. Choose the right. Most of the girls in Emma's Primary class already had one. Emma had thought she wanted one, too, but when she slid it on her chubby finger, it seemed to whet the appetite of whatever small creature was sharpening its teeth on her insides. "My tummy hurts," she told her mom.

"That's natural when you're feeling excited, sweetie. It will pass."

It was time to leave. Emma swallowed hard and followed her mother out of the bathroom and toward the door. Each step of her white stockinged feet, each lift of her patent leather Mary Janes took her a step nearer perfection, nearer accountability, nearer belonging *forever*.

Dad captained the Ford Club Wagon to the chapel and walked by Emma's side from the parking lot, into the building, then down the hall to the Relief Society room, where an oversized bathtub hid behind an accordion door. Emma thought she could smell a hint of chlorine in the air, and she remembered the sensation of plugging her nose as she jumped from the diving board for the first time that past summer. Her tummy hadn't hurt from excitement *then*. She would plug her nose today, too, when her father dunked her backwards into the font, baptizing her by immersion. She was nervous about that part. If so much as a toe floated up to the surface, she would have to do it all again. That had happened to Adam, a boy in her class. She remembered how red his face had looked against the white of his baptismal suit.

Emma breathed in the chlorine and the room full of warm, waiting bodies. The more she breathed, the more her gut clenched and seized. She tried holding her breath instead. Barfing in the font would be far more embarrassing than a baptismal redo. Could you still be washed clean, still be bathed into belonging, if your insides turned out and splashed in the water?

A hymn was playing on the piano. Emma moved her lips in time with the singing. She tried to listen when Mom said a prayer, and she knew she was supposed to listen when Sister Caudill gave the talk about baptism, but it was all lost on her. She was trying not to puke.

Mom's warm hand wrapped around Emma's cold one, bringing her back into the room. "It's time, Emma," she whispered.

Emma needed to say something. Needed to stall for time or relieve the pressure. "What if my hair doesn't go under?" she whispered.

"Your dad is going to do a great job, sweetie. He'll get you all the way under on the first try."

Dad approached. He reached awkwardly for her hand. "Heavenly Father is proud of you, Emma," he whispered. The surprise of his words was a warm glow wrapped around her wrenching stomach.

Together they walked out of the Relief Society room, went their separate ways through the restrooms, and then met again at the uppermost step of the font. The water was warm. It swished around their bare feet, little splashing sounds echoing as they descended. Emma's dress rose on the water, determined to float. She pushed it down, watched the water drag it under, gluing the heavy fabric to her legs. It was hard to walk, wrapped in wet dress. Emma clutched Dad's hand, and he led her down into the base of the tub. The accordion doors separating them from the Relief Society room opened.

Emma heard the sounds of breathing, of restless babies and muffled coughs. She looked at Dad. He looked back at her, a hint of a smile on his lips—as if she looked clean to him already. Maybe getting baptized *was* the right choice. Maybe once she was washed clean, Dad would always look at her like this, always want to hold her hand.

She just needed to get through this without throwing up on him.

Dad took her right wrist in his left hand, just as she had seen other fathers do, then he raised his right arm in the air. "Emma Louise Madsen, having been commissioned of Jesus

Christ, I baptize you in the name of the Father, and of the Son, and of the Holy Ghost. Amen."

He brought Emma's right hand up toward her face, and she plugged her nose, the blue shield of her CTR ring glinting at the edge of her vision. Dad's right hand was on her back, and she was underwater. All of her. Right down to the last curl.

That moment—the moment of immersion—seemed to stretch on and on. Emma felt warm all over. Maybe that was the feeling of all the sins that clung to her hair and dress and skin and toes being washed off. When she came up again, the water still looked clear, but that didn't mean it wasn't crawling with sin. Emma hurried out of the filthy water as fast as her sick stomach and wet dress would let her.

She had done it. She was perfect. She belonged. She had kept her insides from spilling out.

Chapter Ten

Claudia is in the kitchen when the phone rings. She bakes on Saturdays. Sometimes it's an elaborate affair, like last weekend, when she made Bavarian apple strudel, stretching a yellow ball of dough into a thin sheet across the kitchen table, layering it with apples, cinnamon, sugar, raisins, and cream, then rolling it end over end into a casserole dish. Other times she opts for something simple, as she is doing today. Brownies from a box. Always, Claudia deviates from the recipe, adding a healthy dollop of homemade cannabis butter to her confections. Dean, her partner of seven years, swears that it eases the arthritis in his knees, and Claudia appreciates how it whets his dry humor.

She scrapes the side of the brownie bowl with her index finger to sample the batter. It's Dean who answers the phone.

"Hello?" His voice reverberates through the receiver and into the earpiece of the Moab payphone.

There is a long pause. Emma was ready for either of two options: Oma would answer, or no one would answer. This she isn't prepared for.

"Umm . . . hi," she finally stammers.

"Umm hi to you, as well."

"Is . . . does Claudia Dietrich live there?"

"She does." Dean's lips twitch at his conversation partner's obvious and inexplicable discomfort. "And she's generally a nice lady, so you needn't be frightened to speak with her. Shall I put her on?"

"Yes please," Emma exhales.

"It's not a telemarketer, is it?" Claudia asks, wiping her hands on the sides of her jeans.

Dean returns the phone to his ear. "The lady in question would like to know if you are a telemarketer." Claudia whips his thigh with the towel.

"A what? No, no, I'm her granddaughter."

It takes a lot to surprise Dean. Seeing his mouth fall open, Claudia snatches the phone from his hand.

"Hello, this is Claudia." Her voice is just as Emma remembers it.

"Oma. Hi. It's Emma."

Claudia clutches a hand to her chest and sinks into a chair. A three-way battle between shock, worry, and delight plays on her features.

"Emma, my God!"

Emma's not sure what to make of her grandmother's profanity. She's only heard the Lord's name taken in vain a handful of times, besides in the PG-13 movies that she watches at Cami's house.

Claudia collects herself and continues. "I'm so happy to hear your voice. Surprised and happy."

Emma's throat burns. It's hard to talk. She hates when this happens: a sudden surge from zero to ugly cry. "I'm happy . . . to hear . . . your voice . . . too," she gasps.

Oma can hear the red blotches appearing on her favorite grandchild's face, can hear the dam cracking and its wall of water threatening to drown intelligible conversation. "What's happening, Schatz?"

Emma's answer is muffly and convoluted, but Oma pulls these words: "Moab" and "information center."

"You're in Moab? You drove down?"

"Yes. No. I mean, I'm in Moab, but I didn't drive. I got dropped off."

"Can I pick you up?" Oma asks.

"Yes, please," Emma sniffles.

"It'll take me half an hour to get there, okay? But I'm coming. You're at the information center, right? And you'll stay put?"

"Uh-huh. Oma?"

"Yeah?"

Emma hesitates. "Please don't call my parents, okay? I don't think they've noticed I'm gone yet."

Claudia hesitates, too, but agrees. "Okay. I'm leaving now, alright?" Claudia hangs up the phone, removes her apron, begins the hunt for her keys.

"Emma's in Moab?" Dean asks.

"Yes!" Claudia looks under the pile of mail on the kitchen table, rummages through her purse. *Where are the damn keys?*

"Here," Dean says, his hand emerging from the pocket of her down jacket, which she had tossed across the back of a kitchen chair. He gives her the keys, and their eyes meet. He's always like this: calm, steady, sure of the next step. It's what she loves and hates most about him.

"You probably want to go alone?" he asks.

"I think I'd better," Claudia nods. She doesn't feel at all sure of the next step.

"I'll finish the brownies and see what I can do about the guestroom."

"How did I get so lucky?" she smiles, planting a kiss on his mouth before she heads for the door.

"Gotta keep my dealer happy," Dean retorts. And then, "Don't drive too fast!"

The only thing that keeps Claudia's tires from squealing as she tears out of the driveway is the fact that the road is made of dirt. Dust billows red behind her, but the coast is clear in front until she reaches the twisting two-lane highway that leads to town. Claudia drums her fingers on the steering wheel, impatient for the dotted yellow line that is still a dozen curves away. Whoever is driving the forest green Taurus in front of her clearly does not share her sense of urgency.

Emma ran away from home. That much seems clear. "Don't tell my parents," she had said, or something to that effect. It's easy enough to come up with reasons why a spirited seventeen-year-old might want to flee a strict and conservative home. But wanting to flee is different than *actually* fleeing.

"Something must have happened," Claudia says aloud. She often talks to herself when there's no one else around. Not just single sentences, trickling out by accident. Full paragraphs—the movement of air from her lips tickling her mind into movements of its own, prompting still more paragraphs, whose verbosity and lack of structural cohesion would make most high school English teachers pull their hair out in dismay. Topic sentences that act as foils rather than guideposts. Supporting sentences that begin with certainty but trail off into ellipses.

"Heide said she does well in school, she has friends. Why would she up and leave? Why not just rebel from the comfort of home? Graham is a complete *Arschgeige*"—Clauida prefers to deliver insults in German—"but so are lots of dads."

She sits in silence with herself for a moment before continuing. "What if, oh God, please not that. And yet, why not? All that nonsense about purity . . . the layers of guilt. She wouldn't have access to birth control. And imagine . . . imagine trying to tell that *Erbsenzähler* of a father."

Sometimes Claudia's private speeches reveal deep wells of intuition. Other times they devolve into joke telling. Often, they do both.

"There are other possibilities, I suppose. Drugs? I doubt it." And then she laughs. "Maybe something really scintillating . . . like a coffee addiction. A propensity for swearing? A secret longing to wear miniskirts? A crush on the bishop's daughter?"

Claudia veers quickly around the lollygagging Taurus as they enter a brief straightaway. "God, I hope she's gay and not pregnant. Gay and hooked on coffee."

Emma is not gay, nor is she hooked on coffee, though it was her gateway sin (coffee, that is). One second, she was sipping her first latte, feeling invigorated by naughtiness and caffeine, and then bam, she was knocked up. At least it felt that way. In truth, there were a couple weeks' worth of lattes before she bedded the barista (well, *backseated*, technically). And still, Emma couldn't shake her surprise at how fast her world had changed—how fast *she* had changed.

There was only one way to account for it: Emma *wanted* to sin. She wasn't tricked or coerced. She chose this. Never, not even for a day, had she zipped down the straight and narrow path with the breathless zeal and dizzying speed that she now employed in pursuit of the Great and Spacious Building.

Part of this penchant for sin was just plain old curiosity. Emma had always been curious—always lived with a longing, insatiable as an itch, for the rich, wide, and sometimes excruciating world of experience.

Perhaps Emma's exuberance for experience—her hunger for change and movement—came from her grandmother.

There is another car in Claudia's way now, this time an SUV. "*Trantüte,*" she mumbles, braking to match its speed, and her thoughts jolt in a new direction. "Emma has to call home. Soon. I can't let Heide think she's been stuffed in a trunk somewhere." Claudia exhales forcefully through her nose, a sort of half laugh. "Graham will accuse *me* of kidnapping her, I'm sure."

She reaches Moab and turns away from the curving path of the Colorado River. Within minutes, she is at the information center. She hasn't seen Emma in eleven years, but she knows what to look for: curly blond hair, blue eyes, a feisty and fair-complected version of her own daughter. Heide sends her a Christmas card each year, and there's always a picture: three girls in red or green dresses, four boys in white shirts and red ties, a mother who smiles with her mouth but not with her eyes, and a father whose lips are pressed into a flat line that somehow reminds you of a smile without actually being one. In the most recent photo, Emma had been promoted to the back row. She was a bit taller than her mother now and towered over the younger children. She stood next to her father, a conspicuous gap between their shoulders, and leaned forward, away from him and toward her siblings. Claudia had remarked to Dean that the picture would look more natural if Graham were just cut out of it. She let him stay, though, the Arschgeige, hanging awkwardly on her refrigerator.

There's Emma now. Claudia recognizes her immediately. She is ambling back and forth in front of the information center, a jittery bounce in her step. Some people wear their feelings on their sleeves. Emma wears hers in her walk, in the swing, sway, shuffle, or bounce of limbs. She is clearly nervous. The morning sun turns her hair to gold—a bushy lion's mane. "Still untamed," Claudia says to herself, as she pulls up to the curb. "Just a frightened cub."

That frightened cub had already paced more than a mile since talking to her grandmother on the phone. The first steps had been leaps, punctuated by audible squeals and gasps of relief. She was going to see Oma! But then doubt had crept in, like the mists of darkness from Lehi's vision, obscuring everything.

That man on the phone. Who had he been? Did Oma have a husband? If Oma lived with this man—*loved* this man—how much could she really care about a granddaughter that she hadn't seen in over a decade? All this time, Emma had imagined that Oma was pining for her, just as she pined for her grandmother. Now that seems silly. Pathetic, even.

Sure, Oma had sounded friendly on the phone, but it was probably just politeness. What if she politely invites Emma into her vehicle, and then drives her straight back to Provo? What if she takes Emma out for a polite bite to eat, politely wishes her well, and then leaves her standing on a curb somewhere?

Oma said she wouldn't call Emma's parents. But what if she does worse? What if that man on the phone already made Oma call the police? What if he called the police himself as soon as Oma left? Or maybe the man is with Oma now, heading toward Moab. Emma had imagined that it would be easy to tell Oma everything, that the words would just spill out, and Oma would know exactly what to say and what to do. Now she imagines a stilted conversation between herself and two strangers—imagines confessing her sins to a stony-faced Oma in front of this strange man.

"Premarital sex is second only to murder," he would remind her, smoothing his tie.

She can laugh away the bishop's judgments, and she can even laugh away Dad's condemnation (though that laugh has a bitter bite to it). But not Oma's. If Oma rejects her, reprimands her, turns her away—the thought is pure panic.

A voice breaks through the mist. "Emma!" it calls.

There she is: Oma, with no male companion in sight. Her long hair, a haphazard mix of waves and curls, is graying now, but her eyes and smile are just as Emma remembers them. Emma stops pacing and stares. She has come all this way, and suddenly she can't move—can't traverse the five yards between herself and her grandmother.

Oma doesn't seem to mind. She swoops down on Emma in a smiling, laughing embrace. For a moment, she sounds like every grandmother: "Look how tall you've gotten! My God, you look so much like your mom did at your age." And "Are you hungry?"

Emma *is* hungry, but she can't bring herself to say so. Is this the polite bite to eat before Oma leaves her standing on the curb?

Oma appears untroubled by Emma's silence. "Come on," she chirps, pulling her granddaughter by the hand into the street. "There's a great bagel shop just ahead. Do you like bagels?"

"Yeah," Emma manages to exhale, then gives herself an internal shake. *This is Oma. You're finally where you want to be.* Her deer-in-the-headlights face relaxes into a tentative smile.

They cross the street together, two heads of almost the same height, four feet that spring as they step, two hands that clasp together, pulsing excitement and uncertainty back and forth like Morse code. A warm, bready aroma spills from a small bakery and into the street. Oma opens the door. "Order whatever you'd like!" she proclaims, as she shoos Emma in. "I always get pumpernickel and an Americano."

"What's an Americano?" Emma asks. She has seen it on the menu at Juice and Java but never asked about it. With Juice Boy's help, she had been working her way through every conceivable flavor of latte.

Probably not a coffee addict, then, Oma thinks to herself. And aloud: "It's espresso mixed with hot water. I add cream to mine."

"I've only tried lattes," Emma confesses. "Maybe I should branch out. Can I have an americano, too?"

It's one thing for Emma to drink a latte all on her own with her babysitting earnings (or to order them on the house when the Juice and Java manager isn't around). It's quite another thing to expect a responsible adult to buy coffee for her. Is that even a thing that responsible adults do—give coffee to children? In Happy Valley, it certainly isn't. Just like responsible adults don't give children alcohol or marijuana or a gift subscription to *Playboy*.

"Of course!" Oma smiles.

Any fears that Emma had harbored that Oma might be a responsible adult dissipate. Clearly, her grandmother is different than Dad or Mom or the bishop or even Cami's comparatively laidback parents. Telling Oma everything suddenly seems like a sane choice again—like the *only* sane choice. "I guess you're wondering why I'm here?" Emma asks.

"I am, but mostly, I'm just happy to see you." Happy, curious, and worried as hell. Claudia is all of these, but she's not going to push for answers. Claudia *hates* being pushed. Besides, she pushed Heide, and look how that turned out.

Emma licks her lips, her eyes darting between her grandmother's face and the array of bagels. "I think it'll be easiest if I just . . . say it. Like ripping off a Band-Aid."

Oma takes her by the hand. Another Morse code squeeze. "Okay, do you want to order first?"

The woman at the register is staring at them, already listening in for their order. Emma blushes. "Oh, yeah, let's do that."

They order their americanos and bagels—pumpernickel for Oma, everything for Emma—and then sit down to wait. To wait, and to finally stop waiting. Emma draws in a breath, then dumps it on the table: "I might be pregnant."

The words sit between them like a shattered mug of coffee, unsalvageable, indigestible. And yet somehow her grandmother *does* digest them.

"Thank you for telling me. That took courage," Oma says, holding her gaze.

Emma's not sure what she expected, but it certainly wasn't "thank you." She feels her shoulders relax just a little. "I haven't told anyone else—not even the guy. The 'dad,' I guess I should say." She puts air quotes around the word. "I just took off. I couldn't stay. Not that he'll notice. He wasn't my boyfriend or anything."

"So, you took off and came here?"

"I know it doesn't make much sense. I mean, I haven't even seen you since I was a little kid. I just remember feeling like you understood me. It's never been like that with my parents."

Tears well in Emma's eyes, quite against her will. She hadn't cried when the stomach aches started or when she found herself getting up multiple times during the night to pee. She hadn't cried when the pregnancy test showed a blue cross. She'd never once cried, the whole time. And now here she is, breaking down for the second time in under an hour. *What is my deal?* she wonders, and the tears come faster.

Oma moves out of her seat on the opposite side of the table and sits next to Emma, putting an arm around her. "Oh, Schatz," she says. "I'm glad you're here."

"Order for Claudia!" a voice calls out. Oma doesn't move.

"You can go," Emma manages to say, her voice thick and congested. "I'll be okay."

"I know you will," Oma answers, planting a kiss on the top of Emma's golden head as she stands to get the food. She's back within seconds, two steaming Americanos, two toasted bagels, generously spread with cream cheese, a carafe of half and half.

"I'm sorry. I didn't mean to cry," Emma apologizes, wiping her face with a napkin.

"Good God, don't apologize! You can cry, you can scream, you can be silent, it's all fine with me," Oma answers. "I wasn't married when I got pregnant with your mom. I didn't even know for sure who the father was. So I understand a bit of what you're going through. And I cried plenty during that time."

This is news to Emma—the bit about her mother's birth. "I didn't know that. I mean, I kind of wondered since I never heard anything about my grandpa, but I never knew for sure."

Claudia nods. "Well, it wasn't an easy path, raising a baby on my own. There's probably no easy path for you here either. You said you *might be* pregnant, though—not that you *are*. Did you take a test?"

"I took two. One was positive, one was negative."

"In that order?" Oma asks, and Emma nods. Her grandmother's eyebrows lift, "Huh. Are you feeling sick at all?"

"Not right now. It's weird. I felt sick for a couple days, and that's why I took the test. My stomach hurt, and I had to pee all the time."

"I was that way in my first trimester, too. When was your period supposed to start?"

"I don't know. My cycle is pretty random. Maybe a few more days? Maybe a whole week?" Emma says.

"Really?" Oma's voice tilts up in surprise. "But you got a positive result already?"

"Yeah, a positive and then a negative. I took them a day apart." Emma scans her grandmother's face for answers.

Oma looks skyward, her eyebrows arching like question marks. "Well," she says, meeting her granddaughter's eyes again, "I think we ought to take you to the doctor. Your parents don't know any of this? And that's why you're here?"

Emma blushes, feeling childish. "Yeah, I'm sorry. It's stupid. I should have just taken another test. It's not fair of me to just—"

"Emma"—Oma reaches across the table and grabs her hands—"I am so glad you're here," she says, emphasizing every word. "We're going to sort this out, okay?"

Emma nods. Another tear breaks loose. "Thank you."

"I can try to schedule an appointment for first thing Monday morning if you're able to stay that long, but where do your parents think you are?"

"At my friend Cami's house. I told my mom we had to work on a project that might take all day."

"Any chance she'll call over there?"

"Yeah, but probably not until dinner time or a little before. I left a note for Cami in her mailbox to tell her everything, and I promised I'd find a way to tell my parents so she doesn't have to do it for me."

"When does Cami's family check their mail?"

"2:00 or so, same as us. She lives just up the street."

"Hmm, so we have a few hours before anyone is likely to notice you're gone. Unless Cami calls your house asking for you."

Emma's face tightens, "Shoot, I didn't think of that."

"You can say 'shit' if you want," Oma laughs.

Emma's face cracks into a startled grin. It's her first time hearing a real-life adult utter the s word. "Shit," she says, "Shit, shit, shit."

"Shit, shit, shit," Oma echoes.

And then quieter, her voice hesitant, Emma adds, "Fuck." The word tastes delicious. "Fuck, fuck, fuck," she repeats.

Oma erupts into laughter. "Fuck, fuck, fuck," she agrees, and Emma sees herself and her grandmother together in the Great and Spacious Building, heads jutting out over the railing. *Fuck, fuck, fuck*, they say.

"Well, what do you think we should do?" Oma asks.

"I guess I'd better call my mom before she has time to get worried."

"Sounds like a good idea. How about we finish eating, and then I'll take you back to my house? And you can call her from there?"

Emma nods. There will be no polite abandonment on the curb.

"You never told me how you got here," Oma muses, before taking another bite of her bagel.

Emma recounts the story of the ride board and delights Oma with a description of her idiosyncratic chauffeur. For a short while, there is no urgency—just a woman and a girl, talking, laughing, sipping coffee.

Chapter Eleven

Eight-year-old Mikey Johanson steps out the front door, an envelope in his hand. Inside the envelope, are four Kellogg's box tops. Mikey is just days away from becoming the proud owner of a Tony the Tiger frisbee!

He opens the mailbox. There is already mail inside. There shouldn't be, since it's not even lunch time yet, but Mikey is oblivious to such technicalities. He pulls the red envelope from the box, putting his own white envelope in its place, shutting the door, and raising the flag.

CAMI, the red envelope proclaims, with hearts at the corners of each letter. Mikey may be young, but he knows a thing or two about the world. For example, he knows that the color red symbolizes love. A red, heart-bedecked envelope for his sister Cami—a love letter!

This is fabulous news. Almost as good as a Tony the Tiger frisbee. His big sister Cami has been teasing him *all week* about his classmate Becky, just because he happened to mention her name once. "Did you see your girlfriend at school?" Cami likes to trill, ruffling his hair.

Red envelope = love letter = revenge! Mikey rips it open. The contents are disappointing. First of all, the letter is ridiculously long. There are three pages, and every inch of space is covered with words. If they were all drivel over some boy's undying love for Cami, it might be worth Mikey's while, but they aren't. It's clear from the get-go that this is no love letter after all.

Dear Cami,

There's no easy way for me to say this, so I'm just going to blurt it out. I think I'm pregnant. Also, I'm running away, but that sounds really dramatic, and realistically, my parents are going to haul me home within like two seconds, so I'm not really, truly running away. I'm just escaping for a moment. Taking a breath, I guess. When I imagine it, I feel as light as air. I know that sounds weird. You probably don't feel especially light reading this, and I don't blame you.

Mikey stops reading here. What a letdown! There's nothing at all in this letter that he can tease his sister about. He checks the signature at the end. Sure enough, it's not from a boy at all. It's from Cami's best friend Emma. *Emma is pregnant?* He sounds the word out a second time to be sure. *Pr-eg-na-nt.* He hadn't even known she was married! He wonders if Cami will get married soon, too. Then maybe she will move away and stop teasing him about Becky.

It dawns on Mikey now that Cami might be less than pleased with him for opening her mail. He might even get in trouble. Should he glue it shut? Give it to her as is? Throw it in the trash? Stick it back in the mailbox?

"Hey, Mikey!" His thoughts are interrupted. It's Nephi Madsen from up the street. "Wanna play basketball?" Nephi calls.

"Sure!" Mikey hollers back, jogging toward the Madsen's driveway.

"What's that?" Nephi asks, nodding at the red envelope and folds of white paper in Mikey's hand.

"Just some dumb letter to Cami from your sister," Mikey answers, dropping them in the grass just in time to catch the incoming chest pass. The dumb letter is quickly forgotten.

The boys play basketball until their fingers smart in the November wind. Nephi blows into his palms, then rubs them together. "I'm freezing," he complains.

"Yeah, me too." Mikey imitates the older boy's actions.

"Wanna come inside?" Nephi offers.

Mikey does *not* want to come inside. He likes Nephi, but no one wants to go over to the Madsens' to play. Their parents are so strict, especially their dad. You always have to be quiet in their house and remember to take off your shoes, and there isn't much to do there either. They don't even have a Nintendo!

Mikey is diplomatic, though. "How about we go to my house instead? We can play Mario Kart."

This sounds like Christmas to Nephi.

The boys spend the next half hour blissfully racing Toad and Luigi across rainbows and deserts. Then Cami strolls into the room. "Hey, Nephi! I didn't know you were over here."

"Yup," says Nephi, his eyes focused on the screen.

"What's Emma up to?" Cami asks.

"Dunno."

"Is she home?"

Nephi shrugs his shoulders and swerves to avoid a banana peel. Cami shakes her head and walks out. *Boys and their video games.*

Cami is bored. Bored and *lonely*. It's lonely when things are weird between you and your best friend—a fact that Cami has only recently discovered, since things have never been weird with Emma before.

Cami used to look at other so-called best friends and pity them. More often than not, one of these "friends" talks about the other behind her back, or they fight, or they don't spend all that much time together. Emma and Cami aren't like that. They've been best friends since forever. They do everything together, trust each other with everything, tell each other everything. Well, they used to, anyway.

For the last few weeks, something has been off. Cami thought at first that maybe she was imagining it—Emma's sudden distance. But the past week has removed any possibility of doubt. Saturday was Emma's annual lunch date with her dad. Emma had dreaded the meal, of course. She and Cami had spent the afternoon prior practicing their Graham impersonations. "I've observed that you squeeze the toothpaste from the top of the tube, Emma. This is an abomination in the sight of the Lord," Cami had reproached in her deepest voice, and they broke into giggles.

Neither of them laughed the next afternoon, though, when Emma showed up on Cami's doorstep, tear streaked and fuming. "He says I have to go to BYU. That I have to live at home," Emma choked out.

They sat on Cami's bed, shifting between silence and fumbling attempts to find a way out of toeing the line that Emma's father had charted.

"What if you just apply to the U anyway?" Cami suggested.

"How would I pay for tuition? Or an apartment?"

"Maybe you could get a loan? And a job?"

"Maybe," Emma stared blankly at the wall. She knew, of course, that plenty of college students get loans and full-time jobs, but she hadn't expected to be one of them. How would she even begin? Could she sign her own paperwork as a 17-year-old? The things she didn't know felt like an insurmountable tower in her path. The thought of trying to articulate that to Cami exhausted her. "I don't even have a car," she mumbled.

"I'll drive you around, silly. I was gonna do that anyway."

Emma sighed heavily. The hot air had all left her. She sat silent, deflated.

"We'll find a way around this!" Cami squeezed her hand

"Thanks," Emma looked down. "I think I'm gonna go."

"Go home?"

"No. For a walk, maybe."

"Want me to come?"

Emma shook her head. "I think I just need some time alone."

That stung, but Cami tried to smile encouragingly. Emma didn't seem to notice. Something felt cracked between them, and the gap widened with each passing day. Cami tried to span the distance. Tried to cheer Emma up. Tried to make her laugh. Tried to be understanding. But the more Cami tried, the more Emma pulled away.

The girls always met at their lockers after school to ride home together, but this past week, Emma claimed she had to stick around to talk with their math teacher on Wednesday.

When Cami offered to wait, Emma said she felt like walking, anyway. On Thursday, Emma allegedly had a meeting with the English teacher. And yesterday, she didn't even bother to come up with an excuse—she just didn't show up to her locker after last period.

Cami was crushed. What had she done wrong? She had tried raising that question at lunch on Friday, but Emma was evasive—something about "stuff" she had to do and a vague assurance that she would fill Cami in on the details later.

Cami doesn't want to be pushy. She doesn't want to doubt her friend. But she also can't just sit still with this feeling anymore. It's as if an arm or a leg has been cut off. She's lost part of herself, and only Emma can reattach the limb. Maybe Cami will walk over to Emma's and see what she's up to. Maybe they can finally talk about whatever's going on.

Cami slips into her coat and shoes and heads out the door. The wind hits her in cold blasts. Something red flutters in the grass. Litter. She should pick it up, she supposes, but her hands are cozy inside her pockets. She walks on, relieved to reach the shelter of the Madsens' front porch.

Cami rings the bell, and moments later, Eliza opens the door.

"Hey, Cami!" she chirps.

"Hey! Is Emma here?"

"I thought she was at your place? But come on in, you can look for her."

Cami steps in. The house smells wonderful. Cami rarely stays long in the Madsen home; she and Emma both prefer the laid-back atmosphere of the Johanson household. But Emma's house does have one definite appeal: her mother's baking.

Cami follows Eliza into the kitchen. “Hi, Sister Madsen! Mmm, it smells so good in here.”

“Thank you”—Heidi looks up from the dishes—“It must be the pie. Are you girls done with your German project?”

“German project?” Cami repeats.

“Emma said you two are working on a project together today.”

Cami blinks hard. There is no project. Emma must be covering for something, she realizes. There’s somewhere Emma wants to go, someone *else* she wants to hang out with, and she’s using a made-up German project as an excuse. She’s using *Cami* as an excuse. Hurt vies with Cami’s loyalty to her best friend, but loyalty wins. “Oh, yeah, we do. That’s what I came over to talk with her about.”

As soon as the words are out of her mouth, Cami realizes her miscalculation. Emma doesn’t want to go somewhere secret *later* today, she already *is* somewhere that she’s not supposed to be.

Sister Madsen turns away from the dishes to look at Cami. “You mean Emma’s not with you?”

“Umm, no"—Cami scrambles for some way to cover her mistake, to remain loyal to her so-called best friend—“Maybe we missed each other, though and she’s over at my place? I came from the other direction. I was . . . out on a walk.”

“But she’s been gone since before I got up this morning. She said you two were going for a run first.” Heidi’s sentences tilt upward into questions.

“We, umm . . . " Cami stammers. She doesn’t want to lie, and what can she even say? She’s suddenly furious with Emma for putting her in this spot. That is *not* what best friends do. Cami’s hands ball into fists. “I haven’t seen her all day.”

Heidi's face goes pale. Other mothers might be mad, but neither anger nor suspicion come readily to Heidi. As far as she knows, this is the first time one of her children has lied to her. Worst case scenarios swirl in her mind—her daughter, injured or abducted. "Do you have any idea where she might be?" she presses, wide-eyed.

"No," Cami says, shaking her head. She almost apologizes, but why should she? This—whatever it is—is on Emma, not on her.

Heidi has already turned to her daughter. "Liza?"

Eliza shakes her head. She's as mystified as her mother. But suddenly, she realizes she *does* know something. Those notes on her desk. She thought it was a little strange—strange but sweet. When she woke up this morning, she discovered that Emma had left a bundle of letters on her desk, one for each sibling, just saying what she loved about them. "You are the kindest person I know," she had written to Eliza. Suddenly those notes seem ominous. Were they some sort of good-bye?

"She left me a note," Eliza's words come out halting, uncertain.

"A note?"

"It didn't say anything about her going anywhere, just that she loves me and stuff. She left one for all of us—for all us kids, I mean."

"It didn't say *anything* about going somewhere?"

"No, nothing like that. I can show you." Eliza hurries upstairs to retrieve the bundle.

"Cami, do you mind double checking that no one else at your house has seen her? And could you maybe call a few other friends?"

"Of course." Cami's own worry is building, slowly catching up to her anger. Probably, Emma is just doing something dumb. Maybe she's off with a boy somewhere and doesn't want anyone to know. But what boy, and why wouldn't she tell Cami? And who goes out with a boyfriend early in the morning anyway? Something feels off.

***

When Emma walked out of Cami's bedroom a week earlier, she knew her words had hurt Cami—"I just need some time alone." When had she ever not wanted to be with her best friend? But she couldn't worry about that then—not in the aftermath of that awful conversation with Dad. The future she had imagined for herself had just been smashed. There would be no rooming with Cami, no registering for classes together. Emma was on her own, and she would have to figure this out on her own.

She walked uphill from Cami's house, her shoulders slumped, eyes on the ground. Running would have felt better, but she was wearing jeans and couldn't bear the thought of going home to change. She never wanted to go home again. *Live there for another four years?* Attend BYU, surrounded by girls whose highest aspiration was to earn their "MRS degree?" So they could all go on to have miserable marriages like the one she saw modeled every day? It was unthinkable. Emma felt squeezed, compressed. Only two things seemed possible: implosion or explosion.

Clearly an explosion of words wasn't enough. Dad didn't care what she said or how she felt. He was as immovable and unfeeling as the jagged peaks that rose on either side of her as she entered the mouth of Rock Canyon. Emma kicked hard against a rock as she walked upward, smarting at the pain in her toe, but satisfied at how the hunk of stone bounced ahead of her up the trail. She reached the place where it had landed and kicked again, harder. A third time. Then a fourth. She would have kept right on booting it, but a smiling couple was walking toward her down the trail. BYU students, for sure. Young, clean cut, glowing with temple fever. They weren't smiling at *her*. They were holding hands, gazing tenderly at one another as they walked. Emma hoped they would stub their toes on her rock. Or roll an ankle. They didn't. They floated past the stone, as if it didn't exist, their eyes trained on each other.

Emma scowled and kept walking, arms crossed, jaw set, and neck corded. Maybe it wasn't right to hate passing strangers with such fervor. Maybe she ought to have shamed herself into more acceptable feelings—righteous feelings, ladylike feelings. But she couldn't. Not today. Emma scooped up a rock and pelted it against the granite wall of the canyon. A piece of gravel broke loose and tumbled into the scrub oaks. Emma hurled another rock, and another, and another. Tiny rock fragments showered to the ground. Bit by bit, the tension eroded from her face.

She could see it. Bit by bit by bit, the whole canyon was crumbling in, collapsing to the ground. There were the remnants of old rockslides. And there was the way the mountains themselves bent, curved, and cracked. Entire layers of rock were flipped onto their sides or bowed and arced into waves.

She would not let him lock her in place. He may be a mountain, but she would be an avalanche. Emma's eyes blazed, and her ribcage expanded. She continued up the trail, and the scrub oaks gave way to firs, maples, aspens. Her spirits lifted with the trees. This soaring warmth was the feeling that her mother and teachers called "the Holy Ghost" or "the still, small voice." Emma never found it in a pew, never found it kneeling for family prayer. But she found it here. She always seemed to find it here.

It was going to be okay. *She* was okay. Maybe she would roar her way down this mountain in a cascade of rockfall, or maybe she would ripple around it like water. But somehow, she would find a way—*her* way. A verse from the Book of Mormon sprang into Emma's mind. Nephi's words, describing how he came to cut off the head of his unrepentant enemy: "And I was led by the Spirit, not knowing beforehand the things which I should do."

Emma laughed aloud. "Well, hopefully I won't have to decapitate anyone," she jested to an aspen in passing, though the thought of her father's head rolling to the valley floor did carry a certain charm. The aspen gazed back at her, tenderly it seemed, with its pale face and black eyes.

Emma was ready to face this. To begin writing her own story. She turned and walked toward the valley.

Chapter Twelve

If something unexpected were to happen to Graham Madsen, it would have to happen on a Saturday. Weekdays are regimented, Sundays religious, but on Saturdays, a hint of possibility hangs in the air. Graham doesn't notice it, of course. What he notices is that Saturdays are agitating. On some Saturdays, his sons' basketball games are in the morning. Other times, they are in the afternoon. And sometimes—Heavenly Father help him—basketball games are peppered throughout the entire day! Swim meets are even worse. There are weeks in the summer when the children have to be roused from bed as early as 6:30 AM to arrive on time, and still the Madsens don't make it back home until late afternoon.

On one such summery Saturday—now several years past—Graham was denied the comfort of his 7:00 AM run, and so he broke the script and ran in the late evening instead. He felt uneasy, untethered, but he ran anyway. He feared tragedy with every step, but no tragedy occurred. Instead, the mountains reflected the red glow of the setting sun with such vibrancy, that Graham smashed the script still further, pausing his clockwork strides to gaze at the Wasatch Range with something resembling awe. Several minutes passed before his internal clock ticked again, and when it did, Graham did something more unexpected still. *He changed course.* He ran a different way, just so that he could hold the mountains in his sight a little longer. For aesthetic reasons alone, the strictly rational Graham Madsen added more than a mile to the run that he had performed so unwaveringly since the day he and Heidi had moved into their house.

The experience unsettled him. Why would he—a rational man—be so moved by a mountain, just because it happened to be blushing pink? Why would he feel so altered, just from running at a different time of day? Why, for the love of all that is holy, did he stray from his route? It was unsettling but also strangely . . . fun.

Graham changed his script. Saturdays became the day for longer runs—ones that might start at any time of day and might meander, at least in theory, onto any path. Of course, his Saturday running routine did become gradually more predictable. He always ran uphill toward the mountains and through Rock Canyon Park. He always picked up stray bits of litter and put them in the trash cans, always grumbled about thoughtless kids as he did so.

Today, Graham collects a water bottle, an empty Cheetos bag, and a ponytail holder and delivers them to the trash can. He purses his lips and shakes his head, but he feels an undercurrent of satisfaction. All the world is unclean, irrational, irreverent. But not Graham. *He* is steady. He does not waver. He holds to the iron rod. He will run four more miles today—because that has become his Saturday pattern—then return home in time to shower before the boys' basketball games.

All goes according to plan until he reaches his own street and spots something awry. *Litter!* Graham is accustomed to picking up trash in the park, but *right here on his street*? Which neighbor could be responsible for such a crime?

He stoops to lift the piece of paper from the ground. *Dear Cami* leaps from the page. Cami? Cami Johanson? She's always seemed like a tidy, responsible girl to Graham. If she litters, perhaps his daughter shouldn't be spending so much time with her. Another word jumps to his eyes: *pregnant*. He can't help reading the whole page then—not out of nosiness, of course, but simply out of the urgent need to set wrongdoings (and wrongdoers) aright.

Setting things right will not be easy. The letter is a jumble of confessions and apologies. The writer suspects that she is with child and intends to run away from home. She confesses to struggling with her testimony and feels that she has betrayed Cami by not revealing her sins sooner. In other words, Cami was deceived by this friend—led to believe, perhaps, that the friend was a virtuous and upstanding young woman. Graham wonders if this young woman is a friend of his daughter's as well. Has Emma also been taken in by her, deceived as to this girl's character?

For all his distress, Graham knows what must be done. He runs—a blur of purple spandex—toward the Johansons' house, letter in hand. He will take this up with the head of the household.

***

Graham runs, and Heidi stands stock still—a statue, with a dishtowel in hand. She is just as uncomfortable being in control of a situation as her husband is with *not* being in control.

It took every last ounce of Heidi's pluck to delegate some of the work of looking for Emma to Cami. Now, there is nothing left.

"Mom?" Eliza asks, "What should we do?"

There is a long pause. "We'll wait for your dad to get home," Heidi's voice finally croaks out. It's not a comforting answer, even to her own ears. How will Graham respond? She doesn't know because she doesn't know what to make of the situation herself. Is Emma doing something awful? Why else would she lie? Is she in danger? And the notes—why would she have written those notes if she *wasn't* doing something awful and dangerous? Heidi tries to swallow, tries to breathe.

"Cami should be home by now. Do you want me to call her and see if Emma was over there?" Eliza offers.

Heidi manages a nod, and Eliza makes the call. Cami is at home, but there's no sign of Emma; no one there has seen or heard from her.

"I was just about to call some of the girls to see if any of them know where she is," Cami tells Eliza. The words leave a bitter taste in her mouth. What would it mean if some other friend knew what Emma was up to?

"Cami?" Eliza asks. "How worried do you think we should be?"

"I don't know," Cami says. "It feels weird that she didn't tell me anything. And weird that she wrote you that note."

"Yeah, I think so, too."

The front door of the Madsen house swings open. Emma? Graham? Both Heidi and Eliza scamper out of the kitchen and into the foyer, but it's only Nephi.

"Nephi! Have you seen Emma today?" Eliza asks.

"Why does everyone keep asking me that?" He already endured an interrogation from Cami.

"Nobody has seen her all day," Eliza tells him.

Nephi's eyes widen just a little. "Do you think she got kidnapped?" he wants to know, but before anyone can answer him, he interjects, "Oh! I forgot! Mikey had a letter from her for Cami."

"He did? Cami didn't say anything about a letter."

"I don't think he gave it to her. He put it down in the yard when we were playing basketball, and then I guess he just forgot about it. I forgot too until right now."

Eliza rushes to the front door, Heidi at her heels and Nephi trailing behind. Sariah, sensing excitement, follows them into the yard. There's nothing near the basketball hoop, but just downwind, a red envelope nestles into a shrub. Eliza snatches it up. Sure enough, Cami's name is on it, in Emma's handwriting, but the envelope is empty.

"Over there!" Heidi cries, pointing to the side wall of the next-door neighbor's house.

A white paper has blown against it. Eliza reaches it first and hands it to her mother. Heidi looks down. "It's not the whole letter. Just the end."

"What does it say?" Eliza and Nephi ask in tandem.

Some mothers would have read the letter to themselves first, then decided whether or not to share it with their children. In this moment, though, Heidi has no recollection of the fact that she is the parent. She feels so small herself. She reads aloud:

I still haven't figured out how to let my parents know that I'm safe. I don't want them to think I've been kidnapped or call the police, but I don't want them to rush down to get me either. Maybe Oma will know what to do. By the time you read this, I'll already be there, and I hope I'll have sorted out what to do next. If not, I know you can't keep it a secret forever. You can tell Eliza or my mom or your parents. You definitely don't want to be the one to break the news to my dad, haha!

Anyway, I know I've already said it, but I feel like I should say it about ten times more. I'm sorry that I've been a crappy friend. I'm sorry for keeping this all from you. You are and will always be my best friend. I hope you still feel that way, too. I'll call you when things settle down.

XOXO, Emma

"Hey, Mom, what time is my game today?" Brigham's voice breaks through the stunned silence. He stands in the doorway, his face crinkled with confusion as he stares out at his family, clustered together in the grass. Only Nephi is wearing shoes.

Heidi turns Brigham's way but doesn't register the question. She walks past him into the house. Eliza is the one to fill Brigham in, and the news passes like a game of telephone to the remaining siblings—"Emma snuck away to Oma's!"

Joseph and Hyrum join the cluster, and soon all of the Madsen children, except Emma, have assembled outside the kitchen, eavesdropping as their mother makes a call.

"Dean! Is Emma there?" Heidi's voice is desperate.

"Heide! I wondered if we might hear from you." Dean's voice is mild and cheerful, as if he's bending over a fresh pan of brownies and inhaling their aroma, which of course he is.

"Is she there?" Heidi repeats.

"Not here at the house, no, but she called us from Moab, and your mother went to meet her. I suspect they'll grab a bite to eat and then come back here, but I don't know for sure."

"Why did she leave? How did she even get there?"

"I'm just as in the dark as you are. Her call came as quite a surprise."

Heidi takes this in. "You didn't know either? I don't know what to do. Graham will be furious—not just with Emma. He'll be furious at *me*. He doesn't know I'm in touch with my mom."

Dean retired from his career as an attorney precisely to avoid conversations like this one. As a rule, he doesn't enjoy interpersonal drama. He breathes in the brownies once more to bolster himself. "Hmm, you're in a sticky spot. Has he already noticed that she's gone?"

"No, not yet," Heidi answers, "But he'll be home any minute."

"So you could go ahead and tell him the little bit that you know when he gets home. Or you could sit on it until we know more. There's no reason to think Emma's in any danger."

Heidi is quiet for a moment. She's never met Dean. He's just a voice. In this moment, maybe that's all she needs: a voice that *isn't* her own. A voice that isn't panicked. A voice that isn't the angry, unbending one she expects to hear from her husband. And maybe Dean is onto something. If nothing else, she can delay the moment of reckoning. It might not change anything, but it does make doom seem slightly less imminent. Meeting doom at dinnertime sounds preferable to meeting doom the second Graham walks in the door. *What on earth is taking him so long anyway?* Not that she wants him to hurry. "Yes, maybe. Maybe I can just put it off a bit. Collect myself. Give Emma a chance to explain."

"If he hasn't even noticed that she's gone, then I think that sounds like a reasonable idea," Dean responds. "You've done nothing wrong. Emma is what? Sixteen? Seventeen? Almost an adult. You can't control her every action."

He's used to talking people off ledges, however much he dislikes it.

"You're right," Heidi says, the tight line of her lips softening slightly.

"I imagine she has her reasons. She'll tell us about them soon enough." Cool as a cucumber, that Dean. His hand hovers over the brownies. Still too warm to slice. They are his one arena of impatience. He reaches for the knife.

Chapter Thirteen

The Christensen's Spanish-tile kitchen is warm and smells like cinnamon. Dan's mother, Anne, knows the way to his heart. It's a well-worn path by now—cinnamon rolls for breakfast, Kraft mac and cheese with hot dogs sliced into circles for lunch, and lasagna with garlic bread for dinner. She sits down at the island with her son while the rolls bake. "You seem preoccupied, honey. Is something on your mind?" she asks.

Something *is* on Dan's mind, but thoughts pile on thoughts in such rapid succession that he hadn't yet found a pause in which to notice this himself. "Umm, kind of," he says, his face scrunching.

His mother smiles. She is a social butterfly, as smooth and universally welcomed as butter. Dan is the anomaly in his family, the insect floating in the cream, but to his mother, his awkwardness will only ever be endearing. "Well, shall I let you mull it over on your own, or do you want to talk about it?"

"I dunno. I drove a girl down here today. You know, the one from the ride board?"

His mother nods.

"Well, she was really pretty, and I was sort of hoping we would hit it off. I wanted to impress her, you know? But she said some super weird stuff at the beginning of the drive."

"Weird how?"

"Like in a way that made me think she's not the kind of girl I should marry. But the weirdest part is that once I realized that, I was way more comfortable with her. It's like I forgot to be nervous. I didn't worry about what she thought of me. And then we *did* hit it off. At least I think we did. I mean, I'm not saying she likes me in that way or even that I like her in that way, but we had a lot of fun."

"It sounds like you were able to be yourself."

"Yeah, maybe that's it." He pauses, considering. "Do you think that's been my problem all along—the reason girls don't like me?"

"Well," her voice is thoughtful, "they can't like you if they don't know you."

Dan nods, his forehead still creased in thought. "Have you ever met a woman who didn't want to be a mother?" he asks

Anne is taken aback. "Hmm, I suppose I probably *have,* but it's not the sort of thing many people would talk about. At least not in the Church."

Dan has only ever known the Church. He forgets sometimes that there is a world outside of it, and that his mother, who is from the Midwest, grew up in it. Dan met plenty of non-Mormon kids in his schools over the years, of course, but he didn't get to know any of them all that well. The Church has been an ever-present reality in his life, shaping not only "right" and "wrong" but also "in" and "out."

Dan's mom continues, "I'm sure there are women who feel more excited about building careers than raising babies."

"But a Mormon girl? There would have to be something sort of wrong with her, right? Like something bad would have had to happen for her to feel that way?"

"Honey, people are complicated. I don't think it's quite as black and white as that. I mean, I know the prophet says that women should stay home and raise children, but personal revelation matters too. Maybe there are some women for whom that isn't the right choice. Did your new friend say something about that?"

"Yeah. She even said something about not having to get married to have a baby."

"Well, technically she's right, though that does seem concerning."

"I guess she wasn't really saying she doesn't want to be a mom. I think she was saying she doesn't want to get married."

His mom laughs. "Were you pressing that poor girl to talk about marriage?"

Dan blushes. "I guess that was bad?"

"Not the smoothest start, honey. But it sounds like you recovered."

"Yeah, I think maybe she got upset. And I started thinking maybe something bad had happened to her and that's why she wouldn't want to get married. So I started talking about running, and it turns out she's a runner, too, so things got better from there."

"You wear your heart on your sleeve. And someday you'll find a girl who appreciates that. But talking about hobbies before talking about marriage is always a good idea." His mother stands to check on the cinnamon rolls, planting a kiss on his head as she moves past.

People are complicated. Dan repeats his mother's words in his own mind, wishing they were just a little less true.

Chapter Fourteen

Graham Madsen was two years younger than Emma when he ran away from home. This was less dramatic than it sounds. He simply walked out the door of his mother's apartment and didn't return. "Bye, Mom," he murmured over his shoulder. But she didn't answer, nor did she chase after him. In fact, Graham's mother would have no memory of his departure, and several days would pass before she noticed his absence. For some people, liquor dulls everything. For others, it burns from inside to out, until their entire life is a smoldering ruin. For Graham's mother, it accomplished both.

Once, when he was eight years old, Graham hid a nearly full bottle of his mother's whiskey, imagining that if she couldn't find it, maybe she would simply stop drinking. Maybe she would go buy groceries or cook dinner or even just *look* at him. She did look at him, but only after turning the living room upside down in pursuit of her beverage. "Where did you put it, you little shit?" she growled. Graham covered his head with his arms just in time. A hardcopy of *Charlotte's Web*, a gift from his second-grade teacher, hurtled through the air and smashed against his elbow. He yelped in pain. The warm wet of urine burned his thighs.

No eight-year-old feels good about wetting their pants. When you have only one pair, it's even worse. Graham was already the dirty kid, the quiet kid, the awkward kid, the kid in ratty clothes. The next day at school, a pretty blond girl informed him, amidst an echo chamber of giggles, that he smelled like a toilet.

Eight was a rough year. But it was also the turning point. Because Graham, much to his own astonishment, was a "child of record." This means that once upon a time, in some unimaginable world before his father had disappeared into the ether and his mother had disappeared down the bottle, his parents had been active members of The Church of Jesus Christ of Latter-day Saints. And *that* means that as a newborn baby, Graham had received his name and a blessing from a circle of Melchizedek priesthood holders, who held the fussing infant between them in their outstretched arms, bouncing him gently as the words were uttered. And that in turn means that a record was created, with Graham's name on it. This didn't make him a member of the Church, but it generated a paper trail designed to lead to eventual baptism and salvation.

And so, not too long after Graham's eighth birthday, Mormons began knocking on his mother's door. A member of the bishopric. Missionaries. And finally, one of the Primary teachers, a woman with a son who was one grade above Graham. She was the only one to make it inside the apartment. Graham's mother had just begun imbibing her liquid brunch, and those first swigs sometimes put her in a comparatively agreeable mood. Sister Rasmussen, as she introduced herself, made Sister Madsen's mood even better. (Amazingly, Graham's mother answered to this name, albeit with a smirk.) "We're having an activity at the Church this afternoon for

Primary children. There will be cookies and games and lots of fun. I thought maybe Graham would like to come. I'd be happy to take him myself."

"You're saying you wanna take him off my hands and feed him?"

"Yes, I suppose I am." The muscles holding Sister Rasmussen's smile in place appeared suddenly taut.

"Have at it. Take the little pants pisser for as long as you want."

Sister Rasmussen flinched and looked at Graham. "Do you want to come with me right now, sweetheart? You could have lunch at my house. Or should I come back and get you later?"

Graham went with her then and there. The Rasmussen family picked him up the next day for church, too, bringing with them a bag of hand-me-down clothing that he could choose from. He wore his first tie—a purple clip-on—with pride and hardly minded his mother's cackle when she saw him. At church, Graham found something wholly new. A place of *order*. A place devoid of chaos. It was clean and structured and sometimes even quiet. He sat in Sister Rasmussen's Primary class, hanging on her every word.

"Heavenly Father has a plan for you." She looked right at Graham as she said it, and the words flooded him with a warm light. "It's called the Plan of Salvation or the Plan of Happiness."

A plan! That was precisely what he longed for. It had seemed like the whole world was a sloshing sea of confusion and pain. But no, *there was a plan!* Graham made it his mission to learn everything he could about this plan. And then, he would help Heavenly Father conquer chaos!

When he ran away from home, it felt like part of the plan. Graham was going to live with the Rasmussens, after all. He stocked the refrigerator with a few groceries just in case his mother ever decided to eat solid food again. He tidied the apartment one last time. He washed his sheets at the laundromat and left them neatly folded on his battered box spring. On top of them, he placed a brand new copy of the Book of Mormon. What more could he possibly do? He would not make the mistake of Lot's wife and look back over his shoulder.

Graham looks straight ahead now, his eyes on the Johansons' front door. His right pointer finger jabs the bell. Cami rushes to answer, certain it will be Eliza. "We found Emma!" she will say. "She was making out with a boy in the park, and Dad just grounded her for a month!"

But it's not Eliza, nor is it Emma.

"I need to speak with your father." The man at the door is stern, purple spandex notwithstanding.

"Oh, hi, Brother Madsen!" Cami chirps with a little too much pep, but Graham doesn't notice. He plows straight ahead.

"Is he here?"

"My dad? No, he and my mom are out running errands. Is there something I can help you with?"

He should say "no," of course, or that it's something he can only discuss with her father. Any other day of the week, that is what he would say. But it's Saturday, and he found litter right there in his street, and somewhere in the vicinity a child of God is growing inside the befouled reproductive system of an unwed girl. And so Graham, however fleetingly, succumbs to chaos.

"I need to talk with your father about some concerns I have for you, Cami."

"For me?" Cami tilts her head and arches an eyebrow.

"I found your letter—the one from your friend. I suppose you threw it away because you were aghast at its contents, but littering solves nothing."

"I'm sorry, what are you talking about?"

"The letter from your friend. The one who is having a child out of wedlock."

Cami is mute, her face an inscrutable stare.

"This letter." He thrusts the paper forward, and Cami takes it, immediately recognizing Emma's handwriting.

There's no easy way for me to say this, so I'm just going to blurt it out. I think I'm pregnant.

Cami's head pulls back, as if she's been slapped. Emma, *pregnant*? And Brother Madsen—how did he get this letter? Does he not know that it's from his own daughter?

Cami tries to read the remaining words on the page, but they spill back out of her head. They might as well be gibberish. None of it makes sense.

Also, I'm running away, but that sounds really dramatic, and realistically, my parents are going to haul me home within like two seconds, so I'm not really, truly running away. I'm just escaping for a moment. Taking a breath, I guess. When I imagine it, I feel as light as air.

Emma, pregnant, running away. Brother Madsen, out of breath, agitated, his hairline glistening with sweat. Cami can't hold the words and images together. Her eyes skim the rest of the page. The last sentence trails off. *Where is the rest of the letter?* "I don't get it. Where did you find this?" she asks him.

"Lying in the grass, right over there," he points. "Your habit of littering, however regrettable, is just one issue that concerns me, Cami. In fact, it's the lesser issue and *not* the reason I came to speak with your father. Your choice of friends is the primary problem. As a father myself, I would want to be informed if one of my children had fallen in with the wrong crowd, and—"

"I'm sorry, I'm just really confused. I never even got this letter. I don't get how a letter for me ended up by the road."

"This is the first that you've seen it?" Graham's forehead crinkles as the tally of problems in his neighborhood grows. Is there a mail thief on the prowl? A *littering* mail thief? Or could their mail carrier have grown suddenly careless? Perhaps there is a new carrier on the route, and this is what they are to expect from here on out. He jerks his head away from these doomsday tangents. "Well, that's certainly something to investigate further, but it's even more important that you take a hard look at your life and at the young women and men that you are choosing to associate with. Do you know who this letter is from? There must be more pages somewhere."

Graham turns and begins scanning the surrounding lawns. Cami's eyes follow his. They see it at the same moment. A single white paper, caught in the weeds of a neighbor's yard. "Ah ha!" Graham is as pleasantly sickened as if he had caught the fornicating letter writer in the offending act. He jogs toward it. Cami sprints to catch up to him.

The cold ground burns through her socks. They feel paper thin, and for a moment, *everything* feels paper thin. She and Brother Madsen rush forward. Letters begin to come into focus. What if Emma has signed her name!? They are neck and neck.

"Brother Madsen, it's my letter!" she pants, snatching it just in time.

He seems startled—embarrassed, even. "Yes, of course. I thought I'd give it to your father, but I suppose it's fine for you to do that yourself."

There's no way around it. Having handed Cami the first page, he can hardly demand it back now. Nor can he claim any right to this second one. It's hers. He is left to puzzle in private over the smattering of words that he saw: *Church, Book of Mormon,* something about *juice.*

"This . . . this friend of yours. I hope Emma isn't friends with her?"

Cami hesitates. "No, I wouldn't use that word. Emma *knows* her, but I wouldn't call them friends exactly."

Graham's mouth twitches softly with relief, and the ever-present furrow in his brow smooths just a little. "Well, that's good. You'll talk with your parents about this?"

"Of course." She turns for the door.

"I'll follow up with them later!"

"I'm sure you will," she mutters under her breath, but he isn't quite finished.

"Cami!"

"Yes?" She pivots.

"Pluck off the branches that have not brought forth good fruit, and cast them into the fire."

She looks at him quizzically. For once, Graham seems to register the meaning behind a facial expression. Or maybe he had only paused to catch his breath. "Jacob 5:26," he exhales, then turns toward home.

Cami goes inside, too. The front door is still ajar, cold air pouring in, sweeping aside all that once felt warm and safe and sure. How did this happen? Emma—pregnant? It can't be true, but apparently it is. Did she break under pressure from some boy? Cami shakes her head. She's never known Emma to break under *anything*. And yet, Cami thinks of Brother Madsen—his unbending intensity. Even the air around him feels taut. If Emma broke, then he's to blame. Cami's sure of it. She closes the door of her room, plops on the bed, and reads from the beginning.

Dear Cami,

There's no easy way for me to say this, so I'm just going to blurt it out. I think I'm pregnant. Also, I'm running away, but that sounds really dramatic, and realistically, my parents are going to haul me home within like two seconds, so I'm not really, truly running away. I'm just escaping for a moment. Taking a breath, I guess. When I imagine it, I feel as light as air. I know that sounds weird. You probably don't feel especially light reading this, and I don't blame you.

I'm sorry for not telling you all of this sooner. I'm sorry for the way I've brushed you off and avoided

you. I wasn't mad at you and I love you just as much as always. I've just needed space to figure things out—not things about our friendship (you're my BFF), just my own drama.

Maybe none of this will surprise you. Maybe all of it will. I don't really know. Do you remember me asking you once how you know the Church is true? Well, I've never known. And I've tried really hard. I pray about other things and feel like I get answers. But when I pray about church stuff, it's like there's just this blank nothingness. No answer, no burning in the bosom. Just me, wondering why everyone else knows and I don't.

For a long time I thought maybe there was something wrong with me. But

Cami flips to the second page, her brain struggling to keep up with the rapid inflow of words.

lately . . . please don't hate me for this . . . lately, I've been starting to wonder if maybe it's just because the Church isn't actually true. I mean, I know the Church does tons of good stuff and helps loads of people. But maybe Joseph Smith wasn't literally a prophet, and maybe the Book of Mormon isn't literally the word of God, and maybe other stuff isn't quite the way we've been taught. It feels scary to write all of this. Not be-

cause I'm afraid of being struck by lightning but because I'm afraid of disappointing you.

Anyway, about the whole pregnancy thing. I met the guy at Juice and Java. He works there, but none of that is especially important. I doubt I'll ever see him again. I haven't told him a thing. I took two tests. One was positive and one was negative, so I don't really know what that means. I can't ask my mom about it, but remember how I found out she's still in touch with my Oma? It turns out her info has been right there in my mom's address book all along. So, I've decided to go to Oma's in Castle Valley. I know this probably sounds crazy since I haven't seen her since I was a little kid. It probably <u>is</u> crazy, but when I imagine it, I feel weirdly okay—peaceful, even. It's almost like I feel the thing I'm supposed to feel when I pray to know if the Church is true. If I'm really not supposed to do this, then I wouldn't feel that way, right?

The final sentence ends, squeezed against the bottom corner of the page. Where is the rest of the letter? Cami flips the paper over again, as if answers might appear. She is flooded with questions. She needs the next page. She also needs to let Eliza and Sister Madsen know that Emma is safe. Well, *probably* she's safe. How did she get down to Castle Valley, anyway—assuming she's made it? Maybe Cami can tell them where Emma went without telling them why. Of course, she can't do it with Brother Madsen around.

A memory surfaces, one of Emma's many complaints about her father's rigid routines. "He's such a psychopath," she had said. She was sitting on Cami's bed, painting her toenails. Cami can still smell the polish and see the deep shade of pink. "You know how he runs every day at the exact same time?" Emma asked.

"Yeah," Cami had said, opening a bottle of blue polish. Cami's own father always ended up seeming so reasonable after these chats with Emma.

"Well, it's not just that. After he gets home, he goes straight up to his room and clicks play on the same MoTab CD and then does exactly fifteen minutes of stretching. And you *can't* interrupt him, or he totally freaks out. He has this exact order of stretches that he does, and the whole time, he's doing these crazy loud Darth Vader breaths. Like, you can hear him from the other side of his door, even with the music on."

Cami laughed, her hand wobbling as she applied the first brush of blue.

"Anyway, after exactly fifteen minutes of stretching, he shaves, but only every other day. And since shaving takes him exactly three minutes, he takes a shower for eight minutes on non-shaving days but only five minutes on shaving days. Because he has to be done at the exact same time each day, get it? Well, except Saturdays, which are always a little funky, and he's usually in a terrible mood. But anyway, after eight—or five—minutes in the shower, he turns the water all the way to cold, and you always know when it happens, because he lets out this really high-pitched squeal, and then sixty seconds later, the shower goes off, and five minutes after that, he emerges from his room, and ties his tie while he's walking down the stairs. Again, unless it's Saturday, and then it's actually really funny to watch him coming down the stairs because he looks *so uncomfortable.* Like he doesn't know what to do with his hands."

"You've gotta be exaggerating. I mean, there's no way the times are that exact!"

"Oh, they are. Brigham is the one who figured it out. We bet on it, one day, whether our dad had exact times for each of his activities. I figured it was more approximate. But Brigham sat right outside his bedroom door five or six mornings in a row and timed everything. The man is unwavering."

Cami could be remembering the numbers wrong. Maybe it's a ten-minute shower, not eight. Maybe the stretching is only twelve minutes. But in any case, Brother Madsen should be upstairs and indisposed for at least twenty minutes. Most likely, he will head straight up after coming in from his run. She should go now. Only a few minutes have passed since his departure.

Cami heads for the door. In mere seconds, she has made it to the Madsens' house. If Brother Madsen opens the door, she can ask him what that scripture reference was again. If not, she'll listen for sounds of heavy breathing or a shower running and tell Eliza and Sister Madsen as much as she safely can.

It's Brigham who comes to the door. "Wassup?"

Cami hesitates, peering over his shoulder into the house. She can hear the muffled sounds of the Mormon Tabernacle Choir coming from somewhere upstairs. The words are too quiet to discern, but Cami knows them by heart. Lyrics involuntarily echo in her mind. *Come, come, ye Saints, no toil nor labor fear; but with joy wend your way.* She finds her own voice. "Is your dad . . . stretching?" she asks.

"Yup." Brigham grins and releases a Vader breath. "He doesn't know Emma's gone. Apparently, she ran away to our grandma's house."

"How did you know that?" Cami is surprised.

"She left a letter." He shifts his feet, suddenly awkward. "Actually, it was for you. My mom read it. Well, she read part of it. It was just lying in the yard."

"I don't get it. How did it end up blowing around the neighborhood?"

"Did you ever read it?"

"Two of the pages. They were outside, too. But obviously Emma didn't leave them lying in the grass, so the whole thing is super weird."

"Mikey had it," Brigham explains. "That's what Nephi said, anyway. I guess he opened it and set it down, and the wind blew it everywhere. We couldn't find the other pages."

"I'm gonna murder that brat," Cami growls, shaking her head. "Your dad found one of the pages."

"What!?"

"He didn't know it was from Emma. He just saw that it was for me and brought it over. I couldn't believe he didn't recognize her handwriting."

"That's how he is." Brigham's voice has a bitter edge.

Eliza joins them in the foyer. "Did you tell her?" she asks Brigham.

"Yeah. She found the rest of the letter."

"You did? Did she say why she ran away?" Eliza presses.

Cami knew they would ask. She can't tell them, though. Not all of it, anyway. The muffled music still floats down the stairs, and Cami's mind fills in the garbled lyrics. *And soon we'll have this tale to tell—All is well! All is well!* She wishes this were true.

Eliza looks at her expectantly. "Umm," Cami stalls, "it's kinda complicated, but she felt like she needed to get away, and she wanted to see your grandma. She's gonna call your parents later to explain. That's what she wrote, anyway."

They move together into the kitchen. Eliza talking as they go. "My mom called our grandma's house, and our grandma's husband or whatever he is said Oma left to pick Emma up from Moab. So she made it there, and now we just have to wait for her to get to Oma's house and call—hopefully before our dad comes back downstairs."

"Mom should just stay home from our games. If Dad takes us, then it doesn't really matter when she calls," Brigham muses aloud.

Eliza's eyes brighten at the suggestion. "Mom, did you hear that?" she asks.

Brigham repeats the plan. Heidi looks unconvinced. "I don't know. Your dad wasn't going to stay for all the games, and you know how he hates a change in plans."

"What's the alternative?" Brigham presses. "Do you want him to be here to answer Emma's call? Do you want to leave and miss it?"

Heidi sighs. No, she doesn't want that.

"I could pretend to be sick! Or Sariah could!" Eliza volunteers.

"We can't lie to your father."

"You could say *you're* not feeling well. It's true, isn't it?" Brigham urges.

Heidi exhales. She wrings her hands and her eyes dart from Brigham to Eliza to Cami and back. "Damn it!" she exclaims. It's the most dramatic exclamation the Madsen children have ever heard from their mother. Eliza and Brigham look at each other in disbelief.

Their mother continues. "I'm so . . . so frustrated with Emma for putting us in this spot. But you're right. I *don't* feel well. I can't catch my breath, my head is aching, I'm dizzy. It's too much!"

Tears leak from the corners of Heidi's eyes. "Mom, it's gonna be okay," Eliza murmurs, putting an arm around her. "Come on, why don't you lie down on the couch, and when Dad comes downstairs, the boys will be ready to go, and we'll tell him you don't feel well."

Heidi allows her daughter to lead her to the sofa. "They have to leave soon," Heidi protests. "By 11:40."

Eliza glances at the clock.

"I'll go get ready now," Brigham assures his mother, "and I'll make sure the others do, too." He disappears in pursuit of his brothers. Four boys, four basketball games. One at noon, another at 12:45, the third at 2:00, and the final game at 4:00.

When Graham comes down the stairs, Cami is gone, and all four boys are uniformed and waiting in the foyer. Graham nods at them approvingly. "Heidi," he calls, looking down at the Casio on his wrist. "It's time!"

"She's not feeling well," Brigham interjects. "I think she's staying home."

Graham's surprise shows clearly on his face. Illness rarely slows Heidi down. He sees her, then, on the couch.

"What's the matter?"

"I'm not feeling well. Can you go without me?" Her voice tiptoes into the remaining words. "I'm sorry. It means you'd have to stick around for all four games."

He groans with annoyance and turns to walk away but then pauses. There will be no meatloaf tonight, he realizes—not if Heidi is sick. The first and third Saturdays of the month are supposed to be meatloaf nights. Graham had been looking forward to dinner—the one dependable thing in this fray of a day. Well, it can't be helped. "Do you need me to pick up pizza on the way home?"

Every now and then, he surprises her. Today, the surprise smarts. She feels treacherous. "Pizza would be nice. Thank you, that's really thoughtful."

Chapter Fifteen

Oma drives like Emma wants to drive but doesn't dare to. Her father told her in no uncertain terms that if she ever got a speeding ticket or a complaint from a neighbor that she had been driving too fast, he would confiscate her license, so Emma pilots the family van almost as law-abidingly as Graham Madsen himself—ever mindful of speed limits and stop signs, ever vigilant with her turn signal. But *inside* she races past every car on the road, hugging turns and catching air over the dips. Oma does this, or something approximating it, on the *outside*.

"Am I making you nervous? I can slow down," Oma says, as she zips around another tourist-driven sedan. "Dean hates the way I drive."

"I'm not nervous. Dean's the guy on the phone?" Emma asks. They still haven't talked about him. Actually, they haven't talked about Oma's life at all.

"Yeah"—there is a smile in Oma's voice—"we've been together for over seven years now. You'll like him. Even though he drives too slow."

"What's he like?"

"Mmm, what's he like?" Claudia says this as if she's been asked to describe something delicious, like a slice of cake. "He's kind and calm and steady. I mean, I can swing in the blink of an eye from sunshine to storm—not as intensely as I used to, but I'm still a bit . . . bouncy. Dean just takes everything in stride, including me. He accepts me just the way I am."

"He sounds really nice."

"He is, but he's not a pushover. He has strong opinions, but he kind of . . . I don't know. It's like he watches the world unfold as if everything is fascinating and nothing is personal. I don't mean that he doesn't care; he's very caring. But he holds things in perspective. Like, a bomb could go off in the house, and he would assess the situation, do what needed doing, and then build himself a seat in the rubble where he could calmly sit and contemplate it all."

"That seems like a good trait. Especially since I'm a bit like a bomb going off in your house."

Oma laughs. "You are *not.* You're like Christmas arriving early."

"With a Santa belly and all," Emma retorts.

"I don't see a belly. If you're going to have one, it's still a way's off"—Oma pauses, hesitating it seems—"I'm curious. Why didn't you take another pregnancy test—you know, as a tiebreaker?"

"I don't know." Emma sighs and looks out her window, as if the answer might be sitting atop one of the sandstone bluffs or perhaps floating on the surface of the winding river. "If it was positive, I wouldn't have known how to handle it. And if it was negative, I'd obviously feel better, but I'd still be totally confused, at least until my period starts. Plus"—her voice drops like it's found the edge of a cliff—"after the first test result, the positive one, I got the idea to run away. And I felt such *relief.* Like that little blue cross was just a shove out of a situation I don't want to be in. And of course, it could be more than that—a *lot* more than that—but once I had the idea to run away, I couldn't shake it, even after the next test was negative. I guess I didn't *want* to shake it." Her hands rise to her face. "Oh my gosh, that sounds so dumb."

"Not to me it doesn't."

"But I *should* have taken another test, right? And I wanted to because I wanted it to be negative, but then . . . " Her voice dissolves into the whirring of the engine.

"Then it would have been harder to leave?"

"Yeah"—Emma sighs heavily—"Wow, I hadn't even admitted that to myself, and here I am dumping it on you."

"I'm glad you're telling me." Oma removes a hand from the steering wheel and gives Emma's arm a squeeze. "What was it that you needed to leave?"

"Oh, everything. My dad, especially. The ridiculous future that he's mapped out for me. He's trying to make me go to BYU"—Emma shakes her head—"and I don't even believe the Church is true anymore. I don't know what I believe, but I'm not going to figure that out by doing the same old stuff I've always done. I want to be somewhere different with people who don't all believe the same thing. But he's dead set on preventing that. He wants me to keep living at home for my freshman year . . . probably until I get married or whatever."

"I don't blame you a bit for wanting to break free."

"Thanks." Emma is silent for a beat. "I overheard you and my mom on the phone a couple weeks ago. Once I knew you two were in touch, I wanted to talk with you, too. And it kind of felt like . . . like if even my mom has secrets, then why should I keep all the rules? I'd been planning to leave for college, and that was kinda . . . keeping me going, but then my dad shot that down. I guess that's why I had sex—or part of why, at least."

"Because you felt trapped?"

"Yeah, trapped. And mad. But also"—Emma's face twists into a smile—"do you know about the honor code?"

"Honor code?"

"Yeah, to go to BYU you have to be interviewed by your bishop, and it's stricter than the regular interviews they do every year. You have to agree to all this stuff and sign this paper promising that you'll do it."

"What kind of stuff?"

"Obeying the Word of Wisdom—you know, no coffee or tea or alcohol or anything like that. But also stuff like not wearing tank tops or shorts that don't reach the knee. Guys have to shave and keep their hair short. There's stuff about curfew, too. Like you technically can stay out as late as you want, but you can't have boys in your apartment past a certain time, and they can never go in your bedroom. There's all kinds of rules. You have to attend church regularly. Obviously, you can't have sex."

"Obviously," Oma smiles.

"Anyway, the guy I hooked up with is a BYU student, but he works at Juice and Java, so someone reported him to the Honor Code Office for drinking coffee, but the thing is, he doesn't drink coffee. He just works there. I think he *would* drink it, but he doesn't like the taste. Instead, he drinks like three cups of juice every shift. The girls he works with all call him Juice Boy. But anyway, someone reported him to the Honor Code Office, so he still has to go through this whole elaborate investigation, and he's pretty sure he's going to have to quit his job. He can't afford to get kicked out of BYU. I think he has a scholarship or something, so he's trying to follow all the rules. He goes to church every week, even though he doesn't really believe it—you can get kicked out for not going to church, too—and he was obeying the Law of Chastity, or so he says, until I came along." Emma blushes and looks down at her hands.

"It sounds like you guys have some things in common. Feeling a bit stuck. Feeling unsure that you belong in The Church."

"Yeah, we do. But I guess my point is just that hearing him talk about how hard he has to work to *not* get kicked out of BYU made me realize that the easiest way to shred my dad's ridiculous roadmap would be to just make myself ineligible. You know, just sin enough that they won't accept me. But that all seems pretty stupid now. Or at least it's stupid that I didn't make him wear a condom, but it's not like either one of us carries those around."

"I think there's room for hope," Oma says after a pause, "about your pregnancy test, I mean. False positives aren't common, but it seems odd that you got a positive result so early. I've never heard of that. So maybe it doesn't mean anything."

"Let's hope." Emma's hands fidget in her lap. She gazes at the river without seeing it.

"What are you thinking about?" Oma asks after a time.

"About what to say to my parents."

"That's a hard one."

"I guess I should just come out with it? Say that I might be pregnant?"

"I think that makes sense, but it's up to you. I suppose you could also tell them that you're having doubts about your faith or that you don't want to go to BYU. You could say that's why you ran away and wait to see if you're actually pregnant before mentioning that part. I don't know that there's a right or a wrong answer here. Maybe it's just a question of where you're at right now and where you're hoping to go . . . both in your relationship with your parents and in a broader sense."

Emma sighs. "Well, I don't want to go home. Not that I expect to be given a choice in the matter. But beyond that, I wish I knew where I wanted to go."

"Don't we all? In my old, *old* age, one bit of wisdom that I've picked up is that the best way—maybe the only way—to figure out where you want to go is to start by being where you are."

Emma smiles. "You sound like a yoga teacher. My best friend's mom is really into yoga, and she dragged us with her to class a couple times. The teacher is, like, really out there. She wears these flowy pants and a bunch of beads, and she says stuff like that. *Arrive where you are. Inhabit this moment. Greet the present moment as a friend,"* Emma intones in an airy voice.

Oma laughs. "Well, maybe she's onto something."

"Maybe," Emma says. "Cami and I were always too busy giggling to really give it any thought. But that wasn't even the funniest part."

"What was the funniest part?" Oma asks.

"There was this pose she would have us do like a bunch. It's called downward dog. Basically, you have your hands and feet on the ground and your butt in the air, so you're like an upside-down V. But I swear every time she went into the pose, she farted. But she didn't even care! She just acted like it didn't happen. Cami and I would always joke like *inhabit your flatulence. Greet your bean burrito as a friend."*

"You girls are ruthless. Remind me not to attempt any downward dogs around you."

"But if *you* farted in a downward dog, you would laugh, right? Or excuse yourself? Or *something*? You wouldn't just pretend it hadn't happened, would you?"

"I don't know what I would do, but I doubt I could be totally straight faced about it."

"And she was *totally* straight faced. One time, you could smell it, and I wasn't even in the front row. And still, she acted like it hadn't happened—or like it was no more significant than the sound of the air conditioner turning on."

Oma laughs. "Did she tell you to inhale right then?"

Emma giggles. "You think she was being sadistic?"

"It makes you wonder. But either way, if she's denying her own farts, then I guess she's denying part of the present moment. So she wasn't quite practicing what she preached."

"Yes! Exactly! People should own their farts."

"People should own all of themselves. But we generally don't. Here we go," Oma says, pulling away from the Colorado River. "Castle Valley is just over these hills."

The sandstone hills are red and crumbling, dotted with scattered clumps of grass. Even in broad daylight, Emma can't quite make out whether the hills are solid rock or shifting dunes. Oma hangs another right, and they descend. Golden cottonwoods greet them on the valley floor, contrasting the red buttes all around. "It's beautiful," Emma breathes, her lips turning up at the corners. Her smile evaporates in a heavy sigh, though. "My dad is just going to rush right down here and haul me straight back home."

"That does seem likely," Oma concedes. "And yet you still came?"

Emma is quiet, her eyes trace the ridgeline, rising and falling with each tower and turret.

"I suppose," Oma muses, "a little taste of freedom is still a taste of freedom, isn't it?"

"Yeah, it is," Emma whispers, and the words are bittersweet on her tongue.

Chapter Sixteen

As soon as Graham leaves with the boys, Heidi rouses herself from the couch. Being still is impossible. She'll clean instead. For nearly eighteen years, Heidi has dusted, diced, doused, or diapered her way through, around, or away from every problem. The idle mind is the devil's workshop, and idleness of any sort can breed that most uncomfortable of compulsions—the impulse to ask, with naked honesty, why she is living her life this way rather than some other way—so Heidi is never idle. Her mind scurries along, keeping pace with her hands. Swipe left, swipe right, rinse, wring, repeat.

This wasn't the life she pictured for herself. It wasn't the life *anyone* pictured for the bright, pretty young woman she had been when she married Graham. Heidi was liked by virtually everyone she met. She fit in seamlessly—anywhere—shaping herself to the people and situation around her. Heidi did this so fluidly that she was rarely aware of it herself. During the daytime, she was a studious and responsible undergrad. Rarely the best student, but never the worst. In the evenings, she attended parties, drank beer, and flirted with men—in a moderate, middle-of-the road fashion. Never the life of the party, never a wallflower.

Then, toward the end of her freshman year, Graham came along. He was different than the other guys she met in college. Quiet, deep-thinking, earnest, a tad brooding, perhaps, but the way his handsome face lightened when Heidi walked into the room made her feel magical. It was like waving a wand; just by moving toward him, she could transform his solemn, straight-lipped expression into a bashful smile.

Heidi and Graham didn't go to parties together. Instead, they stayed up into the wee hours of the morning, just talking. Not about sports or cars or whatever it was that other college boys were into. They talked about *real* things—philosophy, religion, the meaning of their own existence. Admittedly, Graham did most of the talking, but Heidi liked listening, and when she told him about growing up without a father, he held her hand. He let her cry.

When Graham's heart was broken by the death of the woman he considered his mother, it was Heidi's turn to do the holding. One thing led to another, as it often does—a process that Graham clearly relished in the moment but one that left him wracked with guilt. He confessed his coital transgressions to his bishop and was promptly disfellowshipped. He couldn't take the weekly sacrament or serve in any church callings. He couldn't teach or bear his testimony at the pulpit. He couldn't even offer the prayer in a meeting.

Graham, always on the periphery, became a true outsider then. He sat alone in the back row. Attending church used to soothe him and bring out his gentler side. Now he came home bristly and irritable. Heidi offered to go with him to meetings, and his face illuminated in a hopeful smile.

He *needed* her. That was the truth of it, and maybe that was his main appeal. Who doesn't want to be needed? To matter? With Graham, Heidi would never come second to a bossy mother-in-law or an enmeshed sibling. She was his whole world.

Heidi and her damp rag approach the fireplace mantle. There isn't much dust; there never is. But one by one, she pulls the framed pictures from the oak slab, wiping the tops and shining the glass. There is the yellowed photo of her and Graham on the day they were sealed in the temple. It looks like any ordinary temple wedding photo—youthful faces, white dress—but it isn't. On the sidelines, just beyond the camera frame, Oma bounces Emma on her hip.

The quickest way to lighten Graham's dark moods, it turned out (considerably quicker than attending the full three hours of church with him), was to sleep with him. But this brightening was temporary, followed each time by a backlash of guilt. Heidi tried to talk him out of his shame, and when that didn't work, she decided to break up with him.

"I don't see how we can be together and not *be together*," she told Graham, lying next to him in bed. "But I don't want to keep seeing you rip yourself apart. If this makes you feel that bad, then we should break up."

His hold on her tightened. He didn't say anything, but his breathing grew loud, quick, ragged.

"Graham, it's okay."

But it wasn't okay, or at least *he* wasn't. He curled against her in a tight ball, gripping her arm, his body rocking subtly as he heaved, sobbed, gasped for breath.

Heidi folded herself around him, stroking the back of his head. "Breathe," she said. "I'm here. If you want me to stay, then I'll stay. I won't go anywhere. I'm here, okay?"

It seemed like a reasonable compromise at the time. For her, the pros and cons list tilted ever so slightly in favor of breaking up, but for Graham they collapsed like a ton of bricks on the side of staying together. A small, barely perceptible sacrifice on her part could bring him so much happiness. And making others happy—well, that made Heidi happy. It makes any decent person happy, doesn't it? She could help him heal. She could love him unconditionally—could give him the affection that he missed out on as a child. The thought brought a smile to her lips.

Bit by bit, Graham's breathing slowed. His body stilled and uncurled. He looked at her with glistening eyes. "I need you," he said.

She nodded. His face became suddenly animated, his eyes darting to meet hers. "Heidi," he rasped, sitting upright. "What if we—would you? Would you marry me?"

She looked into his pleading eyes and saw a boy whose entire life had been bent by longing. How could she say "no" to that child? And so, Heidi said "yes," and though a voice inside her wondered what the hell she was doing, some other piece of her glowed because Graham had just broken into the brightest, broadest smile of his life—all because of her.

Thirty-seven-year-old Heidi wipes her twenty-year-old self with the rag. None of the naïve optimism rubs off. She's wondered before, in fleeting accidents of introspection, whether she would go back and do it differently if she could. What would she tell that younger self?

Nothing. She wouldn't tell herself a darn thing. After the wedding photo come framed pictures of the babies Heidi nursed, the toddlers she diapered, the children who clung to her on the first day of kindergarten. Without that first photo and its cheerful martyrdom, none of these photos would exist. And then what would Heidi be? Just a woman, standing at an empty mantel, with nothing to dust.

She works her way across the crowded shelf. Wallet-sized photos fill an accordion frame. Her rag finds Emma's most recent school picture. Even bound by a frame, even flattened onto photo paper with a fake marble background, Emma's eyes spark with a blend of curiosity and independence. They always have.

She was the two-year-old who shrieked "do it self!" when her mother tried to help her with her shoes. She was the five-year-old who boarded the bus and never looked back for the comfort of her mother's smile. Even now, when she is compelled to turn to her mother for help—to ask to borrow the van or to admit that a German assignment is over her head—there is no shine of appreciation in her eyes. There is only barbed resignation. Heidi has tried to raise her daughters to be pleasant and cooperative, but Emma is a fighter—sometimes literally. In fifth grade, she got sent home from school for punching a boy in the face. She never offered any explanation, just tilted her chin in the air and proclaimed, "You can punish me if you want, but I'd do it again." Emma is—has always been, as far as Heidi can tell—utterly, terrifyingly her own person.

Heidi, by comparison, has made exactly two rebellious choices in her life. They were the choices to marry Graham and, several weeks later, to get baptized. Mutti had always pressed her to think for herself, to "show a little spunk!" Finally, Heidi did, shocking her mother with the choice to marry Graham and horrifying her still further by announcing her intention to be baptized into the Mormon Church.

Heidi doesn't regret the baptism. But the marriage? If there were any other path to mothering these children, Heidi would choose it. She knows the pain of rebellion. So, she usually dusts quickly when she reaches Emma's frame. It's easier not to linger. Easier not to acknowledge that her daughter is also on a crash course and has been, seemingly since birth.

But today? Today, the rag slips from Heidi's hand and she holds the bronze accordion, gazing at her oldest child. She gazes so hard that she almost sees her. Then the phone rings, and Heidi blinks.

***

Emma would have gladly postponed the call. She wants nothing more than to spend this moment exploring. The adobe house where her grandmother lives looks like it grew from the earth, and the earth—well, it's unlike any place Emma has ever seen. It's a fairytale valley, ringed by red walls that rise like castles from the ground. Snow-capped mountains peer over the turrets.

This is no fairytale, though. Emma knows this because the phone is ringing in her ear, and any second now, she will embark on the odious task of telling her mother the truth, or at least a portion of it. Fairytale heroines do not telephone their mothers to make incriminating confessions. And yet here she is, the receiver pressed to her ear.

"Hello?" Heidi Madsen's soprano is even higher pitched than usual.

"Hi, Mom. It's me."

"Emma!" Heidi exhales the name in a sharp sigh.

Emma's voice is matter-of-fact. "I heard you talked to Dean already."

Heidi stammers a blend of "yes" and "Emma" and "how could you" in response. And then something about "Dad." There it is again, and again. Three mentions: "Dad." One "Emma," three "Dads."

Emma's jaw tightens. Of course this is what her mother would focus on: how Dad will react. "Mom," Emma cuts her off, "I'm calling to explain. Do you want me to or not?"

"Yes, yes, of course."

"So, the thing is . . . I might be pregnant. I don't know yet. Oma is going to take me to the doctor on Monday to find out for sure."

The silence is total.

"Mom?"

"Pregnant!?" Heidi has slid down the kitchen wall and sits on the floor, knees drawn close to her chest, mouth agape.

"I said *might* be pregnant. Maybe I'm not. But I want to stay here with Oma while I figure it out."

"Emma, how?" Heidi shakes her head as she speaks.

"*How*? Really? You have seven kids."

"That's not what I mean. I just . . . I had no idea, and *who?* Who is the father?"

"No one you know."

"Someone from school?"

"No, Mom. If you must know, I met him at Juice and Java. He works there."

"Juice and Java?" Heidi can't make sense of the words.

"Yeah. It doesn't matter, though. I haven't told him and don't plan to."

"*Doesn't matter*?" Heidi's heart pounds in her ears. "Emma, if you're having a baby, you'll be tied to this person forever. *Of course* it matters."

"Tied forever? What are you even talking about? I'm not getting married, and you keep assuming I'm pregnant. I said *might* be pregnant, remember?"

Emma fills her mother in on the details—the conflicting test results, the timing of her period, her ride down to Moab.

Heidi's replies are breathy. "I don't know what to tell your dad," she says when Emma is done talking.

Emma is quiet for a moment. She stands, twirling the phone cord around her left hand, binding and releasing herself, binding and releasing. "Do you think he'll rush straight down here and drag me home?" she finally asks.

"Probably. I don't know, though. You know how he hates driving at night. And I can't imagine him skipping church tomorrow morning. He'd have to find someone else to teach Sunday School."

"I doubt he'd get gas on a Sunday."

"No, probably not. I'm not sure how much gas he has in his car, but the van is pretty low. I honestly don't know what to expect. Except that . . . he'll be mad."

There is a long pause.

"Are *you* mad?" Emma's voice is small. She feels childish as soon as the question comes out.

Heidi chooses her words with care. "Not mad, no. Worried, surprised. But not mad. I wasn't exactly an angel before I joined the church, Emma."

"That's hard to imagine." Impossible, in fact. Emma pictures her mother accepting a tight-lipped kiss from an ardent suitor. Even that feels like a stretch. "When do you think you'll tell Dad?"

"I guess when he gets home from the boys' games. Or whenever he first asks where you are. I'm not really sure"—another heavy sigh—"I'm not looking forward to it."

"I know. I'm sorry you all have to be there when he freaks out."

"Thanks, sweetie." Heidi's voice is tired and flat.

"Do you want to talk to Oma or anything?"

Normally she would. But there is nothing normal about this. "Not right now. I'll call later."

Heidi imagines that getting off the phone will provide some sort of relief or clarity. That laying down the weight of the receiver will ease the heaviness. It doesn't. Nobody is going to fix this for her. There is no magic wand to re-flower her daughter or, if Emma is indeed pregnant, to render Graham deaf and blind until the baby can be adopted away. She tries to imagine how her husband would react if she took Emma to get an abortion. He would never forgive her, she is certain. And they would be excommunicated, she and Emma together. Yet in this moment, it isn't Graham who has to decide what to do. It's Heidi.

Glassy-eyed and stiff-spined, she shuffles to the broom closet. Mop, bucket, she'll clean the floor, that's what she'll do. In the tumult of the past hour, someone must have walked inside with their shoes still on. Brown smudges bisect the hallway and crisscross the kitchen. A mess that Heidi knows how to clean. She begins in the hall, pushing the damp yellow sponge back and forth in long lines. The mop clicks, sponge straining against its metal backing. One by one, the smudges disappear. She works her way forward, finally reaching the front door, then turns to make her way back to the kitchen. A faint line of brown tracks glistens on the freshly mopped floor. She hears a giggle and looks, bewildered, to find Sariah watching her from the living room.

"Your socks are dirty, Mommy," the little girl offers.

Heidi looks down. The soles of her white socks are damp and smeared with dirt. Sure enough. The mess is hers.

Chapter Seventeen

The second basketball game is beginning now. Graham adheres to his familiar routine: he watches the first ten minutes of the game and then, fatherly duties discharged, grades papers. It's difficult to say which task he finds more loathsome. He managed to grade two papers during Nephi's game, in addition to witnessing his son score two baskets. Brigham's game, beginning now, is longer. He'll be able to get more done. At least he hopes so. He found it more difficult than usual to focus during the first game.

Nephi, Hyrum, and Joseph sit to his left. Nephi is sweaty and slumped forward, clutching an empty water bottle. Hyrum and Joseph are restless with energy and bored of waiting for their games to begin. They take to needling each other.

"Too bad you can't play in Brigham's league," Hyrum goads his older brother. "You might actually score a basket or two."

"Too bad your head is attached to your shoulders and I can't use it as a basketball. It's definitely hollow enough to bounce," Joseph retorts.

Hyrum grins. The game is on. Taunts ricochet off of him like bank shots. "That's cute, Joe. You're adorable when you're mad. You know on second thought, maybe one of the girls' leagues would be a better fit for you."

Joseph's face reddens and contorts. *Swish.*

"Boys!" Graham scolds, without looking at them. "Is there one among you that doth make a mock of his brother?"

Joseph rolls his eyes and crosses his arms. Hyrum wipes the grin from his face and assumes a bug-eyed expression. He gesticulates with his hands, voice somber, as he finishes the scripture for his father: "Woe unto such a one, for he is not prepared, and the time is at hand that he must repent or he cannot be saved!"

"Such *an* one," Graham corrects, glancing down at his watch. Still not time to start grading.

Joseph smirks and jabs an elbow into Hyrum's side.

Something is gnawing at Graham, and he can't quite put his finger on it, possibly because he hasn't tried. Feelings, after all, are a bit like litter—unsightly nuisances to be stuffed down into a trash can and forgotten. This stuffing down was perhaps his earliest lesson in life, the legacy of explosive parents whose feelings left no space for his own. He learned the art of compacting emotion long before Sister Rasmussen took him to Primary, where he mumbled along as best as he could with the throng of well-fed and well-loved children as they cheerily sang:

No one likes a frowning face.
Change it for a smile.
Make the world a better place
By smiling all the while.

Graham doesn't smile often, but he is adept at ignoring his feelings. He is a bit queasy now. As if something is rotting in the rubbish bin. Nine minutes have passed since Brigham's game began. Graham is tempted to follow the secondhand of his watch, but he forces his eyes to the court. He counts in his mind.

Fifty-seven, fifty-eight, fifty-nine, sixty. Finally, the requisite ten-minute milestone is reached. Graham clears his throat, as if clearing his mind of the distracting inconvenience of youth sporting events, then opens his briefcase and retrieves a navy-blue folder. Clipped to its left side is his grading rubric, meticulously detailed, strictly followed. On the right side of the folder, is a stack of essays. Graham pulls a paper from his folder and settles in. Only he *can't* settle. His mind won't focus. And this particular paper is hardly worth the effort. For starters, the student failed to conform to MLA formatting! The margins are all wrong. That's 10% off right there, but it gets worse.

Graham explicitly laid out in his syllabus *and* reminded the class on multiple occasions that he requires *two* spaces rather than one at the end of each sentence. It is his sole departure from the current MLA guidelines. Few things rankle Graham more than an uninterrupted sprint of letters from one sentence into the next. It's like those people who forget to breathe while talking and end up awkwardly interrupting their own speech (completely out of sync with the rules of punctuation) by gasping for air and making unpleasant mouth sounds. Is it really too much to ask that people just breathe in sync with periods and commas?

Two spaces—it makes things so much cleaner. So much easier to process. He continues grading the paper, circling each infraction, but they follow every single sentence. It's too much. "TWO SPACES!" he writes in angry, red letters.

Graham continues to read, his stomach in knots:

Anselm's ontological argument for the existence of God is a waste of time. God cannot be known through philosophical arguments. The whole point of our existence is to exercise faith. Faith is not developed in the halls of secular learning or through so-called rational arguments. It is nurtured first and foremost in the home. Consider the two thousand striplings warriors in the Book of Mormon. Of them, Helaman wrote: "Now they never had fought, yet they did not fear death; and they did think more upon the liberty of their fathers than they did upon their lives; yea, they had been taught by their mothers, that if they did not doubt, God would deliver them. And they rehearsed unto me the words of their mothers, saying: We do not doubt our mothers knew it."

Faith isn't based on rational thought. It is based on feeling. Because of my faith, I know with every fiber of my being that Heavenly Father exists. So what use are arguments like Anselm's? Anselm was just arguing besides the point. The point of our existence is to develop and exercise faith, not reason. I owe my faith to my mother, not to any philosopher or scientist.

The paper is tripe. The student failed miserably in the assignment, which was to analyze Anselm's argument, not to debate whether it is worthy of analysis. And still, the words stir something in Graham. *I owe my faith to my mother.* His thoughts flutter to the mother of his children, and something gurgles to the surface, not unlike what happens when a garbage disposal is clogged. Graham realizes at once that she is the source of his unease.

Something seemed off with her, didn't it? It isn't like her to lie down in the middle of the day. It isn't like her to complain about *anything*. Heidi is like Sister Rasmussen. Always agreeable, always smiling, *making the world a better place by smiling all the while.* That's why he married her. Or at least one of the reasons. To be sure that his children would have the one thing he had always longed for: a cheerful, loving mother. A stable home.

He knew such a thing was possible because he had seen it firsthand in his three years with the Rasmussens. He had *experienced* it. Pam Rasmussen said she loved him, that he was part of the family. If she hadn't died so young of cancer, just months after he met Heidi, she would be in his life still.

This is just how the cancer had begun. With Pam lying down on the couch in the middle of the day. Surely, there is some benign explanation for Heidi's malaise, and still—Graham's insides twist. He wouldn't survive if—no, he can't let his mind go there. He feels a painful urgency to do something nice for Heidi. Something more than just picking up pizza.

"Boys!" His voice is sharp. Maybe it needs to be to pull their attention from the dribbling ball, the rushing players, the cheering crowd. His sons turn and look at him.

"What does your mother like?" Graham asks.

Hyrum and Joseph exchange confused glances. "What does she *like*?" Hyrum asks, clearly at a loss for where this conversation is going.

"Yes, what does your mother do for enjoyment, for example?"

"She cleans!" Nephi chimes in.

"That's not what she does for *enjoyment*." Hyrum puts air quotes around the word.

"How do you know? She spends all day doing it," Joseph points out.

"Yeah, because you guys are slobs," Hyrum retorts.

Perhaps the bickering continues, but Graham doesn't hear it. He is lost in thought. *Cleaning. Yes, Heidi does spend a lot of time cleaning.* It's not really a hobby, he supposes, but it does take up much of her day. Surely, being able to do it better or more efficiently would make her happy? Graham remembers the fancy pens that she puts in his stocking every Christmas. The briefcase she got him for his birthday a few years back. He always gives her books in return, but now that he thinks about it, he isn't at all sure that she reads them. Maybe she lacks sufficient time for intellectual pursuits. Keeping house must be a lot of work. A well-chosen gift might make it easier for her. It's not Christmas, nor is it Heidi's birthday, but today, Graham decides, he will return his wife's kindness with a gift that is really for her.

"We're going to run an errand after Hyrum's game," he announces.

The boys' attention is back on the court, and they don't reply. "Way to go, Brigham!" Hyrum calls.

Graham wishes there were a rule against cheering at sporting events. His brow creases, and he returns to grading, filling the oversized margins with blistering commentary.

"That was some shot!" a cheery voice bellows too close to his ear, and Graham finds himself assaulted by a clap on the shoulder. He turns. Jeff Pingree, whose youngest son is on the same team as Brigham, beams down at him.

Graham can't help liking Jeff. No one can. Still, he wishes the man didn't feel the need to congratulate him on every small success his sons might have.

"Yes, yes," Graham answers distractedly, turning back to the paper.

"He didn't see it," Joseph explains, his voice blunt.

"Didn't see it? Oh no! It was excellent, Graham. Brigham faked right, went left and scored from just inside the three-point line. Nothing but net."

"He doesn't care." Hyrum is even blunter.

"Of course he cares!" Brother Pingree protests, turning to Graham, expecting some sort of self-defense.

"I'm pleased that he's doing well. We have a lot of sporting events in our family, though, and so I just watch the first ten minutes of each one, then I focus on my work." Graham returns unceremoniously to grading.

Brother Pingree's eyebrows are almost at his hairline. He turns to the row of Madsen boys, a clownishly quizzical expression painted on his face. Hyrum and Nephi grin. Joseph purses his lips and turns back to the game. He used to derive satisfaction from being the oldest son, the favorite son, but more and more often, he wonders what it would be like to claim one of the other fathers in the gym. One of the dads who stands up to applaud when their boys rebound or score. One of the dads who discusses the game with you play by play over a burger and milkshake. He thinks of Emma, miles away and doing whatever the heck she wants, and his face scrunches with something like envy. He gives himself back to the game.

Chapter Eighteen

"You did it. How do you feel?" Oma asks Emma, who has just hung up the phone.

"Weird. I feel weird."

Oma nods her head sympathetically, and Dean enters the room.

"Everything okay?" he asks.

"Dean is a fixer," Oma explains. "He smooths people's family dramas."

Emma and Dean have only exchanged a few words so far, but she's already inclined to like him. He was washing a baking pan when she walked in the door—a task her own father would never perform—and the kitchen smelled like chocolate. Dean even readied the bed in the guestroom.

"Your grandma is sugar coating the truth," Dean smiles wryly. "I spent most of my career as the guy people go to when they want their marriage dissolved."

"Yeah, yeah, but there's a lot of smoothing and placating in that process. Besides, you did plenty of other stuff, too." She turns to Emma, and mock whispers, "Dean has this magic wand that he waves, and disputes turn into agreements."

Emma snorts and looks to Dean. "Well, if you think you can wave that wand at my dad and turn him into *not* a jerk, that would be amazing."

Dean smiles, "Alas, I'm afraid my magic doesn't extend quite that far."

"Well, if you're going to refuse to fix all of this for us, there's just one way forward"—Oma smiles conspiratorially at Emma—"Let's get out of here and go do something fun. I mean, I really hope that father of yours isn't going to rush down here tonight and haul you home, but he might. So let's not miss our chance. What do you say to an easy hike? Do you feel well enough?"

"That sounds great," Emma beams.

***

The hike meanders up a sandy wash then climbs into piny-on-juniper woodlands, punctuated by red slabs and boulders. There is no water in sight, and yet the memory of water is everywhere, its comings and goings written on the face of every rock, in the shape of every sandstone tower, in the placement of each grain of sand.

Conversation flows as grandmother and granddaughter walk, finally spilling onto the subject of Emma's parents.

"Why did my mom even marry him?" Emma asks, following Oma uphill.

Oma slows her steps. For a moment, the world is quiet. "It's hard to say for sure. People are messy," she finally answers. "He was sweet to her in the beginning, though . . . and my guess is that she got swept up in the idea of . . . saving him."

"Saving him? From *what*?"

"From himself. Your dad's always been . . . intense. He had such a tragic childhood. I think your mom imagined she could make up for that somehow."

"That's dumb."

Oma laughs. "Maybe so. But it's a pretty common brand of stupidity."

"Well, it's not my brand."

"No, I wouldn't imagine so. Nor is it mine. But I'm dumb enough in other ways."

"I doubt you're *that* dumb."

Oma laughs again. "You need to get to know me better. I agonized for years over the ways I messed up as a parent. I could make a long list . . . but I think maybe the worst thing was that when your mom decided to get married—and *baptized*—I lost it. It was ironic, really, because her whole life I'd been trying to get her to be more decisive and more independent. And then as soon as she made a choice I didn't like, I let her have it . . . and I just kept pushing."

"But that was because you love her and wanted her to be happy."

"Yup, but it backfired. Your mom and I are wired differently. She's always been this really gentle soul. She's happiest when she's making the people around her happy. Which is completely the opposite of how I was growing up. I was always the black sheep—cheeky, opinionated, kind of a rebel. I was pretty careless with people's feelings . . . certainly more careless than I am now, anyway. When I had your mom, I got this idea in my head that being a good parent would mean letting my daughter be her big, loud self because that's what I wished my parents had done. But your mom isn't loud. She doesn't want to take up a lot of space. She never has, as far as I can tell. Anyway, I think maybe the fact that I pushed her to be bigger and louder actually made her trust herself less. Maybe it made her more eager to please people."

"It's gross."

"What is?"

"The way she does whatever he wants. The way she tiptoes around him. She's scared of him."

"Are you sure it's your dad she's scared of?"

"What do you mean?"

"I kind of think she's scared of herself. Scared of what *she* feels when he's angry or unhappy."

"Maybe." Emma doesn't sound convinced.

"It takes a lot of trust in yourself to be willing to sit with the full range of your own emotions. And the less you trust yourself, the more you need the approval of everyone around you. I guess I just wish I had done a better job of nourishing that sense of trust in your mom."

"It's not your fault that she is the way she is."

"It's certainly not *entirely* my fault. Just like I can't take credit for all the ways in which she's wonderful. But if I could go back, I'd try to give her more space to just be who she is. I'd try to be a little more curious and a little less controlling. And if she still chose your dad and the Mormon Church, I guess I'd want to be more relaxed about the whole thing. It isn't my life to live. For a while, though, I was just so furious at your dad . . . at your mom, too. And then I was furious at myself. But the thing is, I think we were all doing the best we knew how to do at the time. Which is all anyone ever does."

"Not *everyone* is doing their best." Emma's voice is emphatic.

"You don't think so? I used to doubt it myself, but what do we really know? Take your dad for example. He's a difficult guy, right? Pretty rigid?"

"That's an understatement."

Oma laughs, scrambles up a rocky slab, pulls her backpack from her shoulders, and plunks herself down beneath a precariously balanced sandstone roof. "Okay, fine. Exceptionally difficult, rigid to the point of rigor mortis. A total Arschgeige."

"Arschgeige?"

"It's basically just an arrogant jerk. But literally, it means 'butt violin.'"

Emma erupts into laughter.

"The point is, even though he's a butt violin—maybe even a full butt orchestra—if we could look at every experience your dad's ever had . . . I mean, the little bit I know about his childhood is awful. If we could look at all of that and at his full genetic makeup and understand his brain chemistry, I think it would be easy to have compassion for him. I think we'd see that he's doing his best—maybe even doing the only thing he can. Which isn't to say that I'm especially fond of him or that I don't sometimes have a bit of fun at his expense. But there's a part of me that has learned to accept him, at least from afar."

"I bet he's a lot easier to accept from afar than up close."

Oma laughs. "Most people are."

"Especially Arschgeiges."

"Arschgeigen," she corrects the botched pluralization.

Emma sits beside her grandmother and gazes out from their rocky perch. The silence is as thick as sand. Emma chews on her lower lip, eyebrows furrowed in thought. "So if everything you're saying is right, where does free will fit in? If our experiences and genes and brains and all of that stuff pretty much decide what we do, then we aren't free."

Oma grins. "Ah, the philosopher's daughter."

Emma smiles in spite of herself.

"It's a good question. I don't have a tidy theory to wrap it up. I just have my lived experience, which is that sometimes I react to my circumstances so automatically that I might as well be a machine. And I see others do the same thing. But there's this little window each time something happens, whether it's something trivial like misplacing my keys or something weighty like a falling out with someone I love. There's this little window in which I can either react or respond. That feels like the free part of me. And the more I lean into it, the wider the window gets. Like if I'm living my life from a really reactive place, which I sometimes do, then it feels impossible to pause and step back and take a breath and do something different. But the more I manage to find that pause, the easier it gets, and the freer I feel."

"But that still doesn't prove that we're free."

"No, of course not. I guess I'm not really worried about proving it. I'm more interested in living it. I'm not a strictly rational being, and I don't aspire to be."

"Unlike my dad," Emma snorts. "Everything has to stand up to his twisted logic."

"And how's that working out for him?"

"Not very well," Emma admits.

"Maybe because he's not strictly rational either. None of us are. Feelings matter. Subjectivity matters. At least when it comes to our own happiness and sense of purpose. And I guess I don't see the point of a philosophy—or a religion—that doesn't help people to live into their lives."

"But if we're not rational—if we're sort of made up of our feelings and our programming—then how does anyone ever choose to break free from their past and leave a religion or pick a different life philosophy?"

"How are *you* managing it?" Oma asks.

Emma blinks rapidly. Is that what she's doing? Leaving her religion? Yes, she is, isn't she? Though she hadn't yet put it into those words for herself. "I don't know. I just never fit into it in the first place."

"Why not?" Oma asks.

"I guess I always saw these inconsistencies—like between what people say and what they do. But also in what's taught. Like we're taught to feel guilty about *everything* and to try to be perfect and we're told that we should *know* the Church is true, but the more I tried to do all of that, the more miserable I felt inside. I feel better—way better—running up into the mountains than sitting in church. And ironically, the Church tells us that our feelings will teach us the truth. So, like, am I supposed to base truth on what I actually feel or on what the Church says I should feel?"

"Hmm, it doesn't sound like your feelings are holding you back from changing, then. It sounds like they're a catalyst."

"Yeah, I guess that's true. And recently"—the corners of Emma's lips tilt upward—"the whole thing . . . the way people take their beliefs so seriously . . . it started to feel funny to me. The way *I* took it seriously felt funny. And laughing about it, even just a little, sort of put space around the whole thing. Maybe that's like the window you're talking about. It's this tiny opening, where you can choose to do something different."

Oma murmurs a soft "hmm," nodding her head, her eyes looking out across the juniper hills.

"I can't always find it, though. That space." Emma's voice is rueful.

"No, me neither," Oma responds. "And I've had more time to practice than you. I still manage to get in my own way a lot."

"Does it get easier? With time?"

"For me it has. I think just putting words to it, like we're doing right now, helps some. It makes it a more conscious process—like you feel yourself reacting, and you choose to pause and settle into your body and for me, there's a sort of stillness there that gets buried, but that pausing digs it back up again. Even if just for a moment. And maybe I have to repeat that process a thousand times in a day. But with practice, that still place stays uncovered for longer stretches, and it gets easier to sink back down into it again."

Oma's words fade into the silence that surrounds them. Time seems to fade, too. It's impossible to say whether one minute has passed or ten since those last words were spoken. Or maybe no time has passed at all? How is it, Emma wonders, that this silence feels like so much more than the absence of sound? As if it's its own entity—a vastness from which sound emerges and into which it collapses again. *Sounding brass and tinkling cymbals*, the scriptorian's daughter thinks to herself. Maybe that's all any of the noise amounts to, no matter how loud or self-important. Her father's angry voice. Her mother's pacifying politeness. The whirr of traffic and chatter that fill Happy Valley. The whirr of stories and expectations that populate her own mind. Sounding brass, tinkling cymbals.

And *this*—this blanket of stillness, this window of possibility—what if this is everything?

Chapter Nineteen

Graham climbs from the Club Wagon, Hyrum, Brigham, and Nephi trudging along behind him. Joseph stayed at the gym; his game begins soon. "Come on, boys," Graham urges as they cross the parking lot toward Smith's Food and Drug.

"What are we getting?" Nephi asks, scampering to catch up to his dad.

"A gift for your mother."

"And snacks?" Nephi's voice loops hopefully upward.

"No snacks." Graham's voice leaves no room for negotiation.

Nephi slows to walk with his brothers, his feet dragging.

They enter the store, and Graham turns to face them. "Who knows their way around the store? We need to find the cleaning supplies."

The Madsen boys exchange glances. "I think maybe it's over that way," volunteers Hyrum, motioning to the right side of the store.

Graham walks briskly, reading the aisle signs rapid fire. Sure enough, there it is.

Glass cleaner, bathroom cleaner, floor polish, disinfectant, sponges, and scrub brushes span the length of the aisle, reaching from Graham's ankles to well above his head. How can he possibly choose from among all of this? He looks up and down the aisle, finally spotting what he needs: a store clerk.

"Excuse me," Graham says to the pimple-faced young man. "I'm shopping for a gift and need a recommendation."

"A gift?"

"Yes, my wife spends a lot of time cleaning. Are there any particular products you would recommend to increase the efficiency of keeping house?"

The young man looks from Graham to the gaggle of boys behind him, clearly trying to discern whether the gentleman is in earnest. The oldest boy is bent over in silent guffaws, the middle one smirks softly, and the youngest appears to be flicking a booger onto the floor. The young man swallows. "Umm, we have a nice selection of brooms. Just over there," he points.

Graham thanks the young man and walks to the end of the aisle. There is a yellow broom made of something straw-like. He is certain Heidi has one just like it. But there are others, too, including one with synthetic green bristles. He remembers what his wife said to him once, in one of her rare unpleasant moments. "Can't we ever just try something *new*?"

His answer at the time had been some version of "no." But now? What better way to show that he cares? To show that she should, under no circumstances, die of colon cancer and leave him behind. "The lifetime prevalence is only 4%," he reminds the cartoonish image of his wife's colon that looms in his mind. So, it would all be quite unreasonable. Graham pulls the emerald-bristled broom from its hook.

"You're buying Mom a broom? As a gift?" Brigham asks, his eyebrows raised.

"Do you have a better idea?" Graham asks, clearly certain that his son does *not.*

"Umm, gee, I don't know. How about flowers?"

The sarcasm is lost on Graham. Flowers. Yes, Heidi does like flowers. A broom, flowers and, for good measure, a mop. He pulls a green-handled one down from its hook on the shelf. "Hold these," he instructs, extending mop and broom toward his sons.

Nephi seizes the broom, mounting it like a horse. Hyrum hoists the mop onto his shoulder, and leaps into the air, clapping his heels together. "Lunatics," Brigham mutters, a trace of a smile on his lips.

They parade to the flowers, where Graham reaches tentatively toward a cluster of pink carnations. "Yellow is Mom's favorite color," Brigham tells him.

"Is it?" Graham's hands fumble clumsily about, as if he's unsure of the proper etiquette for handling flowers. Finally, he lunges for a bouquet of yellows and reds.

***

Meanwhile, Joseph sits alone in the bleachers, his face scrunched to a scowl.

"You've been abandoned!" Brother Pingree proclaims, seating himself next to Joseph on the bench.

"They're running an errand," Joseph mumbles.

"You looking forward to your game?"

"Not really thinking about it."

"Just enjoying the here and now?"

This elicits a snort from Joseph. "I don't know that I'd put it that way." He gazes down at his hands, pressing one thumb firmly into the other, then releasing, watching the skin change from pink to white and back again. "I've got a lot on my mind."

Brother Pingree's eyes widen. *I've got a lot on my mind.* It may not seem like much, but who's ever never known Joseph to be so forthcoming? "Anything I can help with?" Jeff asks.

The boy sighs heavily. He should say "no." Should keep the family secrets, should tiptoe about, careful not to rock the boat. But Emma wasn't careful, was she? Why should he be? Why should he pretend that everything is normal, that his family is normal? His voice lifts in a tide of indignation. "Emma ran away to our grandma's house. We're not even supposed to have any contact with her—my grandma, I mean. I hardly remember her. Who knows how Emma found her address. But my dad doesn't know she's gone yet, and my mom is too chicken to tell him, so we're all supposed to pretend everything is normal until . . . I don't when. Whenever she gets around to telling him, I guess. And then he's gonna completely flip. And who's gonna bear the brunt of that? Not Emma. So yeah, not really thinking about my game."

Brother Pingree's mouth has fallen open, every trace of levity washed from his face. It takes him a moment to regain the power of speech. "Where . . . where does your grandma live?"

"Castle Valley or something like that? I think it's near Moab."

"Do you know why Emma took off?"

"No"—Joseph's lower jaw juts forward—"don't know, don't care."

Brother Pingree exhales audibly and runs a hand through the top of his hair. It strays from its part now and stands up on one side. "That's a lot to hold."

Joseph grunts in response.

"I'm trying to think how I can help. It's not my place to step in the middle of a family matter, but I want to support you . . . all of you."

"It's fine." Pink, white, pink. Joseph presses his thumbs together harder, and the veins in his hands pop into view.

"Do you have my number? Or know how to find it?"

"Yeah, my mom keeps the ward directory by the phone."

"Well, when your dad finds out, call me. Joelle is baking cookies today. I'll come over with a plate of them, as if the timing is totally random. Maybe an interruption could keep the train from going off the rails?"

Joseph nods. "I'll keep it in mind."

A cluster of boys in royal blue uniforms is forming at the far side of the court. "Gotta go," Joseph mutters, pointing toward them with his head.

"Alright, keep your chin up, kiddo. I'm serious about calling me."

"Thanks." Joseph's face is expressionless as he begins his climb down the bleachers. Halfway to the bottom, he turns around. "What kind of cookies?" he calls back.

"Snickerdoodles!"

Joseph's head bobs its approval, and he continues his descent to the floor, where he fades into blue.

Jeff slouches on the bleacher, right where Joseph left him. He has a soft spot for children with difficult fathers, his own dad having been just such a guy. Jeff turns his last interaction with Emma over in his mind. It was just this past Sunday. He'd surprised her by depositing a silver Dodge Viper convertible (matchbox size) next to her on the pew. "To help you get wherever you want to go," he'd said, "obstacles be darned." They seemed like the right words at the time—harmless and possibly helpful. Now he has his doubts.

***

When the garage door groans, Eliza's head jerks upward, and Heidi's body tenses.

"Good luck, Mom," Eliza mumbles, bending back over the dishwasher to remove the last of the clean plates.

Heidi tries to smile appreciatively to her daughter. It comes out as a grimace. She's going to tell him after dinner, she's decided. He's easier to deal with when he's been fed.

The smell of cheese and pepperoni wafts into the kitchen.

"We're baaaack," Hyrum sings out.

"Pizza!" Sariah squeals, rushing into the room.

"Back off, it's all mine," Nephi teases, boxing out to block her path.

A bumping sound and grunt of frustration echo from the direction of the garage. Heidi turns and sees her husband, flowers in one hand, pizza boxes in another, and a mop and broom tucked between elbow and chest. They slant diagonally across his body, barring his entry through the door.

"I got these for you," he stammers. "Are you feeling better?"

Heidi takes the flowers and pizza from her husband's struggling arms. Her face feels hot. "Yes, a bit better," she answers.

"Your cheeks are blotchy. You look pale and red all at once," Graham observes.

"I'm fine"—Heidi grimace-smiles again—"Umm, thank you? It's very kind of you . . . the flowers, the mop and broom, all of it."

"You've never had this kind of broom before, have you?"

"Umm, no, I haven't."

"I thought you might like to try something new."

"Thank you." Heidi blinks. She takes the flowers to the counter, laying them next to the sink, then walks to the table to deliver the pizza. The children are already crowded around the first two boxes, blocking her path.

"But that thou wouldst clear the way before me, and hedge not up my way!" Graham's voice intones behind her. "Nor the way of thy mother," he adds for good measure, and the children part like the Red Sea, allowing Heidi through.

It almost seems like a normal evening. The boys tell their mom about the games, Nephi is reminded repeatedly to wipe his hands on his napkin rather than his jersey, Sariah topples a glass of milk, and Graham barks out a brief lecture on dinner table etiquette. And yet, all of the children, with the exception of Sariah, spend an inordinate amount of time looking from their mother to their father and back again. It might be this failure to look at his food that explains the slow rolling avalanche of cheese and pepperoni that breaks from Hyrum's pizza crust and slides to the floor, landing between his seat and Emma's, which is of course vacant. And it is this event that first pulls Graham's eyes to his daughter's empty chair.

"Where's Emma?" he asks, after chastising his son.

Heidi draws a shaky breath. "Maybe we could talk about that after dinner?"

Graham's body snaps to attention, but before he can reply, Sariah speaks. "Emma went on a trip to Oma's house!" she chirps.

The table falls silent. Chewing stops. Sariah looks to her father and offers this helpful addendum: "Oma is Mommy's mommy."

Graham pushes back from the table, his chair scraping the ground. "Heidi," he barks, and she stands, following him from the room.

Five sets of widened eyes watch their mother's shrinking figure go. The final set, Eliza's, locks on her little sister in an incriminating glare. "You weren't supposed to say anything," she hisses.

Heidi shadows her husband into his office and pulls the door closed behind her.

"Is it true?" he wants to know at once.

She nods, her head barely moving, eyes fixed on the hem of his khakis. "She . . . she said she was going to Cami's, but—"

"When? How long have you known?" he interrupts.

"I . . . not that long."

Graham remembers his wife lying pale-faced on the couch. "Before the games. You found out before the games."

"I didn't know why she left. I was waiting . . . to get more information."

"So you lied."

"I didn't *lie*. I—"

"Deceived," he finishes for her. He turns away. He can't look at her. He paces, instead, up and down the length of the room. "So, what *information* did you get?"

Heidi's breath is shallow and punctuated. "She . . . she went there . . . because . . ." It's hard to speak. The room is spinning.

Graham halts in front of her. "Because why? Out with it!" His voice booms through the house.

Heidi whispers in response. "She might be pregnant."

"Pregnant?!" His echo shakes the room, but for a moment, his face is blank—a white slate upon which any number of futures might appear. Then he comprehends. The letter. His own daughter wrote that letter. That inane, flippant confession, devoid of true remorse. His daughter, a harlot. Blood rushes back to his head, and his fists clench. His daughter defiled, and he the last to know. "Wo unto them who commit whoredoms, for they shall be thrust down to hell." His voice is quiet but as sharp as a knife.

Heidi opens her mouth to speak but finds no words. She shrinks back against the door, watching as Graham traverses the room again, this time faster, his feet pounding the ground, heat emanating from his body.

"To hell!" he repeats. He pivots to retrace his steps across the floor, and his mood shifts with equal swiftness, footsteps slowing, hands rising to his temples.

He stops in front of Heidi. "Who is the father?" He *needs* to know, but Heidi is frozen, mute. Graham turns from her, releasing a sound somewhere between a snarl and a sigh. Again, he paces, wracking his brain. What had Emma said in the letter? Nothing about the father, at least not that he can recall. He remembers the page that Cami picked up. Words arise hazily in his mind: Church, Book of Mormon, and something else. Fruit, maybe?

He turns on Heidi again, his voice accusing. "You must know *something*. Surely you asked her!"

"Just that . . ." Heidi's voice falters.

"That what!?" Graham explodes.

"He works at Juice and Java."

"*Juice and Java*?"

"Over on Freedom Boulevard."

Graham strides up and down the length of the room. "Some fornicating coffee guzzler," he begins, before his worlds spiral into scripture again, "has deprived our daughter of that which was most dear and precious above all things, which is chastity and virtue."

If Heidi maintained any connection to her body, she would shake her head in disbelief. He acts as if he has never made a mistake—the *same* mistake. But it's easiest to ride out Graham's tantrums from somewhere other than her own flesh and bones. She survives such moments as if she is a speck of dust along the baseboard, small and ethereal. Something that all this hot air can just whoosh through.

The heat continues. Graham blazes with judgment as if he never had sex before marriage. As if all of this is impossibly shocking.

And of course, Heidi is still reeling from shock, too—over Emma's disappearance and the reason behind it. But it hardly makes their daughter a harlot. It makes her, well . . . a teenager. Even the fornicating coffee guzzler may turn out to be no worse than any other boy his age. No worse than Graham once was. How, Heidi wonders, can her husband have severed himself so fully from his own past?

His countenance has changed, though. His hands unclench and rise to his temples as he speaks—or quotes, rather:

"O ye fair ones, how could ye have departed from the ways of the Lord. . . ye are fallen, and I mourn your loss . . . How is it that ye could have fallen?"

It seems as if he might linger in the jagged uncertainty of this question, but then, he has swiveled again, his footsteps rapid, his voice hard, a vein in his neck pulsing. "Whoredoms are an abomination before me; thus saith the Lord of hosts."

Heidi is pressed to the door, her hand on the knob. And yet she can't make herself leave. She would have to be fully in the room, actually present, to manage such a feat. Frozen, she watches as Jekyll and Hyde wrestle with the word of God. Back and forth, back and forth. Justice, mercy, brimstone, lament. Damnation, damnation, damnation. He has made up his mind now, chosen his course. He stops walking and turns to his wife, his jaw set and eyes narrowed.

"And if thy right eye offend thee, pluck it out, and cast it from thee," he growls. "If we bring her home, she'll corrupt her brothers and sisters. So we're done with her. Done."

Heidi doesn't have to turn the knob. Graham thrusts his arm forward and does it himself, exits the room, and marches upstairs. Heidi slides to the floor. She would stay here forever if she could, melting perhaps into the floorboards until nothing remains of her but a heap of clothes. Maybe she can become dust after all. But just then, the doorbell rings. She hears a man's voice in the foyer, and Sariah's delighted cry. "Cookies!"

Chapter Twenty

Seven Hours Earlier

The air inside the Madsen home felt thick and hot, charged with electricity. It was a relief to step out the front door, though a too-intense energy still smoldered in Cami's insides. A cold wind whipped her hair, but inside her skull, were heat and smoke and thoughts that raced like wildfire. Had she done the right thing, not telling Sister Madsen that Emma is pregnant? "Might be pregnant," Emma had said. *What does that even mean? You are, or you aren't, right?*

Cami tried to imagine it—Emma with a baby. Would she keep it? Cami had never felt judgmental of her best friend before, but now, how could she feel anything else? Emma had done the second worst thing. *Second only to murder.* That's why she'd been shutting Cami out; either to ease her own path into sin or to keep it concealed. She'd chosen some boy over her best friend. Chosen *sex* over her best friend.

The heat inside Cami's skull felt suffocating. It smoked, billowed, churned. Images formed in gray wisps and charcoal lines. Emma and some boy, stealing away from school. Emma, hauled home from Castle Valley by her furious father. Emma's belly swelling against the fabric of her clothes. The fabric was the only image that appeared in color, and it was *color* that smothered the flames, threw open a window, and cleared the smoke. Yellow with small pink flowers—a fabric Emma would never wear, and yet there she was in Cami's mind, big-bellied, her stomach straining against that hideous cloth as she waddled down the halls of their high school. Cami saw the fabric and knew at once: she belonged by Emma's side, no matter what.

Cami was in fifth grade when her mother had a brief love affair with sewing. It would have been fine if she had contented herself with blankets and curtains, but no, Jennifer Johanson took it all the way. She stitched her love for her only daughter into an assortment of girls' dresses and skirts, none of which were flattering to either seamstress or wearer. The worst of the lot was a shapeless moo moo, yellow with pink flowers. Inexplicably, Jennifer loved it best of all. "This one will feel so good on a hot day like today," she told Cami, handing it to her before school one morning.

Cami's insides had flopped at the thought of being seen in such a dress. She tried to talk her way out of wearing it, but the hurt on her mother's face was so apparent that there seemed to be no other choice. Cami put the thing on, opting not to look in the mirror before heading out the door. She never liked what she saw there. Cheeks still faintly plump with baby fat, body curving in new ways she didn't know how to hide.

Emma came late to school that day, not arriving until recess. Cami couldn't remember why. A doctor's appointment, maybe? All morning, Cami felt tormented by her appearance. She kept her head low but was certain people were laughing at her—a certainty that was painfully confirmed on the playground. A small group of boys and one girl stood against the wall of the school, huddled together around something. Every so often, they looked toward her, where she sat alone, swaying from heel to toe and back again on a swing. And then, all of a sudden, the whole lot of them broke into a run, charging directly at her. Cami looked up in shock. There was nothing and no one else for them to be running at, and so she jumped to her feet and ran, too, hoping to escape the pack, but there were too many of them and only one of her, and she had never been especially fast. A hand hit her back hard, and she fell to the ground.

Before she could lift her head, there was another hand on her back, this one pulling something from the fabric of that wretched moo moo. She turned to find Emma, red-faced, staring down the pack, a Post-it note trembling in her left hand. Emma swung at the nearest boy before Cami could make sense of what the paper said. He cried out in pain and a stream of red broke from his nose. Emma stepped forward again, thrust out her other arm, this time attaching the crumpled Post-it note to the boy's forehead. *MOO!* it read.

"Don't you *ever* come near her again!" Emma shrieked at the now cowering pack. By the time she turned and helped Cami up from the ground, a teacher had arrived on the scene. Emma was sent to the principal's office and then home for the remainder of the day. Cami endured the remaining hours of school alone but *not* alone. She had something none of those jerks had. She had a best friend who would stand by her through anything.

Now, some six years later, it was Cami's turn to be that friend. To see beyond the labels that others might attach. To peel them off, if she could. She felt her judgment crumple like a piece of paper. She wasn't going to wait around for the grown-ups to see the light. She would drive to Castle Valley herself—right now. If she could get her parents' permission, that is.

Cami's elated certainty didn't last long.

"Drive down there *now*?" her mother balked. "No, Cami. I love that you want to do that for her. But you need to leave space for her family to sort this out. If Emma is pregnant, her parents are going to want to be there with her to help her figure out what to do."

Cami let out an exasperated sigh. "Mom, Emma's dad is *nuts*. He's not going to *help* her, he's going to *kill* her."

"He is not going to *kill* her." Jennifer Johanson rolled her eyes.

"Okay, whatever, he's not going to literally kill her, but he's going to be *majorly* uncool. You have no idea how strict he is!"

Cami's mother raised her hands in a gesture of helplessness. "It's just not our place to interfere, Cami. Emma will be back home soon. I bet one of her parents will drive down to get her tonight. Odds are, she'll be at church in the morning."

"And if not?"

"Look, if she isn't back home within a few days, we can talk about you driving down there—maybe next weekend, okay? I just don't see the rush. You don't even know what you'd be rushing into. We don't know Emma's grandma, and besides, if she's as wonderful as Emma seems to think she is, then Emma probably wants a little time alone with her anyway. And you have a math test on Monday, don't you?"

Her Mom might be right, Cami realized—she's certainly right about the math test, but maybe she's a little bit right about the other part, too. Cami wouldn't want to barge in and mess up Emma's time with her grandma.

"Pregnant," Jennifer sighed, shaking her head. "Poor girl. I wouldn't have expected that of her."

The hair rose on the back of Cami's neck. "Everyone makes mistakes, Mom."

"That's true. We do. I just wish for her sake that she'd picked a different one."

Chapter Twenty-One

Dinner is done and the dishes washed. Oma, Emma, and Dean sit outside under thick, fleecy blankets. A fire crackles between them, in a sandy pit dug into the yard. Emma watches the smoke rise into the black of night and traces it upward until it disappears, dissolving, it seems, into the blurred light around the moon. Even with the moon nearly full, there are more stars in the sky than Emma has ever seen.

"It's a shame the moon is so bright," Dean says. "Once it wanes a bit, you'll be able to see the Milky Way if you're still here."

Emma's never seen the Milky Way, except in pictures. She imagines an arc of stardust across the sky. It would look like mist, she assumes. *The mists of darkness*, she thinks to herself and smiles.

She doesn't feel lost in darkness right now. She feels found. Feels held by something great and spacious and good. She wishes Eliza could know Oma. Wishes that all of her siblings could sit here with marshmallows and sticks, telling stories and laughing in a place where the ground is made of sand rather than eggshells.

"Did you ever try to visit again? After my dad said you couldn't come?" Emma asks, spinning her marshmallow slowly over the low flames.

"Yeah," Oma nods. "I did. I mean, I didn't actually show up on your doorstep, but I wrote your dad letter after letter. He wouldn't take my calls. I'm not sure he read the letters either. Your mom tried talking with him, too, but the more she tried, the angrier he got, so then we thought that maybe if we just dropped it, he'd soften with time. But that obviously hasn't happened. Every year or so, your mom tries again and then gets punished with an extra dose of coldness and crankiness."

Emma's marshmallow blazes. She doesn't bother to blow it out. "I hate him so much."

Oma releases a heavy sigh. "I get that."

"You *don't* hate him?"

"I got tired of hating him. Being right, making someone else wrong—even when the facts line up on your side, it's exhausting. And like I said earlier, he's had a hard life."

Emma stares intently into the fire. The orange flames mirror her insides.

"Do you know much about his childhood?" Oma asks.

"No. He doesn't talk about it."

"His mom was an alcoholic. Your mom thinks she must have been pretty abusive, though of course your dad doesn't divulge a whole lot. At a minimum, she was extremely neglectful. And I don't think he has many memories of his father at all—he ended up in prison for something or another. So it was just him and his mom, who was apparently drunk as often as not. Your dad moved in with a friend when he was in his teens, and that's how he joined the church. I think it saved him. Literally, perhaps. His friend's mother took him under her wing, but then she died of cancer, right around the time your parents met."

Emma's eyes blink rapidly, stinging from the smoke. She tries to imagine her dad as a child. All she can muster is a child-sized man, stern-faced and pursed-lipped, wearing a white button-down shirt and living in squalor.

"Some people who come from troubled backgrounds never manage to grow up. I think your dad has the opposite problem. I think he never got to be a kid," Oma muses.

"My sister married a man like that"—Dean stares into the fire—"Your Oma already knows all this, but this guy's whole life was centered around asserting control. For a long time, I thought it was just because he was an asshole. But as I got to know him better, I realized it was because he never experienced the safety that a kid is supposed to have, and he was still reeling from that. Still just trying to control his environment so that he could handle it. I mean, he was also an asshole. But he was an asshole for a reason. My sister ended up leaving him, which was the right call, but I also felt for the guy."

"My mom would *never* leave my dad."

"Sometimes spunk skips a generation," Dean observes.

A ringing sounds from the house. "I'll get it." Oma rises to her feet.

Minutes pass.

"Think it's your mom?" Dean asks.

That is exactly what Emma is thinking. She feels glued in place, though. Whether by the biting cold of the air or by the coziness of the fire or the grandeur of the sky or the weight of what she's just learned about her dad, she can't say.

Oma returns to the yard, her gait slower than it had been moments before. She sinks down heavily into her chair. "That was your mom."

"And?" Emma asks.

Oma chooses her words slowly. "She said your dad didn't take it well, which I know you expected . . . For now, he's saying he doesn't want you to come back home . . . Apparently, he said you *can't* go home."

Emma feels her belly clench as if it's been punched. She waits to feel something else. Instead, feeling seems to drain out of her. No anger, no triumph, no sadness, no fear—just a cold nothing, as if the fire has gone out. "So he's disowning me," she finally mutters.

"It's not actually about you or about anything you've done, Emma. He isn't doing it because of you, he's doing it because of *him*. It's his stuff."

Emma nods. *Of course it's his stuff. It's always his stuff.*

"He might just need a few days to come to his senses," Dean offers.

"You have a home here, Schatz." Oma reaches out and squeezes Emma's hand. The girl's fingers remain limp.

Silence stretches between them.

"Thanks," Emma finally whispers. "I think . . . I want to go to bed."

"Can we get you anything?" Dean asks.

"No, I just need to sleep." She stands to go.

"Hey"—Claudia's voice is emphatic—"we've got you, okay? You're not doing this alone."

Emma nods but doesn't look up. Claudia and Dean watch the slender shadow retreat.

***

At 11:00 that night, Cami's light is still on. Jeff Pingree's mind is swirling. Heidi stands numbly in the shower, hot water streaming her face like tears. Eliza tosses, turns, can't fall asleep. Graham lies rigid on his back, his thoughts marching to battle, maneuvering against unseen foes. Dan Christensen watches *Star Trek: The Next Generation.* "Last episode," he vows to himself.

Oma and Dean whisper to each other drowsily. Emma is awake—has never been more awake, or more desperate for sleep, in her life. "He's disowning me," she murmurs to the dark.

The words should bounce off her. Or roll like water. Wasn't she trying to get away from him? Isn't this what she wanted? Oma said she can stay here, so why does she feel flooded—alone, unmoored, tossed on the waves? Emma can apply to any college she wants now—assuming she can manage to finish high school, save a bit of money, and figure out loan applications. And, well, assuming there's no baby. But she isn't thinking about college right now. She isn't even thinking about babies. She's thinking of her family.

Will her mother stealthily stay in touch, like she has with Oma? Will Emma have to wait until her siblings are grown and out of the house to see them again? She pictures Sariah as an adult—a woman who will barely remember her. Emma wasn't trying to run away from *all* of them. She just wanted her dad to stop controlling the details of her life. She wanted a taste of freedom. Just a taste. And now? Clearly, her father is hell bent on seeing her eat the entire pie. His control feels more complete than ever.

She remembers what he said when he came into her bedroom the day after their lunch date on campus—the day after she threw caution and chastity to the wind. “I’m sending you to BYU for your own good," he gruffed. "I know you don’t understand it right now, but you’ll thank me later. You just rush into things headlong without considering the consequences. You’re not ready to make a decision of this magnitude.”

Recalling these words from 210 miles away, Emma is afflicted with the desire to kick him and herself all at once.

She remembers how he stood over her, his voice growing more agitated when she neither looked at him nor replied. Behind her placid face, she had distracted and amused herself by comparing this particular daddy-daughter chat to the ones that played out every Friday night on *Full House*, when Danny Tanner would enter his daughter D.J.’s room for yet another heart-to-heart. The Tanner family conversations invariably ended with sappy music and hugs. Emma began composing a sentimental score for her present reality. It was hard not to smile just a little at the way it clashed with her father’s voice.

“Are you listening to me?”

“Mm-hmm,” was all she offered, appearing perhaps a bit too pleased with herself.

“Someday you’re going to be a parent, and you’ll get it. You’ll see that everything I do is out of love.”

Emma failed to suppress a snort. Color rushed to her father’s face, and his nostrils flared.

“You are *so* smug, Emma!” he barked. “Lest you’ve forgotten, you don’t have a single privilege that I can’t take away. Not one!”

He slapped his hand hard on her desk to punctuate his words. Something rolled to the floor. Emma's eyes dropped to the carpet. It was the silver Matchbox car that Brother Pingree had given her earlier that day. It gleamed there, shone like freedom, like escape.

Emma trained her attention on it. Her father's voice grew louder, angrier. But she barely heard it. Emma was shrinking, first her ears, then the rest of her head, and then her whole body. Her thousand desires, the complexity of her longings, everything was shrinking down, condensing to matchbox size. There was just one desire left—simple, straightforward, roaring like an engine. *I'm getting out of here.* Emma's mind spoke the words like a prophecy.

She would get away. She would free herself; that would show him. Emma saw herself, now in miniature, leap to the floor. Mini Emma rushed across the carpet and swung the door of the Dodge Viper wide. She climbed in, turned the key, and the car thundered to life. Foot pressing hard to the gas, hands clenched on the wheel, she raced forward, between the legs of the screaming, red-faced giant, and out the door. She caught air over the stairs, landed in the foyer, exited via the front door, and then? *Where was she going?*

She knew in a flash. She was going to find Oma, even if she didn't know when or how. And everything else? Anything that didn't fit in the four-millimeter passenger seat of her silver Dodge Viper? Well, it would just have to stay behind.

There is a lot, it turns out, that can't be squeezed into a Matchbox car. At 11:30 p.m., Emma mourns the loss of Cami, Eliza, and Sariah. By midnight, she misses her brothers, too—some more than others. It's close to 1:00 a.m. before she allows the aching realization that some piece of her still needs her mother. By 2:00, exhaustion overcomes reason. Emma's mind flickers from face to face, calling up school friends, church friends, teachers, neighbors. All of them, she is sure, are sleeping soundly right now. She is just a blur on the periphery of their lives. They won't even miss her.

Cami will find another roommate—a new best friend. Joseph will be the oldest child now. Everyone will carry on, living into a future that doesn't include her. And Emma? She has no idea what her future holds. In the light of day, the wide openness of this mystery might hold a certain sparkle. But not now—not in the middle of a sleepless night. Not when her stomach is queasy, her back aches, and her mind won't quit.

Somehow, eventually, she falls asleep. She only knows this because she jerks awake. Pale light seeps around the edges of the patchwork curtains. The sun isn't up yet, but it's morning—the best time to take a pregnancy test, that's what the girl at the pharmacy had said. Emma climbs from bed, pulls the crumpled box from the bottom of her bag, and shuffles to the bathroom.

She flicks the light on, walks barefoot across the cold tile, opens the box, tears the wrapper, sits on the toilet, and holds the stick in her urine stream. Pee splatters against her fingers, which feels appropriate. Like a metaphor for her life. Searching for answers, getting pissed on. Finished, Emma lays the test on top of the empty box, washes her hands. She sits on the edge of the bathtub and waits, head heavy in her palms.

Seconds tick past slowly. Minutes, slower still. She crafts *Choose Your Own Adventure* endings in her mind. She doesn't like any of them.

Finally, she stands up and looks. Just one line. No cross. *Negative.*

She should feel relieved. She *does* feel relieved. But it's a small feeling, encircled by a big, anxious emptiness. She drops the test strip into the wastebasket and walks to the kitchen to search the cupboards. Raisin Bran. Grape Nuts. A Tupperware container of brownies.

Her hand hovers over the brownies. If ever there was a moment for chocolate, this is it, but her stomach feels off. She picks up the box of Raisin Bran instead, pours herself a bowl, and sits down to eat, alone with the sound of her own chewing and the solitary clinking of her spoon.

"Morning, Schatz." Oma breezes into the room.

"Morning," Emma mumbles.

"You look tired. Coffee?"

"Yeah, thanks."

The sounds of the coffee pot, gurgling and dripping, meld with the chorus of chewing and clinking. Emma stares blankly ahead.

"How are you feeling?" Oma asks, sitting down directly opposite Emma, placing one mug in front of her granddaughter, then cupping the other in her own hands.

"Not great . . . queasy . . . and my back hurts. But I took another test."

Oma's head jerks up from her coffee. "And?!"

"It was negative."

Oma releases a gust of air. "Oh, thank God! I'm so glad!"

"Yeah, me too," Emma says, her face slack. "But then why do I feel so crappy?"

"You're under a lot of stress. Could it be that . . . and a lack of sleep?"

"Maybe."

Oma sets down her mug and reaches forward, taking one of Emma's hands between her own. "We'll get you to the doctor first thing tomorrow, and we'll get this figured out. Just one more day of uncertainty, okay?"

Emma smiles faintly. It's a nice thought—*just one more day of uncertainty*. But of course, it isn't true. Her whole life is airborne.

Oma seems to read her thoughts. "Well, just one more day of uncertainty *about this,* anyway."

Emma nods her head. "I used to feel pulled to the unknown. I used to *like* mystery and surprise. But now . . ." Her voice trails off.

Some part of her wants to say it all—wants to say that she feels so small. That right now, she would grab onto pretty much any scrap of supposed certainty, just not to feel like this. But saying words like those aloud, releasing them from her mouth and giving them substance—that would be its own cliff, its own freefall.

Oma's brow is furrowed, her expression grave. Then, a soft smile breaks at the corners of her eyes. "Do you want to know my favorite memory of you?" she asks.

"Sure," Emma shrugs.

"You must have been about seven, and you were in trouble with your dad. I don't remember what for. It was something little, some normal thing that kids do like making a mess or snatching a toy. But your dad was really steamed about it. He spanked you and sent you to your room without dinner, and of course no one was allowed to go in and console you. And the whole time, I kept imagining how upset you must be. Hungry, alone. I thought you'd be crying. It was at least an hour before I could sneak upstairs to check on you. Your mom had baked bread, and so I grabbed a couple slices when your dad wasn't looking, and went up to your room, thinking I was going to comfort you. Thinking you needed rescuing. Do you know what I found? Do you remember this?"

Emma shakes her head no.

"I walked in, and you smiled up at me, bright as can be, and you said," Oma pauses, laughing, then composes herself. "You said, 'Welcome to Tenju, a world where everything is unexpected.' And sure enough, you had turned your entire bedroom into this magical world, in which nothing was as you would expect it to be. You'd remade your bed with the pillows where your feet should have gone and moved your shoes to the highest shelf of your closet. I have no idea how you reached it. You'd built a house out of dolls and a family of blocks was living inside it. And you were taping together sheets of paper into a giant mural and coloring it like the sky, and you said it was your new carpet."

Emma smiles in spite of herself. "Tenju. I wonder how I came up with that."

The two women sit quietly for a long while, Claudia sipping coffee, Emma lost in thought. Finally, she speaks. "You know, I think that story sums up my whole life." Something has made her forget that only minutes before, getting pissed on seemed the more apt metaphor.

"How so?" Oma asks

Emma draws a deep breath. "Dad, Mom, The Church, my teachers . . . they have all these expectations. It's like my whole life was laid out and decided for me before I was even born. Boys at least get to choose a career, but for girls, there's nothing. No choice. Just this straight and narrow path that you're supposed to follow from birth to marriage to motherhood and then all the way to death. And if the Church is true, then that path just stays the same right on into the eternities. One eternal boring-as-hell line, walked obediently by your husband's side. Or maybe just trailing behind him, since once you get to the Celestial Kingdom, he might have any number of wives. . . . I'm sick of straight lines. I'm sick of being told to stay on the path. Of doing the expected thing. I feel like I was *born* sick of it. I didn't have sex because I fell in love or had some mega crush or something. I just had sex because I wanted to have some *say* in my own life. I wanted to break the rules . . . because it felt like they were breaking *me.* Plus, if I broke them in a big enough way, maybe people would stop trying to fix me. So basically, it came down to sex or murder. Sex was probably still the better choice."

Oma laughs. "Given those options, I'd say so."

"But it was dumb, really. I mean, I should have just gotten drunk instead. Or shown up to my bishop's interview in a miniskirt. Or refused to sign the honor code. There are plenty of other ways I could have proven myself 'unworthy' of BYU."

"But this is about more than just not wanting to go to BYU, isn't it?"

"Yeah. It is," Emma concedes. "But still, I should have planned things better. You know, avoided this whole . . . thing"—she gestures at her belly— "but it's my own dumb fault."

"Or, you know, maybe 50% your own dumb fault?" Oma suggests.

"Okay, fine. 50% my own dumb fault," Emma smiles.

"That second negative test seems really hopeful, but have you thought about what you would do if you *were* pregnant?"

Emma sighs heavily. "A little. I'd mostly just shut off that part of my brain. I already had so much to think about, you know? But last night, I couldn't sleep, and I felt sick, and at some point, I'd thought about literally every other thing I could possibly think about, so yeah. I gave it some thought, but I don't have an answer. Just questions."

"That's a shitty night."

Emma smiles, the sharp edges of her worry softened by the union of empathy and profanity. "Yeah, it sucked. But even though my body's been feeling . . . off . . . the whole pregnancy thing has never seemed real to me. Like, I've tried to imagine myself pregnant, walking through my high school with a gimongous belly . . . and I can't. I just get these cartoony images of my stomach smashing into lockers and my water breaking on the gym floor."

"You've had a lot of change to absorb all at once—your dad blowing up your plans to go to the U, finding out your mom and I were in touch, meeting your guy, having sex for the first time, us seeing each other again after all of these years. It's already a lot to take in, even without a pregnancy."

"Yeah, it is. Either way, my whole life is changing. And it's not all bad, but it's all . . ." Emma searches for the word.

"Hard?"

Emma nods. "Really fucking hard." Then she smiles. "It's a world where everything is unexpected."

Chapter Twenty-Two

By 3:00 AM, Graham Madsen could take it no longer. For hours, he had held statue-still, doggedly denying every urge to move, to roll onto his side, to crack his ankles, or even to scratch his nose. Heidi had climbed wet-haired into the bed (though she knew how he hated that) and curled into a tight ball as far from him as she could get without actually toppling off the bed. He could feel and hear the fitfulness of her slumber—the tiny tremors and jerks, the whimpering exhalations. And still, Graham had not so much as batted an eyelid. Yet here he was, eternities later, wide awake.

There was no doubt that he was in the right as far as his daughter was concerned. Since retiring to bed some seven hours prior (*that* must have been where he went wrong, going to bed early, rather than adhering to his usual schedule), Graham had constructed a half dozen cogent arguments in support of his decision to disown Emma. Several of them were scripturally based, and all of them were, to Graham's thinking, logically sound. How vexing that even when the line of his thoughts was steady and unwavering, sleep should evade him! Yes, it must have been that lamentable breach of routine that launched him into insomnia. He ought to have known better.

The clock on his nightstand read 3:11. He rose, pajama clad, and trudged down the stairs to his office. Graham did his best thinking at his desk.

There was a theme among his arguments for disowning Emma, he realized. Three of them hinged on the premise that his six younger children might also become corrupted if she remained in the household. One argument focused on Emma's direct influence. If she were to continue living at home, she might persuade her siblings to sin. A second argument considered her unintentional influence on her siblings. Simply by following her unrighteous example, they could be swayed from the straight and narrow path. A third argument weighed the impact of Graham's response to his daughter's impurity. A soft response would give the impression of laxity, thereby encouraging similarly licentious behavior in his other children.

Graham's thoughts turned to his upcoming Sunday School lesson. He felt like the lord of the vineyard, grieving his lost olive trees. Graham wished there were some other way, some easier path, but Emma had left him no choice. He pulled his well-worn scriptures—a gift from the Rasmussens when he turned twelve—from the top drawer of his desk and opened to Jacob 5. A question rose from the sea of words: *What could I have done more for my vineyard?* Three times the lord repeated this same question, this same lament.

"Three times," Graham mumbled to himself, and an idea flashed to his mind. *Three times this message of dismay. What other words were deemed worth repeating?*

Labor. It seemed to spring from the page. Graham's finger ran up and down the thin paper, counting. Twelve times. Over and over, the lord of the vineyard and his servant *labored* to save their trees. Graham understood this even better than he understood their grief. How many evenings had he spent reading the scriptures to his children? How many hours sitting with them in Church? How much energy had he poured into their instruction and discipline—into teaching them right from wrong? He had baptized them with his own hands and worked long hours to keep a roof over their heads and food in the cupboards. Surely, Graham had labored as hard as the lord of any vineyard.

Prune. His finger skimmed the page again. Nine times. Pruning—a culling of sorts. A separating of the righteous from the wicked.

Cast. "Sixteen references," Graham breathed. Sixteen times the lord of the vineyard cast wild branches away into the fire or threatened to hew down entire trees, casting them to the flames.

Clearly, justice, not mercy, had to prevail. And why? For the same reason Graham had arrived at himself. Lest the wild fruit overcome the good. Lest the ground of the entire vineyard be cumbered by unnatural fruit. It was a numbers game, Graham realized, nodding his head in sympathy for Heavenly Father's plight. Divine Utilitarianism. No matter how much it hurt, a loving parent must be willing to sacrifice one child for the good of many.

A memory scratched at his conscience. He saw himself, awkward and acne-ridden, just after his sixteenth birthday. Pam had lent him her station wagon and told him to be home by 10:00. He went to a party—his first. He stood against a wall, trying to blend in, whether with the wallpaper or with the mob of laughing, confident teens, he wasn't quite sure. A boy—older, tougher, cooler—had shoved a waxy cup of something golden into his hand. It smelled like his mother.

Graham's stomach lurched. So why did he drink it? Why the heck did he drink it? And how many more did he drink after the first one?

He still wasn't sure about any of that. He only remembered arriving back at the Rasmussens' well past eleven, with a fresh dent in the wood paneling of Pam's car. He remembered the way her nose wrinkled at his smell. The look of disappointment on her face. He was sure they would throw him out. He was wrong.

"Why did you let me stay?" he asked years later, his tongue loosened by the fear of losing her.

"Because you deserve love, and your parents didn't give it to you. I love you, Graham."

"No, I mean later. After what I did. To your car."

Pam shook her head, her pale face earnest. "You're too hard on yourself. Everyone makes mistakes. We all need second chances."

He swallowed hard, but her words were a lump that wouldn't go down. Sure, everyone makes mistakes. But he *was* a mistake. How did she not see it?

After the incident with Pam's car, he had vowed that even if he might *be* a mistake, he would stop *making* mistakes. Then maybe it wouldn't matter so much. If he read the scriptures cover to cover. If he followed every rule to the letter. If he kept his room tidy and earned straight A's. If he lived beyond reproach. Maybe then it would be enough to make him worthy of her kindness.

Graham never drank again. He resolutely avoided sin, shunning even the appearance of evil—well, until Pam died and he sacrificed it all just to be in Heidi's arms, making it clear how unsaintly he actually was.

But why was he thinking of this now? None of this stuff with Emma had anything to do with Pam. And the person he was way back then had nothing to do with the person he was now. He had cast all of that off. He ought to burn it from his memory.

Graham pruned the wild branching of his thoughts and turned back to the Book of Mormon. He read until his eyelids refused to stay open. Until sleep finally, mercifully prevailed.

Chapter Twenty-Three

Cami looks with distaste at her groggy, puffy-eyed reflection in the mirror. She barely slept. She splashes cold water against her face, pats it dry, then rummages in the drawer for concealer to mask the dark circles under her eyes. "I look like a raccoon," she snarls, but then breaks into a smile. It's fitting that she should resemble a creature known for banditry.

Cami doesn't intend to become a bandit, exactly, but in the wee hours of the night, she did concoct a plan, which might involve some light breaking and entering. She glances down at her watch. It's 8:15. Sacrament meeting begins at 9:00. She sits with her family, so she'll have to stay until it ends, but Sunday School classes begin at 10:20 and are divided by age group. Her parents won't notice if she slips away then.

The clock ticks slowly. Cami wishes for the diversion of breakfast, but it's Fast Sunday—the slowest Sunday of the month. Her stomach rumbles its protest. No food or water until dinner time. Thankfully, the Johanson family bends their dinner schedule to make this an easier feat. Dinner is as early as 2:00 or 3:00 on Fast Sundays. The Madsen children, of course, have no such luck. "The Lord cannot look upon sin with the least degree of allowance," their father would remind them, which apparently means that fasting must last for a full twenty-four hours, not a minute less.

Church begins. Emma is not there, and sacrament meeting does nothing to speed the passage of time. It's Fast and Testimony Meeting, and the usual cast of characters has lined up to bear their testimonies.

"I know the Church is true," a parade of primary children will squeak.

"I know with every fiber of my being, beyond a shadow of a doubt that this is the Lord's true church," Brother Armbruster will vow.

"Heavenly Father shows his love for us every single day," Sister Clifton will beam.

Cami wonders which lost object Heavenly Father will have helped Sister Clifton to find this month. Last month, it was her purse, which she had mistakenly placed on the roof of her car while pumping gas. "That explains why Heavenly Father isn't able to help all those starving kids in third world countries," Emma had joked. "He's been busy directing Sister Clifton to her purse."

Stamps. This time it was a misplaced book of stamps. "When we pray for help, even in the little details of our lives, Heavenly Father answers. He *always* answers," Sister Clifton effuses, tears streaking down her cheeks.

Cami thinks of Emma. Emma whose prayers weren't answered. Emma, who asked for a testimony and didn't receive it. *I've <u>never</u> known*, she had written in the letter. *And I've tried <u>really</u> hard.*

Cami knows Emma tried. It isn't fair. Why should it be so hard for Emma and so easy for Cami? The very first time she prayed to know if the Church was true, she felt overcome by a happy warmth. She was what then, maybe eight years old? Cami wishes she could divide her testimony in two and give half to Emma. But she shouldn't have to. Heavenly Father should have answered Emma's prayers! Why didn't He? Surely it mattered more than keys and stamps.

Finally, the closing hymn begins. Cami misses the sound of Emma's voice, rich and warm in the pew behind her. She hears Eliza and Sister Madsen with their clear sopranos, Joseph's bass, Graham's tenor. The alto part is missing. Cami tries to fill it in, but she's never been as good at harmonizing as Emma.

"*Who am I to judge another when I walk imperfectly?*" the congregation sings. "*In the quiet heart is hidden sorrow that the eyes can't see. Who am I to judge another? Lord, I would follow thee.*"

Does Cami imagine a bitter edge to Joseph's voice? And a quiver in Sister Madsen's? As the song enters its final verse, Cami glances over her shoulder. Something seems to pass between Brigham and Eliza. Maybe Hyrum, too? Cami wonders how much they know, how their father has reacted so far, what's going on in their heads. The closing prayer begins, and she turns her thoughts to her own next steps. She'll exit through the side door, where her parents are least likely to see her go. It's just a few blocks to the Madsens' house. If their door is locked, she knows where to find a key.

The meeting ends, and Cami stands to leave, but it's impossible to steer away from every person who wants to detain her for a chat. When she finally manages to slip from the building, she glances over her shoulder before crossing the parking lot and joining the road. In minutes, she's arrived in the Madsens' yard. She tries the backdoor. It's unlocked. The hinges creak eerily as Cami pushes it open. The Madsens are all at church. She shouldn't feel nervous, but she does. She tiptoes to the kitchen without turning on a light.

"Cami!?" Eliza starts.

"Trespasser!" Hyrum forms his hands into a pistol and points it her way.

Cami freezes, blood rushing to her head. "I'm sorry, I just wanted to find your grandma's address!" she stammers.

"It's okay," Eliza laughs. "We're doing the same thing."

"*And* we're going to eat snacks," Brigham chimes in, exchanging a grin with Hyrum.

"Maybe *you* are, but I'm not," Eliza scolds.

Cami's stomach growls loudly, and the boys laugh.

"Cami's on our side," Brigham tells Eliza.

The back door creaks again, and the crew falls pale and silent. Heavy footsteps approach. Joseph strides into the kitchen; they exhale in relief.

"What are you all doing here?" He looks from one face to another.

"What are *we* doing, what are *you* doing here? You belong in Sunday School, young man!" Hyrum returns, his voice deep and reprimanding.

"I asked first." Joseph crosses his arms.

"We're looking for Oma's address," Eliza explains.

"Yeah, what are you guys going to do with it? You can't even drive."

"We wanted to give it to Cami and see if she'd go down there. And then she showed up with the same plan."

Joseph uncrosses his arms. "I told Brother Pingree after sacrament meeting about Dad saying Emma can't come back home."

"He said she can't come home?" Cami's mouth drops open. "I thought he'd be all about *making* her come back."

"Yeah, I thought that, too"—Hyrum nods his head—"but instead, he went all fire and brimstone, yelling scriptures at Mom, and then he like stomped upstairs and when he came back down again, he told us that Emma's out of the family and that if she calls, we're supposed to hang up the phone because now she has leprosy or something."

"So much for eternal families." Eliza shakes her head, then turns to Joseph. "How did Brother Pingree react?"

"He was really surprised. He said if I can get him the info, he and Sister Pingree might go down there to check on her."

"So, Brother Pingree told you to sneak out of Sunday School?" Hyrum looks pleased.

"No. He just asked if I thought I could find her contact info, and I said yes. This seemed like the best way. Anyone know where to look?"

"In your mom's address book," Cami answers. "Emma mentioned it in her letter."

"It's that easy?" Brigham walks to the phone, lifts the slim book and flips through it. "I was sort of hoping we'd have to climb over lasers or something. What's Oma's name anyway?"

"Claudia," Eliza replies. "I don't remember her last name. Something with a B, maybe? Or a D?"

Brigham flips through the pages. "Here it is. Dietrich. Claudia Dietrich. I can't believe it was just right here all along. Dad could have found it any time."

"Why would Dad ever look up addresses? You think he's going to send out thank you notes or something? He hates people." Joseph's voice is hard.

"Not all people. He likes prophets and stuff," Hyrum points out.

Joseph grabs a pen and blank sheet of paper. "Let me see that," he demands, snatching the book from Brigham's hands, then jotting down the number and address. "Alright, I'm heading back before anyone notices I'm gone. You fools should do the same."

"Nah, we're staying for snacks," Hyrum replies.

"Snacks?" Joseph smiles for the first time.

"Skipping Sunday School is already a sin, as is the whole not-honoring-your-father-just-because-he's-a-psychopath thing, so Brigham and I figured we might as well go all in, since we're going to have to repent anyway." Hyrum walks to the counter and begins peeling back the layers of cling wrap from the plate of snickerdoodles.

"Not those, you moron. Mom will notice," Joseph chides, turning back toward them. "Check the freezer. There might be cookies in there."

Sure enough. Two gallon-sized bags are filled to the top with homemade cookies—one bag of peanut butter, one bag of chocolate chip. Joseph and Hyrum each grab a bag, letting the freezer fall shut behind them.

"How many should we heat up?" Hyrum asks the group.

"I'll take one of each!" Cami declares, her stomach gurgling with excitement.

"Two of each for me." Brigham rubs his belly.

The kids crowd around, snatching at cookies, piling them onto a plate. Eliza's pursed lips relax. "Okay, fine, one of each for me, too," she announces.

"Woohoo!" Hyrum cheers. "I knew you had it in you, Liza!"

They sit together, laughing, eating, dunking cookies in milk. "It's ironic," Brigham says. "I think this is just what Dad is afraid of—that Emma will lead us down the path of sin."

"Mmmmm," Hyrum responds in his best Homer Simpson voice, a cookie crumb dangling from his bottom lip. "Si-iiiin."

***

"Sin." Graham's voice fills the Sunday School classroom. He pauses to let the weight of the word settle. "Jacob 5 paints a stark image of the consequences of sin. Five times the Lord of the vineyard threatens to hew down the trees that produce evil fruit. Sixteen times he says he will cast them into the fire. How does the Lord of the vineyard protect his good trees? He does so by pruning off the bitterest branches, hewing down the wildest of the trees, and casting anything that produces evil fruit into the flames. The lesson is clear—"

A white-haired sister in the front row sits with hoisted hand. Now she flutters her fingers impatiently. Teaching Sunday School really isn't so different from teaching undergraduates. Graham sighs. "Yes, Sister . . . Sister Clark?"

"Hall, dear. I'm Sister Hall. That's Sister Clark over there"—she nods with her head toward an elderly woman across the room—"but never mind that. I just wanted to say that while you are right that this chapter has a few stern things to say about sin, the message—to me—feels like one of mercy. I actually did a little counting, too, when I was reading this chapter at home this week. And did you know that this line is repeated three times? It's so beautiful. Hold on, let me find it."

Her finger trembles across the page until it lands on what she's looking for. "Ahh, here it is!" She lifts her Book of Mormon and reads, "'What could I have done more for my vineyard?' Three times the Lord of the vineyard asks this question. And it isn't rhetorical. He actually goes back and does more. He *grieves* over the loss of his trees, and so he goes and nourishes them again. In verse 40, it even says he *wept*!"

"Verse 41," Graham corrects.

"Oh, did I get that wrong?" She looks down at the page. "Sure enough! Verse 41. See, we all make mistakes. Isn't it wonderful that there's mercy?"

A few soft chuckles sound from around the room.

"But mercy isn't offered willy-nilly," Graham counters. "Certain conditions must be met. You say the lord of the vineyard went back and nourished the trees, but he also pruned off the wildest branches and burned them. If he hadn't, the entire vineyard would have been overcome by wild fruit. And this message isn't unique to Jacob 5. It's repeated throughout the scriptures." He commences to prove his point, quoting not one but three separate passages of scripture.

Brother Benson's arm is raised, straight as the iron rod itself. Graham sighs audibly. He would rather call on someone else—anyone else. The man always seems so intent on contradicting him. "Yes? Brother Benson?" Graham practically groans. "You have something to say?"

"Why, yes I do, Brother Madsen. I'd like to suggest that we take a step back here. In the chapter heading for Jacob 5, it says that the tame and wild olive trees represent Israel and the Gentiles. This allegory is about the scattering and gathering of Israel. It's not about me and my little sins or you and your little sins. It's painting a bigger picture. I think we need to zoom out a bit and take the time to understand that."

A vein twitches in Graham's left temple. His fingers wrap around the sides of his neck. "I'm sure that's a very comforting way to view it. It's not about *your* house, you say, it's about the house of Israel. No wild olive trees in Brother Benson's home!"

"Woah, woah—that's not what I'm saying. I'm not claiming that my family doesn't have its own share of challenges. No need to go making this personal. I'm just saying that's not what this chapter is about. It's about the scattering and gathering of the tribes of Israel. It's right there in the chapter heading."

"That's one interpretation of the allegory, but—"

"*Interpretation*?! It's in the chapter heading! Those were written by *Elder McConkie,* you know."

"I'm not contradicting anything in the chapter heading. I'm simply digging a little deeper. Which is exactly what Elder McConkie would encourage us to do if he were still alive. He said, and I quote, 'People who study the scriptures get a dimension to their life that nobody else gets and that can't be gained in any way except by studying the scriptures.'"

Brother Benson attempts to interject, but Graham plows ahead. "*Study* the scriptures, he said. I understand the temptation to skim the Cliffs Notes, Brother Benson, but I'd encourage you to go deeper if you—"

"If I what!?" Brother Benson is on his feet. "If I want to strut around quoting scriptures all day long?"

His wife tugs at his sleeve, pulling him back to his chair. Heidi, who plays piano for the Primary children, isn't there to offer her husband the same service. Graham's face is red and tight. He opens his mouth to retort, but Brother Pingree steps in, his gentle voice filling the room. "It's a good sign that the scriptures can prompt such spirited debate. It means we care about them. Every one of us here cares about discovering truth and about living it as well as we can. I really appreciated Sister Hall's point about mercy. And of course, as Graham put it, the Lord doesn't dole out mercy willy-nilly, but I think that as humans, we tend to fall into the trap of doling out *judgment* more often than we ought. And whether in a Sunday School debate or in more personal matters, maybe one of the takeaways from this chapter is that *all of us* can afford to look for reasons to offer mercy, rather than getting stuck on the reasons to sit in judgment."

Heads nod around the room. Sister Hall glows with appreciation. Brother Benson's blood pressure seems to be returning to normal, and anyway, his wife is keeping a firm lock on his hand. Only Graham is still visibly agitated, adrift.

"In a vacuum, yes, we can afford mercy." Graham paces again as he speaks, his eyes darting about on the floor in front of him. "But we don't live in a vacuum. We live in families and in a society that are influenced by what we condone and what we condemn. As parents and leaders, we have to be strict in how we respond to sin. Otherwise, we unwittingly condone it. Haven't you ever wondered why the scriptures are so full of generational curses—of God punishing the sins of the fathers on their children down to the third or the fourth generation? It's not a literal punishment that God brings about. It's a practical consequence. If you are surrounded by sin, you are more likely to sin. If you are raised in a culture of sin, it's very difficult to break out of. And if you do break out, you have to be *vigilant*"—he almost shouts the word—"not to allow sin back in."

Vigilance. It's how he came this far. If he hadn't been vigilant, how could he have broken the cycle of alcoholism and abuse that he was born into? If he hadn't been vigilant, what might he have done when his mother claimed sobriety and asked him to come home? What might he have done when she showed up at his dorm room, pleading for money? Thankfully, he chose vigilance. He spent his savings to serve a mission for the Church. His vigilance lapsed after Pam's death, of course. But he made up for it by marrying Heidi, by holding to the rod despite the shame and stigma of disfellowship. And from then on, he did everything right—*everything*.

Graham seems to have exhausted himself. He has stopped pacing. He is unsure what to do with his hands.

"Or," Sister Hall timidly suggests, looking as if she'd like to offer Graham a pat on the head, "you could open yourself to the love of Christ, and trust in the power of His Atonement."

Graham shakes his head at some thought or voice that is only his to hear. He returns to the center of the room and picks up his notes. "Let's just read the chapter from the beginning," he suggests, his voice doubtful and deflated. "Who wants to begin?"

"I will." Brother Benson's voice is confident but conciliatory. He begins reading, starting with the chapter heading. "Jacob quotes Zenos relative to the allegory of the tame and wild olive trees—They are a likeness of Israel and the Gentiles," he recites, hardly smirking at all.

Chapter Twenty-Four

Dan Christensen beams up at his mother. It's her first day as ward organist, and she's already played the first two hymns flawlessly, just as Dan knew she would. She returns his smile and walks to the podium.

Anne Christensen's testimony never follows the usual script. As often as not, she forgets or perhaps simply doesn't feel inclined to affirm her knowledge that Joseph Smith was a prophet or that The Church of Jesus Christ of Latter-day Saints is indeed the Lord's one true church. But always, her words leave Dan with a joyful longing to do better, to be kinder, to live as a truer disciple of Christ.

"Good morning, brothers and sisters," Anne begins. "I had a conversation with a loved one yesterday that has been kicking around in my heart ever since, and so I'd like to share it with you. This loved one of mine—let's call him . . . Don, shall we?" She flashes a mischievous smile, and a soft chuckle rises from the congregation, heads turning to locate Dan in the room.

"So, Don found himself in a difficult interaction with someone who didn't share his values. I don't know about you, but I have a tendency to jump to judgment in those moments. Don noticed that impulse in himself but chose to do something really different. He made the conscious choice that, no matter what she said or believed, he would treat the young woman like a daughter of God. Their interaction completely shifted. The difficulty and sense of difference melted away."

Dan tries to swallow the lump in his throat.

His mother continues, "To choose to see someone—*everyone*—as a child of God is *not* to put on blinders. It's not to pretend that everyone is perfect or kind or trustworthy. It isn't about erasing the uncomfortable parts of people. It's about turning the light on, *flooding* one another with light, so that we can see more than the blemishes, more than the imperfections. Don reminded me—and I need this reminder over and over again—that when we choose to see someone as a child of God, we're choosing to see them in the truest possible light."

The lump in Dan's throat thickens, and he blinks back tears. His mother is talking as if he were her teacher. But the opposite is true: her telling of the story and the way she's mapped meaning onto it is teaching him. *When we choose to see someone as a child of God, we are choosing to see them in the truest possible light*. The words feel alive inside of Dan. Like a warm ocean pulsing through him. What if he were to do this in every interaction? Not just with pretty girls. Not just when things seem to be going awry. But *always*. With his roommates. His professors. The people in his ward. Strangers he meets.

People are complicated, Dan thinks to himself, *but they are also children of God*. Gestating deity, that's what they are, if you dive deep enough into the doctrine. But Dan doesn't need to dive right now. His noblest feelings float here at the surface. He's determined to do it: to view and treat *everyone* the way he treated Emma. Better, if he can.

I'll think of everyone I meet as a child of God, Dan vows in his mind. *Beginning now!* The words rise inside him like a cresting wave.

Testimony meeting, it turns out, is the perfect time to launch such an endeavor. Dan prays silently for each testimony bearer. The squeaky children appear cuter and more innocent than ever. The chronic testimony bearers suddenly dazzle him with their consistency. Dan is awash with tenderness toward the lonely widower, the exhausted young mother, the prematurely balding father, the pimpled and crackly-voiced teen. Children of God. His sisters and brothers. All of them.

Chapter Twenty-Five

"Graham is a lunatic," Jennifer Johanson whispers to Joelle Pingree on the way out of the Sunday School classroom.

Joelle laughs softly. "He's not a *lunatic*. He's just . . . a little high strung."

"A little?" Jennifer's left eyebrow arches. It's a facial expression that her daughter Cami inherited, though Cami favors the right eyebrow.

"Okay, a lot. He's a lot high strung."

Joelle's husband Jeff stands behind them. "He's dealing with some pretty heavy stuff right now," he offers. "It's no wonder if he's not at his best."

Jennifer whirls to face him, trying to read how much he knows. Their eyes lock. "You know about Emma, then?" Her voice is hushed.

Jeff nods.

"I'm surprised they're all in church today. I thought Heidi or Graham would drive down there and scoop her up. Or maybe they did? Maybe she's back at the house?" Jennifer wonders.

"No, she's not"—he shakes his head and sighs audibly—"Can I tell you something in confidence? I'd appreciate your advice. You know Emma better than Joelle and I do."

The trio moves together to the far corner of the hall and Jeff dives in. "Apparently, Graham says he's disowning Emma. I have to think he'll soften, but last night he told Heidi and the kids to hang up the phone if she calls. I'm guessing that's why he was so worked up just now. In his mind, Emma's a wild olive branch, who might infect the rest of his vineyard. He's probably convinced himself that it's the right thing to do—you know, to protect the other kids."

Joelle shakes her head. "Poor girl. As if being pregnant isn't hard enough."

"I don't think it's for sure that she's pregnant," Jennifer says, "At least not based on what she told Cami. But regardless, listening to Graham in Sunday School . . . I mean, it's no wonder if Emma acts out. She's a great kid, but with a dad that . . . *rigid* . . . well, just listening to him makes *me* want to go buy a pack of cigarettes or rob a liquor store or . . . "

"Have another child?" Joelle suggests.

"Heck no!" The two women laugh loud enough to turn heads.

Jeff waits for the soundwaves to settle, then leans in, speaks in a hushed voice. "Here's where we need your opinion, Jennifer. Joelle and I are wondering if we should go down there—just drop in and let Emma know she's not alone. My brother lives in the area, so we have a place to stay, and Joseph thinks he can get their grandma's contact info. Maybe I should be asking Heidi instead, but she seems pretty cowed by Graham, and, well, Joseph is clearly itching to do something, so I'm hoping this might keep him out of worse trouble."

Jennifer considers for a moment. "I don't envy you—or Joseph—if Graham finds out, but asking Heidi seems like a dead end. I mean, either she'll be so worried about Graham's reaction that she'll tell you not to go, or she'll say 'yes' and then be in the position of having to hide something from him. If you're gonna go, I say just go. My guess is that Emma would appreciate it. Cami actually asked to go down there last night. I brushed it off then, but . . . well, I imagined Heidi and Graham handling things differently."

"We could take Cami down with us," Joelle offers, glancing to her husband for confirmation.

"Speak of the devil," Jeff nods, looking over his wife's shoulder to the side door.

Cami has just walked in. She sees her mother looking at her, and her eyes dart nervously from one adult face to the next. "Where were you?" her mom wants to know.

"Just getting some fresh air," Cami answers, attempting to breeze past.

"Why do you smell like peanut butter?" Her mother's eyebrow lifts.

Cami stifles a guilty grin, arching her own eyebrow in a mirror image reply. "I don't know. Maybe you're just so hungry you're smelling things that don't exist."

The Pingrees chuckle, and Cami attempts to maneuver past.

"Honey, wait," Jennifer laughs. "You're not in trouble. I don't care if you ate. We were talking about Emma, and I think you're right about going to see her. It sounds like her dad isn't planning to get her after all. The Pingrees might head down there."

"You can ride with us if you'd like," Jeff says.

"I can go?" She turns to her mom.

"When are you leaving?" Jennifer asks the Pingrees.

"Hopefully this afternoon," Jeff answers. "We'd like to make it down there before dark if possible, and I imagine we'll come back tomorrow. Tuesday at the latest."

Cami's face falls. "Shoot, I have a math test first period tomorrow. I don't think I can make it up if the absence isn't excused." Her forehead is creased.

Jennifer's forehead furrows in nearly identical lines of thought. "What if," Jennifer thinks aloud, "what if Brother and Sister Pingree go today and scout out the situation, and assuming everything seems okay down there and Emma's grandma is up for a visitor, then you can leave tomorrow after your test and stay for *one* night."

Cami's face opens into a bright smile. As much as she likes the Pingrees, going on her own sounds better. She had been tentatively planning to sneak away after her math test. Now the sneaking—and the grounding that would undoubtedly have followed—won't be necessary. "I should have saved you a cookie!" she declares, planting a kiss on her mother's cheek before sailing down the hall to her Young Women's class.

Joseph arrives moments later, smelling of brown sugar and chocolate. He slips a piece of paper into Jeff's hand. "Here you go," he mumbles.

Jeff claps a hand on Joseph's shoulder. "That was quick! Anything I should tell your sister for you?"

"I dunno"—Joseph shrugs—"Tell her I'm taking her discman until she gets back."

Brother Pingree chuckles. "I'll be sure to let her know."

Chapter Twenty-Six

Emma and Oma sit side by side on a boulder, pant legs rolled up, feet dangling into icy water. Emma's supposed to be in church right now. The thought fills her with a giddy rush of freedom, like every wall has just revealed itself to be a door. "This is what I needed," Emma exhales.

She had tried to talk Oma into more—into a full-fledged hike—but her grandmother had resisted. "You said your back hurts, and your stomach," Oma had pointed out.

This is the compromise: a casual meander up this glistening creek, just a valley away from Oma's house.

Emma lies back, shaping her body to the boulder. She lifts a hand to shield her face from the sun, then lets it fall, closes her eyes, watches the backs of her lids swirl red.

"When you left our house that last time, did you know that my dad wouldn't let you come back?" she asks her grandmother.

"No. I sensed that something was up. He seemed even madder at me than usual. But your dad was never friendly to me, so I didn't pay it much mind. Your mom called me and told me that night, just a few hours after I got home. I was upset, but I thought it would blow over."

"I heard them talking about it the night before you left."

"Is that why you didn't get out of bed that morning?"

Emma nods, her eyes still closed.

"Did your dad ever explain it to you?"

"No. Well, not unless you count him telling us that you were in the Great and Spacious Building."

"In the *what*?"

Emma sits up again. She drops her head onto Oma's shoulder and relates the story of Lehi's vision. Of Lehi standing alone, munching on the fruit of the Tree of Life, calling out to his family to join him. Of the mists of darkness that rose from the ground, obscuring the way to the tree. Of the iron rod and the narrow path that ran alongside it. That the only way to reach the tree—the only way to land in the Celestial Kingdom of heaven—was to cling to the rod and march the straight and narrow.

"The Great and Spacious Building just sort of popped up out of the mist, somewhere on the periphery," Emma tells her grandmother. "It was like a big party of glamorous, evil people, all pointing and laughing at the other people, the ones eating the fruit. Dad said you weren't coming to visit anymore because you were in the Great and Spacious Building. When he said it, all I could see was you standing on a balcony, popping your head forward and saying 'kuck-uck!'"

Oma laughs. "You remember that? Playing peek-a-boo with Hyrum?"

"Yeah." Emma smiles.

Her grandmother sighs. "What a black-and-white way of viewing the world. So, everyone is either standing at the Tree of Life or lost in darkness, taunting and jeering from some lavish party?"

"Yeah, there's no middle zone. That's what we were taught, anyway. I grew up wishing I was more like Nephi—the good kid, you know? The one who supposedly knows the truth. But now, I feel bad for Laman and Lemuel. Their dad, Lehi, was always lecturing them and preaching to them and going on and on about the certainty of their damnation. When that's what your parent sees in you, well, what's the point in giving them anything else?"

"So, what do you think? Are we damned?" Oma's eyes sparkle.

"I don't know."

"How do you *feel,* Emma? Do you feel cut off from what's good and true and beautiful?"

Emma lifts her head and lets the sound of water wash through her. She takes in the sun-warmed rock against her skin, the singing of the creek as it meets her rocky perch, the dancing poplar leaves overhead. They quiver with the uncertainty of which face to show. They are *alive* with uncertainty.

"No," she answers. "Not damned, not cut off. I feel"—she searches for words—"I feel like I've landed in a new place on the map. Or maybe there is no map? No tree, no path, no rod. Everything feels uncertain, but it's not damnation, it's just . . ."

"Life?"

"Yeah," Emma smiles. "Maybe so. Maybe this is what it feels like to arrive in my own life."

She didn't know this was true until the moment she spoke it. But as soon as the words are out, she feels a trickle of warmth tracing her spine, a burning of bosom, belly, fingers, and toes. It's the feeling of cloud-break, of sunlight streaming in. The feeling that even if everything has gone to shit, it will be okay; it's already okay.

Emma sits beside her grandmother, their hands gritty with sand and their feet clean and cold in the babbling water.

Dean wipes brownie crumbs from his lips and surrenders to the flowing tones of Debussy, crackling on the record player. For over an hour now, he has been lost in melody, lilting and soaring with song, oblivious to all else, including the ringing of the phone.

Heidi sits with Sariah at the piano, smiling forgetfully as her daughter plunks out the melody to "I Am a Child of God."

Graham is in his office, scriptures open on the desk, turning page after page. He finds himself inexplicably taken by the thin, tissue-paper pages, with their gold edges. Some of them ripple and dimple softly at the top. He never noticed before. His hands arrive near the middle of the Book of Mormon, in Alma chapter 26. He intends to read the words. Instead, he lifts a single page and lets it fall into his right hand, which then passes it back to his left. Back and forth, back and forth, the page rises and falls to the rhythm of the piano. The crinkling of paper reminds him of wind. Of something blown loose. For just a moment, Graham forgets to think. He closes his eyes and rocks with the music, his body swaying with the page, his hands conducting the orchestra.

Upstairs, Eliza writes in her journal, earnest reflections, penciled in letters that bubble and swoop:

I've always been taught to honor my father and mother, but the scriptures also say I should love Heavenly Father more than I love my parents.

That means obeying Heavenly Father first. Dad is being like the people who threw stones at the woman accused of adultery. Now I have to be brave and be like Jesus.

Just up the street, Cami petitions her parents. "Please let me bring Emma back here! We have an extra room!"

"The *room* is not the issue, sweetheart," her father tells her.

Jennifer chimes in. "We can't make that choice without her parents' approval. And even if we could, your dad and I would need time to talk about it."

Cami stands in place, looks at them expectantly.

"When you're *not* in the room," her mother adds.

"Fine," Cami groans, trudging to her own bedroom, where she attempts to review her math notes but mostly just picks at a hangnail and stares at the Spice Girls poster on her wall.

Jeff Pingree's hands are on the steering wheel. "What do you say to telling Emma about us?" he asks his wife. They are alone in the car, beginning the drive toward Castle Valley.

His question is nonspecific, but Joelle knows exactly what he means. She's already been thinking about it herself—about telling Emma that she, too, got pregnant out of wedlock. "I think it's a good idea," she says to her husband. "People are so hush-hush about this sort of stuff in the Church. She probably feels like she's the only person it's ever happened to."

He nods his head in agreement. "You don't think Graham and Heidi have told her anything about their own past, do you?"

Joelle laughs. "Umm, no."

The idea is preposterous—the Madsens confessing sexual sins to their children. Of course, Jeff and Joelle had done precisely that, but their kids would have figured it out on their own eventually. Brittany, their eldest, was born seven months and two days after her parents' wedding, which took place in a chapel rather than in the temple. Jeff was barely nineteen and had been filling out his mission papers when "the slip" occurred. Jeff referred to it once this way to Joelle, recalling the event. She had burst out laughing. "You mean when you slipped it to me?"

"Yeah, that," he had blushed.

But the terminology stuck. Brittany's conception was and forever would be referred to between them as "The Slip."

Jeff Pingree hadn't been disfellowshipped for slipping up (and in), but the sting of not getting to serve a mission stayed with him. Not that he would trade Joelle for a mission. But it would have been nice if he could have had both.

"You remember that conversation I had with Heidi, right?" Joelle asks.

He does. As Joelle had explained it at the time, when she told Heidi about her own conversion, The Slip, and the shotgun wedding, Heidi's face brightened with recognition. She became unusually animated, telling Joelle everything—about meeting Graham, her initial feelings toward him, the shame he felt over their sexuality, his being disfellowshipped, how he sat alone on the back row, how she joined The Church to comfort him, but how it had ultimately brought her comfort, too.

Then, there was the follow-up conversation, just days later. Heidi blushed and stammered, her eyes downcast. "That thing I told you?" she said. "About me and Graham? I shouldn't have said anything. I mentioned it to Graham. I thought maybe he'd be relieved to hear someone else had been through the same challenges, but . . . he wasn't pleased. He says that telling people about past sins is the same as denying the power of the Atonement because if I really believe in Christ's power, then those sins never happened."

Joelle had promised never to mention it again. And so, she mentioned it only to Jeff.

"Apparently, if we really believe in the Atonement, then The Slip never happened," she had jested to him.

"Well, that's great because I'm tired of paying the insurance on Brittany's car. It's a relief to know that she's a mere figment of our unbelief."

The Pingree's own car approaches ever nearer to Castle Valley.

Emma and Oma return home from their hike. They eat. Emma showers. She wipes the fog from the bathroom mirror and stares at her damp reflection. She looks tired. Maybe she'll take a nap.

There is a distant knocking, followed by the sound of voices. Footsteps approach the bathroom. Dean's voice: "Emma, you've got visitors."

His feet recede before she can ask questions. It can't be her parents. Dean would have just said "your dad is here" or "your mom is here." Who, then? Emma towels the excess water from her hair, dresses hurriedly, and heads to the living room.

"Brother Pingree? Sister Pingree?"

"Emma!" Jeff's voice is jovial as he and Joelle rise to their feet. "I know it's a bit odd . . . us turning up here. We tried calling, but—"

"Never mind that," Oma shushes him. Clearly this isn't his first attempt at an apology.

"At any rate, there's a very logical explanation for our sudden appearance"—he assumes an earnest expression—"I took cookies to your family last night and learned that you weren't there. It didn't seem fair . . . you not having any cookies."

Right on cue, Joelle thrusts forward a cling-wrapped paper plate.

"You drove four hours to bring me cookies?"

"Nah, just three and half. That was our limit," Jeff answers.

Joelle swats his arm. "We wanted to check on you and let you know we're here to help. *And* tell you how much your brother misses you."

"Which one?" Emma snorts.

"All of them, I suspect, but Joseph in particular," Joelle replies.

"Joseph? That's a bit hard to believe."

"Well, he didn't use the word 'miss' exactly," Jeff concedes. "But he was upset enough to tell me everything."

Emma wonders what "everything" means.

"Admittedly, he also wanted me to say that he's claiming your discman until you get home. Presumably as a sort of security blanket to help him through your absence."

Emma laughs. "I'm sure that's his motive." She hadn't given it much thought—how her dad's declaration that she couldn't return home was affecting the rest of them. She tries to imagine herself in Joseph's shoes, in Eliza's shoes, but she doesn't make it very far. She's still trying to fit into her own shoes. "Well, thank you for the cookies"—Emma glances down at the plate in her hands—"and for coming all this way."

"There are a lot of people thinking of you right now"—Joelle reaches out a hand, placing it on Emma's arm—"We wanted to be sure you know that."

Emma looks down at the plate again. "Thanks," she whispers. "I'm going to go put these in the kitchen. Do you want anything? A drink?"

Dean steps in and lifts the plate from Emma's hands. "I'll take these to the kitchen and bring back drinks. You sit and relax."

Emma settles awkwardly into an armchair.

For a moment, no one knows what to say. Finally, Jeff speaks. "We also wanted to tell you something kind of . . . personal . . . that we're hoping might make you feel a little better about . . . your situation." He looks to Joelle, his eyes pleading for rescue.

Joelle takes the helm. "I was already pregnant with Brittany when Jeff and I got married."

"You were?" Emma's voice is incredulous.

The Pingrees fill in the broad strokes of the story—the embarrassment of confessing to their bishop, the wedding in their local chapel, Jeff's exclusion from serving a mission, the temple sealing a little over a year later.

"How did your parents react?" Emma wants to know.

"Jeff's dad went nuts. Not unlike yours," Joelle replies.

"I had the advantage of being a bit older than you, though," Jeff points out. "I was already away at college. But he still managed to make it very clear that I was a disappointment to the entire family."

"Ouch," Emma says.

"Yeah. It hurt . . . a lot, but he softened with time. He never apologized, but Brittany was his first grandchild, and he adores her."

"What about *your* parents?" Emma turns to Joelle.

"Well, I'm a convert, so it was really different for me. Sex outside of marriage was just the norm. My older brother lived in a hippie commune for a while, so I guess my getting pregnant seemed sort of tame by comparison. My parents were sad and worried. They knew having a baby limited my options. But once they met Jeff, they fell almost as in love with him as I was, so they came around pretty quickly."

"I can't imagine my dad coming around to anything."

Joelle nods sympathetically. "He might not. I mean, I *hope* he will of course, but"—she sighs and continues—"I guess the point of our telling you all this is just . . . so that you know you aren't alone. Lots of people make this same mistake. And some people, like your dad, are going to judge you, but many, many others understand. You can make a mistake without *being* a mistake, Emma."

"I know." Emma's voice is quiet, her gaze directed to the floor.

"*And*," Claudia interjects from across the room, "what feels like a mistake to one person might not be a mistake to another. Maybe sex was a mistake, but maybe it wasn't. Maybe the only mistake was not using a condom."

Emma's head jerks up, startled by the collision of worlds. The Pingrees, kind and nonjudgmental—apart from the implicit judgment that having sex must have been a moral error, albeit a common one. Oma, open and outspoken, boldly uttering the word "condom" in front of the Relief Society President.

"You're right," Joelle says, holding Claudia's gaze and shocking Emma still further. "Each of us has to find and live our own truth. Regardless of how we've been brought up," she adds, turning to Emma.

Joelle's husband looks only mildly bewildered by her assertion. Joelle places a hand on his knee and continues. "I'll let you in on another secret, Emma. So you know that I mean that—about finding and living your own truth. I joined the Church after meeting Jeff and just a few months before I got pregnant. Getting baptized meant I had to stop drinking coffee. And I *loved* coffee."

"Almost as much as she loves me," Jeff interjects.

"*More*, some days," Joelle quips. "It was so hard to quit—not because of the headaches and what not, but just because I loved that ritual of slowing down and sipping this mug of deliciousness. My mom was a big coffee drinker. None of that Folger's stuff in our house. We ground the beans by hand each morning. I remember being a little girl, long before I was old enough to drink coffee, and she'd let me grind the beans for her in this wooden grinder she'd inherited. I loved the sound and the smell, and once the coffee was done brewing, my mom would stop everything she was doing and just sit down and talk with me while she drank it. So naturally, when I was older, we'd drink it together—and just talk. I'm pretty sure that's the only reason I made it through my teen years intact. When I went to college, I was just half an hour from home, so we had a weekly coffee date. Every Thursday, she'd come to my dumpy little apartment and brew a perfect pot of coffee, and we'd sit and catch up."

Joelle looks wistful as she speaks. Her fingers fidget as if this would all be much easier if she had a warm mug to wrap them around.

"Your mom must have been sad when you quit," Emma muses.

"Yeah, she was. Supportive but sad. But I made a concession: once a year, on her birthday, we sat down and I drank a cup of coffee with her. Jeff was horrified at first."

"I was"—Jeff's eyes twinkle—"I was certain it meant she would be banned from the Celestial Kingdom and our marriage would be void."

"Do you still think that?" Emma asks.

"No," Jeff shakes his head. "You live a bit longer and realize everyone has their stuff. Joelle is the most loving person I know. If an occasional cup of coffee keeps her out of the Celestial Kingdom, then it doesn't sound like a place worth going. But I don't think that's going to happen."

"I still drink a cup every year on her birthday. My mom passed away two years ago, so I drink it alone in her honor."

"*A* cup?" Jeff chuckles. "I'm pretty sure I saw some refills going on."

"That's how you keep your coffee warm. It doesn't count as a refill unless you reach the bottom."

Emma speaks into the laughter. "If you ever want company, I'll join you."

Joelle smiles. "I would love that. And your grandma is right. I know this isn't what you hear at Church, but you get to be the one to decide right from wrong in your own life. You *have to be* the one. Whatever path you take from here, I'm not going to judge you. And Jeff won't judge you out loud."

Her husband chuckles. "I'll keep all of my thoughts of fire and brimstone entirely to myself," he assures them.

A ringing sounds through the collective mirth. The phone. Claudia rises to answer it and returns just a moment later. "Emma, it's for you. It's Cami."

Emma bounds from the armchair and into the kitchen. "Cami?" she breathes into the receiver. Her voice is excitement and expectation and edge.

"Emma, finally! I've called like three times today, and no one ever answered!"

"Sorry, me and Oma were on a walk. I'm not sure what her boyfriend was doing."

"*Boyfriend*? Your grandma has a boyfriend?"

Fragments of story spill out on both ends of the line. Cami's plan to come down the next morning. All that Emma's been up to since arriving in Castle Valley. Cami's shoeless race across her lawn to reach the fluttering paper before Emma's father. How Cami felt when she first read Emma's words. How Emma is feeling now. The negative pregnancy test. The ocean of uncertainty. What to do next? There is too much to ask and too much to tell, and so no plotline ever finds completion. Some derailing question or exclamation invariably tips it off course. But no matter. By the time they hang up the phone, something feels healed for each of them. Cami's missing limb is reattached. Emma feels soft and open where she had felt hard and alone. *Cami is coming tomorrow!* And she's promised to bring extra changes of clothes, which is why Cami finds herself standing at the Madsens' doorstep only minutes later.

Cami isn't sure what she'll say if Graham answers the door. It's never happened before, though, in all her years of ringing and knocking, and so the risk seems low enough. Indeed, though Graham sits in his study—the closest room to the front door—he ignores the bell with apparent ease, never even glancing up from the text in which he is immersed. It's Sariah who slides across the foyer in her stockinged feet and gleefully invites Cami in.

Cami looks around as she steps through the door. "Is Eliza here? I, umm—" She is about to layer in the lie she rehearsed on the walk over, but Sariah isn't listening. She breaks into a brief sprint, then skates toward the kitchen, shrilly calling out for her sister.

"Liiiiiza!"

Cami follows behind.

Eliza moves toward them, drying her hands on the sides of her dress. Even after so many years, Cami—clad in a sweater and jeans—can't quite get used to the fact that the Madsens wear their Sunday best from moments after they rise until it's finally time to slip into pajamas again.

"Hey!" Eliza speaks the greeting like a question.

"Hey. I think maybe I left something in your and Emma's room and was wondering if I could look for it."

"Of course. Go on up!"

"Well, actually, could you help me?"

The girls lock eyes over the top of Sariah's head. "Sure. Sariah, you go help Mom with the dishes, okay?"

Sariah wrinkles her nose but trudges into the kitchen, and the older girls scurry together up the stairs. Only when the bedroom door has closed behind them, do they speak.

"I'm going down to see Emma tomorrow after first period. I talked to her on the phone tonight." Cami's voice is low.

"You're really doing it! Is she alright?"

"Yeah, she sounds good. She really likes your grandma."

"Is she actually pregnant?"

"She doesn't know for sure, but it seems like maybe not. She had a negative home test this morning, but she still feels sick, so she's going to the doctor sometime tomorrow. I told her I'd bring her some clothes. For some dumb reason, she only packed two pairs of underwear."

Eliza laughs. "Seems like she could have planned that better. I'd send you with a big suitcase of stuff, but I don't know how we'd get it out of the house."

"I was wondering about that, too. Like, do we need to hide it from your mom? Or just your dad?"

Eliza chews on her lower lip, considering. "My dad is the only one who wants Emma gone. I don't think my mom has said a single word to him all day. She'll probably be glad you're going down there."

"And there's no risk she'll tell your dad?"

"I don't think so"—Eliza shakes her head—"Things seem . . . weird . . . between them." She pulls a duffel bag from the closet, and the two set to work filling it. Another set of pajamas. A week's worth of socks and underwear. Several changes of clothing. "I wish I could go with you."

Cami frowns. "I know. It's not fair."

The bedroom door swings open. The girls jerk their heads up, and Joseph, Hyrum, and Brigham file into the room, shutting the door behind them.

"What's the dealio?" Hyrum asks.

"I'm driving down tomorrow."

"We're going with you," Joseph and Hyrum reply in near perfect unison.

"*Going with me?* How's that supposed to work?"

"When are you leaving?" Joseph presses.

"Right after first period. I have a test. So, I guess at like 8:50 or 9:00."

"That's perfect," Hyrum exclaims. "We'll just pack our stuff in our backpacks, and then Joseph and Eliza can leave from school with you, and you can come pick me and Brigham up."

"Pick you up?" Cami's face is incredulous. "You think they're going to let me march into the middle school and pull you guys from class?"

"We won't go to school. We'll just leave home like usual, but we won't get on the bus. You can pick us up from the park or something."

Cami is shaking her head. "There's no way that will work."

"Why not?"

"I don't know. What if someone sees you? And even if they don't—even if it *does* work—then either my mom or your dad is going to murder me."

"Nah, our dad might kill us, but he won't kill you," Hyrum assures. "Besides, don't you get it? This is the ultimate way to stick it to him."

Brigham and Joseph nod their heads in solemn agreement.

"*Stick it to him*?" Eliza asks. "This isn't about revenge, guys. It's about supporting Emma."

"It's the same thing," Joseph interjects. "He's trying to cut her off, so if we go there or *support her*," he uses air quotes, "then it's good for Emma, but it's also sticking it to him."

Eliza shakes her head.

"Liza"—Brigham turns to her, his face earnest—"don't you get it? He's just using Emma as an example. To say 'follow my rules or else'. Any one of us could find ourselves in her shoes one day."

"Not me! I will *never* get pregnant," Hyrum trills, placing a hand daintily over his heart.

"You know what I mean"—Brigham rolls his eyes—"If we team up and go down there, then we're supporting Emma, but also, Dad can't win against *all* of us. He can't banish us all."

Cami's head begins shaking just as Eliza's goes still. "You guys are brave," Cami says in a way that suggests not only admiration but also, perhaps, a touch of concern about their sanity.

"So, you're saying," Eliza begins slowly, "that if there's just one rule breaker, Dad can use it as an excuse to be even stricter. But if all of us break out—by going down there to show our support for Emma—then he can't use the same tactics anymore. And so maybe he'll give up on trying to control everyone all the time?"

"Exactly," Brigham nods.

"Or he'll murder us," Hyrum grins. "But there's only one way to find out."

"That's very comforting," Eliza replies.

For a moment, everyone is quiet. The boys wait in suspense for a response. Finally, Cami breaks the silence. "Okay, I'm in. I'll drive you."

Eliza's voice is quieter. "I'm in, too."

Hyrum and Brigham each throw an arm around her. "Attagirl!" Hyrum cheers.

Fifteen minutes later, Eliza and Cami carry the duffel bag through the kitchen, where Heidi is wiping counters.

"Hi, Cami." Heidi's voice is careworn, but lilts upward when she spies the bag. "What are you . . . ?"

"I'm driving down to see Emma tomorrow. She said she needs more clothes. Is there anything else you want me to take for her? Or tell her?"

Heidi's voice is thin, as if it might shatter at any moment. "Tell her we miss her. That I wish . . . I could just . . . drive down there, too." Heidi's eyes dart to the front hall. The door to Graham's study is still closed. She wets her lips and continues, her voice gaining strength. "I'm going to call her, at least. In the morning, once her dad is away at work." She seems to stand a little taller as she says this, lengthened by this microscopic rebellion. "I need to know what she finds out at the doctor. She's going tomorrow, last I heard."

"That's still the plan," Cami confirms.

"I'm glad she has you." Heidi manages a weak smile. "Oh, here, wait." She moves toward the freezer, cracks it open, and pulls out a bag of peanut butter cookies. "These are Emma's favorite." She pauses briefly, her forehead crinkling in confusion. She had thought the bag was full. *Oh well.* "Will you take them to her? Send her my love?"

"Of course."

Heidi's smile falters. She seems to be getting smaller again, slipping farther away.

Cami glances from Heidi to Eliza and back. "Well, I'll see you later," she finally says, then slides out the backdoor into the darkness.

***

Well past dark, the Pingrees are still at Claudia and Dean's, the time ticking by so convivially that no one notices the hour until yawning creeps into the gaps between their laughter. Claudia suggests that they continue their fun in the morning over breakfast in town, and the Pingrees rise to leave.

"You've been so hospitable," Joelle says to Claudia and Dean. "I'm certain I wouldn't have been half so gracious if complete strangers had barged into my home unannounced."

"I'm certain you would." Claudia gives Joelle's arm a squeeze.

"You'll think it over?" Joelle says to Emma as she leans in to hug her goodbye.

"Of course," Emma answers. It would be hard for her to think about anything else. Before the yawning began, the Pingrees asked her if she would like to stay with them until she finishes up her senior year or until it works out for her to return home. Emma tries to imagine it—living so close to home, yet not at home.

"Wow," Oma says after closing the front door behind the Pingrees. "That's quite an offer." She tries to read Emma's face.

"Yeah," Emma agrees. "It is. I dunno, though. I don't feel ready to leave tomorrow."

"No," Oma agrees. "We still need to get you to the doctor. Plus, I'm not ready to part with you yet."

They seat themselves on opposite sides of the living room couch, their bodies turned toward one another and legs stretched into four nearly parallel lines.

"I'd miss you . . . if I go," Emma says.

"I'd miss you, too. But I'd see you next month when I drive up for lunch with your mom. And if you won't be living with your dad anymore, there's no reason I couldn't come more often."

"Lunch?"

"Her birthday lunch."

"Birthday lunch?"

"I thought you knew? Huh, I guess I lumped it together with the phone calls, and you knew about those. I drive up around your mom's birthday every year and then again around my birthday, and we have lunch together. Of course, she always insists that we meet somewhere other than Provo—Spanish Fork, usually—so there's no risk of seeing anyone she knows. She always brings me a big envelope stuffed with pictures of you guys and artwork you've made or things you've written for school."

Emma is silent. After a long moment, Oma finally asks, "What are you thinking, Schatz?"

"I'm thinking"—Emma shakes her head faintly as she speaks, her voice flat—"I don't know what I'm thinking."

"I always wished you were there. You and your siblings. Your mom tried more than once to talk your dad into letting me back into the picture, but it never went well."

"*She tried to talk him into it.*" Emma spits the words as if they leave a bad taste in her mouth. Heat roils in her belly. "Did it ever occur to her to just make her own choices?"

It's a question Claudia has asked herself too many times to count, but she has no satisfactory answer. "I don't fully understand your mom. But I know she's never stopped feeling sad about my not getting to be in your life."

"But not sad enough to *do* anything. Not sad enough to, say, take us with her to lunch. Or to just drive us down here. Not sad enough to even *tell* us that she was in touch with you."

Oma's voice is soft. "I think she was equal parts sad and scared."

Emma's voice is not. "*I* think she was one part sad and a hundred parts selfish."

Claudia nods. "Scared and selfish often go together," she replies, then turns her own words over in her mind, deleting the "and." "Scared selfish," she says aloud. "Maybe she was scared into selfishness. Though I guess we never really know what's inside a person, do we?"

Emma *does* know, though. She's watched her mother up close for seventeen years now. It's enough time to learn what she values. First: comfort. Comfort in the form of a surface-level calm, a hollow harmony whose tonality depends on refusal to rock the boat, on cheerful compliance, on placating the person in power. Placating the person in power and demurring to ever step up and take the risk of actually *being* that person. And her children? They are a distant second on the list.

But her mother is Oma's child, Emma realizes. She tries to temper her tone. "Sorry. I know she's your kid and all."

"She is, and I love her to pieces. But you know"—Oma laughs, a rich bell-like laugh—"I heard a saying once about being a grandparent, and I think it might just be true: 'You'd kill for your children, but you'd kill your children for your grandchildren.'"

They ring together with laughter. The hot coals in Emma's belly cool just a little.

"I don't actually wish her dead," Emma concedes.

"What a generous statement!"

Their laughter rises and falls. Emma chews her bottom lip, wondering why her anger toward her mother feels so much messier than her anger toward her father. The coals in her belly are still smoking. Emma's anger toward her dad, when it flares, is quick and hot—a fast, furious, straightforward burning that she can readily vent. With her mother, it's complicated. One moment, Emma might scorch with rage over Heidi's failure to intervene on her children's behalf, but the next moment, Mom is smiling warmly, asking about her day, and offering a plate of homemade strudel. And so, instead of burning down to ash, the coals—partially smothered—smoke and smoke. They billow in small gray puffs of resentment and irritation and the occasional black cloud of outright contempt. And there has been no vent, no window—until this little opening between her and Oma, right now.

Chapter Twenty-Seven

Heidi is exhausted. For the second night in a row, she lies awake, frozen in place, feigning sleep. Again, she hears Graham rise from bed. Again, the creaking of the stairs as he descends. And still, she lies inert. She *could* move, at least in theory. There's no risk of conversation with her husband now that he's left the room. But the connection between her mind and body seems severed. She feels numb. Completely numb.

Emma is awake. Completely awake. Not because she's deliberating the Pingrees' offer, nor even because of her anger toward her mother. Emma fell asleep easily enough at first, but she dreamed of giving birth and woke to a throbbing in her low back and a queasy clenching of her innards. It's hard to say which is most to blame for her inability to return to sleep: her aching abdomen or the strangeness of her dream.

The dream began with a belly ache. An intense cramping that could only mean one thing: it was time. The baby was coming.

Even in the dream, Emma knew it was too soon. Much too soon. She wasn't ready. And surely the baby wasn't either. She couldn't be more than a lump of cells at this point—a mere glob of potential. And yet the pains amplified and accelerated. Emma felt the warm rush of life between her legs. She listened for a cry. There wasn't one. She lifted her head to look and found her baby already standing.

"What are you doing?" Emma asked the baby, who had walked away and was now rifling through Emma's bag and was, it seemed, not a mere glob after all, but rather a fully formed clone of Emma herself.

"I'm getting dressed. I've got stuff to do," the clone baby answered, helping herself to Emma's only remaining pair of clean underwear.

"Stuff?" Emma asked.

"Yeah, I'm gonna apply to the U. Maybe look for a part-time job."

"But you're a *baby.*"

"Am I?" the baby laughed.

No, not a baby. And not quite a clone either. She exuded a confidence and calm that the birth-exhausted Emma envied.

The new and shiny Emma walked toward the door. Old and exhausted Emma felt a tugging. "Ouch!" she cried. "Don't do that. You're still attached." She motioned to the umbilical cord.

"It's time to go, though." New Emma was matter-of-fact. She pulled toward the door. Her progress was slow; Old Emma fell to the floor, then bumped and dragged along behind her younger self, voicing a slew of noisy protests.

Finally, New Emma paused and turned, looking at her miserable old self. "Hmm, this won't work"—she crinkled her brow, considering—"I know!" she cried, her face lifting like the morning sun. New Emma pulled a pair of scissors from her pocket, the blades forming a V around their umbilical attachment.

"No!" Old Emma cried. "You need me! I *made* you."

New Emma paused. They locked eyes. "I know you're scared, but we're okay," New Emma affirmed.

And then, *snip.*

Old Emma expected it to hurt—the severing. Instead, a lightness washed through her. She felt suddenly airy, ephemeral. As if maybe she didn't need so much substance, so much weight, after all.

New Emma smiled at her and reached out a hand. "You can still come with if you want."

"Okay," Old Emma breathed.

Her younger, stronger, more substantial self reached out a hand and hoisted her up with ease. Old Emma was featherlight now, baby light. Inexplicably content to let her newborn self become the mother and take the lead. New Emma opened the door. "Let's go!" she declared, only there was no separate self to hear the words. She was alone in the room. That's when she jolted awake.

Emma's body is leaden now. It aches all over. She wants to slip back into her dream, wants to know what the surefooted version of herself does once she leaves the room. "We're okay," she had said.

Emma doesn't feel okay. Her abdomen is wracked with alternating waves of queasiness and pain. Her armpits are damp, and there is sweat between her legs. Or could that be her period? She gives up on sleep and rises from bed. The room spins. One hand on the wall, she stumbles to the bathroom.

No blood. No period. Just Emma, a spinning room, a throbbing back, and an uneasy belly, contents unknown. She slides heavily to the floor, drawing her knees into her chest and dropping her forehead onto them.

The lightness of the dream is gone, unreachable. She feels the weight of everything—of pregnancy, a baby, motherhood. What other explanation is there for this physical misery? There's a warm rush of fluid. Tears, not blood.

Half an hour passes before Emma finds the will to pull herself up from the floor and drag her pained and exhausted body back to bed.

And still, no sleep. Maybe she needs to eat something. She remembers when her mother was pregnant with Sariah, how snacking eased the morning sickness.

Again, Emma rises, this time shuffling to the kitchen. Grape Nuts, Raisin Bran, bread, leftover soup. Nothing appeals to her. She remembers the brownies she spied the previous morning, and her tongue tingles at the thought, her mouth filling with saliva. It's an absurd thing to eat when you're queasy. "Just one," she says aloud.

The richness of the chocolate distracts her from the pain in her low back. The ecstasy of her taste buds outshines her anxiety over the impending doctor's appointment. So she eats two. Her stomach doesn't feel any worse. She considers eating a third. "It won't fix this," she sighs aloud, meaning the whole of her tangled situation. "It'd probably make it worse," she adds, this time thinking of her queasiness.

She wishes someone would answer back. Would say something reassuring. Would tell her what to do. Not about the brownies. About life. Should she go live in Provo with the Pingrees? Stay here with Oma? But the refrigerator only hums in response, which is hardly illuminating. Emma is struck with the urge to pray—not one of the brief, casual, on-the-go prayers that still bubble up inside her at random. A real prayer. A fall-down-on-your-knees, admit-you're-clueless prayer. The kitchen doesn't feel like the place for it, what with the refrigerator's unintelligible droning.

Emma knows where to go: outside. The natural world has always been her temple, the place where she feels closest to—well, to what, she's not sure.

Her coat and shoes wait by the door. Emma slips into them, sockless and pajama-clad, then steps out into the star-strewn November morning. She gazes up into the expanse until her neck protests, then tucks her chin, slips her hands into her pockets for warmth, and walks, turning uphill when she reaches the road.

***

Heidi thinks she hears the weather seal break on the front door. Has Graham gone outside? What on earth for? Still, she lies inert.

Graham has indeed gone outside. He has slipped his sockless feet into sneakers and his flannel-pajama-clad arms into a winter coat. His feet move rapidly, pulled toward the temple. He's almost arrived now. The grounds are closed and gates locked, but he knew they would be. His steps slow as he traces the perimeter. Any moment now, he is sure, the knot in the pit of his stomach will loosen. The tension in his head will ease. *Thou good and faithful servant*, something will whisper in his mind.

No whisperings yet, and he's walked the western boundary of the grounds. He turns uphill, following the southern edge now, his steps even slower. It will come soon; it *must*. A divine stamp of approval. The heavens will acknowledge the infallible logic of his decision to disown his daughter. Or at least, at the very least, the pain will go away—the terror.

He walks along the east side of the temple, and still serenity evades him. His mind volleys arguments, counter-arguments, justifications, attacks. He arrives at certainty over and over again, and yet something unnamable nags from the edges—or no, not from the edges, but rather from the interior of some locked enclosure.

His logic is sound! So why do images keep intruding on his mind, keep bubbling up from some unseen reservoir: Emma, stomping away from their table at the Cougareat. Emma, silent on her bed, staring at the floor as he tried to elucidate his reasoning—his temper, rising like bile, choking his good intentions. Heidi, feigning illness on the couch. Sariah with her matter-of-fact pronouncement: "Emma went on a trip to Oma's house!" *They had all known.* Heidi and every one of the kids—they had all been part of the cover-up, had all sided with Emma. Sided against him. *Why?*

They stand together like a playground gang in his mind—Heidi and the kids. They stand shoulder to shoulder, just like in those humiliating memories from his childhood. Just like the way the bishop and his counselors stood after disfellowshipping him. But Graham is in the right this time! He isn't the one who should be cast out!

Round and round he circles the temple grounds, but the images only gain momentum. Round and round he circles, but clarity and a calm stomach remain locked behind the gates. He can get no closer. Graham rubs the back of his neck and picks up his pace in frustration. Before he knows it, he is running. His legs are a red, flannel blur in the black predawn. He is a red, flannel blur, careening from his circular orbit.

Graham Madsen runs upward toward the mountains.

Emma Madsen walks and walks until she realizes, quite suddenly, that the pain in her back is gone. Her feet build speed. She runs toward the ridgeline.

Her father finally comes to a halt, breathless, his hands pressed to his head.

Emma stops, chest heaving, and falls to her knees. This is as good of a place as any. Here under the endless sky.

"I need to get this right," Graham moans.

"What now?" Emma pleads.

The red, packed earth chills her knees and shins. The wind whips at Graham's bare ankles. Neither of them notices the cold.

"If I'm doing this wrong, you're going to have to explain it to me," Graham instructs his maker.

"What do I do now?" Emma entreats.

"Oh, shit!" Claudia exclaims. It is not a prayer. These are just the words that spill from her mouth when she goes to the kitchen for a glass of water. Emma's door is open. The brownies are on the counter. Emma is nowhere in sight. Claudia rushes back to the bedroom to wake Dean.

Four pajama-clad figures search in the cold and dark. One scours his mind. Another searches her heart. "Emma!" the final two call.

Emma is beyond hearing. She has broken open. She is inside out. She looks at the sky and feels stars burning inside of her. She looks down at her hands. They are made, unequivocally, of stardust. The whole world is light, and the whole world is dust. The big is small, and the small is big. The simple is complex, and the complex is stunningly simple. Every moment is contained in this moment. And all of this is inside of her—and she is inside of it.

Emma wants everyone to taste this fruit. She scans the horizon and sees two figures moving toward her, as if through a mist. *Oma and Dean!* She calls to them, and they come.

"Emma, thank God! Are you alright?" Oma gasps.

Emma lets out a wild laugh and sings her reply: "*All is well, all is well.*" The hymn has other lyrics, too, but words are made of dust, and time blinks in and out behind a cloud.

Claudia and Dean exchange a glance. Dean shakes his head softly. If Emma isn't alarmed by how she's feeling, then there is no sense in explaining anything to her just now.

"Let's get you home," Oma coaxes.

"Home," Emma echoes, transfixed by the sound of the word. It is made of stars, too. *Home, home, home.* She feels her heels clicking together. *Everything* is clicking together; all the atoms in her body, all the atoms in the whole world, living in perpetual collision. *Click, click, click.*

Oma links her right arm with Emma's left, and Dean links his left with Emma's right. They progress slowly. "Everything—everything is linked like this. Like arms," Emma says in a whisper. Or at least she thinks she does. It's hard to tell thoughts and spoken words apart.

"It sure is," Dean agrees aloud. Or perhaps Emma reads his mind.

Graham's hands finally drop from his head. His legs begin the trek toward home, but he doesn't know what to do with his arms. They hang limp, idle, restless. His fingers itch for pages to turn, a tie to knot, a chalkboard to erase. For problems that are solvable. He remembers the heat of his daughter's hand in his as he led her to the baptismal font. The weight of her tiny, brand-new body asleep in the crook of his arm. He rubs his right hand back and forth across his chest, then circles his cold fingers around the warmth of his own neck, before cramming them dolefully into his armpits.

Oma and Dean keep their arms interlocked with Emma's until they reach the living room couch. "Sit down, Schatz. I'll get you some water."

Emma drops to the cushions, and time floats to the ceiling. She seems to sink deeper into the plushness with each passing moment. Or is the softness sinking into her? She wonders for the first time how long it's been since she left Oma's house to pray. Did the pale beginnings of light shine on the horizon as they came back in the door? Emma tries to calculate what that might mean, but numbers feel slippery. *Is this normal? Was it this way for Lehi? Is this how visions always are?*

Oma returns with the glass of water and notices the crease in Emma's brow, the perplexity in her eyes. "Are you alright?"

"I feel strange," Emma answers. "Dizzy. So clear and so cloudy . . . all at once." Her voice sounds impossibly slow to her own ears.

"Yeah, I'm not surprised." Oma looks at Dean for confirmation and then continues, "Those brownies you ate, they have something in them—a plant—that can make you feel that way. It'll go away, but it might take a few more hours. Do you remember how many you ate?"

The vibrations of Oma's voice creep at a snail's pace from Emma's eardrums to her brain, and finally, Emma's own vocal chords tremble to action. "A plant? Like a vegetable? Two. I ate two."

Oma sighs in relief. It could have been worse. "Yes, a plant, but no, not really a vegetable. Marijuana. It's . . . helpful for arthritis."

"*Marijuana?* The *drug*?"

"Yeah, the drug. I'm so sorry. We should have put it somewhere else. Or warned you," Oma replies.

Emma's eyes narrow, and the skin between them crinkles. Claudia watches her granddaughter's face, waiting for the wave of panic or anger that will surely come.

Instead, Emma's shoulders begin to shake. From her cushioned corner of the infinite universe, Emma expands in a flood of giggles. Claudia and Dean exchange a look—amused, relieved. Emma collapses forward, her head on her knees, convulsing with laughter. "I can't stop laughing!" she finally chortles out.

Claudia can't help a chuckle of her own. It shouldn't be funny. It's *not* funny—accidentally giving drugs to a minor. A minor who might be pregnant. "We're such idiots." Claudia shakes her head, looking at Dean, but her lips still twitch with amusement.

Dean glances down at his watch. "Maybe she can sleep it off?"

"She doesn't look especially tired."

Emma is still bent over with giggles. Suddenly, she lurches upright, her eyes wide. "What if Lehi was on drugs, too!? And Joseph Smith. And all of them."

Emma imagines Lehi ingesting desert plants before each vision. Heavenly Father appearing to Joseph Smith in the woods of upstate New York, offering him a golden plate of brownies. She ripples with laughter again until her sides ache.

"I need to stop laughing," she sighs, lying down on her back and exhaling sharply.

She closes her eyes, steadying her breath. The laughter has shaken everything loose, as if all of the pieces of her mind—every thought and every experience—are now jumbled, waiting to be arranged into something new. She feels it fleetingly, wordlessly: what it all might mean, how it all might shake out. That while we contort our necks, looking to heaven for answers, truth germinates at our feet, gestates in our guts, grows from our own dirt.

***

Ringing splits the stagnant air of Heidi Madsen's bedroom. The alarm clock. The night is finally over, then. Her heavy limbs move and lift mechanically, as if propelled by cogs. She is a mere extension of the ringing alarm, the morning to-do list, her children's needs, her husband's whims. She is a clock, wound and ready, ticking without volition.

He is back in the room now. Soon he will don his spandex and leave for a run. Graham considers not doing this, of course. He just ran, albeit in flannel. But his routine is his iron rod. It doesn't *feel* like iron today. Like everything, it feels flimsy—the lone thread, perhaps, between him and a complete unraveling. Still, he must run.

Wordlessly, Heidi dresses—*tick, tick, tick*. The cogs turn, and she descends the stairs. Lunches packed—*check*. Kids awoken—*check*. Breakfast served—*check*. Next: Coats, shoes, backpacks. Six children to send out the door and onto a bus. *Just six*.

"Joe! Liza! You need to go!" Heidi calls to the children who are now her oldest. It is 7:00 exactly. She knows because Graham just stepped out the front door for his morning run.

They hurry past her and out of the house, throwing goodbyes over their shoulders, with something oddly like enthusiasm. Or nervousness? Heidi turns to watch them go. Her head feels heavier than usual. She wonders fleetingly if it's possible for a head to simply roll off of a neck. The idea holds a certain appeal. She returns to the kitchen and tosses the dishtowel, balled in her clenched hand, onto the counter. Four more children to load onto buses. *Just four.*

***

Graham plods uphill. He is off pace, and he knows it. Two nights with little to no sleep have caught up to him—have *passed* him, given how slowly he is moving. His brow creases with determination. He wills his legs to pump faster. It works for a moment. But his mind is tired, too. It drifts.

He remembers the day Emma was born. The happiest day of his life. Heidi placed the warm bundle of soft blankets and softer flesh into his arms. His entire body warmed, tingled, as if he too were swaddled and safe. Probably it was just heat conduction, his daughter's warmth spreading to him. But for once, Graham didn't overthink things. He had never held a baby before. Now he had *made* one. "You have to support her head," his wife told him, reaching out to show him how.

He cradled his baby daughter with the utmost care. He would protect her from everything. Would give her a childhood opposite of his own. She would never know the pain of abandonment, the bewilderment of being left to fend for herself in a too-big world. He would structure it all. He would build a scaffold around her so that it—whatever it was—couldn't collapse in.

Where did we go wrong? he wonders, still plodding uphill. His anger has exhausted itself. Has burned itself out, leaving behind an incriminating pile of ash. This "we" is his only consolation, however scant—the hope that Heidi might share in the blame.

How did we lose control?

It started when Emma was so little. He remembers her at two years-old, breaking free of his hold, charging ahead as they crossed the street. Three-year-old Emma, yanking her Mary Janes from her feet and hurling them across the room because her mother had dared to put them on for her. Four-year-old Emma, sneaking to the kitchen after her bedtime to eat the cookie she had been denied. She didn't whimper like her younger siblings when he scolded her or swatted her on the bottom. He spanked her when he found her eating the cookies. She didn't even flinch.

"When you spank me, it just makes me want to be badder," she told him, crumbs spilling from her lips.

Emma refused to be guided, scaffolded, protected. Joseph, Eliza—the others were all easy by comparison. Or so Heidi told him, and she would know. Graham wasn't around as much after Emma's baby stage—those blissful early months in which he held his sleeping daughter against his chest or nestled in the crook of his left arm, while his right hand turned the pages of Hegel or Kant.

At seven-months-old, Emma started crawling, and from that moment on, she had no interest in being held. She explored the world on all fours, pulling books from shelves and dishes from cupboards. She climbed onto tables and chairs, knocking things to the ground as she went. She banged on the piano, a battered upright that they had purchased at a garage sale for thirty dollars. The dissonant chords and Emma's shrieking laughter rattled the paper-thin walls of their one-bedroom apartment. "Can't you keep her quiet?" he barked at Heidi one day, after rereading the same passage of Hegel for the fifth time.

"Maybe you could try studying on campus instead," his wife replied, choking back her hurt.

"Fine," he answered, slamming the book shut. If she didn't want him there, he would leave. And he did. He stopped coming home between classes. He took on more hours at work. It was a good thing. Money was tight, and they needed a bigger apartment. Soon enough, there would be more babies to diaper and clothe and feed. Graham would be more careful with these ones. Wouldn't get quite so attached. Would spend less time with them curled in the crook of his arm. It was best to leave that to Heidi.

The ground is level now beneath his feet. Still, his legs protest the effort. He is tempted to walk. "You might as well," he mutters to himself, disgusted by the slowness of his gait.

And so he does; he walks and thinks of Emma. He walks and searches for a storyline, a tidy one to organize the disparate shards of his life. He walks and thinks of the first chapters of the Book of Mormon. He wonders, as he has done before, how it is that Emma ended up so much like Laman, Lehi's wayward eldest. It occurs to Graham, for the first time, to wonder whether he is really such a Lehi after all.

He isn't. He smarts at the realization. Lehi never gave up on his children. He never stopped calling to Laman and Lemuel, urging them toward the Tree of Life. He forgave them everything—*everything*. Is that what he, Graham Madsen, is called to do? To love and forgive without limits? How could he even begin?

The question lands him in such foreign territory that Graham loses all awareness of his actual surroundings. Somehow, his feet still stride forward, but he misses the glow of sunlight rimming the mountains. He doesn't see or hear the passing cars. He doesn't register the shocked whisper of "it's Dad!" or notice the two boys scrambling to hide themselves behind a park bench.

It's late when he gets home. Only Nephi and Sariah are still there with their mother. Graham plants a kiss on the top of all three of their heads. Nephi and Sariah exchange quizzical looks, before Nephi theatrically swipes his hand across the crown of his head, wiping the kiss from his hair and then smearing it onto his sister's shirt sleeve.

Heidi's face is flushed. Her head feels hot, as if Graham's lips had burned her. For a moment, something gurgles up from beneath the numbness. An evanescent geyser of feeling that some might think to call anger. It buries itself almost as quickly as it rose.

She tidies the kitchen, her mind blank and body leaden once again. The remaining children board their bus. She folds a load of laundry and mumbles a goodbye to her husband as he departs for work. Next: grocery shopping. Because it's Monday. Thankfully, the meal plan is already set. The grocery list requires no thought. That is what Heidi wants from this day: to make it through without thinking.

***

Emma is beyond thinking. She is inside out—literally.

"Two brownies really shouldn't be enough to make her puke." Claudia's forehead creases with concern. She chews on her lower lip, considering.

Dean shakes his head. "Everyone reacts differently." That much is clearly true. Neither Claudia nor Dean has ever waxed visionary while tripping on edibles. "I had a buddy in college who puked if he ate even a little bit," Dean says. "It affected his mind differently, too—more like acid."

"Well, that seems to match Emma's experience. We'd better take her in." It is something between a statement and a question. Claudia and Dean sigh in synchrony.

"I don't think there's much a doctor can do for her. She'll have to ride it out. But given that she might be pregnant . . ." His voice trails off.

"Better not to take any chances."

Of course, they are taking a chance, and they both know it. If the doctor asks Emma how she came by two weed-laced brownies, things might not go well for them. But what's the point in discussing this now? Two things are assuredly worse than accidentally giving drugs to a runaway minor: giving drugs to a runaway minor and then denying them access to appropriate medical care. Or giving drugs to a minor and then pressuring them to lie about it.

Claudia turns back toward the couch, where Emma lies in a miserable heap. "They might give her IV fluids."

As if on cue, Emma lifts her head and leans out from the edge of the couch, heaving once again into the large bowl that her grandmother has placed there for her.

"Oh, Schatz. I'm so sorry," Claudia says, moving to her granddaughter's side and pulling her blond waves back from her face. Heat ripples from Emma's head.

"Lehi . . . never mentioned this part . . . of visions." Emma's voice comes out in trembly bursts, punctuated by spitting.

"What an asshole. Do you want some water?"

"No. I don't think I can keep it down."

Again, she heaves into the bowl. Her vomit, which had begun as putrid brownie batter, is thin now and yellow-green.

Claudia waits for the wave to pass. Emma falls back exhausted onto the couch.

"We're going to take you to the doctor, okay?" Oma says, touching a hand to her granddaughter's forehead and frowning. Pot wouldn't give her a fever. But Claudia doesn't say this. She doesn't want to worry her. Instead, she offers, "I'm sure you're going to be just fine, but we want to play it safe. They might give you fluids to keep you from getting too dehydrated, and we'll ask them to do a pregnancy test, too, okay?"

After a brief discussion, Claudia and Dean agree that, while Claudia would undoubtedly get them to the hospital faster, Dean's style of driving might prompt less vomiting from their passenger and will increase the odds that said vomit lands (and stays) in the bowl. They each put an arm around Emma and help her into the front seat of the Subaru.

Chapter Twenty-Eight

Heidi is still numb, her movements automated. She drives to the grocery store, seeing nothing but not crashing into anything either. She maneuvers her grocery cart and pulls items from the shelves with blind precision. Until she reaches the yogurt.

There is no Dannon vanilla yogurt on the shelves this morning. Heidi *always* buys Dannon vanilla. It's Graham's favorite. Actually, Heidi isn't sure that he's ever tried anything else.

She stands, staring at the vacant space where the Dannon vanilla should be. Her feet feel glued to the linoleum. Only her head moves, scanning left and then right. There is yogurt in an endless array of brands and flavors. Heidi is only inches from the Yoplait section. She should reach out her arm. Pick up that container of vanilla. But what if Graham doesn't like Yoplait? Would the store brand be better? She unpeels her feet from the floor and shuffles toward the generic vanilla, only to find herself paralyzed again. Maybe Yoplait is the better choice? Or there's the Dannon plain—might that do?

A minute passes, then two, then three. Still, Heidi stands in the yogurt aisle. Time ceases to exist. Nothing is real, except this void, this eternal indecision. Eleven minutes. Eleven minutes and finally she decides. Yoplait Vanilla. That's what she'll get. She turns toward it, but in that instant, a fellow shopper—a brunette with immaculately rounded bangs, a woman who knows what she wants—lifts the final 32-ounce container of Yoplait vanilla from the shelf and plunks it into her cart.

Heidi's numbness shatters. *Who are you?*—an inner voice roars—*that you can't even choose a flippin' yogurt!*

Her mind screams, and her body wakes, and Heidi knows in an instant—knows beyond thinking—what she needs to do. It has nothing to do with yogurt.

She strides, fists clenched, away from the dairy section, her cart abandoned. The banged brunette steps hurriedly aside, possibly out of politeness or possibly because of the way Heidi's nostrils are flaring. Chest puffed and eyes sparking, Heidi stalks past the cleaning products and out the front door of the store. She knows what she needs to do, and no one—not her husband and not her own demurring self—is going to stand in her way. Heidi is going to see her daughter. And her mother. Come what may.

She clambers into the driver's seat of her Ford Club Wagon, and the engine rumbles to life. She glances at the clock. 9:28, it reads.

At 9:29, Emma slumps in a waiting room, vomiting into a complimentary plastic bag.

The Pingrees wait in a Moab diner. They glance down at their watches and speculate on what could have gone wrong. "Should we try calling again?" Joelle asks.

Jeff shakes his head. What good would it do? "They must still be enroute. Either that, or they're sitting in the wrong restaurant, wondering where we are."

"Breakfast," Dean says in the tone of someone who has just made a mildly interesting discovery.

Claudia looks up at him from where she sits, holding Emma's hair back as she heaves yet again. Claudia stares blankly for just a moment before she understands. "Joelle and Jeff! Shit!"

Dean looks down at his watch. They are already a half hour late.

"Do you want me to go?" he asks.

"Yeah, please do. Emma and I obviously aren't going anywhere."

Emma spits pitifully into the bag.

"Okay, I'll just pop over to apologize and tell them Emma's not feeling well. Then I'll come back." Dean plants a kiss on the top of Claudia's head, gives Emma's arm a light squeeze, and then hurries his steps out the door toward the car.

Heidi is hurrying, too. The van's tires squeal as she pulls into the high school parking lot.

Graham is in his office chair, wheeling from bookshelf to desk, doggedly resisting the thought that serenity, certainty—one's entire system for living—can collapse in an instant. A knock sounds on the door.

"Come in," Graham croaks. He hasn't spoken a word yet today, he realizes. Or perhaps he said "goodbye" to his wife? He can't remember. No matter. It's clear she wants nothing to do with him, anyway. He thinks of the way she shrank back from his kiss, like she'd been scalded. His face burns. It's as if *he* is the one who sinned, the one who's being disowned.

The door opens and an unfamiliar head pops in—close-clipped brown hair, a handsome face marred by a puckered scar, spanning from eyebrow to hairline. “Hey, Brother Madsen,” the face greets him.

Facial recognition isn’t Graham’s strong suit. “May I help you?”

“Yeah, I wanted to talk with you about a couple things. My paper and also, um, the honor code thing.”

“Benjamin. Come in.” Graham recognizes him now. The band t-shirt—Red Hot Chili Peppers today—should have made it obvious. “I see you’ve finally cut your hair.”

“Yeah . . . about that. I was hoping maybe you hadn’t contacted the honor police yet.”

“It’s called the Honor Code Office, as I’m sure you know.”

Ben blushes slightly. “Right, the Honor Code Office. Anyway, my roommate cuts my hair for me, and we meant to get it done before your last lecture, but our whole apartment ended up sick with a stomach flu, so it didn’t happen. Sorry about that. I was hoping you could overlook it this once.”

"Twice,” Graham corrects, his eyes fixed on a stack of paper, neatly aligned with the corner of his desk.

“Twice?”

“I excused it once on the day when I told you to cut your hair lest I report you. If I also excuse Friday’s infraction, that would be *twice*.”

“I was sick.”

“So you said.”

Ben sighs in exasperation. “Look, I know you probably think I’m making that up, but I’m not. And I know I shouldn’t have let my hair grow so long in the first place, but look at this thing.” He gestures to the scar on his forehead.

Reluctantly, Graham lifts his gaze.

"When my grooming is *up to honor code standards*"—Ben's voice floats upward a half octave, taking on an unnaturally clipped quality before sliding back to its usual register—"I get asked about it constantly. Do you have any idea how old that gets?"

"We all have our burdens to bear. That doesn't excuse us from the necessity of obedience."

Ben isn't listening. "Sometimes I say it was a skateboarding accident. Sometimes I tell them to mind their own business. But then I'm either lying or being rude."

"It seems that you might as well tell the truth then."

"No one wants to hear the truth. That my dad was a drunk. That this scar was his last gift to me, right before I went to foster care. You should see the way people look at me when I tell them that."

The room feels suddenly hot. Graham's throat constricts. He must have knotted his tie too tightly this morning. He tugs at it, rubs at his neck. He needs water. Or fresh air. Maybe both. In either case, he needs this conversation to end. "Alright, well, I'll excuse your infraction *twice* then, but only twice. I wrote up a report, but I'll hold onto it . . . for now."

"Thank you! Thank you so much." Ben's voice is breathy with relief.

This should be the end of it. Ben should walk out now. Instead, and much to Graham's dismay, Ben sinks into the empty seat that the department chair delivered a few semesters back. Graham can still hear the man's smugness: "Otherwise, it seems like you're actively *discouraging* your students from attending office hours, Graham."

Which is, of course, exactly what Graham was trying to do. But he wasn't supposed to say that. So, Graham allowed the cushioned seat to take up residence in his office, hoping that no one would ever tarry long enough to use it. Sometimes he stacks books on it for good measure. But where has the pile gone? He spots it, relocated to the windowsill, and silently calls a pestilence down upon the custodian.

Ben sits. He practically *lounges*, one more link in an obnoxiously long chain of students and colleagues who have outstayed their welcome in Graham Madsen's office. Ben pulls his backpack onto his lap, unzips it, and rummages inside. "I have my paper for you, too. I know it was due Friday, but like I said, I was sick. I threw up all day Thursday, so I wasn't able to get it done on time. It's okay if you dock points."

"Ten percent per day."

"I know," Ben nods. "But I was thinking maybe you wouldn't count Sunday? So this would just be two days late." He hands the paper to Graham.

"Why wouldn't I count Sunday?"

"Because it's the Sabbath. We're always told not to work on Sunday, so it doesn't make sense for it to count against us as a work day."

"Did you work on the paper on the Sabbath?"

"No. I finished it Saturday afternoon." Ben doesn't mention that he spent Sunday studying for an Economics test.

Graham is quiet for a moment, then nods his head. "Alright, I'll amend that in the syllabus. *At my discretion,* Sundays might not count toward the deduction."

Ben does a double take. "Really?"

"You argued your case effectively."

Ben grins and wishes Andrea were here to eavesdrop on the conversation. He, Ben Rogers, the catalyst for a syllabus amendment. "Thank you. I actually enjoyed writing this paper, which is weird for me."

Graham doesn't ask him what he enjoyed about it, but Ben continues, unprompted. "I picked the problem of evil. It feels pretty relevant to my life, you know. If there's a god, why do bad things happen to innocent people, and especially to kids? Any halfway decent human steps in to protect a kid from abuse if they know it's going on. So why doesn't God?"

Graham props his elbows on the armrests of his office chair, pressing his fingertips forcefully together. He's not getting out of this conversation, he realizes. Sometimes, bad things—uncomfortable things, inconvenient things—happen to good people. "What did you discover?" he sighs, willing the air to ease the tightness in his throat.

"I tried to question the question, like you said in class. And I realized the question starts with all kinds of unspoken assumptions. That there *is* a God, obviously, but also that God is a certain way—all-powerful, all-knowing, and good in the way we understand goodness. And it assumes that God is interested in us, that humans matter to Him."

Ben wants to add "if God is even a 'Him' at all," but he wonders if a statement like that might also be against the honor code. He's not sure. He signed the thing without bothering to read it. Better not to take the chance. So he skips that part of his thinking and carries on.

"So then I started wondering why we begin with those assumptions. And I realized we *want* God to be that way. So I asked myself why that's the case—why we want God to basically be a perfect, powerful version of us. And I think the answer takes us right back to suffering. Suffering is a fact of life. It's a fact that isn't distributed equally, but it's still a fact for everyone. And it's also a fact that we all die. And that scares us. It threatens any sense of certainty we have. It threatens our sense of self-importance. And so, we reach for this notion of a god who embodies certainty. A god who is the opposite of us—infinite instead of finite, unlimited instead of limited, perfect instead of flawed—but who is also enough like us to inflate our sense of importance. Because then we get to believe we're children of God and that we're going to become gods after we die."

"You've veered from the basic question of what's real and landed in the domain of psychology."

Ben chews on this for a moment before replying. "Okay. But how can you do philosophy without doing psychology? Every philosophical argument is constructed by a human mind. And every human mind is influenced by emotions, desires, life history, all that stuff."

"That's the reason for philosophical training. To learn the rules of inference. To learn what constitutes a sound argument so that you can arrive at truth."

"But more often than not, people still don't agree on whether an argument is sound. The steps might be logical, but there's almost always disagreement about the truth of the premises. Because we're all biased in some way or another. So when you learn about someone's philosophical views, you might think you're learning about how the world really is, but what you're actually learning about is the philosopher's personality, their life history, their biases."

"This is what you wrote about?" Graham looks down at Ben's paper.

"Yeah."

"Well, I hope you argued your case well."

"I tried to. But, of course, I'm also biased, right? I'm double majoring in Psychology. So it stands to reason that I'd think about things with more of a psychological bent. Plus, I've spent a lot of time in therapy," Ben adds with a lopsided grin.

His eyes roam across the mostly bare office walls, landing with a start on the clock. "Oh! I've gotta go!" Ben declares, popping from his seat. "I have to make it work by 10:00," he offers apologetically, as if Graham were asking him to stay. "Thanks for your time. And for excusing me—twice."

Ben's hand is on the doorknob when Graham speaks. "Benjamin . . ."

Ben looks back over his shoulder. It's impossible to say who is more surprised by the words that tumble from Graham's lips: "My mom was an alcoholic." Graham's voice is barely above a whisper. "She threw bottles at me."

For a fleeting moment, their eyes meet. Then Graham turns again to the stack of papers on his desk. Ben Rogers closes the door softly behind him.

It happened three times—the bottle throwing. Other times, it was plates or books or, when Graham was lucky, something softer like a shoe. Her aim wasn't great. But you only have to be pelted in the head with a hard object one time to live in perpetual fear of the next bullseye. Graham monitored his mother with even greater dedication than his classmates monitored football standings or baseball box scores. He knew how many swigs she could take from the bottle before she became dangerous. He knew the warning sounds: the mouth breathing, the heavy shuffling of her feet, the banging shut of cupboard doors. He learned not to get too close.

Learned when it was imperative to keep a couch or a table between them.

He had a dream when he was eight or nine, not long after Pam first took him under her wing. He slept fitfully that night due to an angry knot on the back of his head—this time from a book. When he finally slipped into dreamland, he was building. He was stacking bricks, one at a time, constructing a tidy square around himself. The walls were still too low when his mother entered the dream. She was throwing things. Soft things at first—socks and dish towels. A banana. A tomato. He kept right on building, the walls rising brick by brick. She switched to harder, heavier objects. Books, bottles, then the TV. At that point, Graham knew it was a dream because his mother would *never* throw the TV, for the same reason she never threw a whiskey bottle until after it was drained.

If this is a dream, I can control it, Graham remembers thinking.

His hands began working faster—much faster. Faster than any human could lay bricks in the waking world. *Crash, crash, crash*. Objects banged against the walls, but the bricks held. Nothing could hit him. Soon enough, his structure was fully enclosed. He was safe. *Safe*.

Now he sits, surrounded by the four walls of his office. Graham does not feel safe. The windows on his brick house have been thrown wide. Emma left everything open when she departed. He doesn't know his surroundings anymore. Doesn't know *himself*. What was he thinking, telling a student about his childhood? *The past is the past. It's over—done*. Why on earth did he drag it back up? *Crash, crash, crash*. It's all coming in. Even the bricks wobble, and for the first time, Graham thinks to wonder about the integrity of his foundation.

He has spent the last two days trying to slam doors and windows shut. Banning Emma. Tightening the rules. Tightening his grip. But the ground is shifting beneath his feet. Everything has become slippery. Heidi and the kids are sliding out the windows now. *Crash, crash, crash.*

When does it become safer outside of a house than in? Graham doesn't want to die in here alone, trapped beneath a pile of rubble. His head drops to the desk. *Thump, thump, thump.* Three times he bangs his forehead against the surface. His right hand reaches out and lands on a thick stack of papers. His paper. *The* paper. The one where he lays it all out: the meaning of life. It just needs a few more revisions before he submits it to the *The Philosophical Review.* Well, that's where things stood an hour ago. But an hour ago, Graham had thought the meaning of life hinged on the bringing of order to chaos—the human echo of divine creation. And he had thought that chaos was something external, something outside of him that could be subdued and conquered. Now, he knows only this: he built his house upon the sand.

Graham's hand pulls at the first sheet of paper, crumpling it into a ball. Then the second paper goes, and the third. He lifts his head, crumpling papers faster and faster, more and more furiously until the pile is exhausted. He begins to throw them. To throw them the way some people throw bottles and shoes. He hurls them one after another toward the wastebasket. His aim is better than his mother's. Twenty-two wads of paper in the basket. Thirty-one scattered around it.

His certainty is garbage. Fifty-three crumpled balls. His world—had it all been as flat and lifeless as paper? He hadn't built a home; he had lived inside a dream. A child's desperate dream, designed to protect him from what had been. A dream that instead entombed him, locked him off from what is and from what could be. A dream that has made him an exile from his own family.

"And the rain descended," Graham whispers, his lips barely moving, throat burning, "and the floods came, and the winds blew, and beat upon that house; and it fell: and great was the fall of it."

Minutes pass amidst the rubble. Graham sees nothing. Says nothing. Thinks nothing. Finally, he blinks, shakes his head. His vision comes into focus. He isn't staring at nothing after all. Two crumpled balls of his former life are there, in the corner, stacked one on top of the other. How they have landed like that is a mystery. Like a snowman.

"Like a colon," Graham breathes. And then his eyes widen. *A colon!* How has he never seen it before!? *The answer is right there, contained in the question.*

Graham grabs a fresh sheet of paper. "What Is: The Meaning of Life," he writes. He folds the paper, tucks it into his breast pocket, presses back from his desk and rises. The ground feels alive. Or is it his feet that are coursing with energy? His legs move to the door, his hand opens it.

"I need to cancel my classes for today," he tells the secretary two doors down.

"Is everything okay?" She looks alarmed. Graham Madsen has never cancelled a class before—not once in nearly thirteen years at the university.

"Existential crisis," he considers saying. Or maybe "existential breakthrough?" He pauses for a beat, clears his throat. "Family emergency," he mumbles. *Family breakthrough?* He is back out the door before she can reply, striding down the hall, exiting the building, marching toward his car. It's time to reckon with what is. There's no other way to make this right. And Graham *must* make this right—must bring his daughter home.

Chapter Twenty-Nine

"Hyrum and Brigham Madsen?" the round-faced secretary repeats for the second time, as if Heidi might have misspoken—as if perhaps she said Hyrum and Brigham Madsen, all the while meaning Peter and Paul Smith.

"Yes." Heidi is impatient and out of breath. She raced to the high school, only to find that Joseph and Eliza had disappeared following their first period classes. After a brief flutter of panic, it hit her: they must be with Cami. After all, Cami said she was leaving for Castle Valley after first period. Nothing else makes sense.

"Your sons were both marked absent in homeroom." The round-faced secretary's eyebrows brush her hairline as she says this. "Do you want me to send someone to check if they are in their second period classes?"

Heidi's eyes move rapidly, mirroring the clamor of her thoughts. "Umm, yes please," she finally croaks, and the woman disappears from the desk, leaving her alone in the office.

It makes no sense. The boys walked out the door at the normal time this morning. They've never skipped school before. If it were just one child, she would worry that they had been kidnapped—but all four vanished? They must all be with Cami, then—they *must.*

The secretary returns and delivers the verdict: they didn't show up to second period either. Heidi says nothing, simply heads for the door.

"Mrs. Madsen? Are you alright?" The secretary calls behind her.

Heidi turns, nods. "I know where they are."

The elementary school is just a parking lot away. Heidi traverses it in long steps, her hands shoved into her coat pockets for warmth.

"Good morning, Mrs. Madsen!" the elementary school secretary chirps cheerfully. "Do you need Nephi or Sariah?"

"Both."

"Alrighty. And will they be coming back today, or should I have them collect their things?"

"They'll be out for the rest of the day."

"No problem." The secretary places two calls and then looks up with a smile. "They're on their way. Have a seat if you'd like."

Heidi stays on her feet, bouncing impatiently—heel, toe, heel, toe. Two children are accounted for, at least. But Heidi's sense of urgency, piqued in the yogurt aisle and amplified by the disappearance of four of her children, grows ever more electric. They'll need to pack a few things in case they stay the night. And she needs to call Jennifer. How quickly can they be on the road? And *how long, for crying out loud, can it take children to walk from their classroom to the front office?*

Finally, they arrive, first Sariah, then Nephi close behind her. "Are we getting shots?" Nephi moans.

"No, no shots, honey," Heidi answers, hurrying them out of the building.

"The dentist!?" his voice betrays equal dismay.

"No appointments. We're going to your Oma's house, where Emma is."

"I'm going to meet my grandma!?" Sariah gallops sideways, turning to look at her mom with a wonderstruck beam that reveals every lost tooth.

"Yes, you are." A smile flickers across Heidi's lips, too. It's been nearly six months since she's seen her mother.

Heidi ferries Nephi and Sariah back to the house, then sends them upstairs with orders to pack their things for an overnight visit.

She'll call Jennifer and then do her own packing. She's reaching for the receiver when the phone rings. Heidi jumps, but it's Jennifer on the line.

"Cami took my kids with her when she left this morning," Heidi blurts.

"What!?"

She fills Jennifer in.

"That nervy little—"

"I don't blame Cami. I just thought you should know."

"Well, I'll be confiscating her keys as soon as she gets home."

"Don't do that on my behalf. I've appreciated her help with all this Emma stuff."

"That's why I was calling you," Jennifer breaks in, "to talk about Emma, I mean. I heard Graham won't let her come home?"

Heidi's mouth tightens. "That's right."

"Men are *ridiculous*," Jennifer sighs. Heidi doesn't respond, and so she continues. "Look, I don't want to put myself in your business or assume I understand things that I don't, but my guess is that banning Emma isn't *your* preference. So I wanted you to know that Steve and I talked it over, and we'd be happy to have her here until things blow over with Graham—or if they don't, then until the girls go off to college. Emma is already family to us. If she wants to be here and finish out her school year, we'll do whatever we can to help her . . . if it's okay with you."

Heidi is silent. It's a terrible kindness, what Jennifer is offering. A kindness that Heidi is determined not to need. "Thank you, but I'm working on a way to bring her back home."

Working. Heidi is struck by the word, as if someone else had said it. It rings inside her. She isn't going to sit about, hoping and praying. She's done pressing her back to the wall and idling in yogurt aisles. She's going to actually *do* something.

Heidi holds down the button in the phone's cradle, then dials her mother. Sariah appears in the doorway, a canvas bag over her shoulder and a teddy bear in her arms. "I'm ready to meet Oma!" she trills.

"Grab a snack, go to the bathroom, and hop in the van," Heidi says, lifting her mouth away from the receiver. The phone rings and rings in her ear. How many times has Heidi told her mother to get an answering machine?

"If anyone wants to talk to me that badly, they'll call back," Claudia always insists.

Heidi slams the phone down in exasperation. Oh well. It's not as if she needs permission to go see her own daughter. She quickly packs, rustling up extra socks and underwear for her older kids just in case.

By 10:15, they are on the road.

As it turns out, eight-ninths of the Madsens are on some road or another. Only Emma is stationary, lying on an exam table, waiting for the results of the urinalysis.

"I'm amazed you had anything left to pee out," Oma says as they wait.

"No kidding," Emma agrees.

Mostly, though, Emma and Claudia sit in silence, Emma's left hand entwined with her grandmother's right.

It is one of those moments. A moment between moments. A waiting that is more than just waiting. A threshold between a past that can never be reclaimed and a future that will arrive with or without consent. A space as swollen, as pregnant, as fit to burst as Emma imagines her belly might be some eight months hence.

Claudia has imagined this, too. She remembers her own grief and fear in the wake of her unexpected pregnancy with Heide, the weeks of indecision, her mother's unexpected offer to pay her way to Amsterdam for an abortion. The sleepless nights and finally, the decision to have the baby. It was a choice that she could barely explain to herself, let alone to anyone else. A decision confirmed by the unexpected rush of joy that poured into her just as a tiny, red, wailing human burst out of her womb and into her arms. Claudia isn't sure that the joy would have been possible without the choice. She wants the same things now for Emma: joy, of course, and the freedom to choose her own next step. That will all be much easier if she isn't pregnant.

"Please," Claudia prays to some unseen power.

She prays, and she cradles the hand of the nearly grown child of that tiny, red, wailing, unwanted, and then oh-so-very-wanted human. Claudia prays and marvels at the way life can change in an instant. Everything can be given to you, or taken from you, in the blink of an eye, in a rush of fluid or a puff of breath. Is there any more brutal or beautiful truth? We live and die a thousand times in our finite lives. Or so it seems to Claudia. We lose people. We lose pieces of ourselves. Hopes, dreams, possibilities, relationships, identities, abilities. And still we find, over and over again, reasons to keep living. A thaw for every freeze, a flow for every ebb. The pull to throw ourselves back into the sting of wind and sand and to warm to the glow of a sun that rises and sets, rises and sets, over and over and over again.

Life changes in an instant. Sometimes, for the better. Like when her daughter entered the world. Like when she met Dean—in the grocery store, of all places. She was looking for croutons and found *him*. Like when her granddaughter hitched a ride and arrived back in her life.

The door opens, and the doctor steps into the room. In an instant, both Claudia and Emma's bodies snap to attention.

"Well, I've got some good news and some not so good news," the doctor announces.

Chapter Thirty

Joseph called shotgun before they even made it out of the school.

"Then you have to navigate," Cami warned him.

He sits now in the front seat, a map unfolded across his lap. "I think there's just one more real town between here and Moab," he announces as the car speeds out of Wellington with two hours left to go.

"I told you we should have stopped for food!" Hyrum groans.

"Just eat the lunch mom packed you," Eliza tells him for the third time.

"I don't want to. I want a burger and fries," he moans.

"If I had an eject button, I would have launched you out of this car already," Cami gripes.

"Middle schoolers," Joseph shakes his head.

"Hey, don't lump me in with him. I'm not whining," Brigham protests.

"Buurrrrrrger!" Hyrum moans louder, clutching his stomach and collapsing sideways onto Brigham.

"Get off!" Brigham laughs, shoving his brother, only to find himself pushed backward onto Eliza.

"Ouch!" she cries. "Guys, seriously, chill out."

Joseph's voice sharpens in a near perfect imitation of his father. "Boys, don't make me pull over!"

"Did you hear that, Hyrum? Dad's going to give you a warm bottom," Brigham goads.

"A warm bottom?" Cami laughs. "Do I *want* to know what that is?"

"That's what he used to call spanking when we were little. Giving you a warm bottom," Eliza explains.

"When we were *little*?" Hyrum objects. "He spanked me less than a year ago."

"That's just because he doesn't like you." Joseph turns in his seat and pats his brother's knee in mock consolation.

"Don't be a jerk," Cami chastises.

"No, it's totally true," Hyrum says. "Dad hates me . . . and Emma. He loves Joseph and Sariah, though. And he sorta tolerates Liza and Brigham and Nephi."

Cami shakes her head. "Okay, I'm sorry, but I'm just going to say it. Your dad is nuts. I don't know how you guys have turned out so normal."

"Noooormal?" Hyrum repeats in an airy voice. "She thinks we're normal!" He flops onto Brigham again.

"He's not really *that* nuts, though, right?" Eliza appeals. "I mean lots of parents spank their kids."

"But they don't *ban* them from the house," Brigham retorts. "They don't pull them out of bed in the middle of the night to punish them. They don't yell scriptures at them."

"He doesn't really *yell* them . . . usually," Eliza answers.

"Whatever, they don't *raise their voice* in scripture."

"Dad is totally weird," Joseph breaks in.

"I can't believe you're the one saying that. Hyrum is right, you're totally his favorite," Brigham says.

"Well, he is. I go over to friends' houses and see how their parents act. None of them are at all like Dad. He's not just a weird dad, he's a weird person.

"I wonder what Oma will be like," Brigham muses.

"I remember her a little," Joseph answers.

"And?"

"She laughed a lot. And I remember her driving Matchbox cars with me on the floor."

"I have one memory of her," Eliza chimes in. "But I've never been quite sure if it's real or if I made it up. It's just of sitting on her lap while she read me a story."

"You were what, like *one* when you guys last saw her?" Brigham asks.

"Three," Eliza answers. "I was three. Hyrum was one. But besides that one memory, all I remember is that I used to have nightmares about her."

Hyrum's interest is piqued. "Nightmares? Why nightmares?"

"It was a bit later, like when I was in preschool. I remember dreaming that she was some sort of villain and was trying to kidnap me."

"That's probably just because of the stuff dad said about her back then," Joseph surmises.

"What did he say?" Brigham wants to know.

"That she went with Laman and Lemuel to the Great and Spacious Building," Joseph snickers. "I remember because I was all worried that maybe she'd taken some of my Matchbox cars with her."

"I bet she's awesome," Brigham says. "The fact that Dad doesn't like her counts as like twenty points in her favor."

"Or maybe she's a serial killer," Hyrum suggests. "And for once, Dad was being totally reasonable."

"Emma talked about her some," Cami volunteers. "She remembers quite a bit."

"Like what?" Brigham and Joseph ask at the same time.

"Jinx!" They cry.

"Liiiike," Cami raises her voice to speak over them and they fall silent. "Little things. Like playing with her and your dad getting mad at them for laughing too much or being too loud or whatever. She sounds really fun. And Emma overheard when your dad told your mom that your grandma couldn't come visit anymore."

"Really, what did he say? Do you know what she did to piss him off?" Joseph asks.

Eliza aims a reproving glance at the front seat. "Don't say 'piss.'"

"Yeah, you're headed straight for the Great and Spacious Building with language like that," Hyrum jokes.

"Fine, what did Oma do to *ruffle his delicate feathers*," Joseph amends.

"It was something about her trying to make Emma be like her. Like he just thought she was a bad influence, I guess."

"So, she didn't actually *do* anything?" Brigham asks.

"Not from what Emma told me."

"Dad's such an asshole," Joseph shakes his head.

Eliza's mouth falls open. "Joseph!"

"Sorry, butthole. Such a butthole."

"That's still rude."

"Butt*head*?" Hyrum ventures.

"Butt*wipe*?" Brigham tries.

"Butt*odor*?" Hyrum takes a turn again.

"Bully," Cami says with finality. "Your dad is a bully."

Chapter Thirty-One

The rigid contours of an address book press against Graham's hip crease. He leans back in the driver's seat of his boxy, gray Camry, stretches out his right leg, and removes the book. When he plucked it from the counter that morning, he didn't know why he was doing it. It was a rare act of impulsivity. It felt . . . inexplicable . . . transgressive . . . necessary. Suddenly, it's clear why he needs this book. He flips it open and finds the entry for his mother-in-law with ease. Has Heidi been in touch with her all these years? Or did she just hold onto the address? Is this how Emma figured out where to go? Graham shakes his head with amazement. A mindless impulse guided him to the exact information he needed. "I was led by the Spirit, not knowing beforehand the things which I should do," he mumble-quotes the prophet Nephi. Being like Nephi is just as good as being like Lehi, isn't it?

That is what Graham is thinking as he buckles his seatbelt: *I am like Nephi of old*. It is equal parts assertion and aspiration. Graham is driving down to Castle Valley with no clear picture of what he will do or say or how his daughter will respond. He is holding to the rod, pressing forward blindly, *trusting*. Trust. It's always been the most difficult thing. The most dangerous thing. But it must be done.

"Trust in the Lord with all thine heart," Graham whispers, hands clenched tight at ten and two. "And lean not unto thine own understanding. In all thy ways, acknowledge him, and he will direct thy paths." Graham has never quoted this scripture before and is pleased to discover that he knows all the words (and the reference to boot). The verse steadies him—not completely, of course, but just enough that he manages to press his foot to the gas and reverse from the parking space. He aims toward the interstate. The Lord has directed him to go to his daughter in Castle Valley, and that is precisely what he intends to do. Which is why it surprises him when he finds himself hanging a sudden left onto Freedom Boulevard. This is not the way to the interstate. It's the way to—well, Graham isn't quite sure. There's a Smith's Food and Drug down here. He's been there often enough. But there's no reason on earth for him to go grocery shopping right now. So why did he turn? A strange spasm of the arms? A fleeting fit of mental confusion?

He sees it, then. He sees it and knows. He *is* Nephi. He *is* being guided by the Spirit, and just ahead of him on the straight and narrow path sits Juice and Java. He can still hear Heidi's trembling voice: "He works at Juice and Java. Over on Freedom Boulevard."

What's inside this small and squat but metaphorically great and spacious building? Graham answers aloud, his voice a low buzzing: "The fornicating coffee guzzler."

His daughter's defiler. *Here.*

Graham hesitates. It would be nice to have more specific instructions from Heavenly Father, broken down into succinct steps, if possible. What is Graham supposed to do? Burst in and call the fornicator to repentance? Demand child support on Emma's behalf? *Behead him?* Oh, how Graham would like to behead him! But even Nephi—righteous prophet, beheader of villains—was only told what to do one baby step at a time. *Trust.* That impossible word again.

Somehow, Graham—a man who loves nothing more dearly than a plan, a schedule, a checklist—does the impossible. He opens his car door. With no concept of his next step, he exits the Camry. He feels unsteady on his feet but presses forward, walking toward the entrance. Surely, everything will become clear—the mists of darkness will lift—once he's inside. Maybe he'll just confront the lad who works here, who will then fall weeping and penitent at Graham's feet. Only, what if there's more than one lad? How will Graham know whom to confront?

He opens the door and enters. As soon as he looks to the counter, Graham is shocked out of his nervousness, bludgeoned out of uncertainty.

"*You* work here?" he gasps.

"Brother Madsen," Ben stammers, his face flushing. "Um, can I make you some juice?"

***

Nephi sends a kick to the back of his mother's seat. "I'm thirsty," he moans.

"Nephi! *Please* stop kicking my seat," Heidi entreats for the third time. "It's too early to stop, okay? That's why I reminded you to get a drink before we left."

They are only a half hour into the drive, and boredom has already set in.

For the first twenty minutes or so, they played the alphabet game. Beginning with "A" and working toward "Z," they each called out letters as they found them on road signs, semitrucks, stores, and restaurants. "Q" is always the hardest. Nephi got lucky. "Q for Quest!" he called out, as a Nissan minivan raced past.

Within minutes, he had reached "Z" and won the game. They began a second round but soon gave up.

Signs are scarce now and stores nonexistent. They drive in silence. Nephi kicks again.

"Nephi!" Heidi's voice has an uncharacteristic edge.

"Sorry," he mumbles.

He crosses his arms and stares out the window. Minutes pass before he speaks again. "So why did Emma go to your mom's house?"

Heidi opens her mouth to answer, then closes it again. She had imagined that all of the kids knew the full story by now. Certainly, Graham's crazed scriptural recitations had been loud enough for them to hear, so she had absolved herself of the awkwardness of explaining. "Well," she begins, then pauses. She *almost* says "your sister made a mistake and was afraid of getting in trouble." But that is just a sweetened version of her husband's take on events. It's the same old Dannon Vanilla yogurt that she's been feeding herself and her children for years. Emma isn't the only one who made mistakes.

Finally, she finds words—imperfect still, but better. "I don't understand it all the way, but Emma remembers Oma from when she was little. She felt like she needed to get away, and seeing Oma probably sounded really special to her. She should have talked to me and your dad about it, though."

"Did you tell Dad we're going to Oma's house?"

"Umm, no."

"Dad says Oma's a bad person."

"Are those the words he used?"

"I dunno. It was something like that. Sariah asked him why we don't ever see her."

Sariah interjects, "He didn't say a bad *person*. He said a bad *influence*."

"Same difference. Is she, Mom? Is she a bad influence?"

"No, I don't think so. I think she's wonderful."

"Then how come you haven't taken us to see her before?"

"Because your dad . . . felt really strongly about it." The words sound pitiful to her own ears.

"When *I* get married," Sariah says sweetly, "if my husband tries to tell me I can't see you, Mommy, then I just won't listen. And I'll let you see my babies, too, no matter what he says."

The trill of words lands like a punch to the solar plexus. Even a seven-year-old child can see it: this is *her* mess, not just Graham's. Blaming it on him won't fix a thing. Just like cowing to him hasn't fixed anything. Heidi feels acutely aware of the seatbelt strap pressing into her chest. She tries to breathe into it, to push it forward by expanding her lungs. If this is her mess, then it's within her power to clean it up—or at least to make things a little better. *It has to be.*

Nephi is talking now. "I bet he'll be mad we're going there today."

Heidi lets the air rush out. "I bet he will. And you know what?"

"What?"

"It'll be okay." She feels vaguely hysterical once the words leave her lips. She's not sure whether it's laughter or tears that she's holding back. *Just keep driving*, she tells herself. But it's rare that a mother of young children is permitted to do just one thing.

"What does Oma look like?" Sariah wants to know.

For every answer Heidi provides, her daughter has another question. How old is Oma? Why doesn't Heidi have siblings? Why does Dad think that Oma's a bad influence? Why doesn't Oma go to church? Why doesn't she send presents at Christmas time? Does Sariah look like her at all?

Heidi wonders at the sudden flood—at the breaking of a levy that she hadn't known existed but had clearly helped to maintain with her own wall of silence. "I think you have her eyes," she answers. "So does Emma. Emma looks a lot like your grandma. I do, too, I think. But Emma *acts* more like her."

"Is Emma a bad influence?"

"What do *you* think?"

"No. Except maybe a little bit for running away."

"Yeah, I think that seems right."

"Are *you* a bad influence?"

Heidi is taken aback by the question. "Why do you ask?"

"You didn't tell Dad where we're going, so it's the same as running away."

"It's not the same as running away, sweetheart. I'm a grown-up, and we're going to go back."

"Dad won't let Emma come back. So it isn't her fault she has to stay there. Maybe Dad won't let us go back either."

"Your dad will let us go back."

"But what if he doesn't?"

Heidi takes a deep breath. "Well, we'll just go anyway."

"But you always do what he says."

Heidi hesitates, and Nephi punctuates the silence with another kick to the back of her seat.

"Well," she finds her voice, "there's a first time for everything."

***

A dozen questions batter the inside of Graham's skull. "Do I want juice?" is not one of them. He stands mute, mouth agape.

"Professor?" Ben asks.

Still nothing.

Ben knows it looks bad—a BYU student working in a coffee shop. And right after Brother Madsen agreed not to report him to the honor police! The silence can only be an icy demand for explanation. "I know how this must look—me working here. And I don't blame you at all if you don't believe me when I say I don't drink coffee. But you can ask my manager. He gestures toward a woman, talking on the phone behind him. She'll tell you."

"I don't care what you drink," Graham croaks.

Ben's surprise at this assertion is quickly swallowed by his far greater surprise at what his professor says next.

"I care whether you fornicated with my daughter."

"What!?" Ben is flabbergasted.

"My daughter!" Graham pounds the counter, spilling the beet-red juice that waits there. It runs up the sleeve of his white button-down shirt and splatters the front, but he doesn't notice.

Somewhere behind him a customer halts her approach. "That was my drink," she exclaims in protest, but no one hears.

Ben shakes his head, his face slack. His hands seem to move of their own accord, wiping at the spill. "I really don't know what you're—"

"Emma is my daughter!" As the words explode from his lips, Graham suddenly remembers that there may be other male employees at this establishment. Benjamin may not be the culprit.

But even a man illiterate in body language can read what happens next. Ben takes an involuntary step backwards, his face scarlet, eyes blinking rapidly. "Emma? Emma's your daughter?" he sputters.

"Yes, my *child*! She's *seventeen*!" Oh, how Graham would love to behead him.

Ben shakes his head as if to clear his mind of this nightmare. "She . . . she said she was eighteen . . . that she goes to UVSC."

"Well, she lied. She's still in high school, and now she's pregnant. You've ruined her. *Ruined* her!" Graham's face is red and twisted. His voice echoes through the room. A bell jingles as a customer hurries out.

The manager is at Ben's side now. "Sir, I'm going to need you to lower your voice," she says.

Graham hadn't noticed her hanging up the phone. Hadn't noticed the change in Ben's demeanor. The boy is shaking from head to toe. Graham can't look away. Ben's complexion has changed from red to white, his eyes are wide—too big for his face. He looks like a kid—a kid who has just been punched by someone twice his size.

"I'll cover this shift on my own," the manager tells Ben, her voice soft. "Take a break, or go home, or do whatever you need to do. And *you*," she barks to Graham. "I don't ever want to see you in here again. If you have a personal problem with one of my employees, then address it privately—not here."

She stares him down, unblinking. He is a child, dismissed. Graham looks down to find his own hands trembling. He shuffles out the door. *It wasn't supposed to go like this*. He was supposed to be like Nephi. Was supposed to be guided by the Spirit.

He stands by his car, unsure of what to do. He'll go to Castle Valley—to Emma. But what will he do when he gets there? And what if it fails just as spectacularly as this did? He imagines Emma and Claudia, standing shoulder to shoulder. Imagines himself dismissed.

Graham is shaking now, his complexion white. In the distance, a bell rings. He sees a figure approaching. Graham wipes his eyes, looks up. *Benjamin*.

"Look, I can't undo the past," Ben's voice is choked, his face still pale, "but I want to do whatever I can to make this right. I want to help Emma. I'll do whatever you say." He doesn't fall weeping at Graham's feet. Maybe this is the next best thing.

Graham swallows hard. He feels empty, drained, spent. His voice is hollow. "She ran away from home. She was afraid to tell us. I've been sort of . . . hard on her lately. I'm going to get her now. Come." He gestures with his head toward the Camry.

Ben swallows. "Like right now? In your car?"

Graham nods. Ben shuffles to the passenger door, and they climb in, one to the left, the other to the right, doors closing in strange harmony.

***

"Well?" Emma and Claudia urge in perfect unison.

The doctor had paused, perhaps for dramatic effect. "Some good news and some not so good news." And then nothing. A span of silence, in which the audience was left to wonder and worry and observe the whiteness of his coat.

Finally, he resumes. "Well, the good news, young lady, is that you're not pregnant."

Claudia shoots upward with a shrill screech of relief. Emma releases a barely audible puff of air. Before they can wonder about the not-so-good news, before they can puzzle at Emma's myriad symptoms, he continues. "Now the other part, which isn't good news per se but is very manageable, is that you have pyelonephritis. That explains the vomiting, the back pain, the abdominal tenderness, and the fever, as well as your high white blood cell count. I'm going to start you on an antibiotic, and you should begin feeling better within a few days."

"Pye-what?" Claudia asks.

"Pyelonephritis. A kidney infection—a *double* kidney infection in your granddaughter's case, which isn't uncommon. It likely began as a bladder infection and spread. When you're sexually active"—he turns to Emma—"you need to be more careful about hygiene. Always urinate as soon as possible after intercourse to clear any bacteria from the urinary tract."

"So, I was never pregnant? The test was just wrong?" Emma tries to take this in.

The trouble isn't that there is no space inside her for this new information. Quite the opposite. She is hollowed out.

Empty. There is nothing for the doctor's words—"you're not pregnant"—to grab onto.

"A urinary tract infection can trigger a false positive. It's rare, but it happens. In any case, your pregnancy test today was negative, and pyelonephritis explains all of your symptoms."

Both Oma and the doctor study Emma, monitoring her reaction. She knows she's supposed to say something. She shakes her head. "All that stress. For nothing."

"Not for nothing," the doctor objects. "It should drive home the importance of taking precautions to avoid an unwanted pregnancy. Regardless of your religious beliefs, there are good reasons to practice abstinence until marriage."

Claudia looks for and finds the telltale ridge just above his knee—a subtle folding of his pants, right where his temple garments end.

The doctor continues, "There is no better protection against pregnancy and STDs than abstinence. And there's also the negative psychological impact of having sex at such a young age. I assume this has been an unsettling experience for you. Instead of just putting it behind you, think about what you can learn from it. And that goes not only for your sexual activity but also for your experimentation with drugs." His face is stern as he stares down at Emma over the top of his spectacles. "You're on a slippery slope, and it doesn't lead anywhere good. You may need to reevaluate who you spend time with. Whoever gave you those brownies is not a friend worth having. Now, all of that said, if you absolutely refuse to practice abstinence, then I suggest you make an appointment with a gynecologist and get a prescription for birth control. And you"—he turns to Claudia—"ought to purchase your granddaughter a box of condoms if she's going to carry on in this manner."

"I absolutely will. After we have a long talk about abstinence. And drugs. Thank you, doctor," Claudia answers solemnly.

As soon as he leaves the room, Emma trembles with laughter. It hurts her stomach, and so the resulting sound is somewhere between a giggle and a moan. "I'm sorry I can't be your friend anymore," Emma tells her grandmother.

"I'm sorry I'm not a friend worth having," Claudia returns, wrapping her granddaughter in a hug.

"At least I got a vision out of the whole thing," Emma smiles wanly.

"And you're not pregnant." Claudia's smile is anything but wan.

"I'm not pregnant," Emma echoes.

***

Ben takes in the view from the passenger seat. He is surprised to see that they are leaving Provo. "Where did Emma *go*?" he asks, breaking the silence.

"Castle Valley."

"Huh?"

"Castle Valley. It's about three and a half hours from here."

"Three and half hours!" He had assumed that Emma had "run away" to stay with one of

her classmates. Or maybe, worst case scenario, that she had hopped on a bus to Salt Lake and was now waiting around in a dumpy diner for one of her parents to rescue her. This is, he now realizes, not going to be a quick excursion. "I'm gonna miss my classes," Ben says.

"Yes. Me too. Only in my case, that is without precedent. Whereas in your case, missing class seems to be par for the course."

Ben rolls his eyes but says nothing. There are so many questions he would like to ask. When did Emma find out she was pregnant? How is she taking the news? Is she actually going to have the baby, or . . . ? And if she has it, will she keep it? Also, why Castle Valley?

He hasn't seen her since the night they had sex. It's been nine days. He knows because he's counting. She just . . . disappeared. Stopped coming in for lattes. He always thought it was weird that Emma wouldn't give him her number. She would just show up near the end of his shift, and they would hang out. "When can I see you again?" he would always ask.

"When are you working?" she would answer.

It made no sense then and all the sense in the world now. *A high schooler.* Does that make him a pedophile? He's only two years older than Emma, but still—*sex with a minor?* And unprotected sex, at that. *I'm such a piece of shit,* Ben thinks to himself.

It's hardly a new thought. His father had said precisely those words to him often enough, usually with an additional descriptor attached, like "stupid," "worthless," or that most versatile of all words: "fucking." His old therapist referred to this piece-of-shit mantra as a core belief. In high school, she had him fill out a thought record every day for weeks on end. He can still picture it. *Daily Dysfunctional Thought Record*, it said on the top.

If he were to fill it out now for his dysfunctional thought du jour, he would write this:

Situation: **got my professor's underage daughter pregnant & now I'm stuck in a car with him**

Emotions (Severity 1-100%): **stressed as hell, 100%.**

Automatic Thoughts: **I'm a piece of shit & I've ruined her life & possibly mine**

Cognitive Distortion: **labeling & catastrophizing**

Rational Responses: **I made a mistake. Things are going to feel really hard for a while but not forever.**

Outcome (Severity 1-100%):

Outcome. That's where he's stumped. Ben has no idea how this will turn out. How could he? He wonders what Brother Madsen expects of him. Wonders what Emma expects of him. He breaks the silence that surrounds him. "So . . . what do you want me to do when we get there?"

Graham sucks in air through pursed lips. "Well, if in fact she's pregnant, then you'll need to propose."

Propose? Ben feels his heart drop in his stomach. He's yanked to a cliff edge. He hangs from a single word: "if." Professor Madsen said "if."

"*If* she's pregnant?" Ben repeats.

"I haven't talked to her, so I don't know the details. There was something about conflicting test results."

Ben steadies himself with a long exhalation. Maybe the situation just became less catastrophic. But *propose*? "I don't think Emma wants to marry me, even if she is pregnant. I haven't heard from her in over a week."

"Well, it's not always about what we *want,* is it?" Graham snaps. "I want my children to obey the Law of Chastity. I want to be in my office right now. Yet here I am, structuring my day not around what I want but around *what is.*"

What is: the meaning of life. Graham sees the words again, separated by a colon. He sees the crumpled balls, stacked on his office floor.

Ben glances over at his professor. Graham's knuckles are chalk white against the black steering wheel. He's at a cliff edge, too, Ben realizes. "I hear you," the younger man sighs.

Graham says nothing.

"The only thing harder than acceptance is non-acceptance. My therapist used to say that." Ben doesn't add that the necessity of acceptance does not equate with the necessity of a marriage proposal. He would prefer not to enrage his driver. And anyway, milk before meat.

Graham considers Ben's words. What is *non*-acceptance? *Control,* he thinks. That's what it's always been for him, anyway. If he had tried to control his daughter less, would things have turned out differently? He thinks of Emma's persistent complaints, many of which begin with "no one else's parents" or "all my friends get to." None of Emma's friends are, to Graham's knowledge, defiled or pregnant. It seems unjust that lax parenting should reap greater rewards than his conscientiousness.

"Maybe if I hadn't tried to control Emma quite so much she wouldn't have rebelled," Graham admits into the silence. Perhaps he hopes to be contradicted. Hopes that Ben will be privy to the inner workings of his daughter's mind, privy to the unexpected ardor of her filial devotion, to a secret yearning to live up to her father's expectations.

"Seems plausible," Ben agrees.

Heat rises to Graham's face. "Did she . . . say something about that?" There's a quiver in his voice.

Ben tries to recall. "She didn't really tell me the truth about her life. She said she goes to UVSC and lives with an aunt. So, I don't know how much stock to put in anything else she said. But she always seemed to me like she was running from something. I've been that person and sometimes I still am, so I get what it looks like. And if you were trying to control her, no matter how good your motives, well it probably just made her feel more trapped. More desperate to run. She's spunky."

"Always has been," Graham laments. *What could I have done more for my vineyard*? The words drift again into his mind.

It's as if Ben hears the question. "I took a Human Development class my first semester at BYU. And something the professor said stuck with me. He was talking about being a parent, and he said you have to prioritize the relationship over the rules."

"How's that supposed to work?" Graham scoffs. "You can't parent without rules."

"Yeah, I don't think that's what he was saying. I think the point is to not get so fixated on the rules that you're putting more energy into them than into your actual relationship. I latched onto that kind of stuff in the class—parenting advice, you know? I didn't have a good model for parenting, and odds are I'll be a dad someday . . . maybe a lot sooner than I thought"—Ben swallows hard—"so I need to learn that stuff. I was little when my mom died . . . She had cancer."

Graham thinks of Pam. "My mom died of cancer, too," he says. "My *real* mom, the one who took me in, not the one who threw bottles." He's never phrased it this way before, never quite thought of it this way. But of course, it's the truth: Pam was his real mother.

Something else rings true—*relationship over rules. That's what Pam did*, wasn't it? When he crashed her car and she responded with love rather than anger? It had made him want to do better. *Better*, rather than badder. He hears Emma's tiny voice: "When you spank me, it just makes me want to be badder."

"When you try to control me," she might as well have said.

The meaning of parenting is to accept your children as they are. The words descend on Graham's mind. The voice that speaks them isn't his. Nor is it the sonorous speech one might expect from a member of the all-male trinity. It's a soft voice. A feminine voice. *Pam's voice.*

It pierces him like a sword. He feels beheaded. An old way of thinking topples from his neck, rolls about at his feet. A new skull, airy and light and wholly unnerving sprouts from the stump. Graham isn't sure which head is his.

Chapter Thirty-Two

"Any news?" Dean asks, walking back into the exam room and looking from Emma's supine form to Claudia's upright one.

"She's not pregnant. It's a kidney infection," Claudia tells him.

Dean lets out a sharp exhalation, almost a whistle. "Are they admitting her?"

"No, she can go home with us. They're going to pump her with fluids first, though, and start her on an antibiotic and something for the nausea. Though they don't seem to be in much of a hurry," Claudia sighs. "How did you explain things to Jeff and Joelle?"

"I told them Emma's sick and that we think it's something she ate."

Claudia laughs. "You're such a lawyer," she says, shaking her head.

Dean stays with Emma, and Claudia steps out to hunt for a payphone. She wants to move her legs, release the pent-up stress from her body, but mostly, she wants to call Heide with the news.

***

What Eliza wants most is a bathroom. "I have to pee really bad," she says for the second time, her voice apologetic.

"Me too," Cami sighs. "I think we're getting close to Moab, though."

"Why don't you just pee on the side of the road like civilized humans?" asks Hyrum, who demonstrated his civility some twenty miles back.

"We turn up here," Joseph tells Cami, pointing off to the left. Straight ahead sits Moab, with its promise of public restrooms.

"I'm gonna drive into town first. We can turn back around after we use the bathroom."

"Girls," Hyrum shakes his head. "Don't stop at a gas station!" he advises, as the first buildings begin to appear. "Stop at a McDonald's or Burger King or something. The bathrooms are always cleaner."

"Nice try. You just want food," Cami replies.

"I don't *just* want food. I also want the two of you to have a pleasant and sanitary bathroom experience."

"Riiiiiight," Cami scoffs, but she passes two gas stations without a word, then swings a left into a Wendy's parking lot.

"You da bomb, Cami!" Hyrum proclaims before bounding from the car, his speed matched only by Eliza's.

When the girls emerge from the bathroom, they find all three boys in line, waiting to order.

"I can't watch them eat fries and not have any," Cami says.

And so, all five kids wait in the languorous line until finally, they are squeezed into a booth, where their chatter falls away as their mouths fill with food.

"What time did you tell Emma you would get there?" Eliza asks Cami, her french fries dwindling to crispy nubs.

"I said 12:30 at the earliest." Cami looks down at her watch. "It's 12:28 now."

"She's gonna be surprised to see the rest of us," Hyrum grins, not bothering to swallow before he speaks.

"Cute. You should give her that exact smile when we roll up. The chewed-up bun is a really nice effect." Cami is one of the gang by now.

Hyrum broadens his grin. A chunk of ground beef tumbles from his mouth and onto the table.

"Ewww, you're disgusting," Joseph says, throwing a napkin at his brother as Brigham and Cami giggle.

Eliza turns the conversation toward the practical. "I hope there's room for all of us," she muses, a crease emerging between her eyebrows.

"It'll be fine," Cami reassures her. "Emma said there's a big guestroom. We can all crash on the floor in there. It's just one night."

"I wonder what Mom's going to do when we don't come home from school." The line on Eliza's brow doesn't soften.

"Ahh, she'll figure it out," Brigham says. "She knew Cami was going down here."

"I know she'll figure it out. But what will she *do,*" Eliza emphasizes.

Her question goes unanswered. Hyrum has balled up his straw wrapper, dampened it with Sprite, fixed it to the end of his straw, and blown it full force at Joseph's face.

"Gross, you moron!" Joseph peels the wad from his cheek and pelts it at Hyrum, delivering a sharp kick under the table that misses its target, meeting Brigham's shin instead.

"Ouch!" Brigham cries out. A half dozen heads turn to look in their direction.

Cami rolls her eyes at the fresh outburst of sibling discord. "Alright, children, time to go." She rises from the table and begins bussing the trash. Eliza joins her.

Table cleared, they troop to the parking lot, the boys still bickering and assigning blame. Cami rummages for her keys. She pats her jean pockets, reaches into her coat pockets, scours her purse.

"Uhh, Cami," Brigham's voice interrupts her searching. He nods his head in the direction of the driver's seat.

There, wedged between the seat and the center console, Cami's keys glint in the sun.

"Nooo!" She thumps a hand to her forehead, pulls at the door handle in dismay, then turns in a bewildered circle, as if help might materialize in one direction or another.

A few blocks away, Dean opens the front passenger door for Emma. She moves slowly but supports her own weight.

"You alright?" he asks.

"Mmm hmm," she confirms and ducks into the car.

She *is* alright. A bit of color has returned to her face. Sure, she's exhausted and aching, and true, none of this feels quite real to her, but at least she's not puking. And she's not scared. Not pregnant!

In half an hour, they will be back at Claudia and Dean's. Oma will tuck Emma into bed, and Emma will fall asleep before she has time to recall that Cami ought to have arrived by then.

"I wonder if Cami called while we were out," Oma will reflect to Dean. Maybe Heide is right about needing an answering machine.

And of course, Cami will indeed have called while they were out. It is the first thing she does, once she stops spinning in circles.

Three times she and Eliza call, always with the same result: interminable ringing. So, they try Cami's mother instead. The answering machine picks up.

"I guess we have to call a locksmith," Cami moans.

It takes seven rings before someone finally answers. "Thisburt," a voice slurs.

Thiburt? Cami wonders to herself. "Uh, are you the locksmith?" she asks aloud.

"Yep."

Cami explains the situation. Then, when it becomes clear that the man on the phone—he's named Burt, apparently—grasped almost nothing she said, she explains it again. And again.

"At Wendy's, you say?"

"Yes."

"Alright, gimme 'bout twenty minutes."

If time is a line and each moment is a dot upon it, then the series of points that make up these twenty minutes are round and full. Burt bumps about his bedroom. With the shades down and the light off, it's impossible to tell which clothes are the least dirty, the least wrinkled, so he just dons the first shirt and pair of jeans that he finds. He takes deep breaths, or tries to. He knows the sunlit drive will be too much. Too agitating. That he will arrive rattled, unwell. His eyes will throb, his adrenaline surge, his movements grow even more uncoordinated. But he hasn't worked in days, and he's determined to do this.

Within these twenty minutes, Claudia, Emma, and Dean will (like Burt) move not only forward in time but also across space, beginning the drive from the hospital back to Castle Valley.

Dan will hug his parents goodbye, will promise to return soon, then climb into his station wagon, where he will travel through space-time and, it will seem to him, cross spiritual dimensions as well. Dan is still praying for the people he meets. He pronounces blessings on the passengers of every car he encounters, or at least he tries to. Traffic occasionally picks up to a degree that makes this untenable. Still, he has the sense that he's connecting with the people he passes—that he understands them in some way. They're his brothers and sisters. They have, all of them, inner lives and outer worlds as rich and complicated as his own. He can feel it. Can feel *them.* Some of them carry pain beyond his imagining, and yet *not* beyond his imagining. Dan's eyes tear up with the lightness of love and the weight of what it is to be a spiritual being having a human experience.

Maybe this is what Jesus felt in the Garden of Gethsemane, he thinks, *only amplified many times over.* He imagines the Son of God crossing space and time, suffering every sin and pain and disappointment that humanity would ever know. Perhaps time isn't a line. Perhaps it can all be collapsed into a single moment, can all be felt in one wordless wave.

It is true, in this moment, that three of the Madsen children are grumbling impatiently at the edge of a parking lot, but perhaps it is equally true that they are giggling infants, or that they are wrinkled and old and ready to pass through the veil. Maybe it is only a matter of perspective. A question of where you stand and how carefully you look.

Time passes. Or perhaps perspective merely shifts. Cami has given Burt the twenty minutes he asked for, followed by another twenty on top of it.

"Is this guy ever going to show up?" Joseph sighs.

Graham sighs, too. A heavy, rattling exhalation.

"What do you think is wrong?" Ben asks him. They stand shoulder to shoulder on the side of the road, staring down at the engine.

"I have no idea," Graham confesses, slump-shouldered.

He's never been the sort of guy who tinkers on his own car. He can jump a battery or change a tire if he absolutely must, but this—whatever this is—is beyond him.

Everything had been fine until a few miles back when the car grew suddenly jerky and the check engine light came on. Perhaps Graham should have pulled over right away, but they were in the final stretch before Moab, maybe thirty minutes from town. Surely, they could make it! Surely—but they didn't.

The engine hiccupped and sputtered. Graham drew in deeper and deeper breaths—oceanic breaths. Vader breaths, his children would say.

"What are you doing?" Ben asked.

"What do you think I'm doing? I'm breathing."

"Yeah, but like *really* loud."

"It's calming," Graham assured him.

"You don't look calm," Ben laughed.

"Well, your interruptions aren't helping. It's a proven technique." That's what Graham's high school track coach had told him, anyway. This was the first time that Graham had thought to employ it in a moment of stress, though. He felt rather pleased with himself, and this fact—the fact that he could feel something else alongside the angst and alarm—seemed to him a further demonstration of the efficacy of the technique.

Ben attempted to imitate Graham's breathing. The car filled with the whooshing of their shared exhalations. Only the engine was louder. *Hiccup, sputter, hiccup, sputter*. And then it died. Graham let out a final shuddering breath and turned on his hazard lights before coasting onto the shoulder, where they are now parked. Stranded.

"I guess we better flag someone down," Ben says, stepping toward the road.

He waits. A few dozen seconds tick past, and a vehicle approaches. Ben lifts a hand, but the car races by, sending a rush of air strong enough to ripple even his tidily cropped, BYU-standard tresses.

Several minutes yawn past before another vehicle comes near. It slows. "They're stopping!" Ben tells Graham, who is still staring forlornly at the engine.

But they don't stop. Instead, the car arcs into the opposite lane, giving them a wide berth, both driver and passenger rubbernecking shamelessly.

Ben throws his hands up in exasperation and turns to Graham. "Who does that?" he protests, his voice incredulous.

Graham looks up from the engine. Somehow, he has managed to smear his face and the chest pocket of his once white shirt with grease. "And by chance there came down a certain priest that way: and when he saw him, he passed by on the other side," he answers, as if this might be illuminating.

Ben tilts his head quizzically.

"It's from the parable of the Good Samaritan," Graham explains. He succeeds, quite without precedent, at saying this in a tone that doesn't suggest that his conversation partner is an uninformed imbecile.

A third automobile draws near, from the opposite direction. Again, Ben lifts a hand, albeit without much hope.

"This one will stop," Graham says. He doesn't know how he knows this, and for a moment the evidence seems stacked against him. The vehicle slows but passes them by

Its driver is busily whispering supplications, but he swings a U-turn and pulls in behind them. Graham stares at the car—a station wagon, wood-paneled like Pam's.

A young man—clean cut, gangly, a bit duck-footed—climbs out and approaches Ben. They both give a start. "Hey, I know you," the gangly youth grins.

"Yeah, you're in my ward, right? At the Y?" Ben asks. Ben may not be the most enthusiastic participant at church, but he still attends three times a month—the minimum required to avoid expulsion from the university.

"Yeah. That's crazy to bump into you way down here!"

"No kidding. I'm Ben."

"Dan." Dan extends his arm. They shake hands. "Looks like you and your dad are having some car trouble?"

Chapter Thirty-Three

Insecurity gnaws at the edges of Heidi's resolve as she nears Castle Valley. She's doing the right thing. She's sure of that. But she's made so many wrong steps before this one. How will her daughter respond to her arrival?

Her daughter, at the moment, is nonresponsive. She is deep in a haze of sleep.

Somewhere between mother and daughter, an older man, noticeably red in the face, emerges from a pickup truck. "You the ones got locked out?" he asks the pack of loitering youths.

"Yeah! We worried you weren't coming," Cami says.

He grunts and walks over to the driver-side door. "Looks like your keys are right there in the car," he observes, peering in the window.

"Yeah, that's why we called."

"Alrighty," he says, returning slowly to his truck for tools.

Cami and Joseph sit down beside the others on the curb to watch. The show is neither as fast-paced nor as eventful as any of them hoped. Apart from Burt's heavy breathing and occasional groans, not much seems to happen. He picks at the driver-side lock for some time, then steps back, staring at it with an expression of distaste, before repeating the process again. Eventually, he moves to the passenger-side door, where the same scene plays out.

"Is it not working?" Cami finally asks, rising from the curb.

"You got tricky locks," Burt says, wiping his forehead. "Think I'll give the trunk a try."

"The trunk?" *What good will that do?*

But he is already hard at work, brow furrowed, breath labored. There is a pop, and the trunk opens. "There you go," he proclaims, moving slowly toward them.

"How is that supposed to help?" Joseph makes no effort to hide his disdain.

"There's a bit of a crack between the seats in the back. You kids are small. I expect you can get an arm through, maybe figure out a way to fold one of the seats down."

All five children stare at him open-mouthed.

"Since I couldn't get the front door open, I won't charge you full price. Twenty dollars should do."

Cami fumbles in her purse, then hands him a bill.

Burt returns to his truck and drives away, his back wheel climbing the curb as he rolls slowly out of the lot.

All five kids walk to the back of the car and stare into the trunk.

Cami probes at the back of the seat. Sure enough, with effort she can sneak a few fingers through, but nothing more.

"This is ridiculous. I can't believe I just gave him twenty dollars."

"I can't believe anyone is that bad at their job," Brigham adds.

"What would MacGyver do?" Hyrum wonders. "Maybe we can make an extendable arm out of stale French fries and reach through to get the keys."

Cami shakes her head and trudges back to the payphone.

She almost has Claudia's number memorized now. This time the line is busy. Three times, she calls, each time with the same beeping in her ear.

Claudia stands in the kitchen, receiver in hand. Five rings and the Madsens' answering machine picks up. Claudia hangs up and tries again. Three times with the same result. "Heide picked some time to stop being a homebody," she complains to Dean.

"Maybe a mechanic can help," Joseph suggests to Cami.

"I guess it's worth a try."

And so they do try, Cami thumbing again through the yellow pages. A woman answers the call. Thankfully, she seems to grasp their situation the first time Cami explains it. "We don't usually handle that, but I'll go check with the guys and see if one of them can help. I'm going to put you on hold for a minute."

"Okay," Cami breathes gratefully, but her gratitude doesn't last or at least not for as long as the hold does. It stretches from one minute to two and then three and beyond until an automated voice demands that she insert more coins.

She reaches into her purse, searches her wallet. It's full of pennies. Nothing she can use. She looks across the parking lot to where the Madsen kids sit in a line on the curb. "I need more change!" she calls.

By the time Eliza reaches her with a fistful of coins, the call has dropped. Cami groans.

"Just call back," Eliza suggests.

Of course, the line is busy. Eliza looks over Cami's shoulder at the listing in the phone book. "Hey, is that the place you're calling?" she stabs a finger at the page.

"Yeah."

"Look, it's right over there!" Sure enough, there it is, just a few buildings away on the opposite side of the road.

"Boys!" Cami calls. "We're going on a field trip!"

"Hyrum's in the bathroom," Brigham shouts back.

"He'll probably be awhile," Joseph adds, smirking.

Cami sighs. *Can't anything just go smoothly?*

Ben has asked himself that same question once or twice today. After nearly half an hour in the car with Dan, Ben knows as much about the Brazil Campinas Mission as he ever really wants to know. Dan is a good guy, though, and his quirkiness is amusing. Ben needs amusement. He leans forward between the seats. "I like your scented temple," he says, unable to resist a little snark. But snark, as a rule, sails right over Dan's head.

"Thanks! I hung it there to impress a girl." Dan blushes at his own confession.

Ben laughs, not unkindly. "Did it work?"

"No, but I like seeing it there anyway. As a reminder, you know."

Ben doesn't ask what a piney fresh temple reminds Dan of. Such a question might precipitate testimony bearing, and Ben has endured enough awkwardness for one day.

Graham, apparently, has not. "It's unclear to me what sort of reminder a temple taped to an air freshener is supposed to serve as."

Graham is not being snarky. He's just not good at polite conversation.

Dan laughs self-consciously. "Yeah, I guess it seems kinda dumb, right? But it reminds me of this thing I figured out when I was trying to impress that girl. She was sort of mixed up, you know? Like about Heavenly Father's plan. And at first I felt pretty judgmental, but then I tried to just accept her as she was and treat her as a daughter of God, and it's like all these really cool parts of her emerged, just because I was looking differently. So that's kind of my focus now. Trying to view everyone as a child of God. That's why I picked you guys up."

Ben considers a cautionary retort. Something along the lines of *you should be careful, Jeffrey Dahmer was a child of God*, but he opts for courteous appreciation instead. "Well, we're glad you did."

If he was still listening, Graham might echo this sentiment, but he's elsewhere now, turning Dan's words over in his mind. *Tried to just accept her as she was and treat her as a daughter of God.* Acceptance. The word has sprung unbidden into Graham's field of awareness more than once today. Is this what the moment of clarity in his office points to? The stacked balls of paper? *What is: the meaning of life.* Not changing what is, not resisting what is, not battling it or even bringing it into order. Just *accepting*?

Somewhere in the course of the past few hours, Graham has come to accept Ben. He can't say when or how it happened. He isn't any more pleased about the prospect of his daughter being pregnant than he was at the start of the drive, but his anger has dissolved. Graham sees pieces of himself in the younger man. He doesn't want to be the one to cast Ben out, to disfellowship him or stand shoulder to shoulder with the Honor Code Office in condemnation. Not only does he not want to be the one to do this, he doesn't want *anyone else* to do this. He almost likes the kid.

If Graham can accept his daughter's defiler—not *approve* of him, exactly; not hand him any gold stars or write him a recommendation letter for the Celestial Kingdom, but not begrudge him any good thing either—then surely he can accept his own daughter, too. Accept her as she is, not as he wishes her to be. *I have to*, he thinks to himself, *but can I?* The words of Nephi arrive on Graham's lips: "I will go and do the things which the Lord hath commanded, for I know that the Lord giveth no commandments unto the children of men, save he shall prepare a way for them that they may accomplish the thing which he commandeth them."

Dan turns to look at Graham, a puzzled expression on his face. It takes Graham a moment to realize that he quoted the scripture aloud.

"Sorry, I was talking to myself."

Dan returns his eyes to the road. Tumbleweed and puffs of sand blow sideways, pelting the vehicle. "It's a rad scripture."

Ben, not unreasonably, wonders how Graham's apparent determination to follow the Lord's commandments might impact him. "So, uh, is there a particular commandment you're thinking about?" He hopes it is a commandment from the comparatively warm and fuzzy God of the New Testament, rather than the wrathful deity who burned Sodom and Gomorrah.

"I'm thinking about Emma. I'm thinking . . . I need to accept her as she is. To *love* her just the way she is." The words leave Graham's mouth, and warmth fills his chest. He can almost feel the bundle of blankets pressed to him—his daughter, newly born.

Ben settles back against his seat, smiling. "I'm sure she'll appreciate that," he says. His eyes meet Dan's in the rearview mirror, and so he explains, "Brother Madsen isn't my dad. I've sort of been . . . dating . . . his daughter, and she ran off to her grandma's in Castle Valley, so we're on a reconnaissance mission."

Dan's mouth hangs open. His eyes dart from side to side as his brain plays connect the dots. They are in Moab now. The repair shop is just ahead. He pulls in, parks, his mind aswirl. "I can wait around . . . to make sure you guys are all set," he manages to stammer.

Graham has already unbuckled his seatbelt and opened his door. "Thank you. I'll come back out and let you know what they say." He pauses, his hand still on the open door. "Are you driving to Provo today?" he asks Dan.

Dan nods mutely.

Thick creases line Graham's forehead. He shifts his weight from side to side, not looking at either Ben or Dan, who exchange a wondering glance. That strange warmth still tingles inside him. "I think . . . " Graham begins to speak but trails off.

"Therefore, you are?" Ben quips.

"Smart aleck," Graham says, but he's smiling now. He looks Ben full in the face. "I think if you want to go back to Provo that's fine. I think you were right. Emma won't want to get married. And she might view my bringing you down here as a bit . . ." again his voice drops off.

"Tyrannical?" Ben offers impishly.

Graham winces. "Can we go with 'heavy-handed'?"

"Sure. Heavy-handed works," Ben grins in reply.

Graham turns to Dan. "Can you drive him?"

"Yeah," Dan manages to say, though his brain is shot through with a fresh onslaught of bullet points demanding connection.

Emma won't want to get married. Brother Madsen's words echo in Dan's skull. He hears Emma's voice, layered in. *You don't have to be married to have a baby.* For a moment, Dan can't hear anything else. Can't see anything else. Girls are born pure and good. Something must have happened to her. Someone must have treated her badly. *This guy*. This Ben character. *He* is the one. He got that poor girl mixed up—mixed up and pregnant.

By the time Graham has entered the repair shop, Dan has spun in his seat. Ben feels himself yanked forward by the front of his shirt.

"Woah, man, what the hell!?"

"If you weren't a child of God, I'd put my fist through your face," Dan sputters.

Ben lifts his hands in baffled surrender. "What are you even—"

"You got her *pregnant*!? Do you have any idea what that will do to her life? Her *salvation*!"

"Do you . . . *know* Emma?" Ben tries to make sense of senselessness.

Dan releases Ben's shirt, his fury quickly spent. Tears spill from the corners of his eyes. "I drove her down here."

Ben watches him warily. Dan swipes at his eyes, then looks at the dangling, pine-fresh house of God, as if for answers.

"She . . . was the one you were trying to impress?"

Dan nods.

"Woah. Hey, I didn't mean for it to happen. I feel like a total jerk. It's not for sure that she's pregnant, though. I mean, I really hope she's not."

The car feels too hot. Dan rolls down the windows, and the two young men fall into glassy-eyed silence, punctuated only by Dan's occasional sniffles. Each gazes wordlessly ahead. A gaggle of kids approaches, most of them teenagers.

Ben's eyes come into focus, and he marvels at how much one of the girls reminds him of Emma. Dan has precisely the same thought at precisely the same time. It isn't Emma, of course. She is sound asleep in Castle Valley.

Heidi is in Castle Valley, too, pulling into the driveway, gravel rumbling beneath her tires. Sariah is already unbuckled, bouncing up and down with the gravel. "This is where Oma lives?" she pipes.

Cami sends an elbow into Eliza's rib. "Those two guys are totally checking you out. One of them is cute."

Joseph hears and scowls in their direction. "That's disgusting. Eliza's like twelve, and they're like thirty."

Cami laughs, "They are *not* thirty."

"And I'm *fourteen*," Eliza adds, though she doesn't relish the intensity of the men's stares.

"Still, it's gross," Joseph insists.

"I think you should open up a can of whoop A, Joe. Defend your sister's honor," Hyrum suggests.

"I think you should—" Joseph begins his retort but doesn't finish.

The wood-paneled doors swing open. The cradle robbers climb out, each giving Eliza one final lingering gaze before they walk together into the repair shop.

"That was just *wrong*," Hyrum says.

"They didn't even try to hide it!" Cami laughs, shaking her head.

Eliza's steps slow. "I'm not going in there. I'll wait outside."

"I'll stay with you," Brigham offers.

"Me too," Hyrum says. "Someone will need to defend your virtue once they kill Brigham."

Cami and Joseph walk to the door alone. Joseph reaches for the handle, when Cami suddenly throws an arm out, blocking him. "Is that your *dad*?" she hisses.

"No," Joseph answers reflexively. Then he looks—really looks. His eyes widen. Joseph lurches to the side of the door, away from the windows. "We can't go in there," he says, his face stricken.

"No duh," Cami replies.

***

Claudia hears the crunching of tires on gravel and hurries to the front door. It will be Cami, she thinks, and throws the door wide. Her daughter and two youngest grandchildren climb from a Ford Club Wagon. Claudia squeals and races toward them. "I don't know who to hug first!" she trills.

Heidi and Sariah move just as quickly toward her, landing in a group embrace with Sariah sandwiched in the middle. Only Nephi hangs back, tracing lines across the gravel with his big toe.

Claudia finally disentangles herself and moves toward him. "I'm so happy to finally get to meet you. I hear you're quite the basketball player. You had a game this weekend, didn't you?"

He nods. It hadn't occurred to him that this unknown woman would know things about him.

"How'd it go?"

She smiles so warmly that Nephi forgets he was still debating whether to let himself like her. He tells her about the shots he made, then follows her into the house, where they peer together into the freezer and he smilingly informs her that mint chocolate chip happens to be his favorite. Dean scoops ice cream into bowls, and the matriarchs talk in excited whispers, and the words that rise over the clinking of spoons hardly seem to justify their animation—"kidney," "antibiotic," "sleep."

Suddenly, though, Heidi's voice is at full volume. "But where are the other kids?"

Claudia's forehead knits in confusion. "Other kids?"

***

The other kids are embroiled in hushed debate.

"He's our *dad.* I know he's strict, but come on guys, let's just go in there," Eliza is saying, not for the first time.

"You're out of your mind!" Joseph and Hyrum are in agreement for once.

"What's the worst that could happen?" She wants to know.

"Umm, he could murder us. Or ground us for life. Or drag us home."

"*Or* we could all just ride to Oma's house together," Eliza protests.

"Where he probably has some fresh torture plotted for Emma!"

"And we'll get dragged into it," Brigham chimes in. "Liza, you said you wanted to *support* her, remember? Showing up there with Dad is the exact opposite of supportive."

Eliza bites at her lower lip. "Fine," she mutters. It's not that she thinks her brothers are wrong, exactly. It's just that she *wishes* they were wrong. She wishes that love was the defining thread weaving her family together. Wishes that kindness rather than conflict was the default. And who doesn't, on occasion, live based on what they wish were true rather than what actually is? And when living on a wish, who doesn't do the occasional weird, inexplicable thing?

And so, it's not really all that strange that, when Hyrum sounds the alarm ("He's coming!") and the shop door swings wide, and all five kids crouch down on the far side of the parked station wagon, Eliza reaches out her pointer finger, running it across the dusty door until three crisp words gleam on the faux wood: *GOD IS LOVE.* She will feel awkward about this when she realizes that she left the message for her oglers.

Graham walks out of the repair shop. The two men follow closely behind him. They are all talking together. Graham isn't the sort to banter with strangers, but his children don't have time to marvel at the oddity of his behavior. They need a new hiding place, and fast.

The three men have stopped now and stand in a cluster on the passenger side of the vehicle.

"The tow truck should be here within an hour, and then I'll ride with him to the car," their father is saying. "Thank you for your help."

"Hey, happy to do it! We're brothers, after all," one of the men replies (not the one Cami referred to as "cute"), clapping Graham on the shoulder.

Graham lets out a soft snort but nods his head. "I suppose we are. And you," he turns to the other man, the cute one, "I'll be in touch. I have your email address."

The kids crouch low as they rush from the driver side of the wagon to the back of a nearby dumpster. The sounds of conversation fade for them into unintelligible mumbles.

"I'll see you in class on Wednesday," Ben reminds his professor.

"Right!" Graham shuffles his feet, then smiles self-consciously. "That's going to be a bit . . . strange, isn't it?"

"A bit," Ben agrees.

"Well, we'll manage. I don't plan to report you to the Honor Code Office, on the condition that you try not to," Graham's lips twitch soundlessly, as if he can't quite bring his mouth to form the words, "try not to do any more fornicating until you're out of my class," he finally manages.

Ben gives a salute.

Graham pulls his briefcase from the front seat. He'll wait inside for the tow truck. He backs away from the vehicle, waving goodbye with an awkwardness that suggests a lack of practice with such gestures.

"Bye!" Dan shouts. He looks down as he pulls at the door handle. The words *GOD IS LOVE* shine up at him. *He sure is*, Dan thinks to himself.

The mysterious appearance of these letters on his car feels like a divine hug. A heavenly pat on the back. "You're on the right track. Keep it up," Heavenly Father must be saying.

"Look!" Dan beams to Ben, pointing at the car door. Ben walks around to inspect.

"Cool," he nods. For Ben, the words prove only one thing: that they left a car parked in Utah. That there are Mormons milling about. Perhaps these things happen in the Bible Belt, too.

Graham doesn't see the words until the station wagon pulls away. The sun glints on them then. *GOD IS LOVE.* Dan wrote them; *he must have*, or so Graham concludes. But they feel like the right words for this moment. *God is love.* To be a servant of God is to be a servant of love. To wield the priesthood—the power of God on earth—can only mean to wield the power of love. Graham has been doing it wrong. Maybe it was shame that kept him from seeing this sooner—from seeing *himself* sooner. It usually is. Graham doesn't feel shame right now, though. He feels resolve.

Chapter Thirty-Four

In mere seconds, Heidi's brain manages to enumerate—in graphic detail—a slew of separate but equally horrific fates that could have befallen her children. A fiery car wreck. A flat tire, followed by roadside abduction. A wrong turn down a deserted road, then an empty fuel tank, then death by dehydration. Heidi wasn't always this quick to rush to worst-case scenarios, but when her first baby came into the world, life transformed from a tentative adventure into something high stakes, perilous, fraught with landmines. Mutti is saying something to her, but it's hard to hear over the racing of her own heart. "What?"

Claudia holds out the phone. "Cami's parents? Do you know their number?"

Heidi nods blankly and dials, amazed that her fingers know where to go.

Thankfully, Jennifer picks up. She had a voicemail from Cami. Something about keys getting locked in the car. A mention of Wendy's.

Heidi hangs up the phone and turns to her mother.

"They're at Wendy's?" Claudia asks.

"Yeah, it sounds like it. They locked the keys in the car. Jennifer didn't actually talk to them, but Cami left her a voicemail."

Dean looks up from the kitchen table, where he and Nephi have been having an exuberant conversation about the Utah Jazz. Dean's right arm is hoisted high, wrist flicked in a seated imitation of a jump shot. "Do you want me to go get them?" he asks.

Heidi would *love* for him to go. She feels shaky and exhausted. But her kids have never met Dean. She *hopes* none of them would be willing to climb into a car with a strange man. She tells him as much.

"I could go along!" Nephi suggests, his voice uncharacteristically bright.

Dean smiles. "Okay by me. I could use some guy time. Your grandma refuses to talk sports with me."

"Do you mind driving my van?" Heidi asks. "You'll need the seats."

"That's fine."

She tosses him the keys. Nephi leaps into their flight path and executes a grinning interception. Dean matches his smile, and they head out the door together.

***

Graham stares down impatiently at the woman at the desk. He asked her how much longer it will be until the tow truck driver arrives, and she's taking her time replying.

"An hour or so. Ricky's still out on a call." She sighs, as if it is a great inconvenience to be bothered in this way, though she can't be *that* bothered, given that she doesn't even look up from her magazine. "Give Him the Sex of His Dreams," the cover proclaims, and then in a slightly reduced (but still bold, firm, in-your-face) font, "The Amazing Middle Eastern Technique That Will Actually Double His Pleasure."

Graham tries not to wonder what this technique might be. He focuses instead on the apparent indifference of the receptionist. *An hour or so.* She said the exact same thing twenty minutes ago! Apparently, she is oblivious to the passage of time, lost in lusty reverie, but Graham is not. His irritation rises.

God is love, God is love, God is love, he reminds himself, grinding his teeth in time with the repetition. He should have asked that Dan kid for a ride to Castle Valley, but it's too late now. Graham glowers down at his watch.

If the driver makes it here in about an hour, picks Graham up, and they ride together to the car and tow it back to the repair shop, then the absolute soonest a mechanic could possibly look at it would be around 4:10, some two hours hence. This optimistic timeline, Graham realizes, is unlikely.

"What time do you close?" he asks.

"Five."

Graham groans. There is virtually no chance that his car will be drivable by then. "What happens if I *don't* wait here? Can the driver tow the car without me?"

She lowers the magazine halfway and stares at him over the top, as if to verify that he is in fact for real. "He doesn't need you. You said you *wanted* to ride along."

"Yes, I did. But *you* said it would only be an hour, and now more than twenty minutes have passed, and you're *still* saying an hour."

"I didn't say it would be an hour." She lifts the magazine again.

Heat rises to Graham's face. "You most certainly did!"

"I said *or so*. An hour *or so*. Looks like it's going to land on the side of *or so*."

Graham wants to yell. He wants to chastise her for shoddy customer service, as well as for her utter lack of propriety. Her eyes are glued to the pages of that smut. There's no point, though. He realizes this, and the heat drains out of him. He takes a breath. "I'm going to step out for a walk. If I'm not back in time, ask the driver to go get the car without me."

"Whatever floats your boat." She doesn't look up.

Graham walks up Main Street, in the direction of his car. He won't make it there on foot, of course. But somehow it feels like the more purposeful direction, and he needs to move, needs to clear his head. He wonders if he should call Claudia. Would she come pick him up? His heart pounds harder at the thought. There must be some other, more palatable option. A taxi? Does Moab have a taxi service? He could check the phone book. Make a call. But it must cost a small fortune to hire a ride all the way to Castle Valley, and then he would still be at Claudia's mercy, with no exit if she closes the door in his face and no way to get back to town without again relying on a taxi or on her willingness to drive him. *And why should she be willing?* After the way he treated her? She wasn't blameless, to be sure, but perhaps Graham was too harsh. Too heavy-handed, if you will.

He'll need to get a hotel room for the night. It's really the only option. With luck, the car will be fixed and ready to go by late morning, and he'll drive to Castle Valley then. He'll arrive altered and penitent, but still as a man in control of his own destiny. He'll inform Emma of his intention to be a better father, and then take her back home again. *Tomorrow.*

For now, he needs a place to stay and a phone so he can let Heidi know that he won't be home for dinner. *Heidi.* He hasn't slept a night apart from his wife since the last philosophical conference he attended, nearly a year ago. He thinks of the comfort of her slumbering body just inches from his. He thinks of Middle Eastern sexual techniques and feels his body flush with heat. Quickly, instinctively, he banishes this line of thought from his mind.

Graham remembers passing a motel on the ride in, maybe a mile or so up the road. He wishes he were carrying a backpack rather than a briefcase. Wishes he had different footwear, but it can't be helped. At least his Oxfords are broken in. Graham tucks his chin against the desert wind and walks.

It's fortunate that Graham moves forward with such singular focus, because if he looked to the right in the first minute or so of walking, he might have noticed five youthful bodies, scampering to hide themselves behind a parked car. And if he listened really, really hard, he might have heard excited voices over the whirr of passing traffic.

"Where's he going?"

"Who knows."

"I still can't believe there's only one locksmith in town. Are you *sure* about that?" This voice is Joseph's. He turns to Cami as he speaks.

"Go look for yourself if you want!"

Joseph disappears to the payphone. The others watch him from across the lot. He flips through the yellow pages of the phone book, then whirls about with a triumphant "ha!"

(This, Graham might have heard even without paying attention, but he's well past them by now.)

Joseph inserts a quarter, dials seven digits, then pivots toward the group again, just to be sure that they fully appreciate his brilliance.

"I swear there was only one locksmith," Cami says, rising to her feet and walking to join Joseph.

She peers over his shoulder, and he stabs exultantly at the page. Sure enough, there are *two* locksmiths listed, neither of whom is Burt. Cami stares in confusion, rustles the pages, and finally realizes her error. Burt was the only locksmith on the *preceding* page, but the listings continued from there. She could have sworn she checked the next page, though.

"The pages were a bit stuck together," Joseph admits, the phone already pressed to his ear. "Oh, hi, umm, my *friend*"—he places ironic emphasis on the word—"locked herself out of her car."

Cami smiles and gives a sheepish shrug.

Twenty, or so, minutes later, two vehicles pull into the Wendy's parking lot—a tow truck, followed by a Ford van.

***

Graham is barely surprised by the unrecognizable reflection in the motel bathroom mirror. Why should he expect to look normal? Nothing else is normal today. His hair is disheveled and his nose pink from the sun. Shadowy circles rim his eyes. Grease streaks his face, neck, and collar. Red juice stains darken his right sleeve and polka dot the front of his shirt. He is a mess. Outside and in. It's Monday, but Graham feels as if he's lived through a year of Saturdays. How he longs for a Sabbath! A day of rest. A day of normalcy.

He washes his hands and face, then smooths his hair. He considers stripping out of his shirt and scrubbing the whole thing in the bathroom sink, but he has nothing else to wear, and he'll need to go back out for dinner. And so, shirt still on, he attempts to spot clean the sleeve. The deep red spreads like watercolor, billowing outward in shades of pink.

Fed up, Graham twists the faucet off with a bit more force than is strictly necessary, then yanks at the knot on his tie, pulling the red-and-blue striped number from his neck and tossing it onto a chair. Next goes his shirt. He pulls at one button at a time, again perhaps with a trifle more vim than is needed. A button pops loose and flies to the floor. "Shit!" Graham cries out. He stomps his feet against the carpet. "Shit, shit, shit!" It is the first time Graham has sworn since three-year-old Hyrum urinated into his open briefcase.

The shirt, still stained and one button lighter, joins the necktie on the chair, and their owner flops face down onto the bed. It's been three nights since he slept properly. Mercifully, he sleeps now—almost immediately—though "properly" might not be the term for it, given that he is on top of the covers, with his shoes still on.

Graham sleeps, and Emma awakes. She dreamt of laughter. Of sitting on the warm earth, a mist hanging over her head, laughter ringing from her belly, her heart, her lips. She dreamt of laughter and wakes to the sound of giggling. She blinks her eyes in confusion. It takes a moment to get her bearings. She is in Oma's guestroom. *Not pregnant.* But the laughter?

Slowly, Emma sits up and scoots her legs so that they hang over the edge of the bed. Her feet find the floor. Gingerly, she rises and walks to the door. There's more giggling. *It sounds like Sariah.* Emma wants to go investigate, but the IV fluids have made their way through her system, and her bladder screams protest. She turns toward the bathroom.

It's there, plunked down on porcelain, that she hears voices. Oma's. Sariah's—that squeaky chatter can't possibly belong to anyone else. And then, the opening and closing of a door, followed by a volley of vocalizations. Exclamations, laughter, voices layering on top of voices.

Emma finishes, gives her hands a cursory rinse, and rushes as quickly as she can (which isn't in fact all that fast) to the living room.

"Emma!" several voices cry at once.

Emma smiles, looking from one face to the next. Cami, who rushes toward her with a hug. Her mother. All her siblings. *They're all here. Everyone except Dad.* "What are you guys doing here?"

"I came to meet Oma!" Sariah chirps, squeezing herself into the middle of Emma's and Cami's embrace.

"I wanted to check on you," Heidi says. She means to say more, but finding the right words feels like trying to find the right yogurt.

"And *we* just wanted to piss dad off," Hyrum offers. Eliza kicks him in the shin. "And uh, show you that we don't hate you and stuff," he adds. "But hey, listen—I was just about to tell Mom this, too . . . Dad's in Moab."

"What!?" Heidi's face goes white.

The story tumbles out in a tangle of exclamations and interruptions. By the end, Emma has sunk onto the couch. "I don't want him showing up here," she says, deflated.

"I doubt he'll get here tonight," Joseph offers. "The sign on the door said the repair shop closes at 5:00. Last we saw, he was walking away from there with no tow truck in sight."

"At least Judgment Day won't come until tomorrow then," Emma sighs.

"Emma, never mind what he thinks! He's just wrong!" The forcefulness of Heidi's voice stuns the room into silence. "He was wrong to react the way he did, and I was wrong to go along with him for even a minute. I know I'm not very good about standing up to him," her voice wavers. "Actually, I'm terrible at it. But I'm going to do it for once. You're not alone in this, okay?"

The room is silent, but Heidi's words echo inside Emma, the emptiness filling with sound and sunlight.

Hyrum steps forward. "Me too. I'll stand up to him."

"We all will." Joseph's voice is gruff. It is the most tender thing Emma has ever heard him say.

"We're all with you," Heidi says, her brow creased with the effort of trying to read the expression on her daughter's face.

Emma looks up at the nodding heads, at faces so familiar that she wonders if she's ever looked at them properly before this moment. *We're all with you.* The words seem plausible. Her whole family—patriarch aside—is with her. A sense of familiarity brushes against the edges of her mind. Her dream, she realizes; her dream had something to do with all of this, but just as quickly, the feeling is gone.

"I'm not pregnant," Emma tells her mother.

"I know," Heidi nods. "I'm so glad, but I was with you either way."

"*I* was only gonna be with you until the first time you asked for help with a diaper change. I was for sure disowning you after that," Hyrum cracks, and the conversation quickly devolves into back-and-forth banter about baby poop until Heidi breaks in, addressing her mother over the din.

"Mutti, what do you think of these interesting grandchildren of yours?" Heidi may be attempting to change the subject, but a smile twitches at the corners of her mouth.

"I think they're perfect," Oma replies.

***

Graham's mouth is twitching, too. He looks as if he has tasted something sour. It's 4:30, and the tow truck has only just headed out of town to get his car, or so that obscenity-ingesting magazine enthusiast at the repair shop just told him. He grips the phone tighter, as if to wrangle control of the situation.

"So they'll look at your car tomorrow," she is saying. And then something about Billy or maybe Willy having a dental appointment first thing in the morning, and how that might delay things further.

"What do you expect me to do without a car?" Graham sputters.

"I expect nothing." She sounds bored as she says it. As if she's picking at her fingernails, which she is. "It's up to you what to do. You seem to be the one with all the expectations. No offense."

No offense. As if she can talk to him like that and then, by tacking on those two words, retain a gold star for customer service.

He opens his mouth, ready to offend in return, but he finds himself unexpectedly tongue tied, his lips opening and closing soundlessly, fishlike. He remembers a quote from the prophet Brigham Young: "He who takes offense when no offense is intended is a fool, and he who takes offense when offense is intended is a greater fool."

Graham feels foolish enough already. There's no sense in making things worse. He sighs. "I guess it is what it is," he says, more to himself than to her.

"That's about the most reasonable thing I've ever heard from a customer." She sounds slightly less bored.

"Well, it's tautological."

"Excuse me?"

"What I said—'it is what it is.' It's a tautological statement. So, of course it's reasonable. It's true by definition."

"Umm, riiight. Do you have any more questions about your car, or are we good to go?"

"We are who we are. That would be tautological, too."

"Yeeeah. Okay, well if you have any questions, just give us a call."

She hangs up. Graham holds the phone limply in his left hand, forgetful of its presence. His right elbow drops to his left knee, and his right hand tucks under his chin. He curls in on himself in thought.

"It is what it is" *is*, of course, an inherently reasonable and true statement. But it's one that Graham Madsen has rarely lived. When the most basic tautology stands in contrast to your way of being in the world, that's a potential indicator that you've been doing it wrong. *Very wrong,* Graham thinks to himself. All this time, he's been bellowing truth claims, while resisting the most basic truths of all.

The phone, still in his hand, begins howling. Graham returns it to the receiver and rises to his feet. *It is what it is.* What's the use in getting all worked up? Maybe he'll grab an early dinner.

Chapter Thirty-Five

Claudia and Heidi stand elbow to elbow at the kitchen counter. Dean and the kids muck about the yard, dribbling a soccer ball through a maze of juniper and prickly pear. Cami and Emma sprawl in the guestroom, their limbs draped across the sky-blue duvet, and their heads sinking into plump white pillows that make Cami think of clouds. She wants to ask Emma everything. *Who is this Juice and Java guy? What's sex like? Is Emma going to do it again? What about the Church?* But Emma is clearly exhausted. Maybe it's best to just float here awhile longer. Cami reaches for her friend's hand and gives it a squeeze.

The sensation of Cami's fingers wrapped around hers ignites something in Emma's mind. Her dream! It comes blazing back.

Emma stood in an open field. The iron rod stretched out beside her, leading to the Tree of Life. On her other side, the Great and Spacious Building hovered. She loitered between them, blank with indecision. She needed to choose a destination, something to strive for, but she didn't like the available options.

A warm hand wrapped around her own, giving her fingers an affectionate squeeze. Lehi's wife Sariah stood beside her, smiling. "Follow me," she said and tugged Emma's hand.

"Where are we going?" Emma worried that this might be some alternate route to the Tree of Life, which really didn't seem like her scene.

"Here. We're going here," Sariah said, halting just a few paces from where they had begun.

The mists of darkness were thicker here. Emma couldn't see a thing. "Why here? I don't get it," Emma asked.

"So you can taste the fruit."

"What fruit? There's nothing here." Emma tried to head back in the direction she had come from. She wasn't quite sure which way that was, though. She turned in a circle, straining her eyes into the mist. *What was she even looking for?* The iron rod? The Tree of Life? Some prophet to tell her what to do? The Great and Spacious Building? People she could point and jeer at? Emma didn't want any one of these, but she couldn't stay in this shapeless mist forever.

"Emma, sit down." Sariah's voice was warm and kind. Like Oma's voice. And so, Emma sat.

As soon as her body met the earth, she felt a prickling on her tongue. Sweetness blossomed in her mouth. Sensation flooded her body—the warmth of the ground, a breeze against her face, floral notes in the air. Every part of her felt awake and alive. The mist hovered overhead. At the ground level, all was clear.

"I don't get it," she said, turning to Sariah. Only Sariah wasn't there.

"Yes, you do," a voice answered from somewhere inside her.

"Yeah, I guess I do," she admitted. Because she *did*. It was the same message, delivered over and over again: *it's all right here*.

"What are you thinking about?" Cami asks.

Emma exhales, and the images disappear with her breath. "I'm thinking . . . that we waste so much energy trying to reach a place that we think is outside of us."

Cami rolls to face her. "You mean, like, coming down here?"

"Maybe. Or like me trying for so long to get a testimony. Or thinking that if I go to the U, then I'll finally be happy. But, like, everything is right here."

"Right where?"

"Right inside me. Right *everywhere*."

"Huh," Cami says. She wants to understand but isn't sure she does.

"I can't explain it very well. I just . . . feel it."

"Like a testimony?"

Emma laughs. "Yeah, I guess so."

It will be a while before she can articulate the rest, even to herself. Before she can find words to express that everyone is at the Tree of Life; everyone is in the Great and Spacious Building, all clinging to some iron rod or another, all stumbling through mists of darkness. We are all Paul, and we are all Saul. Emma ran away to Castle Valley and consumed mind-altering baked goods to figure this out, but someone else will figure it out in Provo, possibly while eating a cheeseburger, and someone will learn it in the Big Apple, and someone else has already figured it out in Lagos and in San Salvador and in Beirut. Joy, suffering, love, loss, life—they are everywhere. And to live—to really live—is to be with what is. Someday, Emma will have words for this.

"I guess," she says for now, "I'm okay with not understanding everything. I kinda *like* a bit of mystery."

"How about the rather frightening mystery of your dad showing up in Moab?"

Emma grimaces. "That one I could do without."

***

Belly full, Graham walks north. There's no sidewalk here, just a wide shoulder. Passing trucks spit gravel and exhaust. Perhaps he should have walked the other direction, but the patches of Moab that Graham has seen aren't exactly scenic, and the promise of a view of the Colorado River is more appealing than the view of gas stations or strip malls—or, for that matter, the drab confines of his motel room.

He hears the rustling of cottonwoods as he approaches the river, and at first, he mistakes the sound for running water. Graham is not surprised to see that the Colorado flows toward Moab from the direction of Castle Valley. His whole day has been an upstream struggle. A dog paddle against the current. But he's giving up the struggle—that is what he tells himself, anyway. He still imagines, perhaps, that acceptance is a one-time act. That you can surrender once and then be done with such indignities.

He's ready to let the river take him—just this once. He stands at the edge and closes his eyes. He is wrapped in the sound of wind and water and leaves. A gust rocks him gently onto his toes, and the setting sun bathes the left side of his body in light, but it seems to Graham that some other current, some other pulse of energy, pulls him to his right. He opens his eyes and looks upstream. He passed a sign, just before reaching the river. *What did it say? Sixteen miles to Castle Valley?* Far too many to walk.

That's what makes it so strange, especially to Graham, when he begins walking. It seems an awful lot like kicking against the pricks. But it doesn't feel that way. It feels like letting the current take him. Like flowing with what is. Maybe it's the same pull that took him to Juice and Java, the same mysterious energy that softened him toward Ben, the same force that brought Dan to their aid. Or maybe Graham is just not the sort of person who is able to hang out at a crossroads. Staying here by the river, returning to the motel room—every option feels like sitting at a stoplight. Every option except for one: proceeding—on foot.

"Dude. You're like dressed in a suit. Do you need a lift?"

Graham is *not* dressed in a suit—he doesn't even have a jacket—though he did put his tie back on before leaving the motel room. It covers that gap where the button fell off, plus he hoped it might distract from the stains on his shirt. He eyes the scruffy young men, whose dirt-caked van has rolled to a stop across the road from him. They look like they need a shower and laundromat as badly as Graham does. Normally, that would be a strike against them. At the moment, Graham is oddly disinclined to assign strikes.

"Can you get me to Castle Valley?"

"Pretty close. We're camping by Castleton. Should be an easy walk from there."

Graham has no clue where or what Castleton is, but he likes the sound of an easy walk. He steps forward, and the backdoor of the van slides open, pulled from within. He is greeted by a young woman with a sunburned face. He hesitates, then climbs in beside her, onto a bench that has clearly been used as a bed. There is a sleeping bag balled up on the floor, and a pillow is crammed against the opposite window. The whole van smells of sand, sweat, and something skunky.

He doesn't see the joint in her hand until after he slides the door shut and the van begins to move forward. "So," she says, letting out a puff of smoke, "you coming from work or something?"

"Sort of," Graham answers.

She coughs. "What's your story?"

"My story?" Graham looks at her.

"Everyone's got a story."

"I deal in facts, not stories. And the fact I'm most concerned with right now relates to what you're holding in your hand. That's illegal, you know."

"I do know"—she nods her head smiling—"Want some?"

"No, I want you to put that out!" He shakes his head, flabbergasted, then leans forward toward the driver. "Have you been smoking drugs, too? If so, I need you to let me out of the vehicle."

"Nah, man. I'm the designated driver. You're cool. I've got you."

"Andy's a square. You don't have to worry about him," the girl tells him. "I'm Prudence, by the way."

"Prudence. Not exactly fitting, is it?"

She bursts into snorting laughter, followed by a round of heavy coughing.

"You've got me there. My poor parents. I'm literally the exact opposite of everything they wanted me to be. You got a name?"

"Graham."

"Like the cracker?"

"Yes, I suppose so," he answers, tight-jawed.

"So you're supposed to be what? Sweet and easily digestible? Seems like you got the wrong name too. You strike me as a bit, well, buttoned up."

Graham would normally stiffen at such impertinence, but it isn't possible for his body to get any more rigid.

"First time I've ever seen a guy in a suit walking this road," she continues.

"It's not a suit. Just a shirt and tie and some nice slacks."

For some reason, Prudence finds this hilarious. "If you say so, Graham Cracker."

Graham's face flushes. "Do your parents know about this?" He waves his hand in a way that seems to indicate not only the joint but also the whole of the van, the whole of her life perhaps.

"About what? That I'm on a trip with my friends?"

Buttoned up though he may be, Graham feels a quiet delight in her pun, though he's not sure it was intentional.

"That you take herbal supplements," the passenger in the front seat calls back, turning to them with a grin.

"Oh that. Yeah, they're not stupid."

"Well, they can't possibly approve," Graham says.

"Tell me, did your parents approve of everything you ever did?"

"No," Graham concedes.

"Yeah, because they're not supposed to. If they did, it would probably mean you're not living your life very well."

"Failure to individuate!" the front seat passenger interjects.

"You and your psychobabble." Prudence shakes her head, then turns to Graham to explain. "Cameron went to college before he started dirtbagging."

"Dirtbagging?"

"Yeah, like living in this van, climbing all the time."

"Climbing?"

"*Rock* climbing," she says. She doesn't explicitly say 'duh', but the tone of her voice conveys it effectively. Graham is already exhausted by the conversation and queasy from the smoke. He decides to sit in silence. Prudence has other plans. "Okay, so back to your story."

"I don't have a story," Graham says through clenched teeth.

"Bullshit. You're walking up this road in *nice slacks.* You have a story."

"Okay, my car broke down."

"Yeah? I didn't see a car."

"That's because it broke down like thirty miles north of Moab."

"And yet we found you here. Asking for a ride to Castle Valley."

"I didn't ask. He offered."

"I *did* offer," Andy confirms.

"What's in Castle Valley?" Prudence presses.

Graham sighs. He's not getting out of this one. It is what it is. "My daughter," he answers.

"Oooh, you have a daughter! Has she successfully . . . what was that word, Cameron? *Individuated?*"

Something like pained amusement flickers across Graham's face. "Yes, a little too successfully."

"Oh good! That's so healthy! And you're *letting her*, right? You're not trying to, like, muscle her into being like you, are you? Because a girl walking down this road in *nice slacks* would just be too damn weird."

"Let the guy tell his story, Prudence!"

"Okay, okay. So you're going to see your daughter. I'm listening."

The van is silent. Cameron is still swiveled halfway around, watching Graham and waiting, it seems, for some riveting revelation. Andy glances back and forth between the rearview mirror and road.

Graham sighs heavily. *Amor fati*, he thinks. Love of fate. If it is what it is (and it always is), why not go with it? Lean into it, even?

"My daughter Emma," he begins. And then he just keeps going. Five minutes pass and ten, and still, he is talking. He wonders at his own flood of words but feels powerless to stop them. He goes with the current.

They know everything now—Cameron, Andy, and Prudence. They know what it felt like to hold Emma as an infant and what it felt like to lose her to toddlerhood. They know what her father hoped for her, and even more, what he feared. Maybe they can read between the lines enough to see how his fears tangled themselves around the fragile, tender love of a man who had rarely been loved properly himself.

"You know why she had sex, right?" Prudence muses.

"Because of the temptations of the devil," Graham answers.

Prudence snorts. Cameron laughs. Andy smiles diplomatically.

"Okay, sure. Because of Satan," Prudence says. "But *also* because *you* have been trying to control every detail of her life, and she needed a way out. And so she decided to bust it all to hell."

"Now who's full of psychobabble!" Cameron accuses. "She probably just had sex because it feels good."

Graham is possessed with the urge to cover his ears.

"Okay, fine, that too," Prudence says. "But I guarantee she was also looking for a way to break free. I mean, I would do the same thing. I *did* do the same thing, more or less. But the cool part in your daughter's case is that it *worked.* She got to see Grandma. She got away. And Dad's even coming to apologize! Because that *is* what you're doing, right? Tell me you're not going to deliver any lectures when you get there."

Graham has to think about this for a moment. "No, I'm not going to lecture her," he says after a pause.

"You'll apologize then? For being an asshole?"

"Probably not with those precise words."

Prudence talks so fast that Graham wonders how she manages to process anything at all.

"I mean, okay," she jumps back in, "the pregnancy bit is super crappy and complicated. But she can get an abortion. And you said she might not actually be pregnant, so if she's *not*, then it seems like she made a great choice for her life. And there's no doubt that she's made a great choice for *your* life."

"For *my* life?" He had been on the verge of voicing his strenuous objections to the notion of Emma getting an abortion, but as soon as he latches onto one thing Prudence says, she's taken off with another.

"Yeah. Because it's changed you, right? From everything you've said, you were a complete asshole until like maybe twenty-four hours ago. And now, you're not. You're only—what would you guys say?" She leans forward and slaps Cameron and Andy on the shoulders. "Like 60% an asshole?"

"Ahh, cut the guy some slack," Andy protests.

"40% max," Cameron says. "And who isn't at least partially an asshole?"

"Oh yeah, I wasn't trying to be mean," Prudence tells Graham. "I'm like 80% an asshole—at the very least."

"I noticed," he replies, sending Prudence into another fit of snorting.

Andy raises his voice to be heard over Prudence's laughter. "Hey, what street are you trying to get to, dude?"

"Buchanan," Graham replies.

"Buchanan, Buchanan, Buchanan," Andy mumbles. "I'm pretty sure that's like in the middle. I'll drop you off a bit before where we turn to camp by Castleton."

"What's Castleton?" Graham asks.

"A tower. Sandstone. It's really iconic. We're climbing it tomorrow."

Cameron and Andy launch into enthusiastic descriptions of the route they plan to climb. Graham thinks of Dan's rhapsodic monologues about his mission. He's never spent so many hours of a single day in conversation with people in their teens and twenties before—not even when he *was* in his teens and twenties.

"This should be a good spot!" Andy proclaims, pulling to the side of the road. "We turn off a little further ahead, but Castle Valley is all of that down on our right."

Graham looks out into near blackness. The lights of a few houses scatter in the distance. But for the moon, he wouldn't be able to see anything else.

"You need a headlamp?" Prudence asks.

"Yes, but I don't want to take yours. I'm sure you need it," Graham says.

"I've got two. This one's pretty old and beat up, but it works. Take it." She presses it into Graham's hand.

"So I just walk that way?" Graham points to the right of the van.

"Yeah, you might have to knock on a door to get directions. Or just wait for a car. The main road runs basically parallel to this one. If you get onto it, someone will come along eventually. And I'm pretty sure all the other streets intersect it, so once you're there, it's just a question of ticking off streets one by one until you find Buchanan. I think it's somewhere sort of middlish."

Somewhere sort of middlish. It's not a lot to go on, but at least he has a headlamp.

"You'll be fine. You have good luck," Prudence tells him.

"How do you figure?" It's Graham's turn to snort.

"Well, we picked you up. And that Dan kid you were telling us about, he picked you up. And your daughter's boyfriend didn't knife you or anything. Seems to me like you're pretty lucky."

"Thanks," he says, "for the ride . . . and the headlamp."

They say their goodbyes, and Graham steps into the darkness. A voice calls out.

"Hey, Graham Cracker!"

Graham turns. The beam on his light finds Prudence's head, sticking out of the van window.

"You're blinding me with that thing!" she complains, holding out a hand. Graham aims the light lower, and Prudence continues.

"Hey, I was shitting you. About my name being Prudence. It's Brittany. And good luck with your daughter. Tell her we think that your asshole quotient has dropped way down since she last saw you, and we hope she'll give you a second chance. Oh, and Cameron says you should pick her some flowers."

Flowers. Where is Graham supposed to find flowers in a pitch-black desert?

"Thanks . . . Brittany."

She waves and the van rolls away.

Graham walks. Again. How many miles has he walked in this unending day? In this unmooring stretch of days? This walk is a bit different than the ones that preceded it, though. For one, he's walking across rocks and sand, winding between scrubby little plants that he can't identify. For another, he can see nothing outside of the circle of light ahead of him. His eyes tire from the effort of discerning shapes, distance, depth. He shivers. He needs to walk faster to stay warm.

He picks up his pace, and almost immediately, his ankle scrapes against a cactus.

"Ouch!" he cries. And then: "Shit!" His second episode of profanity in this decade. His second time swearing today. He finds it strangely consoling—the profanity, not the cactus spines. And so he continues.

"Lucky my ass," he huffs, thinking of the girl formerly known as Prudence.

He bends down, shining the light at his ankle, where two spines poke out from his sock and three more cling to the hem of his nice slacks. He begins to pull them one by one, but there must have been another spine he didn't see at first because now the side of his hand smarts, too. He thinks of Saul kicking against the pricks, which weren't cactus spines, of course. They were more like cattle prods, or so he read somewhere. He wishes Heavenly Father would stop prodding him. He's on the path, after all, isn't he? Doing what he's supposed to do? *Why can't it just be easy?*

"I know, I know, because it is what it is," Graham mutters aloud.

As if in response, the light on his headlamp nods off, on, then off again. Graham pulls it from his head, slides the switch back and forth, to no avail.

"Damn it all to hell!" he cries, kicking at the sand—thankfully *just* at the sand.

He swears and kicks, but his heart isn't fully in it. A little part of him seems to float above, watching. *Isn't this fascinating?* that part of him says. *I wonder how it will turn out. It might make a funny story when it's all done.*

He imagines who he might tell the story to. Prudence would eat it up, of course, but that is neither here nor there. Ben, maybe? Ben would enjoy hearing about this. Heidi? She didn't answer when he called to tell her he wouldn't make it home. He left a voicemail. Told her he was in Moab. That he'd had a change of heart. (Actually, what he said was that "upon further consideration, the best course of action seems to be to bring Emma back home.") Heidi must have listened to the message by now. Graham wonders how she felt. How she *feels*. Surprised? Pleased? Upset? Envious, perhaps, that he will get to see her mother? Heidi must miss her after all of these years. Graham feels a pang of guilt. There's no sense in rehashing the past right now, he tells himself. This moment is hard enough. "Sufficient unto the day is the evil thereof," Graham mumbles.

But what *is* Heidi thinking right now? Graham has never been any good at predicting how people will react to different situations. That's one of the things he loves about Heidi: he doesn't have to do much predicting. She's nearly always the same—satisfied, content, pleasant, obliging. Well, except for these past few days. He hopes that this is what she wanted—for him to change his mind, to accept Emma as she is. If so, then surely she's pleased that he came here?

"As long as I don't die in the desert," he says.

It feels less dark, less lonely when he speaks aloud. It feels less dark, and it *is* less dark. The longer he stands there without the headlamp, the better his eyes adjust. The moon is nearly full. Graham looks down at the ground and can clearly make out the prickly pear that assailed him. He turns in a circle, surveying the area. Castleton Tower rises up behind him, like a finger pointing to heaven. Or flipping him off. *Probably both.* Graham turns back toward the valley, toward his daughter, and he walks.

Chapter Thirty-Six

Emma and Cami saunter together into the kitchen. "You're up!" Heidi chirps. "How are you feeling?"

"Better, actually," Emma says. "Maybe the antibiotic is already working. Or maybe the kidney infection wasn't making me as sick as I thought. I think something I ate upset my stomach, too," she explains, throwing a furtive glance at her grandmother.

"Well, don't push it. Sit down! I'll grab you a drink." Heidi touches Emma's arm as she speaks.

Emma takes a step away. "I'm okay. It feels good to stand for a bit." She looks around the kitchen. Spaghetti sauce simmers on the stove. Water boils in a pot, waiting for the addition of noodles. Claudia chops carrots for a salad, and the scent of garlic bread fills the air.

"We just need to get the strudel in the oven, and then we can eat. The Pingrees are coming over for dessert," her mother tells her.

"They're still in town?"

"They pushed back their departure once you got sick. They're driving back first thing in the morning." Heidi walks to the dining room, a bedsheet folded under one arm, and in her hand, a silver mixing bowl containing a thick ball of yellow dough.

"I'll help," Emma offers, following behind her.

"I don't want you to overdo it," Heidi objects.

"Mom, it's fine. I like this part." She always has.

Together Heidi and Emma spread the fresh, white bedsheet across the dining room table. They work wordlessly—a dance in which each knows her part. Heidi hoists the dough from the bowl and begins stretching it, pulling with one hand, then the other, balancing it on her fist, letting gravity carry the sides slowly toward the ground. The dough is the size of a large platter now, still thick and opaque. She sets it on the sheet and, standing at the head of the table, begins stretching again, lifting the dough on one side to pull at the still dense center. Emma stands to her left, gently stretching and pulling too. She knows what to watch for—knows that the thick yellow wrinkles in the dough are more likely to split, so she works carefully around them. For a proper strudel, the dough must be pulled so thin that the sheet beneath it becomes visible. Mother and daughter circle the table, stretching and pulling.

Heidi lets out a jagged sigh, and Emma looks up surprised. A hole—a big hole, right where her mom is working. Emma makes holes often enough, but not her mother. Emma takes in Heidi's face—pale, pained. "What's wrong? It's just a hole."

"Just one more hole," her mother gasps, "that I should have prevented."

Emma is dumbfounded. "Huh?"

"I *let* him do it. I let him pull at all of you, I let him cover every one of us in holes."

Emma doesn't have to ask what she means. She can see it as clearly as the dough on the table. Dad pulling at Hyrum, pulling at her, pulling at every last member of the family. Anything and anyone can break if stretched far enough.

"I just pretend the holes aren't there," Heidi continues. "I surround them with apples and raisins and pretend they never happened."

Emma isn't sure how to answer. She errs on the side of smoothing the awkwardness. "Well, apples and raisins *are* delicious," she offers. The words leave a sickly saccharine taste in her mouth. She lifts one side of the dough, drawing it toward herself and puzzling over her own feelings: discomfort, awkwardness, protectiveness of her mother, but also annoyance—resentment.

Then it clicks: she has never been one to tiptoe around her father, to sprinkle sugar over the holes he makes, but in her relationship with her mother, she sometimes does exactly that. She stuffs down her anger, pulls at herself—all to maintain some shallow semblance of peace or some image of herself as *not an asshole*.

She speaks. Her voice, measured at first, quickly builds to red-hot intensity. "You're right. You've *let* him treat us the way he does. You're the one person we should be able to count on, and you never step up. You let him treat us like shit. You let him treat *you* like shit." Emma's throat constricts. "Why!?" She doesn't feel annoyed anymore. Nor does she feel resentful. She's *pissed*.

"I don't know why. Maybe I'm just . . . weak," Heidi whispers, her voice choked.

"That's a *choice*. Just like it was a *choice* to not let us see Oma all these years . . . not even tell me *you* were seeing her!"

Heidi seems frozen in place, apart from the tears that stream down her cheeks, landing on the strudel. A sprinkle of raisins might go a long way toward easing the tension, but Emma stands with balled fists. Finally, Heidi nods. "You're right," she says. There is no sugar in her voice. "I'm sorry. I know words aren't enough. I'm going to try to do things really differently."

"Good," Emma answers. Her voice is sharp, but her fists uncurl.

They resume the wordless dance, spreading paper thin apple slices across the stretched dough, working carefully around the hole. Next come the raisins and the cream. Grabbing one end of the sheet, Emma lifts, rolling the dough onto itself over and over and over until it's a thick log. Somewhere in the center of it is a hole—a place with too little dough, too few apples, a place where raisins might fall through. But it's rolled up so tidily, curled and cradled in the hot casserole dish, and bathed in melted butter. From the outside, you would never know. But Emma knows, and her mother knows, and the spell of polite pretending is broken.

***

Graham has wandered for forty days in this desert. Or so it feels to him. His right foot is wet and numb with cold from a poorly executed creek crossing. He suspects that a stray cactus spine is still stuck in his lower leg, though he can't seem to find it in the dark. He tore his nice slacks, snagging them on a juniper branch. He feels unraveled. And yet, he presses on.

"We did travel and wade through much affliction in the wilderness," he mumbles, recalling the words of the prophet

Nephi, who fled with Lehi, Sariah, Laman, Lemuel, and the rest of their family from Jerusalem.

It all ended well for Nephi, though. The Lord guided him to a place that they named Bountiful for its abundance of fruit and honey. They camped there, and God instructed them to build a ship, and on that ship, Nephi and his family sailed to the Americas, where they found a land of plenty and grew into a great nation.

Graham doesn't need anything quite so grand, but he would really like to find his mother-in-law's house. "Please," he whispers into the darkness. "*Please*."

A coyote howls a distant reply. Graham fears this is the only answer he will get. It isn't, though. He walks several more paces and then he finds it—a road. How did he not see it sooner? A straight, flat, dirt road. It seems to Graham that it's paved in gold.

"Thank you!" he breathes, hope and energy renewed.

He can move quickly now, and he does, nearly running. He passes an occasional house, all of them dark. Lights surround him at a distance, though, some far to his left, some to his right, some up ahead of him. This road is bound to get him somewhere. And it does. Before long, he finds himself at a junction. He squints his eyes to read the sign in the moonlight. *Buchanan Ln.* This is it. He is already on the right road.

"Lucky," he says—or tries to say. His jaw is growing increasingly stiff from the cold, and the word comes out garbled.

Light shines ahead of him, across the intersection and up a hill. *That must be it!* Graham rushes forward so eagerly that he fails to register the change in terrain, the increasing rockiness of the road. He stubs his toe hard. He doesn't even bother to swear, though. Nor does he notice (or care) that the sole is now peeling back from the toe of his Oxford. An hours-ago version of Graham wanted to arrive here as a man in control of his destiny. Now, it is enough simply to arrive. Well, until he actually does.

Here he is now, outside Claudia's house. The number is illuminated by a porch light. The windows glow gold. Graham can see inside them. Claudia must be hosting a dinner party. There are so many people gathered around the table. It takes him a moment to understand. *Wait, that's Heidi.* Sure enough, her van is parked in the driveway. His children. They are all here. Smiling, laughing, talking together. *Content.* They are all perfectly content without him. Their spirits will not be improved by his presence, he is sure of it.

Suddenly, arriving isn't enough; it's *too much.* For what feels like the hundredth time today, he wishes Heavenly Father would offer him detailed instructions, like he did for Nephi, when Nephi was commanded to build that ship. Graham longs for a plan—a syllabus. "How Not to Destroy Your Family's Happiness 101," the course might be called.

Graham walked across highways and a desert, but now he can't bring himself to step up to the door. He sinks down onto a boulder in the front yard and folds in on himself. He doesn't belong here. He doesn't belong anywhere. He's made too many mistakes. Done too many things wrong. He *is* a mistake. *He* is wrong.

He hears a confirming peal of laughter from inside the house. His family is happy. They are well. There is nothing he can offer them that they want. He won't stay here. He *can't* stay here.

Wearily, Graham stands. He moves with heavy steps back toward the road. He feels it before he sees it. A presence. Something living. Something *beautiful.* He looks down just in front of his toes, and there it is. A single flower, bent. Trampled, in all likelihood, by his own two feet as he hurried toward the house. It's bent, and somehow . . . perfect. Graham leans down and plucks it from the gravel. As if by magic, the flower begins to glow. Graham begins to glow. He looks up, disoriented. Headlights are shining on him. A car rolls into the driveway. Doors swing open.

"Graham!" Jeff and Joelle call out in a surprised chorus.

Jeff walks to him, claps a hand on his arm. "You look rough, buddy. Did you just get here?"

Graham nods, clinging to the small aster in his hand. *Purple.* He hadn't noticed until the headlights shone on it. The flower is purple.

"Let's get you inside." Jeff guides him by the arm toward the door.

"I'm . . ." There seems to be sand in Graham's throat. "I can't . . . go in."

Jeff looks him full in the face. "Why not?"

"They're happy. If I went in there . . . I'd ruin it. I owe them an apology, but I'm not sure . . . how to even begin."

"Well, it will have to start with going into the house, won't it?" Jeff says, draping his arm across Graham's shoulders.

Graham grimaces in reply.

"You look pitiful enough at the moment that your family might be willing to forgive you a great many things."

Graham emits a shrill laugh—almost a yelp—but allows himself to be led to the door. A single ring, and it swings wide. Claudia's mouth falls open in surprise. Her head tilts, and her arms cross over her chest.

"Graham is hoping to come inside and offer an apology," Jeff tells her, his hand giving Graham's arm a gentle squeeze.

"Really? Well, I look forward to hearing that," she replies archly and steps to the side. "How about if you leave your shoes here by the door, Graham? They look like they've seen better days, and cleanliness is next to godliness, or so I've been told."

Graham bends down and unties his Oxfords. He slips his feet out, one foot wet, one dry, both socks stained red from the desert sand. He follows Claudia into the dining room.

"We have a visitor," Claudia announces. "And apparently, there's something he wants to say." She sits down at the table. Graham stands awkwardly off to the side.

His frozen jaw seems to stiffen more at the sight of his family. He wonders if he'll be able to form words. He looks from the faces around the table to his soiled socks and then back again. His wife. His children. Cami. Some guy he's never seen before. There are two seats waiting for the Pingrees, who are loitering politely in the foyer so that he can abase himself with some semblance of privacy. It's too much. He needs a sympathetic face—just one. He looks at Heidi. Just at Heidi. *God is love*, he reminds himself. And for a second—just a single, fleeting second—he imagines that he can see what his wife feels. Fear. Anger. Shame. Hurt. Longing. Love. But maybe those are just his own feelings.

He clears his throat. It's a mournful sound—the opening notes of a requiem. "I . . . owe you an apology," he croaks. "I've been too harsh the past few days . . . Actually, I'm *always* too harsh. I want to do better. And I'm especially sorry for how I reacted to your news, Em—" His voice cuts out. He scans the faces again and realizes that his daughter isn't at the table.

Heidi reads his confusion. "She just went to lie down. She's been sick. Not pregnant, just sick."

Graham gasps in relief. Relief because Emma isn't pregnant? Relief because he said the thing he needed to say? Relief because no one has made a move to throw him back outside again? He doesn't know. He just knows that now that he's released that pent-up breath, everything else is flowing with it. His face crumples, and he buries it in his hands, shoulders shaking. Heidi rises from the table, puts an arm around him and guides him toward the bathroom.

Hyrum is the first to break the stunned silence. "That was literally the weirdest thing that's ever happened in my whole life."

"It wasn't weird. It was beautiful," Eliza sniffs.

"Maybe it was both," Claudia smiles, her eyes wide and glittering.

***

There is a knock on the guestroom door. Emma rolls groggily in its direction. She had felt so good before making the strudel, and then suddenly, she was drained, dizzy, a bit queasy again. Maybe it's her mom at the door, wanting to check on her. The possibility isn't annoying to Emma.

The door opens. Her father stands there. Or rather, a filthy and ragged man who bears a resemblance to her father stands there. Emma's heart pounds. She feels a jolt of adrenaline.

"Can I come in?" he asks.

"I really don't feel up to a lecture." Her voice is as hard as granite.

"I'm not going to lecture you. I want to apologize."

Emma snorts, not unlike Prudence. "I didn't think that was in your repertoire." She rolls, turning her back to him.

"Emma, please. I know I've been . . . " He searches for the right word. He finds it. "I've been an asshole."

Emma rolls back to face him. She stares open-mouthed. It is, of course, no surprise that her father has been an asshole. But it is earth-shattering that he knows it—that he knows it and is admitting it. *He's even using the word!*

"I don't know where to begin," he says, sinking down onto the corner of the bed farthest from his daughter. "I feel like I've lived a whole life today, and I don't want to go back to living that other life, the one from before today."

Emma says nothing. She watches, transfixed. The struggle for words is evident in the crease of his brow, the opening and closing of his mouth, the little puffs of breath that come and go.

"I got confused about what matters. I let fear drive me. I've tried to control things that aren't mine to control. I've tried to control *everything*. And, well, I haven't treated you like a child of God. That's my job . . . my calling as a parent, and I haven't done it. I've been too fixated on trying to change you to notice how wonderful you already are. I'm sorry. I'm . . . so sorry." He wants to look up at her, but he can't.

"Dad"—Graham is surprised to hear laughter in his daughter's voice—"you had me at 'I've been an asshole.' That was the best thing I've ever heard you say."

Graham looks up. "I've been an asshole. *I* have been an asshole. I have been an *asshole.* I *have been* an asshole, but I'm going to try—"

"I get it!" she laughs.

He remembers the flower, then. He reaches out his hand and offers it to his daughter.

"Umm, thanks. It looks a bit crushed." A quizzical smile plays on Emma's lips. "Did you put it in your pocket or something?"

"No, I found it in the driveway. I think maybe I stepped on it." He doesn't mention that he also smashed it against his face and sobbed on it like a child. "There might be a metaphor in there," he muses.

"Well, thanks."

"It's purple," he adds, the way a preschooler might.

"Yeah, I see that."

"Purple was Pam's favorite color." He looks Emma full in the face. Apparently, these words are supposed to mean something to her.

"Pam?"

"Pam Rasmussen. She took me in. I ran away from home, too. I was a bit younger than you, but well, I guess you could say my mother was an asshole, too. And Pam saved me. And I've always thought it was because she gave me the Church. But I think," Graham stammers, his eyes falling back down toward the floor, "well, I think the most important thing she gave me was the experience of being accepted as I was."

Emma stares hard at her father. "How come I've never met her? You've never even mentioned her. I mean, why are you just telling me all of this now?"

"She died of cancer just a bit before I married your mom. Your mom reminds me of her . . . always smiling, always kind. I don't know, Emma. Talking about Pam, it stirs up . . . a lot of feelings. I guess I'm not very good at talking about feelings, or at sorting through them, so not talking about the past just seemed like the easiest way to . . ."

"To not have feelings?"

Graham nods his head.

"You know that doesn't actually work, right?"

"I'm catching onto that."

"Good. Maybe you can stop taking stuff out on us, then." Even lying in bed, Emma manages to tilt her chin at a haughty angle.

Graham swallows the bitter cup. "I'm going to try. But odds are, I'm still going to step on you every now and then."

"*Step* on me?"

"Like the flower. I'm going to try not to. It's just, well, I find change . . . difficult."

"I've noticed."

Graham stands up from the bed and begins to pace. Three long strides, a turn, then three strides back. He stops suddenly. His hands rise to the top of his head, his fingers entangling themselves in his hair. He twirls around to face his daughter. Emma steels herself for a scriptural recitation.

"I'm *really* going to try, Emma. But at some point, I'm going to mess up. And it's okay," Graham's face contorts, as if bile has risen in his throat. He sighs heavily, dropping his hands to his sides. "It's okay for you to voice objections when I do."

Emma's eyebrows rise. "You're telling me to call you out when you're being an asshole?"

A smile flickers across Graham's countenance, gets swallowed by a look of grave indigestion, and then rises to the surface again. "Yes. But gently?"

Emma scoffs. "Because you've always been so gentle with us, right?"

"Fair point." Graham raises his hands in surrender.

"Okay, let's say I did want to call you out *gently*. How would you suggest I do that?"

"I don't know." His words fumble, his hands fidget, and then he finds it. "Purple," he says, meeting her gaze.

"Purple?"

"Maybe you could just say 'purple.'"

"Okay. Purple it is." Emma grins and reaches a hand up toward her father. Graham returns the hand—and the smile. They shake on it.

"Does that mean you'll come home with us?" he asks.

"Does that mean you'll *let* me?"

"Of course I'll let you. I want you to."

"You'll let me, but won't *make* me?"

"I very much doubt that I have the power to make you do anything, Emma."

"I'll think it over."

"You should apply to the U. I was being heavy-handed."

"Heavy-handed? Dad, you were being a complete tyrant."

"Hey, that's what . . . never mind. I'll tell you about that later."

"Tell me about what later?"

"Don't worry about it for now. I concede that I was being a tyrant. I'm going to step out and let you rest. Do you need anything?"

"No, I'm okay," she says.

And she is. Amazed, baffled, okay. There is one thing she wants, though.

"Dad, wait!"

Graham turns to look at her.

"You know you look like shit, right?"

"Yes, I am aware." He nods grimly.

Emma's smile stretches from ear to ear. She's two for two on swearing at her parents today and somehow, hasn't unleashed the wrath of hell.

***

"This is quite the turn of events," Oma says, entering the guestroom later with a plate of food.

Emma sits up in bed, shaking her head. "He apologized to me. That's literally never happened."

"He apologized to everyone else, too."

"Do you believe him?" Emma wants to know.

"I believe he's sincere in this moment. What about you?"

Emma nods slowly. "Me too. I would never in a million years have seen this coming, though, so it's kinda hard to believe it can last."

They sit together, considering. "Well, at least for now, the Arschgeige is trying to harmonize with the rest of the orchestra," Oma says, and they break into giggles.

"But he's still an Arschgeige."

"Hell yeah, he is. But we've all got some Arschgeige in us. And who knows, maybe your dad will have a bit less of it going forward."

Emma tries to imagine this—tries to imagine what her life might look like with a father who is quirky and opinionated and far too particular but *trying* to go with the flow. She might be able to forgive him, she thinks, not yet realizing perhaps that forgiveness is rarely a one-time act.

"I can't believe I'm saying this, but maybe I'll go home with them. I don't know what's going to happen next—with my dad, with my family. My mom is acting different, too . . . in a good way. I've got less than a year left at home. Part of me really wants to see how it would play out."

"Sounds like the same part of you that built Tenju." Oma's eyes sparkle.

Emma laughs. "Yeah, I think it must be. I like that part of me."

"Then you should listen to her. If things go south, I'll come get you. All the parts of you have a home here anytime you need it."

Chapter Thirty-Seven

Months later

Graham steps up to the podium. He trains his eyes just above the sea of faces, clears his throat, and begins: "Our new bishop"—Graham nods toward Jeff Pingree, who sits on the stand—"has asked me to give a talk today on the subject of forgiveness. And I can't help feeling a little persecuted, because the bishop knows me well enough to know that forgiveness happens to be something I've needed a lot of in recent months. But Jeff"—Graham turns theatrically toward his friend—"I forgive you."

The congregation laughs softly.

"If you've been in this ward for a while, you're probably expecting me to quote fifty or so scriptures on the subject of forgiveness. And don't worry, I won't disappoint. We'll get there. But I want to start first with a story—my story.

"I had a chaotic childhood . . . to put it mildly. But when I was fifteen years old, I was taken in by an LDS family. They offered me kindness and love and a home, and they offered me the gospel. I came from a home that had no structure, a home in which nothing was predictable or safe. And then suddenly I was offered the opposite experience. And it was such a positive change that I imagined that this *structuring* of experience was the key to happiness and the meaning of our lives. I thought that we give meaning and purpose to our lives by reining in chaos, by bringing order to ourselves and our surroundings. In essence, I thought the point of life was to control things. To make them predictable. To walk a straight, narrow, unyielding line. And then, I had children."

Graham faux grimaces, and the adults chuckle.

"My oldest daughter, in particular—Emma, who is a freshman at the U now but is visiting us today—has a talent for showing me just how little control I actually have."

He gazes down at his daughter, who is sandwiched between Cami and Ben, wearing a sleeveless dress. He had suggested to her that since she was coming to church, perhaps she could, just this once, dress like a practicing Mormon—even though she isn't one. "Purple," she said.

"It was just a thought!" Graham threw his hands in the air.

She laughed. "*My dress* is purple." Purple, sleeveless, and several inches shorter than Graham would have liked. But it is what it is.

He continues his talk. "I'm beginning to understand how little control *any* of us actually have. I know that's not a popular thing to say. We like to imagine that if we keep the commandments, there are certain guarantees. Our life will turn out a certain way. It's an attractive proposition but one that doesn't hold up well under the testing of years. People get sick or lose their jobs. Children run away from home and call you a tyrant, more than once, to your face."

Again, the laughter.

"And sometimes, they call you other things. Things that you can't say from the pulpit."

The laughter builds.

"My mother-in-law has a great term for me. She's been using it for years, apparently. She calls me 'the Arschgeige.' Apparently, that's German for 'the butt violin.' I'm still not quite clear on what that means, but it's certainly evocative. My kids have taken to using it, too. But only occasionally—only, I'm told, when I'm really being a butt violin."

Graham pauses, waiting for the laughter to die down.

"The thing is, sometimes, regrettably, when our kids or spouses or friends or neighbors call us out, they're right. My kids have been right too many times for me to count. Sometimes, they see me with more clarity than I'm able to see myself. I'm amazed by their willingness to give me another chance. Their willingness to forgive. I'm slowly learning to forgive myself.

"I used to think that self-forgiveness was lazy—that self-flagellation was the nobler path. But I'll tell you from my own experience, you can't tear yourself apart and build up the people around you. You can't judge yourself harshly and still remain open and generous to others. You can't collapse in on yourself in shame and at the same time extend your hands outward. You have to choose. What's it going to be? Forgiveness for yourself, or for no one? Compassion for all, or for no one?"

Graham's throat feels tight. His eyes are strangely damp.

"Sometimes, in the Church, we get really fixated on the notion of perfection. That's the goal: To be perfect like Heavenly Father. We get so focused on that destination that we devalue the path we're on. The path of flailing—of falling down and getting back up again. The path of forgiving, loving, growing, of being in this moment right here, no matter what kind of moment it is. In this moment, I'm still a butt violin. But I'm also a child of God. You are probably also, in your own unique way, a bit of a butt violin. And you are a child of God. Forgiveness grows in the holding of this tension.

"It's easy to get hung up on commandments and rules. But they are just fingers that point us toward God; they aren't God himself. God is love. And love is second chances. Love is forgiveness. Love is trying again to be a little kinder to ourselves and to one another. Love is choosing to accept people as they are. When we do that, then God is right here in this room. When we instead harp on the rules and the details and technicalities. Well, we're just left with a bunch of pointing fingers.

"I should know. If you've been in this ward for long enough, you've probably seen me point a finger once or twice. Please forgive me. I'm a work in progress."

"And a butt violin," Hyrum whispers to Joseph, and they both snicker.

Eliza leans toward them. "Yeah, but he's *our* butt violin."

No one contradicts her.

***

"Oh wow, *this* is worth the drive from Salt Lake," Ben says, practically drooling at the spread on the Madsen's dining room table. His hair is long again. It doesn't matter, now that he's transferred to the U.

"You should go there, too," Emma had prodded him. "Get financial aid or something. Two more years is a long time to keep pretending you actually want to be Mormon."

She was right, and so he did. He took out a loan, and he transferred. Even though, as she told him, "If we're both in Salt Lake, it doesn't change anything. I still just want to be friends, okay?"

And they are friends. Good friends. Weirdly, Ben is also friends (or something like it) with her father. Shortly after their return from Moab, Ben provided Graham with the name and number of a therapist—the same one that Ben saw for many years, in fact. Graham doesn't know anyone else who's been to therapy. Or rather, he doesn't know anyone else who *admits* to going to therapy.

Ben is still enthusiastically ogling the food.

"Are you saying our dad's talk *wasn't* worth the drive?" Hyrum quips, elbowing Ben in passing.

"Nah, the talk was great, man. Did you hear that, Graham?" Ben raises his voice so it reaches into the kitchen.

"That I am a mighty orator?" Graham asks, coming into the room.

"Exactly," Ben nods.

"You were great, Dad," Emma says. "Though I got a little stuck on the child of God thing."

"Oh, good," Joseph groans. "Just what we wanted, a lecture on the perils of theism."

"I have nothing against theism!" Emma protests. "I've never said there's no god, just that if there is one, it probably doesn't have a beard and wear white robes and make up rules about what kind of underwear you should wear, okay? Plus, I don't feel like I need to appeal to some notion of deity in order to have a meaningful life."

Joseph's eyes are still rolling.

"Woah, that can't be good for your eyeballs," Cami laughs.

"All I was going to say about the child of God thing," Emma continues, "Is that he could have used some other phrase that would be more universally relatable. There are other ways to describe the fact that we're all beautiful and special and worthy of love."

"It was *church.* What do you want him to say?" Joseph snorts. "That we're all unique snowflakes?"

"No, silly." Hyrum raises his arms like a conductor. "That we're all unique butt instruments in a grand anal orchestra."

Brigham opens his mouth to claim the role of butt bassist, but his mother interrupts him. "Enough talk of butts!" She has lost count of the number of times she has used that exact phrase. "Time for a blessing."

"Who wants to say it?" Graham asks.

"I will," a male voice from the far end of the table volunteers. Dan Christensen smiles bashfully to his fiancée, a sweet-faced BYU sophomore who sits beside him, wondering why on earth her beloved has brought her to this circus.

He will explain it to her later like this: "People are complicated. Isn't it rad?"

Acknowledgements

Releasing this book into the world, what I feel more than anything is gratitude for the whole of the journey—a gushing sense of *how on earth did I get so lucky?* I don't have words big or loud or sparkly enough to convey my feelings, so I'll settle for a flood of thank yous.

Thank you to my children for making me laugh over and over again. Humor has a magical way of shaking the best of us loose, so it can live and breathe in the world or on the page.

Love does that, too. Thank you to my family for being my anchor. Your consistently loving presence in my life helps me to face down the fear that is always part of living into one's dreams.

Thank you to the many friends and family members who have read drafts or portions of this book and offered feedback, cheerleading, or both. Rebekah Jensen, this book would never have happened without you. Keith Aron, thank you for loving the Madsens like I do and for offering valuable perspective and such an inquisitive ear. Suzy Jensen, Raven Lee, Judy Tiesel, Cathy Thomas, Liz Caras, Bridget Bellocq, Deb Schweitzer, Margot van Eck, and David Miller—thank you, thank you, thank you!

I'm grateful, too, to the places and more-than-human beings that have buoyed and inspired me in my writing—the high deserts of southern Utah, the red sand that stains my socks, the juniper berries waxy on my tongue. Also the endless green of the Kentucky farm where I live, with its wood thrushes, red-tailed hawks, and occasional eagles. Thank you to the Silver Maple who grows a few feet removed from my writing desk. I have spent as much time looking at you as I have at my computer screen, but you, dear, never tire my eyes.

I am conscious of the irony of thanking a tree when the bodies of trees make up the physical pages of this book. Thank you to those trees, as well, and really, to the whole of this world. We are all so interconnected it makes me ache with joy and grief.

Finally, thank *you*, reader, for your time and trust and presence. I hope our paths cross again.

www.ingramcontent.com/pod-product-compliance
Lightning Source LLC
Chambersburg PA
CBHW020742020826
48980CB00019B/698/J

* 9 7 9 8 9 9 8 8 9 4 9 0 9 *